Josie Lloyd grew up in Essex, and studied
English and Drama at Goldsmiths' College.
Her first novel, *It Could Be You*, was published
in 1998. She lives in west London.

Emlyn Rees grew up in Wales and now lives
in London. His first novel, *The Book of Dead
Authors*, was published in 1997.

come together

JOSIE LLOYD AND EMLYN REES

ARROW

Published in the United Kingdom in 1999 by
Arrow Books

3 5 7 9 10 8 6 4 2

Arrow Books Limited
Random House UK Limited
20 Vauxhall Bridge Road, London, SW1V 2SA

Random House Australia (Pty) Limited
20 Alfred Street, Milsons Point, Sydney, New South Wales 2061, Australia

Random House New Zealand Limited
18 Poland Road, Glenfield,
Auckland 10, New Zealand

Random House South Africa (Pty) Limited
Endulini, 5a Jubilee Road, Parktown, 2193, South Africa

Random House UK Limited Reg. No. 954009

A CIP catalogue record for this book is available from the British Library

Papers used by Random House UK Limited are natural, recyclable products
made from wood grown in sustainable forests. The manufacturing processes
conform to the environmental regulations of the country of origin

Typeset by SX Composing DTP, Rayleigh, Essex
Printed and bound in Great Britain by
The Guernsey Press Co. Ltd, Guernsey, Channel Islands.

ISBN 0 09 927927 4

For our sisters, Catherine and Kirsti, with love.

Acknowledgements

Huge thanks to Vivienne Schuster and Jonny Geller – the best agents in town. And to everyone else at Curtis Brown, for their invaluable support.

To all at Random House, for being fantastic from the start. Special thanks to 'The A Team': Andy McKillop, our publisher, and Lynne Drew, our editor, for their friendship and professional advice, but most of all, for making this so much fun. Also to their back-up (Thomas and Jo). To Susan and Rachael, Mark and Grainne, Ron and the sales team and Glenn. And last, but not least, to Simon (you know who you are!) for sorting our heads out and helping us drink the minibar dry . . .

To the one and only Dawn Fozard for being brilliant throughout.

We'd also like to thank all our other mates for their various confessions, anecdotes and feedback. Especially: James & Helen, Paddy, Harriet & Matt, Lozza, Katy, Ruth, Lok, Tim & Danni, Mark & Charlie, Lucy, Emma, George, Daniel, 'Barry' C-G, Kirsti, Henny & Alan, Mands & Chas, Anna, Phil & the Mollster, Kate, Carol, Vicks, Ali, Jonny P, Lorna, Chris & Paula, Rupert & Toni, Ray & Anna, Simon & Caroline, and Lizzie.

Thanks, as always, to our families who've never stopped spreading the word. Most of all, our wonderful parents for backing us up all the way.

And to John Eminson and David Proudlock, for being the best English teachers ever.

1
Jack

The Ideal

Say you're a girl. Say you're a girl and you're at a party, or in a pub, or in a club. Say you're a girl and you're at a party, or in a pub, or in a club, and I come up to you.

Say you've never set eyes on me before.

Some things you'll know immediately. You'll see that I'm just under six feet tall and of average build. If we shake hands, you'll notice that my grip is strong and my fingernails clean. You'll see that I have brown eyes which match my brown hair. And you'll see that I have a scar across the centre of my left eyebrow. You'll guess that I'm somewhere between twenty-five and thirty years old.

Say you like what you see enough to talk to me.

We'll chat and, if things go well between us, you'll find out more. I'll tell you that my name's Jack Rossiter. If you ask me about the scar, I'll tell you that my best friend, Matt Davies, shot me with an air pistol when I was twelve years old. I'll tell you that I was lucky not to lose an eye and my mother wouldn't have Matt in the house for a year. I'll tell you that Matt is less volatile these days and that I'm comfortable with the situation to the extent that I now consider it safe to live under the same roof as him. I'll tell you that he works for a City law firm, but I won't tell you that he owns the house and I pay him rent. You'll ask me what the house is like and I'll tell you that it's a converted pub in west London and that, yes, we have kept the pool table and dartboard and bar, but, no, we haven't given visiting rights to the violent alcoholic who used

1

to sit scowling in the corner. I'll also tell you that the garden is large and wild.

You'll ask me what I do for a living now and I'll tell you that I'm an artist, which is true, and that I make a living from it, which isn't. I won't tell you that I work in a small art gallery in Mayfair three days a week to make ends meet. You'll look at my clothes, which will probably be Matt's clothes, and wrongly assume that I'm rich. As I won't, throughout all this, mention a girlfriend, you'll probably correctly assume that I'm single. I won't ask you if you have a boyfriend, though I will check your finger to see if you're engaged or married.

Say we end up going back to your place or mine.

We'll have sex. If we're lucky, we might even enjoy it. If we enjoy it, we might even do it again. And then we'll sleep. The next morning, if it's your place, I'll probably slip away before you wake. I won't leave a number. And if it's my place, you'll do the same. You won't kiss me goodbye. Whoever's left in the bed will finally wake up. And they'll find that they're alone. But this will be good, because this will be what they want.

* * *

Confessions: No.1 Contraception
Place: the toilet between carriages B and C on the 2.45 p.m. Intercity train from Bristol Parkway to London Paddington.
Time: 3.45 p.m. 15 May 1988.

Behind the toilet door, a young man, aged seventeen, was standing in front of the mirror with his trousers and boxer shorts round his ankles, holding a curry-flavoured novelty condom in one hand and an erect penis – his penis – in the other.

I can be accurate on this. Not because I was sitting in carriage C, staring at the TOILET IN USE sign, bladder threatening to burst, wondering what kind of person could be selfish enough to hog the bog for the best part of twenty minutes. And not because the track vibrations on the approach to Reading became so intense that I marched up to the toilet door and gave it a good kick and saw what was going on inside. But because that young man was me.

OK, so right now it would be fair enough to assume that I could be any one, or possibly all, of the following:

a) A pervert
b) A curry-lover
c) A lunatic

And, on the information disclosed so far, these are fair enough assumptions. Any jury would probably have convicted me on all three counts. Though on the curry-loving charge, the fact that I could barely touch my knee with my mouth, let alone any other part of my anatomy, may have raised a reasonable doubt.

So bring on the defence.

Seventeen-year-old men, as any man who's successfully, and no doubt gratefully, evolved beyond that age can vouch for, are strange creatures. Stretched between adolescence and maturity and doused with hormones by the bucketful, it's an age of self-discovery, where questions are asked, answers are sought, and frequent masturbation is indulged in on the side. It was no different for me. I asked the usual questions. Does God exist? Can there ever be world peace? Why does pubic hair have a finite length, thereby denying the possibility of pelvic topiary? And wouldn't it be gross if boil-in-the-bag was just what it said? And I waited in vain for the answers. And, in between waiting, I jerked off.

A lot.

There were probably prize dairy cows whose yield was less than mine (but, considering the fact that they would only have been milked twice a day, this isn't so astounding). On average – i.e. excluding fire, flood, earthquakes and other acts of God – I jerked off three times a day. And variety was the spice. I spanked the monkey over the bathroom basin. I strummed the banjo on the back of the bus. I choked the chicken under the duvet. I bashed the bishop during *Songs of Praise*. I jerked, I

3

squirted, I wanked, I tossed, I tugged and I glopped. But throughout this period of onanistic experimentation, there was one thing I'd never tried: the Rich Man's Wank.

For anyone unfamiliar with this term, the RMW is simply performing the act of masturbation whilst wearing a condom. Precisely what this has to do with rich men, I'm not sure. I can only assume it's a habit brought on by having too much time on their hands. (Too much something, anyway.) For me, though, on 15 May 1988, in the far from erotic environment of the British Rail toilet between carriages B and C, it served another purpose. It was the condom itself, not what it was designed to act as a barrier against, that interested me.

The plain fact of the matter was that I'd never tried one on before. My contact with them had so far been restricted to watching with admiration as my school friend, Keith Rawlings, had performed his then legendary party trick of stretching a condom over the top half of his head and hyper-ventilating through his nose until the condom swelled up like a Zeppelin and finally went the way of the *Hindenburg*, exploding to a round of astounded applause. Now, whilst I could see the impressive theatricality of such a feat, it wasn't a party audience I was planning to impress that day. It was Mary Rayner, a girl I'd met at a party at Matt's parents' house the weekend before, a girl who lived in London, and a girl who'd invited me to stay with her whilst her parents were away in Majorca. A girl, in other words, who I had high hopes would be charitable enough to relieve me of my virginity. Hence the curry-flavoured condom. In the toilet. On the train.

In less than two hours, there was the possibility that I might be called upon to use one in earnest. The moment I'd mentally and physically prepared for, developing a wrestler's grip in my right hand into the bargain, was almost upon me. So what did I do? I did what all red-blooded, self-confident seventeen-year-old men do: I panicked. Good and long. I sat there in carriage C, drumming my fingers on my wallet, thinking of the three sealed condoms that I'd hurriedly bought from a machine in a pub. What if they didn't fit? What if they were too small, or – excruciating – too big? What if they split or fell off? I'd end up lying next to Mary, apologising profusely, that's what. And if that happened, chances were Mary would never give me another chance. I'd remain a virgin. Christ, I might even die a virgin. I squirmed in my seat, visualising my epitaph: HE DIED AGED ONE HUNDRED WITHOUT A SINGLE SHAG TO HIS NAME. RIV – REST IN VIRGINITY. So I picked up my wallet and hurriedly walked up the aisle to the toilet for a dry run before the main event.

And there the defence rests.

Mary, however, I'm pleased to report, didn't. Rest, that is. From the moment we reached her bedroom and stumbled across the floor and tumbled into bed, rest was the last thing on her mind. This was my first experience of the feeling I'd later come to call 'In'. I was In with her. I was In bed. And soon I was In her, too. The feeling of In flooded me, right up to the point where it flooded out.

* * *

The Beginning
It's Friday morning, June 1998, and I have a problem.

Worse, I can't remember her name.

She sighs and mutters something incomprehensible in her sleep, rolls over to face me and wraps her arm around my waist, leaves it there, sweating against my skin. I glance at the LCD display on my alarm clock on the bedside table: 07.31. Then I look at her: a tapestry of brown hair obscuring everything apart from her nose. It's not a bad nose, as noses go. I stare back at the ceiling, caught in a crossfire of conflicting thoughts.

On the one hand, this isn't an altogether bad situation to be in. Here I am, heterosexual and single, lying in bed next to a naked woman, who, though the information at my disposal is limited to the shape of her nose and a collection of drunken memories, is reasonably good company and reasonably good in bed. To the best of my knowledge, nothing overly weird took place last night: no shacklings, break-downs or expressions of undying love. We met at a club, danced and flirted, and cabbed it back here in the early hours of the morning.

The sex was good. A sweaty parcel of rolling eyes and heavy sighs. We moved well together, considering we hadn't before. There was no speaking. Sometimes I like it like that. No voice contact. No mind contact. The situation was stripped as bare as we were. There was no pretence that what we were doing was anything other than physical. And afterwards, as we sat there sweating it off, drinking from the two pint glasses I'd filled up with water from the bathroom tap, The Ideal continued to hold true.

Proof of this lay in the fact that she didn't:

a) Squeeze my hand
b) Stare lingeringly into my eyes
c) Ask me how come I didn't get lonely not having a girl-friend
d) Go for the intimate route by sharing my cigarette like a spliff
e) Suggest we get together again soon

Instead, she:

a) Kept her hands to herself
b) Stared at the ceiling
c) Told me that the best thing about sleeping around was that no two guys were ever the same
d) Lit her own cigarette
e) Told me that she was going to Australia travelling for three months

Then we stubbed out our separate cigarettes and I hit the light and we slept.

So far so good. The perfect one-night stand. A few minutes ago, when I woke, I felt good about myself. Or maybe smug is more accurate. All the usual Single Fears had been swept away. Yes, I was still capable of pulling. Yes, I was still capable of having sex with a stranger. In other words, yes, I still had what it took.

On the other hand, this isn't exactly a good situation either. It's a Friday morning and – I check the clock again and see that another two minutes have flicked by – I have things to do. As easy as it would be to nestle here in post-coital comfort, maybe even lift her hand from my stomach and hold it, protract the illusion of intimacy a little while longer, the time has come for us both to get up and get on.

Careful not to disturb her, I move into a sitting position and lift the dead-weight of her arm from my body and lay it back on the sheet. From this elevated position, I can see her clothes lying in a pile by the side of the bed. I wait for a couple of seconds, reassuring myself that she's still asleep, then slip out from beneath the duvet and quietly go through her clothes until I find her wallet in her jacket pocket. I pull on some shorts, slip out of my bedroom and walk through to the kitchen.

Matt is there, already suited and booted, his black hair still wet from the shower, perched over a bowl of dry cereal and a mug of steaming coffee. He opens his mouth to speak and I raise a finger to my lips. I sit down opposite him at the table and take a swig from his mug.

'She still here, then?' he whispers.

'Yeah.'

'What's-her-name? Chloe's neighbour?'

Chloe is a girl we went to school with, but never went with at school. As a result, she managed to graduate from potential girlfriend to girl friend.

'Yeah, what's-her-name. That's the one.'

He nods his head, taking the information in, then asks, 'Good lay?'

'Okay.'

He grins. 'Noisy.'

I smile back. 'Tell me about it.' I toast him with his mug of coffee. 'Happy birthday, by the way.'

'You remembered? Bless you, mate.'

'Even got you a present.'

'What is it?'

'You'll have to wait till tonight.'

'A.k.a. you haven't bought it yet.'

'A.k.a. wait-and-fucking-see.' I hand him back his mug. 'So who's coming tonight?'

He lights a cigarette, inhales. 'Usual crowd, plus extras.'

'Single and female extras?'

'Might be.'

'More info.'

'Wait-and-fucking-see yourself.'

'Psychos and mooses, then . . .'

He isn't going to be drawn. 'Like either would put you off . . . Maybe neither. Maybe both.' He prods the wallet with his finger. 'Memory loss?'

I open it up and flick through the ID. 'Not any more.'

'So?'

'So what?'

'So what's what's-her-name's name?'

'Catherine Bradshaw,' I read. 'Born Oxford, sixteenth October 1969.' I pull out her tube pass and study the photo, turn it round to face Matt. 'Marks out of ten?'

'Seven.' He peers closer, reconsiders. 'Make that six. She looked better last night.'

'They always do, but—'

'The camera never lies,' he says, finishing off my sentence.

'Precisely.'

'Correct me if I'm wrong, but isn't S&M coming round today?'

S&M is Matt's nickname for Sally McCullen, because he reckons my brain gets bruised from just thinking about how great she is.

'Yeah, at ten.'

He checks his watch, whistles low. 'Cutting it a bit fine, aren't you?'

I walk over to the thermostat control and spin it round to

maximum. 'Plan A,' I say, pouring myself a pint of water from the chilled bottle in the fridge. 'Sweat her out.'

'And if that fails?'

I down the water, wipe my lips. 'It never does.'

But there's a first time for everything.

The clock display winks over from 08.40 to 08.46. The heating has been running at max for over an hour now, and I can only conclude that Catherine Bradshaw's ID has been falsified and that, rather than being born in Oxford, she was actually born in Bombay. In the summer. In a heatwave. Next to a furnace. At high noon. My iced water cheat has failed. With the summer sun beating down on the closed windows and the radiators boiling, I might as well be locked in a sauna. Sweat bleeds from my brow. The pillow which props up my head has transformed into a hot-water bottle, the duvet into an electric blanket. Bradshaw, however, is playing it literally and metaphorically cool. Not one groan of discomfort. Not one request for the window to be opened, or water to be brought. Nothing but the regular pattern of her breathing, and the relaxed expression of deep sleep on her face. The ice maiden.

Plan B.

'Catherine,' I say, sitting upright. 'Cath?' I guess, louder this time, shaking her shoulder. 'Cathy?'

'Mmmmm?' she finally replies, her eyes still closed.

'You've got to get up. I've got to get going. I'm running late.'

She burrows into her eyes with her knuckles and looks at her watch. 'It's not even nine,' she complains, pulling the duvet tighter round her shoulders and closing her eyes again. 'I thought you said you weren't working today . . . I thought we were both going to take the day off . . . Pact, you know? We made a pact.'

This is true. This was the justification for extending the evening beyond the club.

'I know,' I say, 'but the gallery's just called. They've got an American collector interested in some of my stuff,' I lie. 'He wants to meet me. This morning. He's flying back to LA this afternoon, so I haven't got a choice.'

9

'Okay, okay,' she says, sitting up, 'I hear you.'

By the time she has showered and dressed, it's a quarter past nine. She walks through to the kitchen, where I'm sitting staring blankly at the surface of the kitchen table. As table surfaces go, it's not a bad one to feign preoccupation with. It was Matt's idea, cannibalising the pub sign that used to hang over the front door. Shame we couldn't have left it hanging there, but some of the Churchill Arms' ex-locals weren't too bright, kept homing in on it and seeking lock-ins in the middle of the night. I continue to stare. Winston Churchill stares disapprovingly back. *Never, in the field of human relationships . . .* OK, OK, let's get this show on the road.

I don't offer her:

a) Coffee
b) A lift home
c) Small talk

Instead, I push my mug away, get to my feet and say, 'Right, let's get going.'

I flick my memory back to her wallet as I walk to the front door and her footsteps clack across the tiles behind me. She lives in Fulham, so she can catch the tube.

'The tube's only a couple of minutes' walk,' I tell her as we step outside.

I close the door behind us and we walk twenty yards down the street until we draw level with Matt's Spitfire.

'Yours?' she asks as I rest my hand on the roof.

'Yeah,' I say, and moving swiftly on. 'You want to keep going to the end of the street and then take a left. The station's about four hundred yards further on.'

Instead of saying goodbye and walking off out of my life and back into her own, she scans the other side of the road. Her eyes eventually settle on the bus stop.

'It's okay,' she says, 'I'll bus it. It'll be quicker.'

'Fine,' I say, although it definitely isn't, 'I'll see you around, then.'

'Yeah?' She looks at me uncertainly. 'I've left my number in your room. On a fag packet. On the bedside table.'

'I thought you were going to Australia?'

'I am. But not for six weeks.'

'Oh.'

We stand looking awkwardly around for a few seconds.

'Are you going, then?' she asks.

'Sure. Right now.' Pointlessly, I pull at the door handle. I grimace. 'Keys. Forgot my keys.' I half wave at her, avoiding eye contact. 'See you around.'

'Yeah, you said.'

I walk quickly back to the house and shut the door behind me. I check my watch: twenty past. Slowly, I creep round the living room door. Using the bar, which runs along the back wall, for cover, I peer out through the window on to the street. Catherine Bradshaw is now standing at the bus stop directly opposite the house. I sink to my knees and stare up at the empty row of optics. Shit. I'm tired. I'm knackered. Sally McCullen, a woman I've spent the best part of the last two weeks obsessing over, is due here in just over half an hour. And Catherine Bradshaw is waiting at one of the least-visited bus stops on the planet, without magazine or newspaper or book or Walkman, with nothing better to do than idly watch the front door to Matt's house and wait for me to reappear and drive off in a convertible, which isn't mine, to meet an American art collector, who doesn't exist.

A voice inside me is saying, *So what? So what if you don't reappear and thereby confirm her suspicion that the whole gallery/ collector routine is just an elaborate scam to get rid of her? So what if she's still waiting for the bus to arrive at ten o'clock when you greet McCullen on the doorstep?* We've only just met. We aren't going out. *So,* the voice continues, *why couldn't you have been honest with her? What's the big deal? Why couldn't you have just told her thanks for the shag. It was fun. But the door's that way. Wouldn't life be simpler now if you'd just done that? Well, wouldn't it?*

But a range of other voices disagree.

There's the selfish one: *she's Chloe's neighbour and mate and*

11

*Chloe is your mate. Dump on Catherine, dump on Chloe by associa-
tion. Carry on that way and watch your social circle collapse into a
flat line of inactivity.* The insecure one: *you don't want her, or anyone else for that matter, going through life propagating the opinion,
or even just keeping it to themselves, that you're an arsehole.* The
decent one: *you're a nice guy and nice guys leave nice girls feeling
nice about themselves.*

But, while I suppose all of these voices are speaking the
truth, none of them is telling the core truth. In fact, the core
truth has nothing to do with reasoning at all. Nothing so intelligent. It's down to conditioning, plain and simple. It's down
to the way I've been programmed. Not something I consider,
just something I instinctively am.

It's easy to kid yourself that when you bail out of a relationship you simply swap your couple habits for single ones. I
broke up with Zoe Thompson between 6 and 9 p.m. on
Saturday, 13 May 1995, between the time I returned from a
weekend of heart-searching and tears at my mum's house and
the time her father came to collect her from the rented flat we'd
spent the past fifteen months turning into a home. We'd been
going out with each other for just over two years. In the
months that followed, alterations in my lifestyle and emotional habits included:

a) Stopping using fabric conditioner and watching holes
   inexplicably appear in my socks
b) No longer replacing my toothbrush every three months, so
   that it reached the point where it felt like I was brushing
   my teeth with a strip of shag-pile carpet
c) Using my fingernails rather than nail scissors to trim my
   toenails
d) Turning the bed sheet over every couple of weeks rather
   than washing it
e) No longer feeling guilty for talking to someone of the
   opposite sex who wasn't safe (i.e. a mate's girlfriend, or a
   long-standing girl friend of mine who Zoe got on with, or
   a friend of Zoe's)

f) Wearing condoms during sexual intercourse

g) Sleeping with a pillow hugged between my arms rather than a person I loved

h) Lying in bed on my own on Sunday mornings, wishing I still had someone I cared about enough to want to spend the day with her

But other habits I'd developed during the time I'd been going out with Zoe continued to thrive, despite the fact that she was no longer there to thought-police me, because they'd now become mine. These included:

a) Going to sleep on the right side of the bed, despite the fact I now had a double to myself on which I could have sprawled at any angle I chose

b) Doing my washing up after each meal instead of performing a crockery and cutlery blitz at the end of each week

c) Savouring the taste of vegetables and salads, rather than dismissing them as items made obsolete by the advent of vitamin pills

d) Leaving the seat down on the toilet

e) Watching *EastEnders*

f) Attempting to steer the conversation away from football results when in mixed gender company

g) Looking women in the face rather than the cleavage whilst addressing them

h) Understanding that other people's egos, in spite of what outside appearances might lead you to believe, are just as fragile and easily cracked as your own

Now, I'm not a shrink and I have no way of explaining why some of these Zoe-learnt habits have stuck whilst others have dropped away. What I do know is that those that are left are for real, as much a part of me as my fingerprints. And that includes the other people's egos bit.

Sure, chances are Catherine Bradshaw is going to be just as glad to see the back of me as I am of her. Chances are that leaving her telephone number was probably just her way of making me feel better, or making her feel better, or both. Chances are that even if I do call her she'll probably deny all knowledge of me, or develop a hitherto unknown talent for speaking fluent Latvian the moment she recognises my voice. But, equally, there's a slim chance that she does give a damn. And that possibility means that if I treat her like crap, I'll end up feeling like crap myself. So spin it round: treat her good and feel good as a result. Selfless and selfish side by side. The perfect combination for a clean conscience.

Luckily, Matt's car keys are hanging on a dart on the board in the kitchen and so, within a few minutes, I'm waving across the street at Bradshaw, climbing into Matt's Spit, adjusting the seat and mirror and slipping the key into the ignition. Driving round the block, I ponder over the facts that I'm not insured, and that Matt might well react by holding a knife to my throat and making me eat my recently dismembered genitalia if he so much as suspects that I've taken his pride and joy for a spin. I park the Spit in a side street, well away from the bus stop, cut the engine and switch on the radio.

Four songs, one traffic update, one news flash and two cigarettes later, I risk getting out and walking up the street to take a peek. Just as I'm approaching the corner, slowing down to peer round and check that my road is now a Bradshaw-free zone, a bus drives past. I freeze, my eyes connecting through the window with those of Catherine Bradshaw. I watch as she shakes her head and raises her middle finger in salute.

There are some thoughts you don't have to be telepathic to pick up. Arsehole is one of them.

It's late afternoon. I'm leaning back against the wall in my studio, smoking a cigarette, gazing at the canvas propped up on the easel that I've just repositioned by the French windows overlooking the garden. Sunlight fills the room with the kind of bright light you get from an unshaded bulb.

The studio's at the back of the house. Uniform white ceiling and walls, broken up by sketches and colour studies. The floorboards are unvarnished, left how I found them when I ripped up the beer-stained carpet shortly after moving in. Matt was cool about it, partly because the room was a mess anyway – little more than a storage space for the boxes he'd never quite got round to unpacking after he'd shifted all his stuff from his parents' home back in Bristol – and partly because he knew I couldn't afford to rent anywhere else. With the carpet gone and the walls repainted, only the pool table remains as a testimony to the Churchill Arms' glory days.

One thing I told Bradshaw last night was true: I don't work Fridays. Not regular pay cheque work, anyway. That happens Tuesdays, Wednesdays and Thursdays, down at Paulie's Gallery. Paulie calls me his manager, but seeing as I'm the only person who works there, I don't get too power-happy about the title. What I actually do is sit at the desk at the front of the gallery and flick through magazines or novels, and wait for the phone to ring, which it rarely does – unless it's Paulie checking up on me from whatever Med-based gin palace he happens to be at. Occasionally, someone will come in and browse, maybe ask me a question or two about one of the paintings. Even more occasionally, maybe three times a month, they'll buy something and I'll run up the till and fix them with a receipt, arrange delivery or collection. But mostly it's just reading, or gazing out on to the street, watching people go by.

But Fridays, Fridays along with Mondays, I own. Fridays and Mondays, the only thing I have to manage is myself. And I try to do just that. I try not to leave the house, not unless it's vital, like popping down to LoCost on the corner to buy cigarettes and cans of Pepsi Max, or having to grovel to my bank manager over The Bottomless Hole (a.k.a. my overdraft). I try to respond to my alarm clock at the same time I would if I was aiming to get to Paulie's to open it up on time (10 a.m.), I shower and, if he's there, I chat with Matt while he eats his breakfast. Then I go through to the studio and switch on the radio for company. I light a cigarette, select a brush and pick up where I left off.

All this I try, but quite often I end up getting up late and taking things from there.

I continue to gaze at the canvas. Apart from the dose of morning Bradshaw-aggro, it's been a productive day. Ten through till four, with an hour off for lunch. Everything has gone according to plan. Apart from the needing a radio for company part. I haven't. But that's been part of another plan.

'So,' McCullen asks, coming back into the studio, standing between me and the canvas, blocking my view, 'are you pleased?'

McCullen is five foot eight and slim. Her hair is blonde and hangs like straw half-way down her spine. She has a sexy laugh.

'I don't know,' I say, and not just because I can't see the canvas, but because I've been concentrating too long. I need to get away from it for a while, rest my eyes before I can view it objectively again. 'What do you think?'

She turns round and faces me. 'I like it.'

I'm pleased; I like her too.

A lot.

We met two weeks ago at a party my sister, Kate, threw to celebrate her twentieth birthday. Kate is a student at UCL, History and Spanish. Her boyfriend's name is Phil. He does French, also at UCL. He met McCullen on his course in his first year and they became good friends, managed to stay good friends, and moved into a shared house last year. Kate and McCullen became mates. That's our connection. That's how I ended up talking to her in Kate's kitchen to begin with.

Kate had already told her a lot about me, and the painting I'd given Kate for her birthday was hanging on the living room wall, so it was easy to get a conversation going. McCullen asked me about my painting. She'd done art at school, still went sketching some weekends. I asked her why she'd stopped and she blamed her parents, said they'd told her that she should keep it on as a hobby, but meanwhile get some vocational qualifications. I told her about the limited success I'd had so far – the three paintings I'd sold to collectors and the promising notices I'd got after I'd sneakily held an exhibition at Paulie's for my work a couple of months before. She asked me what I was working on at the moment and, because I was drunk, and because she was wonderful, and because she'd side-stepped all my subtle approaches and obviously had no intention of going home with me, I told her I was planning a series of life studies. I asked her if she'd sit for me and asked her to please, please, please say yes.

And, miraculously, she did.

Or, rather, she asked, 'How much?'

And I replied, 'I was rather hoping you'd do it for nothing.'

And she said, 'No way.'

And I suggested, 'Twenty pounds?'

And she said, 'Thirty.'

And I said, 'Done.'

And why not? I just had been.

McCullen walks over to the sofa, giving me a clear view of the canvas again. I look from her to it and back again. Somehow the two don't connect. Not because the painting is a bad likeness, just that during the hours I've been translating her body from three dimensions into two, I've stopped seeing her as a whole being, more a collection of contours and shades. Now that she has form again, she's resurrected. No longer an object I want to study, but a woman I want to touch. Very badly indeed.

In truth, this thought has been flashing sporadically in and out of my mind since she arrived this morning, about three minutes after I'd finished parking Matt's Spit inch-perfectly back in its space and readjusting its seat and mirror. I fixed her coffee, made small talk and showed her the studio. She undressed in the bathroom and returned to the studio with a towel wrapped round her. I made a show of setting up the canvas, tried not to stare at her as she walked across the room, and generally tried to put her at her ease.

'How do you want me?' she asked.

Now. Over the pool table. In the shower. On a beach. In an aeroplane. Covered in whipped cream and melted chocolate.

The answers kept coming and in any other circumstances I'd have selected one of them and gone for it. But I was a professional, right? I was an artist and she was a model. I was paying her to be here and she was here to take her clothes off for money and art, right? Right. End of story.

'Over on the sofa,' I told her. 'Just lie down and make sure you're comfortable.'

She walked over and, with her back to me, unwrapped the towel, folded it neatly on the floor, and lay down on her front on the sofa.

'How's that?' she asked.

Well, from an aesthetic point of view, *that* was just fine. The pose, with the side of her head resting on her crossed hands, eyes towards me, looked natural, as if she were waking from a deep sleep. The light was good, too. A block of shadow slanted across the lower half of her legs. It was pretty much perfect.

'No,' I said. 'No good. How about if you lie on your side facing me . . .'

Well, I mean, artistic integrity is all well and good, but there have to be some perks to compensate for the poverty and isolation, don't there?

She rolled over, covering her breasts with her arm. 'That better?'

'A bit,' I said, 'but maybe you should move your arm; try resting it on your hip.' She moved her arm. 'That's better.' I glanced between her and the canvas, frowned, then looked back at her again. 'Now just angle your leg ever so slightly. A bit more. Great. That's just great. Perfect.' I nodded in genuine agreement with myself. 'Comfortable?'

She lay there motionless. 'Yes, I'm fine.'

I stared, motionless too, transfixed. 'Good.'

What can you say about obsessions? They're the special forces of human behaviour. If being single, as I truly believe it is, is a state of siege – you create a set of demands in your mind and refuse to surrender your single status until your Uberbabe comes along – then obsessions are the fifth column who, just when you think you're safe and in control, scale your walls and burst through your windows with their machine guns blazing. No defence is strong enough to keep them out.

And that's how it is with McCullen. Since meeting her, I've suffered from an almost continuous barrage of visions of her and visions of being with her. Most worrying of all, many of these visions have been little short of heretical, blatant affronts to the Single Code I've chosen to live my life by. I've visualised:

a) Walking down the street with her, holding hands
b) Lying in bed beside her at dawn, watching her face as she sleeps, at peace
c) Sitting opposite her at an alcove table in a restaurant, sipping wine and staring into her eyes

Not, in other words, regularly quoted passages from the Single Guy's Bible. This said, though, there are other traits of my Uberbabe I doubt she has the potential to fulfil. I can't, for example, visualise:

a) Being separated from her for six months by circumstances beyond my control and knowing that she'll still be there for me when I return
b) Moving into a flat with her
c) Asking her to marry me

But, in spite of this knowledge, she comes closer to being my Uberbabe than anyone I've met since I split with Zoe. And, right now, close is close enough.

'Are we done for today, then?' she asks.

'Yeah. Thanks. You've been very patient.'

She picks up the towel and wraps it round her. 'So what happens now?'

A good question. And one which I've spent a considerable amount of time addressing over the last few hours. The answer I want to give goes somewhere along the lines of, 'I don't have to leave for Matt's party for another three hours, so why don't we put them to good use by hitting the sack?' But, meanwhile, back in the City of London, Planet Earth, McCullen has given no indication over the course of the day that this is a request she'll readily oblige. So instead, I settle for something a little more ambiguous.

'Well, we could crack open a bottle of wine . . .'

She smiles. 'No, I don't mean now as in now now. I mean with the painting. It's not finished, is it? So you'll need me to come back for another sitting, won't you?'

'Oh, right. Sure. Yeah.' Like I know that's what she meant. 'A couple more sittings should do it. If you can bear it, that is.'

'No problem. It's been fun.' She massages her shoulder with her hand. 'Apart from the aches and pains.'

'You didn't get bored?'

'No, you're good company. I suppose you're used to it, keeping people entertained while they sit for you.'

This is better. We get on. She likes me.

'Yeah, I suppose I am,' I say. 'And the wine? I've got a bottle in the fridge, if you're interested . . .'

She considers this proposition for a couple of seconds, then says, 'No, I'd better get going. Got the in-laws to deal with tonight.'

My stomach lurches. Before I can stop myself, I blurt out, 'In-laws? Don't tell me you're—'

She laughs, flicks her hair back from her face. 'Married? God, no. They're not real in-laws. Just my boyfriend's parents. It's his mother's birthday.'

The B-word. I might have known. I can't believe she hasn't mentioned him before.

'I didn't know you had a boyfriend.' The disappointment is there in my voice. I try to sound sociable, and enquire, 'Long term?'

'Three years.'

'Serious, then?'

'Guess so.'

There's a slight hesitation in her voice. Enough to make me probe further. 'I hope you don't mind me asking, but doesn't it bother him, you posing naked for me?'

'Well, it would if he knew.'

We both smile. 'I see.'

'I mean, it shouldn't. It's not like there's anything funny going on. It's not like I'm being unfaithful, or anything like that.'

'So why not tell him?'

'Because he'd just end up getting insecure and jealous. It's just not worth the grief.'

'Do you love him?'

'Yes,' she says, crossing the room to go and get dressed, 'very much.'

OK, so matters aren't exactly following the traditional seduction script. It's more like starting on the final page and reading back. The object of my desire has gone from naked to towel-wrapped and is now getting dressed and will shortly leave. And, what's more, she's just told me in no uncertain terms that she's in a three-year relationship with a man she's in love with. And *very much* in love with at that.

This would be enough to knock most people's obsessions cold. But not mine. I focus on the one flicker of hope in an otherwise dark universe: the fact that she's prepared to deceive the man she loves to be with me. And that she's going to repeat the deception next week. Sure, as signals go, it's more of a nod in a crowded room than a red flare bursting in the night sky, but it still means I'm in with a chance. Conclusion: her turning down my offer of wine to be with her boyfriend is a bad rejection, but there's always next week . . .

And on the ego front, it's not like I haven't suffered worse before.

* * *

Confessions: No.2 Virginity
Place: Mary Rayner's parents' house.
  Time: 6 p.m. 15 May 1988.
  Mary: 'Have you got one?'
  Me: 'Yeah.'

Mary: 'Well, are you going to put it on, or what?'

Me: 'Yeah, of course.'

Mary: 'It looks kind of funny.'

Me: 'It's curry-flavoured.'

Mary: 'That's disgusting.'

Me: 'I know. I'm sorry.'

Mary: 'Jesus, it stinks.'

Me: 'I said I'm sorry.'

Mary: 'Haven't you got anything else?'

Me: 'No, it's all the machine had.'

Mary: 'Okay, then. Put it on.'

Me: 'Okay.'

Mary: 'Where are you going?'

Me: 'The bathroom.'

Mary: 'What for?'

Me: 'Don't worry, I'll be back in a minute.'

Mary: 'Happy now?'

Me: 'Yeah.'

Mary: 'Come here, then.'

Me: 'Okay.'

Mary: 'Ouch.'

Me: 'Sorry.'

Mary: 'Here, let me help you.'

Me: 'Thanks.'

Mary: 'You haven't done this before, have you?'

Me: 'Yeah, loads of times.'

Mary: 'Liar.'

Me: 'Not.'

Mary: 'There, that's better.'

Me: 'There?'

Mary: 'Yeah, right there . . .'

Real-time description of the act itself: one, two, three, four, five, six, seven, eight, nine, ten, eleven, twelve, thirteen, fourteen, fifteen, sixteen, seventeen, eighteen, nineteen, twent—'

Mary: 'Is that it?'

Me: 'Yeah, how was I?'

Mary: 'Crap.'

Matt's Party

Unsurprisingly, things didn't last long with Mary Rayner. Longer than nineteen and a half seconds, sure, but not much. I stayed over at her house that night and we had sex the following morning, and this time I managed to last the length of one commercial for Diet Coke and three songs – though, technically, as I later pointed out to Matt, I could claim six, since the second song was 'Bohemian Rhapsody' – all courtesy of Capital Radio. Even Mary had to concede that under her expert tuition I'd graduated from 'crap' to 'okay' in the space of twenty-four hours. The future looked bright. I was pleased. My mission had been reasonably successfully accomplished. We left her house before lunch, snogged outside Ealing Broadway tube station and then I headed back to Bristol. I called her once after that, but she didn't call back. I never heard from her again.

Nostalgia-wise, I'd like to think that it was circumstances that kept us apart – her living in London, me living in Bristol, both of us too skint to afford the train fare on a regular basis, both of us too wrapped in studying for our A-levels to afford the time to get to know each other better. But it wasn't. What it actually came down to was, quite simply, that Mary had had better and I'd never had it so good. We both moved on for different reasons: Mary, because she didn't want to settle for 'crap', or even 'okay'; and me, because I'd been initiated into a wondrous new world, and now that I'd managed it with one girl (twice), I wanted to try it with more girls (as many times as possible).

As rites of passage went, it was a rough crossing, but well worth the ride. Everything changed after that weekend in London. I returned to Bristol packed with confidence, shut myself in the kitchen with the phone and called Matt. I told him everything, and then he made me tell him everything all over again. And though I tried to hide it from my voice, I relished every moment.

The Monday after, Matt walked Laura Riley, a girl in his maths class who he'd fancied for months without ever having had the bottle to tell her, home from school and kissed her by the bus stop on her street. He asked her out. Two weeks later, his parents went to the Lake District for the weekend and Matt and Laura lost their virginity to one another in the bottom half of the bunk-bed he'd slept in since his seventh birthday.

That Matt lost his virginity so soon after me might have been down to coincidence, but I doubt it. Competition is a more likely theory. Or, rather, the competitive streak that's always coloured our friendship. Post-puberty and pre-Mary, I'd say that seventy per cent of our conversations revolved around the discussion of sex on a theoretical level. How did we get it? What was it going to be like when we did? Once I'd uncovered the answers to both these questions, our friendship was no longer based on an equality of ignorance. The see-saw shifted, with Matt, the boy, looking up at me, the man, and me looking down at him through the eyes of experience. The only way available for him to restore the balance that had previously existed between us – to even the scores, so to speak – was to score himself. So he did. With Laura Riley. In his bunk-bed.

Of course, it didn't stop there. I met someone else, the see-saw shifted again, and he broke up with Laura and caught me up. Aside from the fifteen months he went out with Penny Brown, which – coincidentally, of course – occurred over the same period I was going out with Zoe, I don't think we've stopped competing ever since. And chances are that tonight – I open the door to BarKing, Matt's chosen venue for his birthday celebrations – will prove no different. We're both single. We're both on the pull. And even though we no longer have anything left to prove and our friendship has evolved beyond the point of who's done what first, sports-wise we'll both still be looking to tip the see-saw back in our favour. A one-night stand. No complications. Just another chalk mark on the board. A bit of harmless fun.

I scope the bar for faces I recognise, and for faces I like the look of. BarKing is a renowned target-rich environment, which is why Matt chose to come here. It doesn't advertise itself as a Singles Bar, but effectively that's what it is. By design, it's noisy and busy and the few tables available seat twelve. Not somewhere, in other words, that's likely to be awarded many stars in *The Couples' Guide to Intimate London Night Spots*.

The cursory visual inspection confirms that this is the case tonight: one stag party, one hen party, and a lot of smaller gender-segregated groups in between. You can count the engagement and wedding rings on show on one hand, and I'm sure I'm not the only person who's already done just that. Looks vary, but the dress code boils down to a common residue: labelled clothes and groomed hair and faces. People are here to advertise themselves in the hope of finding a buyer. And I, thanks to Matt's wardrobe, blend in just fine. Matt has been here, we worked out, ten times before and has pulled on two occasions, giving him a twenty per cent success rate. This is my sixth visit and I've pulled once, giving me an equal rating. As far as BarKing is concerned, the see-saw is even.

So far . . .

I spot Matt at a table on the far side of the room, but instead of immediately threading my way through the maze of bodies to reach him, I pull back to the bar and order a bottle of Bud for myself and a traditionally spiked birthday cocktail for Matt. While I wait for Matt's witch's brew to be mixed, I survey his group. Matt's not big on birthdays, favouring the just-a-good-excuse-to-get-drunk-with-your-friends approach, rather than anything more organised. Chloe is there, our right-hand girl, but Bradshaw, I'm relieved to say, is not. Then there are Andy and Will and Jenny, some of Matt's work mates, Carla, Sue and Mike, who Matt was at Uni with, and Mark and Tim, who have come up from Bristol for the weekend.

There are only a few people I haven't met before – obviously the 'extras' Matt referred to in the kitchen this morning. Of these, two are guys, three are girls. Of the girls, only one doesn't immediately set the psycho and moose alarm bells ringing. She's sitting on Matt's left. She's in profile. She looks good. Matt spots me and waves, shouts something that gets swallowed up by the babel of voices between us. I wave back, then check out Mystery Girl one more time, before turning to pay for the drinks.

A friend of mine called Paddy once summed up the basic dilemma faced by single guys when out on the pull something like this:

The way I see it, you've got two options: short term and long term.

Short term, you set out with the attitude that all you want to do is get laid. That means you're duty-bound to go for closure with every woman you think you've got a chance with. So you chat them up and you see whether they're up for it or not. Say they start banging on about the fact that they don't sleep around, or hate being single, or are fed up wasting their time on guys who are too immature to commit to a relationship – then you cut the conversation cold and you move on to someone else. And you move on and you move on, until you meet someone who, if she hasn't just said yes already, has given you enough pointers for you to conclude that she soon will.

Then there's option two: the long term. The defining difference between this and option one is that here you think with your brain *as well as* your dick. The approach is the same. You see someone you like and you chat them up. Only here, if you like what you hear as well as what you see – and, let's face it, at the end of the day, long term, it's the mind inside the body that really matters – then you don't blow her out of the water just because she isn't going to get her kit off with you before dawn. Instead, you think, *Hey, I like this person. This is someone I'd like to get to know better.* And so you try. You do all the old-fashioned stuff: you swap phone numbers, you call her up, you fix a date, and you take things from there.

And it's something you've got to decide right from the start of the night. The two options are mutually exclusive. Choose option one and whoever you pull, you pull because

26

in your head they equal sex. Chances are you won't be able to think of them in any other way after that. Choose option two and you've got to resign yourself to the fact that, for tonight at least, you're probably going home alone.

Paddy got married two months back, so it's not hard to suss out which option he chose. Me, I'm still in the habit of taking option one.

I reach the table and there's a series of all rights and hellos and how-the-hell-are-yous from the various people assembled, depending on how long it's been since I've seen them. The Mystery Girl's chair is empty, but a coat is hanging on its back. I reach Matt and place his birthday cocktail before him. He's groaning before it even hits the table.

'Jesus,' he mutters, staring at the lugubrious, curdled mixture, 'when are we going to grow out of this shit?'

'When we're old and married.'

Resigned to the fact that neither dotage nor marriage are possibilities in the near future, Matt picks up the glass and downs its contents.

'Happy birthday,' I say, handing over a caricature of him I've had framed.

He looks at it and laughs, passes it down the table. 'Nice one. Thanks. Here,' he tells me, wiping his lips and lighting a cigarette, pushing Mystery Girl's chair across and creating a space next to him, 'grab yourself a chair.'

By the time I've managed to find a spare chair and get back to the table, Mystery Girl has returned. I push my chair in next to hers and sit down.

'Hi,' I say, turning to face her, 'I'm Jack.'

27

2

amy

Oh God.

This can't be happening.

It can't be possible for one human being to feel this bad.

I can hear a strange wheezing sound which must mean that I'm breathing (nothing short of a miracle having smoked approximately 4,000 fags last night). However, I have a nasty suspicion that I'm going to have a brain haemorrhage if I don't get up.

This is easier said than done. Overnight, I've developed jelly joints. In one slick move, I manage to trip over my discarded fuck-me boots, stub my toe on the radiator pipe, and whilst hopping in agony, lose my balance, lurch head-first through my plastic bead door and concertina into the tea chest in the living room.

There's a moment of silence. I can feel the morning breeze on my bum as I lie prostrate on the matted rug, my ancient RELAX T-shirt having ridden up in the fall.

And then it happens.

There is a wobbly empty bottle sound and the undeniable reason for my current hangover from Satan rolls off the chest and hits me on the head.

I groan at the sight of the whisky bottle and slowly, horribly, the events of last night start to re-emerge through the haze of pain.

I'm going to throw up.

When I come up for air from the U-bend, I assess the damage in the bathroom cabinet mirror. It's less than ideal.

Amy Crosbie of Flat D, Pemberton Villas, Shepherd's Bush has disappeared. OK. Own up. Who let the warthog in the bathroom? Who was it?

How have I transformed so totally from the swishy-haired, Wonder-bra'd babe who left the house last night at 8.30 p.m. into this Grateful Dead lookalike? I clamp two palms to my head to calm the latest creation of my pillow hairdresser and stick out my tongue. It's green.

Being an optimist, I count the good points before the bad:

1. It can't get any worse (I have to admit that this is usually top of my good points list)
2. At least Jack didn't stay and I'm spared the indignity of him seeing me in this state
3. ?

I can't think of number three, because number two is top of the bad points list. I let out a croak of despair.

Jack didn't stay.

The only decent man I've met for months did a runner. Scarpered back to Blokeland at the crack of dawn without so much as a goodnight kiss. And the truth is I don't blame him. I made a complete and utter berk of myself.

This is too much of a calamity for me to be able to process all on my own. I call H, my best mate.

H: (sleepily) Hmmm?

Me: (A pause, just so that she'll know it's me) Blachhhhhhh! (I inject this greeting with as much post-puking throaty misery as I can muster)

H: Blachh-blachh-blachh? Or just blachh?

Me: Blaaaaaaaaaaaaaaaaaaaaaaaaaaaaaaaaaaaaaaachh!

H: I'll be right over.

I love H. She understands me.

Twenty minutes later, H is pushing her bike into the bike pile-up in my narrow communal hall. She looks sickeningly healthy having had a QNI (Quiet Night In) and probably loads of DSS (Deeply Satisfying Shagging) with Gav (latest bloke).

She kisses me and declares that I stink like a brewery and my teeth are orange.

I grunt, but I'm pleased with myself because I have made it down the three flights of stairs to the front door, signifying my re-entry into the human race. This has taken some fast work.

So far I've swallowed three Nurofen-plus, downed two cups of black coffee each with a tablespoon of demerara sugar (dreadful, I know, but this is a crisis) and force-fed myself no fewer than four effervescent vitamin C tablets. I am now flying on four thousand per cent of the recommended daily allowance and I'm not sure, but I think I can now speak.

In the kitchen, H hoists herself on to the counter whilst I put the kettle on.

'I take it you didn't pull,' she says matter-of-factly. 'What happened?'

I can tell she's disappointed, having assumed the role of Wardrobe Mistress last night. It was on her fail-proof promise of pulling that I was cajoled into wearing my if-it-was-much-shorter-it'd-be-a-belt black dress *with* Wonderbra *and* fuck-me boots (which, incidentally, I bought as a joke with no intention of ever wearing). I'm more of a jeans and chunky trainers girl, but H said a very definite 'no'. She even made me go round to her house before I left so that she could assess my potential. I got a wolf-whistle and a massive vodka and tonic from Gav, whilst H gave me a staggering nine out of ten (ten out of ten is reserved for my wedding day) and a gentle push into the night to wreak my feminine wiles on the divine Matt.

I know this all sounds a bit dramatic, but H knows my horrible secret. A secret which has developed into somewhat of a crisis lately. Oh God, I can't even bring myself to think about it, but the truth is . . . I haven't had sex for over six months.

I guess this technically makes me a virgin; after all, it must have sealed up by now. Whatever it makes me, it's not normal for a healthy twenty-five-year-old girl. This naturally leads me to the conclusion that THERE IS SOMETHING WRONG WITH ME.

H disagrees. She thinks it's only a matter of time. However, even she has become increasingly desperate for me to get a boyfriend, since she's through that all-important three-month relationship gestation period with Gav, gone on the pill and has started referring to him as her 'partner'. This has separated us in some seemingly small but psychologically huge way. As a result, H is on a personal crusade for me to get laid in the first instance and thence ensconced into a matching H-and-Gav-style cosy relationship.

Fine by me.

It was H, not me, who got completely over excited when I mentioned that Chloe had asked me to go to Matt's birthday party. Moreover, that Matt had specifically requested my presence, only having met me once. (An occasion on which I visibly swooned.) I think H saw the invitation as an oasis of hope in the barren desert of my single life and stupidly I allowed her enthusiasm to rub off on me.

So now here we are at the post-mortem and I feel I should justify what went wrong. Truthfully.

I start by softening the blow a bit. 'I did sort of pull,' I say as she chucks her Marlboro Lights over to me. I know that twenty minutes ago I made a solemn vow never, ever, to smoke again, but self-denial has never been one of my strong points. Despite the fact that my voice is two octaves lower and I feel poisoned to my core, I take one out of the pack.

'Who, Matt?' H asks, peeling off her top. She's got a trendy new vest underneath.

'No, not Matt, although he is gorgeous. No, he wasn't interested. I think he got too pissed.'

'Who then?'

I hand back the cigarettes and she takes one. I hold out a lit Cook's match. 'His flatmate.' I light my own cigarette before squeezing the teabags out against a fork. 'Jack.'

Even the mention of his name sends me into a shame spiral.

'Details, please,' says H, settling back and cupping her hands around her mug.

I talk her through the evening: the crowd at BarKing, the drinking, the flirting, the dancing, the leaving, the long walk back to my house, the endless cigarettes, the sitting close together on the floor and, eventually, THE CHAT. By that point, Jack and I seemed to have covered just about everything apart from our sex lives, slugging back the whisky and lolling by the sofa like old mates. I couldn't imagine conversation ever running out between us, there seemed to be so much to say. We'd nearly finished the bottle by the time the hitherto avoided subject came up, at which point I was definitely the worse for wear – physically and emotionally.

'So? Who's the lucky bloke in your life at the moment?' Jack had asked, filling up my whisky glass again.

I'd been playing with the candle wax, but then , staring into the flickering flame, the whisky hit me. I suddenly felt incredibly drunk and overwhelmingly sorry for myself. 'No one,' I whispered.

Jack touched my hand and looked into my eyes. 'Whoops. Have I hit a raw nerve?'

'No. Not really. Yes, I suppose. It's just . . .'

'What?'

'Nothing.'

Self-pity overtook. I felt a fat tear plop out of my eye and splash on to my lap.

Jack pushed my hair away from my face. 'Hey, hey. Come on, it can't be that bad, surely?' he soothed.

'Oh Jack,' I gulped, as tears, snot and mascara began to slide down my face. 'I think there's something wrong with me.'

'What do you mean?'

'I haven't had sex for ages. I'm hopeless at getting blokes. I don't think they find me attractive.'

Jack laughed softly and stroked my neck. 'Don't be ridiculous. You're very attractive.'

'Matt doesn't think so.'

'Matt!' Jack's fingers froze in my hairline.

'He's a typical case. He invited me to the party and when I got there, I completely turned him off.'

Jack sat upright, looking startled. 'You fancy Matt?'

I nodded dumbly. 'But there's no point, is there?' I sniffed (ineffectually) and wiped my nose on the skirt of my dress. 'He's never going to sleep with me. I just have to face it. No one wants to shag me. Not even you, do you?'

I can't bring myself to repeat any more. H and I have made it into the sitting room and now face each other at either end of the sofa. I bury my head in shame. She cups my knee reassuringly.

'I think you're taking this far too seriously,' she says, giving her verdict. 'Okay, so maybe you frightened him, but that's not the end of the world. He was probably flattered in a strange kind of way.'

Has she not been listening? Does she not understand the new-found depths of humiliation in which I am currently diving without an aqua-lung? This is worse than the time I tried to seduce Boris, the sexy German photographer at college. Convinced of the chemistry between us and dying of lust, I appeared late one night in black lacy underwear, rubbing my calf along the doorpost of his room. I was halfway to his bed, giving him my best sexy pout and sliding my bra strap down my arm, when he put down his magazine and told me he was gay.

The Jack situation is definitely worse.

'H!' I wail. 'He was *not* flattered.'

'He was probably worried about not being able to . . . you know . . . do it.'

'He was showing plenty of signs before I mentioned I'd gone to the party to seduce Matt,' I snap.

'So why did you tell him then?' H asks.

Good point.

I get up and start pacing – well, shuffling across the square foot of clear carpet by the window. 'I don't know. I was drunk and maudlin and it just sort of popped out.' I fold my arms. 'The thing is, I like him,' I muse. 'He was the first bloke for ages that I could talk to. And he was a good dancer. *And* he's cute. We had such a laugh until . . .' I clasp my head in my hands. 'Oh God, I'm such a klutz.'

H ignores this. 'I bet he's going to call you.'

'He can't. He left without taking my number.'

'But he knows where you live. There's directory enquiries.'

'You don't understand.'

'Listen. You drank a bottle of whisky between you. So you said a few things. So what? There's nothing wrong with showing a bit of vulnerability.'

Vulnerable is one thing. Vulnerable is OK as long as you stick to harmless revelations like taking your teddy bear to bed occasionally, or admitting that *Top Gun* is still one of your favourite movies. Telling someone you've just met (and that you really fancy) that you're the most desperate, needy, sex-starved woman on the planet is quite another.

'You're absolutely mad if you think he's going to call. He won't. I know he won't,' I sulk.

At that moment, the phone rings.

We both stare at it and H raises her eyebrows in an 'Oh yeah?' sort of way.

'What do I say?' I panic.

'I don't know, just answer it!'

Not only have I revealed that, in my hungover state, I suspect that H could be right and there is a God after all, but I have procrastinated too long. Just as I pick up the phone, the answer machine clicks in. There's a squawking, wailing cacophony from this mechanical error before the line goes dead. I look at the receiver disbelievingly before rapping it on my forehead.

'Ring 1471,' says H enthusiastically, sitting up and crossing her legs.

I dial.

'Sorry, we do not have the caller's number. Sorry, we do not . . .'

I slam down the phone. 'Shit!'

We stay in silent analysis for a while.

'I bet it was him,' says H, hugging her cushion.

I know she's wrong, but I've got to cover things from every angle. 'Okay, supposing just for a moment – just for a moment, mind you – that hypothetically that was him. How do I explain that I've made a mistake and I don't fancy Matt at all, but I want him?'

'He'll call back, and when he does, don't mention last night. Be bright and breezy. Say you've had a drunken memory loss and you don't remember him leaving.'

'Yeah right!'

'I don't care what you say. He's rung, so he's keen. Proof that five minutes of rubbish behaviour doesn't cancel out eight hours of top girl impressiveness.'

H is making me feel better. This is why she's employed as my best mate.

I admit, cautiously, that there's hope. That Jack cares enough to call, that I deserve his call and furthermore that when (not if) he does call again, I will be cool.

K U L E: Kule.

Five minutes later the phone rings again. H crosses both sets of index fingers for me and I roll my eyes at her. Even so, I know I'm putting on my best sexy voice when I pick up and casually purr, 'Hi.'

'Darling is that you? Thank God you've got that awful answering machine off.'

It's my mother. My fragile hot air balloon of hope explodes.

H reaches out and sympathetically squeezes my arm as I shake my head. I hold out the phone so that she can hear the familiar maternal prattle. I'm in such a state of anti-climax that I don't realise until it's too late that I've agreed to go shopping. I hang up and rub my temples.

'What are you doing today?' I ask.

H gives me a look. 'Not going shopping with your mother, if that's what you mean.'

I clasp my hands in a humble prayer position. 'Please? Pretty please? I can't do it on my own.'

'You'll have to. And anyway, it'll take your mind off things.'

It doesn't take my mind off things. The whole world has turned into reminders of Jack. Barking is the place from which my mother is zooming towards me at the moment. Barking . . . BarKing – where we met. See! And then there's a poster at Notting Hill Gate with Leonard Rossiter on it. Rossiter – Rossiter. I can't escape.

Between Shepherd's Bush and Lancaster Gate I have admitted to myself all may not be lost with Jack. Between Lancaster Gate and Marble Arch I have convinced myself that Jack has a heart, and simply will not be able to forget what a great time we had together before I mentioned Matt. Between Marble Arch and Bond Street, I know with great clarity that we are fated to be together. Between Bond Street and Oxford Street, I admit that the reason for this is that Jack could well be my perfect man.

I mean, just look at the vital statistics. Good height (six footish), big eyes like pools of melted Dairy Milk, great sense of humour, cute scar on his eyebrow where Matt shot him (poor babe). Groovy clothes – definitely a Paul Smith T-shirt, so obviously rich. Lives in a converted pub – converted pub – how cool is that? (And with a garden big enough for lazy summer barbecues.) And the best bit? He's an artist. A real-life bona fide creative success story.

WOW.

I'm vaguely aware that I'm mooning round the tube platform like a sad cow, but my brain is otherwise occupied and I'm starting to talk out loud. Jack and I have everything in common. OK, so I lied about my job (but being a temp isn't exactly impressive), but I did do Art History A-level, so in theory I *could* have worked at Sotheby's. But apart from that, we both like Indian take-aways and we've both experienced relationships lasting over two years. I mean, *perfect* match.

He told me about Zoe, his ex, but I didn't really let on about Andy, my last boyfriend. I told him the good bits – that Andy was older than me (thirty), a very wealthy money markets trader and that we lived together for a while in a penthouse apartment in Islington. Of course, I neglected to mention that Andy was the biggest control freak, passive-aggressive, tight-fisted bastard on page forty-nine of the *A-Z* and that our relationship was an utter disaster. This was because Andy and I only had one thing in common: we were both in love with him.

A pattern of behaviour, I have sworn to H, I will never repeat. And I won't with Jack, because Jack is Different. As I climb the stairs two at a time and lurch out on to Oxford Street, my heart is thumping happily. Could this be the first flutter of love *already*?

Mum is waiting for me in the Dickens & Jones coffee shop (it's a tradition thing). She's already bought me a bath bun and a tin pot of tea and I can't suppress my disappointment. I've been harbouring hungover fantasies of a gallon of Coke and a bacon butty. I guess this'll have to do.

'Now have you sorted out the flat?' she asks, as I melt into the plastic seat.

'Um, er, well, nearly.'

This is a lie. I moved in four weeks ago and I've yet to unpack properly.

Mum roots through her shopping bag and pulls out a spiral-bound pad. 'I've made a list of things you need. I thought we'd get a few bits and pieces.'

This is a very kind offer, but I'm so *not* in the mood. Mum's list of flat improvement bits and pieces will include things like a pink fur toilet seat cover and matching bowl surround.

'I've got everything. Honestly,' I say brightly. 'All ship-shape. It's really very homely.'

She looks disappointed and puts the pad down on the Formica table. 'Oh well then, let's get you something nice to wear. You're not going to attract anyone nice if you insist on slouching around in those clothes.'

Ha, that's rich! It's not as if she's a fashion icon herself. After all, she's wearing one of those all-purpose T-shirts that triples up as a beach bag and evening top and headdress depending on which way you twist it. She gave me one for Christmas last year and is mortified when I tell her it got lost in the move. After a while, I can't stall her any longer. We hit the shops.

Three hours and twenty minutes later we've made it as far as Marks and Sparks and tempers are fraying. I am rapidly metamorphosing into the petulant fourteen-year-old of days gone by.

'No, I don't want a green satin-effect body blouse, I wear T-shirts to work. No, no, Mum, Mum, put that velour dressing gown back, it's summer, it's too hot.'

Eventually she agrees to come into Warehouse and winces at the loud music. I try on a slip dress and come out of the changing room to do a twirl.

'It's a bit shapeless, dear,' she says.

'It's meant to be,' I hiss.

Mum grabs the price label and executes a sharp intake of breath. 'But it's only two pieces of material!'

At this point I experience a complete sense of humour failure.

'You've no bloody taste! And anyway, I like it!' I shout and storm back into the changing cubicle, yanking across the curtain on the way.

She's waiting outside on the street by the time I've got dressed.

'I was only trying to help,' she says sniffily. 'There's no need to be rude.'

'I'm sorry,' I sigh, and take her arm. 'Come on, let's get a drink.'

The pub is too smoky for her. I love it. I'm gasping for a cigarette, but it'd be fatal to light up now and incur her wrath. I think she knows I smoke, but I'm still not going to let on, pathetic creature that I am.

In the corner, I open the window and ply her with a restorative gin and tonic before she finally gets things off her chest.

'Darling, I'm just so worried about you. You haven't got any job prospects and it's just not natural you living up here all by yourself. I mean, why don't you think about a proper career? You could always go back and train to be an accountant or something. Barbara Tyson's daughter up the road is doing very well, a big salary and . . .'

I tune out. I've heard this a hundred times before. I don't want a bloody career and I'd rather work in an abattoir before

I set foot inside an accountancy firm. I resent the fact that she thinks I've failed because I'm not doing something that she can brag to the neighbours about.

Anyway, who does she think she is? I wouldn't swap my life for hers in a million years. All that suburban living with trips to B&Q and Slimmers World and a cosy little job in the local council. To me, that's not success, and neither is working your arse off crunching numbers all hours of the day and night.

But I know the reason I'm riled is that in some ways she's right. I have failed to make a go of things and I'm shocked by how cynical I've become in the last three years. When I finished college, everything was different. *I* was different. Brimming over with enthusiasm, all set for my glittering career. I wanted to work in the fashion industry. I didn't care how I started, I just needed a break. But the break never came, and six months after hoicking round my CV and practically begging for a job, any job, I gave up.

So I'm temping. Nine to five, no hassle, until I sort out what to do next. 'The temping is going well,' I say archly, interrupting her with my well-worn spiel. 'The jobs are interesting and it's a *very* good way of seeing what's around. If I like somewhere, there's every possibility that I could take a permanent job – if I wanted to,' I add. 'I've got tons of options open at the moment.'

I make this sound convincing, thrilling even, and she nods, satisfied. I hate her for swallowing it. Everybody, but everybody knows that temping leads from nowhere to nowhere. I've got more likelihood of being the first female astronaut on Mars than landing an even vaguely interesting career as a result of a temp job. However, this is *my* rut and it's very comfortable thank you very much.

'And there's another thing,' Mum says shyly, fiddling with her beer mat.

Here we go. The real reason for her visit.

'It's just that at your age I was married and thinking about a family. And well, I was wondering . . .'

'Ye-es?'

'Well, I know you're very close to Helen and if there was anything you wanted to tell me, about the two of you . . . well . . . I would try and understand.'

I don't believe this! My mother thinks I'm a lesbian.

Great.

I interrupt her warped train of thought before she damages my reputation any further. 'Mum, there's no need to worry.' I take a deep breath and cross my fingers, hoping this will cancel out my tempting fate. 'I've met someone. A man,' I add, pointedly.

I can almost hear the Hallelujah chorus in my mother's head.

'It's early days,' I mutter, unnerved by the look of radiant joy that has lit up her features. 'So I don't want to say too much at this stage.'

'Oh darling,' she chokes. 'That's, well, it's wonderful, such a relief. I was beginning to think . . .'

'I know what you were beginning to think,' I say through gritted teeth.

She finally clocks my warning tone. 'Of course you must be feeling sensitive. It's so exciting falling in love.'

I down my gin and tonic and switch off. I can tell I'm going to pay for this.

I hate Sundays. I loathe and detest them. There's nothing to do, except watch *The Waltons* and the omnibus *EastEnders*. And if you're single, it's pants.

Everyone knows that if you've got a lover, Sundays couldn't be more different. People in couples reserve Sundays for joyful cosy togetherness.

I hate them all.

I bet they're down at Café Flo right now, holding hands under the papers, glowing from their lazy morning shagging. Or they're zooming round in their convertible cars, laughing together and looking cool. Or, even worse, they're out in the country having a lovely boozy time with other couply friends, or just lying on the sofa watching vids together. And I bet every one of them takes it for granted. Bastards.

I'm sulking. Jack hasn't called and it's 1.30 p.m. All morning I've been daydreaming about him asking me out for lunch, followed maybe by a stroll in the park, then the cinema? I've worked it out in such detail that I've begun to believe it will happen. But it's not going to happen. The phone is in my eyeline and it's silent. I've already checked it's plugged in correctly at the socket and I've even called the operator just to reassure myself that there're no faults on the line.

I'm lying on the sofa with my cheek pressed into the cushion, staring at the stain on the carpet. I can't phone anyone just in case he rings, can't eat anything just in case he asks me out. I've already given myself three sweaty orgasms out of sheer boredom, but I'm still full of frustrated lust. I've even tried to transmit telepathic waves. All to no avail. It's a glorious day and I'm stuck inside. A prisoner of my own hope.

When H calls, I nearly jump out of my skin.

'No news then?'

'Nada.'

'We're going down the pub. You coming?'

'No. I don't know. I've got things to do,' I stall.

'Like what? It's Sunday!'

'Just things,' I say defensively.

H sighs. 'You're waiting for him to call, aren't you? It's not going to do any good you know. He'll ring when he rings. There's no point in watching the phone, you'll go bats.'

I hate the fact that she knows me so well.

'I know that. I'm busy. I'm going down the gym,' I bluff.

'What?'

'The gym, you know – exercise.'

'Oh well, suit yourself. You know where we are.'

'Thank you.'

'Weirdo,' she mutters.

I stick my tongue out at the phone. I have no intention of going to the gym. I think I'll go for a walk.

The walk is good. Shepherd's Bush is not a particularly

inspiring place, but at least it's relatively couple-free and I don't notice the winos and junkies as I'm deeply engrossed in giving myself a good talking to. By the time I've walked round the green a few times, I'm on a carbon monoxide high and I've worked out a strategy.

It's fairly convoluted, but the gist of it is this. Jack must know I fancy him. Forgetting the last blip of our encounter, things couldn't have been better so he must know that I want to see him. However, Jack's a cool guy and he has things to do. He's an artist. He's probably busy. And that doesn't mean that he's not thinking about me, it's just that I wasn't booked into his Sunday schedule. And anyway, since he's so cool, he probably won't ring me until tomorrow. Tuesday at the outside. And Matt probably needs some attention. He did get ignored on his birthday by his best mate because of me. So the thing to do is not to wait around, moping, but to get prepared.

Preparation is power.

I decide not to go to the pub as that will just be a diversion. Instead I walk to Boots in Notting Hill and indulge in some shopping therapy. This is immensely enjoyable. I love Boots. It's my favourite shop, except perhaps for Hamleys. I buy girl toys: Badedas bath stuff, expensive shampoo and conditioner with free hair oil, a bumper pack of nail files, three nail varnishes, tweezers, a loofah, mud pack, a new lipstick, a box of coloured tissues (always handy to have by the bed), Oil of Ulay, bikini-line wax, fake tan and a pack of twenty-four super sensitive condoms.

Excellent.

Back at the flat, I do some home-making and am pleased with the results. I don't do anything as ambitious as stripping off any of the Anaglypta wallpaper, or Polyfilla'ing the crack in the kitchen wall, but I do arrange my books on the dodgy shelves and put up the framed picture of me and H on our travels in Thailand.

We were single girls on tour then and we had the time of our lives. In the photo we both look thin and tanned and we're sitting back to back laughing our heads off. That was the holiday where we went island-hopping for three weeks, but got stuck on one beach. H got two shags in and copious snogs and I fell in love with three blokes simultaneously. Toptastic!

I sort out the black bin liner of odd socks and jumpers that has been hanging about by the front door for ages and am surprised how quickly the time goes. I like being a woman on a mission.

I run a huge bath and assess my body in the hall mirror. Naked, I'm not so bad if it's just me looking at me. On a good day, I'm a curvy size eleven and a half.

However, how am I going to look through Jack's eyes? Put it this way. If I did a public striptease, people would ask for their money back.

It's time to diet.

As soon as I decide this, a hunger pang shoots through my stomach like a bolt of lightning and my brain is suddenly crammed with images of all the yummy fattening food I'd like to eat *right now*. I have to get in the bath to ignore them. I lie in the steam with my mud pack on and think about how different I'm going to look in a week.

I spend the evening virtuously nibbling Ryvitas and reading a book called *Power Women* which someone gave me for my last birthday. It's very interesting.

On Monday morning I'm up before the alarm, which is a first. Mornings are so relaxing when you're up at 7.00 a.m. The birds are singing and I listen to Radio 4 for a change, as part of my new intention to get with the world. I think it's important that I should catch up with what's going on.

After my second cup of tea I fish out *Power Women* from under the bed and position myself in front of the bathroom mirror. It's time for some positive affirmations.

'I am a unique, compassionate and loving person,' I read aloud. I look up at my reflection to see whether it has clocked this.

'I am a Power Woman. I can change the world in which I live.' I look up again.

'I look great, feel great. I love myself . . . And Jack is going to ring me today,' I add for good measure, before snapping the book shut and cleaning my teeth.

I pull out the bathroom scales and weigh myself. I'm a pound heavier than yesterday. How can this be? I've deprived myself of food for over twelve hours; I should be at least a stone thinner by now.

I look back up in the mirror. 'I look great. I feel great. I love myself,' I say threateningly.

Elaine at Top Temps has got me a job at Boothroyd, Carter and May, a firm of stuffy management consultants in Portland Square. Janet, their receptionist, is on holiday and I'm going to fill in. Lucky, lucky me.

I stand in the lift with a vague sense of gloom. I can't believe I'm doing yet another temping job. When am I going to get a career, I wonder? I envy people who are very clear about their career choices. People who say, 'I'm going to be a doctor.' And do it. All I can say is, 'I'm going to be a?'

A bored receptionist for a week, that's what.

I have five guidelines for the first day of a new job:

1. Find out my direct line number and call H with it
2. Locate computer games on PC, find the loo and the kitchen
3. Find out who is responsible for signing my timesheet and make them a cup of coffee within the first hour of arrival
4. Find out name and description of the big boss to avoid embarrassment
5. Never, ever stay past 5.30 p.m. and always take a lunch-break

The person responsible for my timesheets is Ms Audrey Payne. On sight I christen her Vinegar Tits. She doesn't seem to like me very much, but then I don't think she likes anyone, humour not being something that she's encountered yet in her life. I make her a coffee, and every time she walks past I rattle the keys on the PC and look efficient.

At 11.30 Elaine calls. 'I hear you're getting on well.'

Fooled them again. Out comes my copy of *Hello!* and the nail file. I know it's cliché to read *Hello!*, but it's an essential item as a temp. I'm sure it's called *Hello!* because it's such an ice breaker. There's not one person I've ever encountered in an office who doesn't have a guilty itch to flick through a copy when they see one. As a temp, if you let them indulge in their (in my opinion healthy) need for escapism, then you've got a friend for life. *Hello!* It works every time.

I spend an hour at lunchtime in Portland Square, sitting on my hands and watching the pigeons. I tell myself that even though I have eaten a Tesco Metro low-calorie chicken sandwich in under a minute, it was satisfying, and no, I am definitely *not* hungry. I recognise a woman from the office walking towards the bench and I have to occupy myself frantically with my purse to avoid contact. I have no desire to speak to her and answer all those questions about Why I'm A Temp. Once you're further than about two feet from the reception desk, I think it's always a good plan to maintain a them-and-us attitude at all times. Involvement always leads to misery and I've discovered that non-attachment works fine for me. It means that I never have to sign leaving cards for people I don't know, gossip about tawdry office affairs, or stand in the pub after work with a bunch of people bitching about the management.

By 2.15 my stomach is eating my liver in protest. I find a packet of cornflakes in the kitchen and eat five handfuls in desperation before washing them down with a gallon of tea.

Between 2.30 and 4.15 I play an uninterrupted game of computer Solitaire, chat to H for half an hour about being a Power Woman whilst picking stray cornflakes off my jumper, play with the paperclips on my desk, type a label for Vinegar Tits, frank the post and before I know it, it's time to go home. All in all, a fairly stress-free day.

That is until I get home and discover that there are no messages on the machine. I mutter affirmations in the shower and then watch *Brookside*.

Still nothing happens. By midnight, I feel a bit wobbly. It's all very well being a Power Woman and in control of my own life, but it's incredibly dull.

It's Tuesday and I'm still calm. Emaciated, but calm.

I spend most of the day toying with the idea of going to the gym. Of course, as soon as the chances of me exercising move up the scale from remote to possible, my body goes into spasm. By mid-afternoon I've developed premature arthritis and a low-level pneumonia-type feeling. However, I know my body and its tricks. It's forgetting that I'm a Power Woman.

I get to the gym by about 7.00 p.m. It's packed and I'm feeling like a bit of a spare part. What am I doing here?

This is definitely not my natural habitat.

I'm dressed in paint-splattered leggings, my *circa* 1984 school trainers, which I had hoped might look retro and cool (but don't), a T-shirt that has gone grey in the wash and odd socks. Cindy Crawford eat your heart out.

I squeeze past the super-fit blokes on the pecs machine to the cabinet in the corner and riffle through it to find my gym induction sheet. I dust it down and set off on the stationary bike.

It takes just two minutes to reduce me to a beetroot sweat-ball. I hop off and try my luck on the MarathonMachine. The girl next to me is wired up to a state-of-the-art Discman and is sprinting in pristine Reebok kit. She's doesn't appear to be sweating and I deduce from this that it must be easy.

Undeterred by her odd look, I rev up the speed and try to catch up with her, but my legs won't go fast enough and I shoot off the back. I ignore her snigger as I clamber back on, jumping my feet on to the plastic casing whilst I slow the machine down to a walking pace.

Walking's good. There's nothing wrong with walking.

I concentrate hard on the calorie counter which doesn't

seem to be moving. After twenty minutes I've burned precisely forty-two calories. That's about three cornflakes.

I'm seriously worried about my level of fitness. By the time
I get on the step machine, my heart is telling me it's about to
pack up. I make an executive decision to come to the gym
every day from now on. And if I do that, take it slowly and
don't push myself at first, then I'll get fit sensibly. There's no
point in burning out early is there now?

I consult my induction sheet and give the press-up machine
a go, but I think it's broken. I certainly can't make it budge.
Exhausted, I flop on to a floormat for sit-ups. I only manage
five, but console myself with the thought that I don't really
want a flat stomach. Flat stomachs are so *eighties*.

By 7.35 I'm in the changing rooms, my hair plastered to my
face. I'm not looking, or for that matter feeling, my best. With
a great deal of effort, I bend down and untie my trainers.

'Amy?'

I slowly look up. Up past the matching slouch-socks, up the
toned, tanned legs, up the perfect cycling shorts to bare midriff
and neatly enclosed breasts in Elle top until my eyes stop at the
orthodontic advert smile.

It's your basic nightmare.

It's Chloe.

'Are you all right?' she asks.

'Yep, fine,' I say, raking my soggy hair away from my face.
'How are you?'

'Great. Did you have a good time the other night at Matt's?'

I'm experiencing mild panic. She must know about me and
Jack. I nod dumbly. Hello? Where is my personality?

'You left with Jack, didn't you?'

'Nothing happened,' I blurt.

'That's not what I heard.' She gives me a teasing wink.

I clear my throat. 'What did he say?'

Thank God I'm red already and she can't tell I'm blushing.

'Nothing much. He was pretty plastered by the time he got
back to Matt's. You mustn't take much notice of him. To be
honest, he's a bit of a tart.'

47

'Really?'

'He's *dreadful*! He shagged my neighbour Cathy the other day and chucked her out without even so much as a cup of coffee. And he leches after all the nude models he paints. We tease him all the time, but you know blokes like him . . .'

'Yeah. I kinda figured that.' I suppress the urge to throttle her, but maybe something in my tone suggests to her that all is not well.

'Of course, I wouldn't blame you if you did want to . . . you know. He's quite cute.' She cocks her head at me.

'You seem to know him pretty well,' I mutter.

'Known him for years. We were all at school together.'

'Oh yes, he told me. I forgot.'

I'm a liar. I could recite his every word at gunpoint.

'He's a good mate, actually. Always game on for a laugh. You should come out with us more often.' Chloe beams at me.

I experience the emotion hatred.

'I'd like that. I had a great time. Actually I was going to call Matt and thank him, but I don't have his number.'

Inspirational, my girl. Inspirational.

Chloe unzips her bag and whips out a thick personal organiser. I ogle as she rips out a crisp lavender page and scrawls the number on it with her funky but obviously expensive ink pen. She hands it over.

'Cheers,' I say, trying to sound nonplussed whilst I carefully fold it up.

She smiles at me, leans forward and kisses my steaming cheek. 'Excellent. I'll see you soon then.'

She's almost out of the door when she turns back. 'Oh, by the way, I did give Jack your number. I hope you don't mind.'

It takes a packet of chips and three pints of Stella with H to digest this information. We go over every possible meaning. My thoughts are that Chloe is trying to warn me off because she likes me and doesn't want me to get hurt, or that she's trying to make Jack seem more attractive by making him out to be a rogue. H is having none of it, but then she doesn't like Chloe much. She says that Chloe is deliberately stirring because she doesn't want her cosy inner circle of friends upset, and for all we know, she probably fancies Jack herself.

Chloe went out with H's brother's friend once and by all accounts was a bit of a bitch. I met her at a party about a year ago just as the relationship was ending and she got drunk and cried on my shoulder. Then I met her again at H's brother's wedding and we've sort of stayed in touch ever since. I like her, but I agree with H that she's not a girl's girl, but a boy's girl. They're altogether different.

'Ah,' I say, 'but if that's the case, why did she ask me to go out with them and why did she give Jack my number?'

H shrugs and shakes her head, 'Dunno. I don't trust her, though. Anyway, you haven't got a problem, you've got his number now.'

'Yes, and he's had my number for days, but he hasn't bloody rung it, has he?'

H sips her pint thoughtfully. 'Are you sure you really want him? It doesn't sound like he's particularly trustworthy.'

'He hasn't found the right girl, that's all,' I smile, before a worrying thought comes into my head. 'What if Chloe tells Jack she saw me and I looked a state?'

'For God's sake!'

'But maybe when I told him I fancied Matt, he believed me and has written me off and doesn't fancy me at all.' I plunge into a monologue of self doubts and further reasons for his silence, before H silences me herself. She stands up with her empty glass.

'This is really getting on my tits,' she warns.

Over the next pint, H dispenses practical advice. She says that if she were me, she'd call Jack and suss out the situation for herself. But she's not me. She's much braver. I tell her that if he really wants to get in touch he will. I'll just have to wait. H says I'm being defeatist, but it's easy for her to say, she's got Gav.

I'm drunk by the time I get home and I'm feeling sorry for myself. Jack still hasn't rung, even though Chloe must have said something by now. I'm not going to call him. He had my number first, so it's up to him. It wouldn't be cool to call him, despite what H says.

I snuggle up with *Power Women* and drop off instantly.

On Wednesday, I wake up and I can't move. Every muscle in my body is in shock. At first I think I've been in a bad car accident and then I remember the gym. I haven't even opened my eyes yet and already I've got a bad feeling about today.

In theory, my morning routine should go roughly as follows:

7.00 a.m.: Alarm goes. Press snooze button.

7.20 a.m.: Alarm goes again. Press snooze button again.

7.40 a.m.: At third alarm, get out of bed. Wash face, put kettle on. Run bath.

7.45 a.m.: Consume tea. Do positive affirmations. Get into bath.

8.10 a.m.: Emerge from bath with washed and conditioned hair.

8.15 a.m.: Dry and attempt to style hair (always a disaster).

8.25 a.m.: Open wardrobe. Assemble and don outfit of choice. (Ironing optional.)

8.30 a.m.: Consume bowl of cereal or toast (depending on milk situation).

8.35 a.m.: Double-check I'm properly dressed. Clean teeth. Assemble kit for possible chores, i.e. dry cleaning, shoe repairs, etc. Apply make-up.

8.40 a.m.: Check and recheck contents of bag. Locate keys.

8.45 a.m.: Leave flat.

Today I wake up at 8.45 a.m. It's not a good start.

Why is it that when I oversleep, I always wake up at the exact time I'm supposed to leave the house? Weird.

Vinegar Tits gives me a lecture on punctuality and I resolve to poison her. I put through calls to the wrong people and generally Fuck Up all day. I console myself with a BLT at lunchtime with extra mayonnaise. There seems to be no point in being thin now.

I spend the afternoon having run-through conversations with Jack.

Me: Hello?

Jack: Hi Amy, it's Jack here.

Me: (Confused) Who?

Jack: You know, from the other night. I had a fantastic time. You were amazing. Honestly, I've never met such an intelligent, sexy . . .

No scrap that. It's never going to happen.

Me: Hello?

Jack: Hi, Babe, it's Jack.

Me: (Super cool) Hi, how are you?

Jack: Lonely without you . . .

Blah! He's making me puke.

This goes on and on. I've rehearsed it all, except the conversations where I've rung him. However, by the end of the afternoon, I've got so used to talking to him that I know he will call. It must be impossible for one human being to think about another one this much without them picking up some kind of vibe. Surely?

There's only one message on the answer machine when I get home. It's from H telling me to call her when I've called Jack.

I can't back out of it. I psyche myself up by flicking through a few pages of *Power Women*. 'Don't give away your power to other people . . . Women who get what they want are always *proactive* . . . etc.'

I stare at the filofax page with Jack's number on it. Just do it. Do it. Do it. Come on, pick up the phone.

Jack's phone rings four times. I squeeze my phone to my ear. My knuckles are white. I feel so exposed. I'm ringing inside his house!

Then the answer machine clicks on. It's Matt's voice.

'Hi, Matt and Jack aren't here right now. Please leave a message after the tone and we'll get back to you. Beep.'

And then something strange happens. Out of nowhere, a chipmunk becomes lodged in my oesophagus.

'Hi, this is . . .' I begin. Then nothing. I'm so shocked by the sound coming out of my mouth. I try again. 'This is Amy. Um.' More silence, then the beep.

I have single-handedly left the worst message *ever* on an answer machine. *Ever*. In the history of the world. And I can't do anything about it. I put down the phone as if it has given me an electric shock and start to flap my hands about. I'm burning up.

I rip the phone out of the socket and switch off the plug of the answering machine, open the window and hurl *Power Women* into next door's garden.

Thursday: melt down.

I am catatonic at work. I've realised that my problem is much bigger than the Jack answerphone incident. It has expanded to encompass my whole life. Unwittingly Geoff steps into this personal crisis.

Geoff is a consultant at Boothroyd, Carter and May and he's been hanging around the reception area all week. This is because he's the office Billy No Mates. He can only be described as a damp squib. There's nothing remotely attractive about him. He has rectangular glasses, a bald patch and a body odour problem.

Such is my state of mind that when Geoff asks me out for lunch, I agree to go. *I go on a date with Geoff!*

He takes me to an Italian restaurant and orders spaghetti which he splatters down his tie. He's very nervous and obsequiously flattered that I've agreed to go out with him. I don't really connect with this, because I'm having an out-of-body kind of a day. Conversation is getting a bit stilted and I start to prod my lasagne with my fork.

'You don't seem very happy,' observes Geoff.

Top marks to Einstein over there.

I shrug. 'I'm okay.'

'What are you thinking about?' he asks (stupidly).

So I tell him.

I let rip.

I tell him that I'm thinking that people only attract people that they *can* attract. For example, Elizabeth Taylor attracted Richard Burton because they were more or less as attractive as each other. And I have attracted Geoff. So that must mean that I'm the same kind of level of attractiveness as Geoff. And that, quite frankly, makes me want to top myself.

I don't know what came over me. I've never said anything so unkind to a virtual stranger before. We stare at each other for a while and then I smile nervously, but Geoff looks really upset. With shaking hands, he pulls some cash out of his wallet, drops it on the table and scuttles off.

Fortunately, because no one speaks to Geoff, he doesn't have anyone to bitch to, so there's no showdown at the office. However, I spend the afternoon in deep remorse.

When I get home, I pluck up the courage to reconnect the phone.

Immediately, Mum calls for one of her 'chats'.

'Darling. How's that lovely new man of yours? I'm dying to know—'

'He's not lovely and he's not mine!' I yell.

I'm having some sort of personality collapse.

Jack still doesn't call. H comes round and we have a barney when I refuse to allow her to pull me out of my black mood. She tells me that I'm being pathetic and there's no need to take it out on everyone else. She's got a point, but I'm beyond seeing it.

'You don't understand,' I say spitefully. 'You don't know what it's like to be dumped even before you had a first date.'

She takes a tough line. 'This has got nothing to do with Jack,' she says, infuriatingly calmly. 'You've finally cracked and it's the temping that's done it. I knew it would.'

'So what if I have a shite job and a shite life? That's my lot. I can't do anything else,' I snap. 'I'm hopeless at everything.'

She refuses to rise to this. 'That's utter bollocks. You're not trying. It's as if you've given up. You know you want to get into fashion and make a go of things, but you're too scared.'

'Oh shut up! That's ancient history. It's too late anyway.'

'It's not too late, you're just being stubborn.'

'Oh, and what would you know? You with your swish job in television and Gav to come home to. What would you know about being at a dead end?' I say, but I'm losing it and my voice starts to shake.

'Having a boyfriend is not going to solve all your problems, Amy.'

'Thank you very much, Claire Rayner,' I choke. 'It may not be the answer, but it'd be a bloody good start, because you have no idea how much I hate being on my own. Dealing with all this . . . shit,' I spit, as I start to blub. 'But if you hadn't noticed, I can't pull anyone. I can't even pull Geoff, because he's realised the truth – that I'm a horrible person and my life is going nowhere . . . and . . . and . . . I'm going to end up in my thirties, a bitter, twisted failure and . . . and . . . I'll die a vi-ir-ir-ir-ir-ir-gin.'

H gives me a big hug, opens the box of coloured tissues, makes me a cup of herbal tea and puts me to bed. She reassures me that everything will be fine in the morning.

Right. Fuck them all! No more wimping about. I've had it. I've expended far too much energy waiting for that fucker to call. One measly little call was all it would have taken, but oh no, he's just a selfish *bastard*! Well, I'm through with wasting my time on him. He's not going to put me through any more of this agony. This week I've lost and regained half a stone, argued with everyone, including H, and for what? Answer me that? Sweet Fanny Adams.

So that's it. Jack Rossiter is out of my life for good. I mean, doesn't he know who I am? He should be round here begging for a date, making my phone wires melt, turning my flat into a bloody florists. Well, do you know what? He can Fuck Off.

54

Take his bloody floozies, fancy clothes *and* all his arty bollocks and Shove It.

Boy, I'm in a feisty mood this morning. I am Tarzan; who needs to be wimpy Jane? I am a Power Woman after all.

I don't need men. Men and all their smelly genitals, disgusting toenails and hi-fi snobbery. Who needs them? Not me. No siree.

I stand on the doorstep and take an invigorating breath. Huh! No stupid man is going to get one over on me ever again. Today is the last day of the temp job and THE FIRST DAY OF THE REST OF MY LIFE.

Unfortunately, I slip on the front steps and snag my tights.

However, I refuse to be fazed and I think my new attitude shows. People get out of my way on the tube and, in the office, people's greetings wither on their lips. I cruise through the day with brutal efficiency. I even tidy up the stationery cupboard which certainly impresses Vinegar Tits.

At 5.30 on the dot I hand her my timesheet. This is the part of temping that I usually detest most. People make such a fuss about signing your sheet, quibbling over the hours and making you feel like you're some kind of prisoner on parole. Not today though. Vinegar Tits looks me up and down as I stand to attention by her desk.

'Thank you, Anna, for all your hard work,' she says. 'I must say that today you've been most, um, diligent.'

'It's Amy actually. You're welcome.'

'Well we won't be needing you next week. Janet's back from holidays, but I'll be in touch if anything comes up.'

She doesn't mean it and that's fine by me. I'm out of here.

I stride over to the Top Temps offices. Elaine has a Friday night party for all the temps which is impossible to avoid when dropping off your timesheet. It's supposed to make us feel like we're one big happy family and not the scourge of the planet that everyone else seems to think is the case. Actually, these parties are just embarrassing. Temps don't have much respect for themselves, let alone each other.

The offices are tropical. There's a platter of curling

sandwiches on the reception desk, a couple of bottles of pop, and a Blue Nun wine box. Elaine is halfway through this already, her smudged eyeliner giving her panda eyes.

'Stay, come on, stay for a drink,' she slurs, chucking my timesheet in her in tray.

I decline her offer and tell her that I'm going out. She tells me that she'll call me about more work next week.

I use the office phone to leave a message on H's mobile. I tell her that she has no choice, we're going to paint the town red.

Blood red.

I hum my way up the stairs to the flat, excited about the prospect of a girls night out. I'm going to get shit-faced. Beyond shit-faced. I deserve it. I might even indulge in a few Class As if they make an appearance. There's nothing that could possibly stop me. I'm In Control.

I put the key in the door. I'm not even going to so much as *look* at the answering machine. I wouldn't give it the satisfaction of knowing that I care. Because, quite frankly, I don't. Even if there were ten messages from Jack-Fuckwit-Rossiter, I'd wipe them all off. And if he were to call again, I'd just tell him to drop dead.

The phone starts as I open the door. Great, that'll be H, ready to make plans.

I lunge for the phone.

'Hello,' I chirp.

There's a small pause.

'Hi, Amy, it's Jack. I just wondered what you were doing tonight.'

And I know this is bad. Really, really bad. That in two seconds I undo the work of two decades of the Women's Liberation Movement. It's just that I'm so happy to hear his voice. So pathetically grateful that he's called at last, that I hear myself saying, far more enthusiastically than I mean to, 'Nothing. Why?'

3
Jack

The Phonecall

'Nothing. Why?'

Well, the why's the easy part. The why I can do standing on my head with my hands tied. Because it's a Friday night and I'm home alone. Because, Amy, despite the fact that last week you told me you fancied Matt, I'm still hoping you might fancy me, too. Because I haven't had sex for over a week and you haven't had sex for over six months. Because, Amy, we therefore have a mutual need. And, yeah, because I fancy you, too.

The nothing, though . . . the nothing's the tricky bit. The nothing comes as a surprise. The nothing's – well, it's just too *honest*. I mean, there are meant to be rules to this game we're playing. There's a manual and inside the manual there are regulations. There are things single people do and things they don't. They do:

a) Meet someone at a party and click with them and file them as an Option in the Pend folder marked PSM (Potential Shag Material)

b) From time to time, find themselves on a Friday night, mateless and dateless, and flick through the PSM folder in search of an Option

c) Occasionally decide to call said Option up and suggest a meet

But they don't:

a) Answer the phone in person at any time, because they understand that answerphones, like Rottweilers, are there to guard them from unwanted intrusions into their lives

b) Pick up the phone on a Friday night if they're in alone, thereby making whoever's called think their social life's just been read its last rites

c) Confirm this impression by using the word 'Nothing' when asked what their plans are for the night

And we're meant to abide by these Rules of Engagement, because they've been designed to protect our status as Single People. They constitute our Declaration of Independence and it's our duty to endorse them at all times.

Only my rules, Amy, obviously aren't yours. With one word, you've gone and ripped the manual up. You've chucked me on the hot spot. In bare feet. And you've left me there with no choice but to convert your nothing into a something. I reach for a cigarette.

'Well,' I say, perching on the edge of the armchair, 'I had this thing where I was meant to be working tonight. Got some portrait I swore I'd finish by Sunday in time for this guy's fiftieth birthday. Only I finished it about an hour ago and . . . and . . . I don't know . . . It was good meeting you last week. We had a laugh, you know, and I thought maybe we should do it again. So, I thought I'd give you a call. On the off chance. See what you're up to, kind of thing . . .'

'Are you asking me out for a date, Jack?'

Direct. Fine, I can do direct, too. 'Well, yeah, that's one way of looking at it.'

'Okay.'

'Okay as in you're considering it, or okay as in yeah, let's do it?'

'Okay as in I've considered it, and okay as in yeah, let's do it.'

I smile at her mimicking me. 'Okay, I'll sort out a restaurant. We can go for a drink first, if you like.'

'I like.'

I smile again. 'You know Zack's?'

'Sure.'

'See you there round eight?'

'Okay, see you there.'

At first, when I replace the phone receiver, I can't help feeling like I'm slipping a six shooter back into a holster after a gunfight. However, apart from a slightly increased heartbeat, I'm A-OK. I've survived a Live Phone Conversation. And it went well. Amy was friendly, pleased to hear from me. I asked her out for a date and she said yes. We're going to meet up. Tonight. So it's a result. Billy the Kid 1. Calamity Jane 0.

But then the realisation hits me: *My God, I'm going on A Date*. A *Date*, for Christ's sake. As in drinks and dinner. As in hours of small talk with someone I hardly know. As in the kind of evening I quit doing once I realised there were other, less complicated paths to sex.

What the hell am I playing at?

Be calm.

I pull heavily on my cigarette and try to convince myself that this is not as bad as it looks. Amy's nice. She's attractive. She's fun. Plus, I *do* want to see her. Why else would I have called? And it's not like I don't know her. After all, I spent the best part of a night with her, didn't I? And she's keen. And if she's agreed to see me, she can't be as keen on Matt as she made out. So this is a perfectly natural thing to be doing.

I sort of blame Chloe for the bizarre direction my evening's heading in. I stare at the piece of paper in my hand: Chloe's handwriting; Amy's number. Chloe palmed it off on me on Monday, after she'd grown bored of me grumbling about the *still* unresolved McCullen situation. She said I should give Amy a call, reckoned I was just frustrated and a good, uncomplicated shag would simmer me down. And then Amy – at least, I'm pretty sure it was Amy – phoned up and left a weird and brief message on Wednesday night. Her getting my number must have been down to Chloe. Can't think of anyone else who'd dare. She's always pulling stunts like that with me and Matt, making sure her boys are happy. And we return the favour, set her up from time to time with blokes we know.

Sometimes I wonder if it wouldn't make more sense if Chloe and I just cut out the middle men and women and gave each other a go. It's not like I've never considered it and it's not like we don't flirt. I talked it through with Matt one time just after I'd split with Zoe. We'd got drunk with Chloe the night before and she'd crashed next to me in my bed. Matt had woken us up with coffee in the morning and found Chloe cradled in my arms. Once she'd gone home, he asked me if anything had happened and I told him no. Then he asked me why not, and I told him that I loved her, but could never fall in love with her. Same as for him, she was my friend. There'd be too much pressure on us to make it work. And, besides, I already knew her too well. What would there be left to discover? I don't know whether he believed me. I wasn't even sure if I believed myself.

I look across the living room and check the old Marlboro clock above the bar: six-thirty. Things to do, things to be . . .

I go up to Matt's bedroom and pull open his wardrobe door and for the thousandth time count myself lucky for having a best friend who doesn't have a sharing problem. Got to hand it to the guy. There are clothes in here for every occasion: dinner jackets, tails and suits, labelled shirts and jeans and jumpers. Coming here's like hitting the shops with an AmEx gold card: you just take your pick. (Always ensure your flatmate has the same build as you.) I just pray that, with all those fat-boy City lunches he indulges in, he doesn't go turning into a bloater. That would be me scuppered on the clothes front. Probably have to resort to a lard-based diet to match his weight. Either that, or get a real job and an AmEx card of my own. And until the end of this year – the deadline I've given myself for making a success of my painting – that just isn't going to happen. I select some stuff and hit the bathroom.

A lot of girls I know regard personal hygiene as a gender issue: girls are into it, guys aren't. End of story. They are, to a degree, correct. Leave a guy on his own for a year. Cut him off from civilisation and, more importantly, the prospect of sex. Do all this and there's a pretty good chance he'll go to seed. Socks and underpants will be worn in rotation, unwashed until they start to itch, or their smell starts to rival the crust of unwrapped cheese in the fridge. Small Saharas of dust will creep unnoticed across the surfaces. The stove will come to resemble a road kill as the pan splashes pile up. And ridges of black dirt will threaten to prise finger and toenails free from their digits.

That said, though, put the same guy back in his normal habitat and the story's plot takes a different turn. Give him a date with a ten per cent chance of a lay and he'll be racking up more deodorants and body lotions than Cleopatra. The point, I suppose, is this: with guys, hygiene is a sex thing. You get clean, you get laid. It's that simple. Take young guys, guys at the stage of evolution where they still think that if the socks aren't running away, they're safe to wear. These guys don't care how mucky they get. Put them within a hundred yards of a dog's turd and, chances are, they'll end up rolling in it. It's only when they hit sexual maturity that they get with the programme. They notice that when they stink, girls think they suck. Crap at mathematics, as they may be, they're suddenly capable of working out the following complex series of equations themselves: Bad breath and mucky teeth = No kissing; Poor lower body hygiene = No sex.

And I'm no different. Take tonight. And not just a ten per cent chance, either. The way I see it, it's more like fifty per cent. Play my cards right and tonight might conclude with a quick stroll down Sure Thing Avenue to Kit-Off Manor. And to ensure that this *is* the case, I do the hygiene thing. Big Time. I shower, scrub, shave, sort my hair, brush and floss my teeth, clean my ears, trim my nails, rub in body lotion and stroke on aftershave. Then I dress: Calvins (a.k.a. Pulling Pants); clean socks; and Matt's clothes (clean and ironed, as always). I check myself out in the mirror, smile as I will at Amy later on over dinner. And my overall impression? I'm convinced. So let's hope she is, too.

Downstairs, I fix myself a beer and chuck on a CD. Zack's is only round the corner, so there's no rush. All that's left to do is choose a restaurant and book it. Somewhere fun and, out of necessity, not too expensive. Somewhere we can relax and have a laugh. Or, rather, that *would* be all that was left to do if I hadn't already done it. But I have. Four hours ago, before I even thought of giving Amy a call. Four hours ago, towards the end of my second session with McCullen. Four hours ago, when I decided to book a table at Hot House, guessing that it was the kind of place McCullen would think hip. Four hours ago, about one hour before I realised for the second time in two weeks that she still wasn't up for it.

Mount McCullen: Base Camp

McCullen rang the doorbell round ten this morning. This time I was ready for her. No Catherine Bradshaw lurking demoni-acally by the bus stop. No sleep deprivation tying up my tongue. No hangover pulsing in my brain. Nothing, in other words, to hinder my second attempt at the conquest of Mount McCullen.

When I opened the door, she kissed me (on the cheek) and even went so far as to give me a quick hug (platonic). This was encouraging. Not the height of pash, sure, but First Contact nonetheless. And inside, she was all smiles, too. No apprehen-sion and twitchy fingers and furrowed brow, like last week. A quick coffee, some chit-chat about a party she'd been to with Kate, a bit of gossip here, a bit of slagging off there. Just like we'd known each other for years. Then through to the studio, where she stripped without a trace of inhibition, before taking up her pose on the sofa. And if all this was good, what came later, as we broke for a mid-afternoon drink in the garden, was better.

The sun glared down like a headlight from the clear blue sky: blinding. McCullen, wearing nothing more than a towel (mine) and pair of Ray Bans (Matt's), was sitting next to me on one of the three wooden benches in the garden. Four recently emptied beer bottles lay on the yellowing grass by our bare feet, sparkling in the sun. A disc of shade, cast by the Bud parasol which mushroomed out of the centre of the old pub table in front of us, cooled our skin. Between us, resting on the wooden slats of the bench, was an ice box, packed with beers. I pulled two out and flipped their tops against the table's edge, passed one to McCullen and raised the other to my lips, drank.

I turned to face her, watched her light a cigarette and stare across the garden. For the first time, I saw freckles on her face. It wasn't surprising I hadn't noticed them before, even after all the time I'd spent studying her indoors. There had, after all, been other bodily features which had drawn my attention. They were faint. Not the loud kind that tempted you to pull out a pen and join the dots, but the kind you worried the merest gust of wind might blow away like confetti. Her head turned and, not wanting to be caught staring, I lowered my eyes and gazed down at the fine hairs showing on my thighs at the bottom of my shorts.

There was no doubt about it. This was perfect. This was a Moment. Serene. There was me. And there was her. And there was sun and there was beer. I hadn't been able to afford a holiday abroad for three years, but this was the kind of situation I'd imagined over all those cold winter nights with no warm body to hold close to mine. These were the kind of colours that had washed the blues away. And, even if it hadn't been McCullen's face I'd pictured there beside me on the beach, it hadn't been far off.

'So,' I said, turning back to face her, 'tell me about your man.'

'Why?'

'Just curious, that's all.'

Which, obviously, was far from being the whole truth and nothing but.

There are two schools of thought on raising the topic of partners with someone you've got your sights set on. There's your Passive School and there's your Active. The former supports the theory that the less you mention the other person's partner, the less they think about them. And, once they're no longer thinking about them, there's no reason why they shouldn't just be thinking about you. And once that's happened, you're in. And then there's your Active. Cut to the chase. Raise the boyfriend subject for debate and you're going to know pretty quick exactly what it is you're up against. I'm more into that. It saves time.

She smiled. I don't know whether it was because she'd guessed I was making a pass and was embarrassed, or because just thinking about him had that effect. Naturally, I hoped it was the former.

'I don't know where to start.'

'How about the beginning? A very good place. It worked for Julie Andrews, anyway.'

So she told me. She told me that his name was Jonathan, but everyone called him Jons. She told me how they met at school when she was seventeen. She told me he was handsome and sang in a band. And just when I was reaching for a sick bag and cursing skipping Professor Passive's lectures, Luke Skywalker suddenly underwent a remarkable transformation into Darth Vader. McCullen's smile switched to a frown and she drew back the curtain on the Dark Side: the coke habit which he couldn't afford; the paranoia; the way, being at university up in Glasgow, he kept tabs on her, insisted on them hooking up every weekend; the way he dirted her friends; the fact that he'd freak if he ever found out that she was modelling for me.

It's funny how sometimes bad can be good. The worse she made him sound, the better I knew my chances were. Jesus, I almost came round to liking the guy.

And then she said, 'I don't know, sometimes I wonder why I'm still with him.'

Which made me think: *Houston, we no longer have a problem*.

But then she said, 'That's stupid. I didn't mean that. I love him.' She glanced accusingly at her beer bottle, slowly shook her head. 'Alcohol and sun. Always spaces me out. Forget I said that.'

Which made me think: *Ground Control to Major Tom. Your circuit's dead, there's something wrong*.

And so I went for the ultimatum, threw her into what I refer to as The Worst Case Scenario: the prospect of marriage. 'You think you'll end up marrying him?' I asked.

She shrugged. I couldn't blame her; I would have done the same thing if faced with such a predicament. 'I don't know,' she said. 'Maybe. Not yet, though.'

'Why?'

She considered this for a few seconds, then said, 'Too young, I suppose.'

'He your first real boyfriend?'

'How d'you mean?'

'First guy you've stayed with for a long time,' I fished.

'First and only . . .'

'How so?'

'There's never been anybody else.'

I have to admit I was shocked. 'You're kidding?'

She turned to face me, looked me in the eyes. 'No.'

'Don't you ever . . .'

'What?'

'Well, wonder . . . Don't you ever wonder what it would be like with another guy?'

She leant forward, ground her cigarette out on the lawn. 'Sometimes.'

'Which times?'

'I don't know.'

And I gave her the look, the one where your eyes do all the talking for you. 'Times like now?'

'Maybe.'

And that was it. She was hooked. I smiled, narrowed my eyes, went for closure. 'Maybe yes, or maybe no?'

'Maybe I don't know.' She lit another cigarette. Smoke drifted from her lips. 'What about you? You got a girlfriend?'

'No.'

And we sat there, staring at each other as she finished her cigarette and I finished my beer. The thing was this: sure, McCullen had yet to make a firm decision about me, but she was close, close enough to make me tingle. But if not now, then when? Tonight? It had to be tonight. Looking at her now, I couldn't bear the thought of it being any later. Restaurant. More talk. More word games. Then decision.

By that time I was running my eyes up and down her body and wishing she wasn't wearing a towel. And then I realised that sometimes you can be your own genie: you can make your own wishes come true.

'Come on,' I said, 'break's over. Let's get back to work.'

And that's exactly what we did. Whilst McCullen settled back on the sofa, I went through to the kitchen, picked up the phone and blew out the party I was going to with Matt and instead booked a table for two at Hot House. Sussed as I thought I was, though, what I didn't realise was that McCullen was even more into the extended flirt than I'd guessed. Forget me putting my desire on hold for a few hours, this was going to be a serious campaign. Later on, her reply to my invitation to dinner said it all:

'That's a sweet thought, but not tonight. Jons is down from Glasgow tomorrow and I've got to be up early to meet him at the station.'

And after she'd kissed me goodbye on the doorstep (again on the cheek), and I'd watched her walk down the street, I realised that my problem was that, when it came down to it, even though she was definitely into me, she was still into Jons. And until she was more into me than him, I didn't rate my chances of getting into her. Physically, that is. It was going to be a case of watch this space. Which I would.

With binoculars.

Day and night.

Without rest.

It wouldn't be the first waiting game I'd played.

* * *

Confessions: No.3 Bondage
Place: my bedroom, Matt's pad.
  Time: 3 a.m. 13 April 1997.

Matt's always warned me off repeats. His thinking on the matter can be summarised as follows:

a) The whole point of a one-night stand is that it lasts for one night
b) Repeat encounters breed familiarity
c) Familiarity defeats the point of being single

And this was the moment I learnt to accept his word on the matter as final.

There I was, spreadeagled on my back on the bed, naked as the day I was born. Sitting astride me, equally naked, was Hazel Atkinson. Atkinson and I had met down at Barry's house on New Year's Eve. We'd sloped off upstairs some time in the early hours of New Year's Day, bagged a room and locked the door behind us. I'd emerged the next morning round seven and persuaded Matt to get up and get me back to London as soon as possible. It wasn't that the night had been bad; it hadn't. And it wasn't that I hadn't liked Atkinson; I had. It was more that the night had been weird.

Atkinson has a penchant for activities that people of my parents' generation would describe as 'kinky'. Or, put another way, she enjoys tying men up and making them squeal. Now, I'm no prude. I'm more than happy to give something a go, even if that something borders on the psychologically disturbed. So back at New Year, I'd let her tie me up and, sure enough, I'd squealed. The best I can say about the experience is that it was educational. But, like Latin at school, it wasn't something I wanted to specialise in. End result: I hadn't returned Atkinson's calls and had made a point of failing to attend any party I knew she'd been invited to.

Silly me.

11.30 p.m. 12 April 1997, however, and who did I see through my drunken eyes, standing at the bar in Klaxon? None other than Hazel Atkinson – looking great, looking available, and looking straight back at me. Normally, of course, I'd have run a mile. Barry had told me that Atkinson, following my strictly adhered to avoidance technique, had grown to regard me as somewhere below an amoeba in the chain of evolution. But I was drunk and I'd been blown out so many times in the last hour that I'd dismissed the idea of pulling from my mind. So when she came over and talked to me and so obviously wasn't angry with me, what else could I have done but invite her back to mine?

So back to the bed.

She'd tied my hands to the bed-head, my feet to the base. But that was cool; I knew what was coming next. A bit of chastisement. A load of word games. Her telling me what to say and me then saying it. And then would come the good part of the proceedings: the sex – surprisingly, and pleasantly, straightforward.

Shame is, Atkinson saw things differently.

'Right, you piece of shit,' she told me. 'I'm going to teach you a lesson you're never going to forget.'

I'd been here before. 'I've been a bad boy, haven't I?' I asked, playing along, finding the whole routine every bit as ridiculous as I had first time round. 'I'm a sick puppy and I have to be trained.'

'You don't know the half of it.' She glared down at me. 'When did you say Matt was back from Bristol?'

'Why?'

'Just tell me.'

'Tomorrow morning,' I said, confused. 'About nine.'

She checked her watch. 'Seven hours. Good. You might make it.'

'What are you talking about?'

She didn't reply, just climbed off the bed and started to get dressed.

'Do you know what your problem is, Jack?' she asked as she sat on the side of the bed and pulled her boots on. I tried to wriggle my hand free, couldn't. Tried my other hand and my feet. No luck there, either. The tights she'd used to bind me were just that: tight. She stood up. 'You pissed off the wrong girl.'

And with that, she walked out of the bedroom and, a few seconds later, I heard the front door slam.

And I waited.

And soon the cramp set in.

And my mouth dried out to cracking point.

And I waited some more.

A lot more.

Until I realised she wasn't coming back.

A whole shoal of thoughts swam round my mind that night. I doubt I've had a concentrated period of plain thinking like that in my life. Most of them were nonsense. Paranoia that I was going to die, or that Matt would never return, or that Atkinson would, armed with a bull whip and an electric nut-cracker. But the Big Thought which kept surfacing throughout was this: if I die, I'll die without having found the person I want to spend my life with. She'll still be out there, alone, not having found me either. And there'll be no one to blame but myself. Perhaps this was the lesson Atkinson wanted me to learn.

Finally, I saw Matt standing in the doorway, stunned.

'Don't say it,' I managed to croak.

'Don't say what?'

'I told you so.'

He sat down on the bed and started to unfasten my feet.

'Atkinson?' he asked.

'Yeah.'

'Thought so.'

* * *

Going Out

I experience an unusual sensation as I'm shutting Matt's front door behind me. My stomach feels like something's nesting in it. Something with feathers. Something that tickles. At first, I put it down to drinking in the afternoon on a mostly empty stomach, and consider stopping off *en route* for a bag of chips. But finally, I recognise it for what it is: nerves. Nerves and excitement. The cause is obvious: Amy. Or, more precisely, going on A Date with Amy. As much as I wish differently, there's no other possible explanation. I'm interested. In her. In seeing what A Date with her will be like. In seeing whether I'm still capable of pulling this kind of stuff off, or even enjoying it.

Zack's is great. Zack's I love. Truly, if Zack's was a woman, then I wouldn't be meeting Amy there tonight. There'd be no need. I'd be married to Zack's and raising little Zackettes on an island far, far, far away. It's all sofas, small tables, big open spaces, dim lighting and chilled music. And just for an added bonus, it's near Matt's pad.

A five-minute pavement hike gets me there good and early, round 7.30. It's fairly quiet for a Friday. But the night's still young. All those other people with real jobs are probably still trapped in post-work drinks, yet to make the break back into their personal lives.

I perform a quick table scan, select one in the corner, away from the pool table, not too near the music speakers, away from distraction. I sling Matt's jacket over the chair against the wall, bagging my seat. I'll make sure Amy sits opposite me. That way, her viewing choice will be limited to me or the brickwork, giving me a fighting chance of holding her attention.

I take my wallet and go and barfly a while, chat to Janet, who owns the place. And Zack? I once asked; I once got told. Zack's Janet's ex-husband. He ran off with his secretary. Janet stung him in court for a fat wodge of cash, named the bar she bought with the proceeds after him, just to rub it in. Janet's been thirty-six for the three years I've known her and shows no sign of getting older. She's fun, some might say eccentric, and we pick up our conversation where we left it Tuesday night, like I've only been gone five minutes. I'm drinking the second bottle of Labatt's she's donated to the Starving Artist Fund, when I hear a voice behind me.

The voice says, 'Hi, Jack.'

And I check out Janet's expression.

And Janet's expression says, *Lucky you.*

And I turn round and see that she's right: I am.

Amy's standing there with the kind of wide smile that makes it impossible not to smile right on back. This kind of rattles me. A good sort of rattle, though, it has to be said – more baby than snake. Last time I saw her, what with all the freaking out she was doing about her recently deceased sex life and her unrequited crush on Matt, her lips had been all squished together like, for want of a kinder description, a pair of mating slugs. Now, though – well, I have to, and am more than glad to, admit – they've got a K and an I and an S and an S written all over them. Clothes-wise, she's wearing a funky little black skirt and grab-me grey top. She looks good. Seriously. Beautiful. And confident. She holds my stare and, as she does, my nerves come surging back. I smile, then the words come pouring out.

'Hi, Amy,' I say. 'You look great.'

'Thanks. It's good to see you.'

'What are you having?'

'Vodka and tonic.'

'You want lemon in that?' Janet asks, fixing the drink.

'Lime. Thanks.'

Janet slices and slots a wedge into the glass. I take out my wallet, but Janet, bless her, just waves her hand, passes the drink to Amy. 'Don't worry, Jack,' she tells me, 'I'll put it on your tab.'

'Thanks,' I tell her, meaning it.

Personal memo: give Janet that painting you're always promising her. Apart from friendship and everything, it's not like you don't owe it to her in kind.

Amy and I look at each other for a few seconds and she takes a sip of her drink, then looks round the bar. It's weird how you can spend a night with someone, getting smashed and listening to them pouring their heart out into the small hours of the morning, and then still end up suffering a silence laced with apprehension next time you meet. Just talk, I tell myself. Kill the silence off.

'I ditched my jacket over there,' I tell her, pointing to the table.

71

We go and sit down, both light cigarettes, inhale, exhale. We pick up our drinks and take swigs.

Finally, she says, 'I guess I should start by apologising.'

'What for?'

'Acting like a complete berk last Friday night.'

This is my prompt to disagree, to no-no-no-you-weren't it a bit. She looks genuinely embarrassed, so it would be the gentlemanly thing to do. But it would be pointless. She'd just end up thinking I got off on emotional outpourings, that I was an emotion junkie. Which I don't and am not. Not in this situation, anyway. Not now. Not with someone I hardly know. Not when it was Matt she was upset about.

'Saturday morning,' I correct.

'What?'

'Saturday morning. You acted like a complete berk last Saturday morning. Round about six. Friday night you were fun. Saturday morning, too, for that matter. Right up till six.'

'When I did the berk bit?'

'When you did the berk bit.'

'Well, I'm sorry, anyway.'

'It's okay. Everyone's allowed to go berk from time to time. It's one of our democratic rights.'

'It still scared the hell out of you, though, didn't it?'

'No,' I lie, 'of course not.'

'Oh, right.' She smiles for the first time since we sat down. 'So I shouldn't read anything into you sprinting off out of my flat like your arse was on fire?' She raises her eyebrows. 'Was that just your way of greeting the dawn? Your regular morning routine?'

I laugh and, as I do, I remember how it was with her last Friday. The fact that I spoke more to her than I did to Matt on his birthday – an act of treachery I can still hardly credit myself with. The fact that she cracked me up. And, most telling of all, the fact that when the fork of freak-out lightning fried her brain, I actually hung around and tried to calm her down, put off my then inevitable runner for a *whole half hour*. I remember why I liked her. Because she was direct. Because there wasn't

72

any bullshit. Because she was the first girl I'd met in ages who I hadn't ended up playing psyche games with.

'Okay,' I reply, 'I did a bunk. But it wasn't because of you. I was just shattered, that's all.' I risk a laugh. 'Jesus, we must have got through the best part of a bottle of whisky once we got back to yours. My brain felt like someone was using it as a pin cushion.'

'I didn't feel too hot myself,' she admits. 'Went for the Banana Recovery Plan.'

'The what?'

'The Banana Recovery Plan,' she repeats. 'You know . . .' But since I obviously don't, she spells it out for me: 'Bath And Nurofen And No Alcohol.'

I smile. 'Have to remember to try that next time.'

'Works every time.'

A silence follows her words. It's like we've dealt with the tricky bit – the bit about her flipping out about Matt and me skipping out. And, what's more, we've done it without mentioning Matt's name. That leaves just the two of us.

So where do we go from here? Options are multiple, of course. Freedom of speech and all that. Problem is, the three topics I want to raise – the me and the her and the how we get it together – are the only three topics that are strictly out of bounds. There's a time and a place for such things. And Zack's at just gone eight is neither. There's other stuff to come first. More drink. More talk. A meal. A cab ride home. Be patient, my brother, I tell myself. Be patient and thou shalt get thy just reward. And so I open my mouth, primed to fire off some quip to turn the conversation liquid again. Only Janet shows up and shatters the silence for me, offering to get us more drinks. Well, it would be rude not to. We graciously accept and Janet saunters back towards the bar, a conversation piece if ever I saw one.

'So tell me,' Amy says, briefly turning round and glancing at Janet. 'How come I've been coming here about once a month for the last year and the woman behind the bar doesn't even recognise me, and yet she knows your name and knows you well enough to run a tab for you when it clearly says on the sign above the bar "No Credit"?'

'Because I practically live here. Matt's place is just round the corner. Janet's a mate.'

And, with the log-jam busted, the conversation flows on. We talk and, as we talk, I play the Poirot game, gradually filling in the blanks in our drunken conversation last week. By the time we're stepping out of the cab and walking into Hot House, I've got Amy's history taped. Her curriculum vitae, now filed under Pend, reads:

Name: Amy Crosbie
Age: 25
Marital Status: SINGLE
Qualifications: English, Geography and Art A-levels; degree in Textiles
Employment History: Various temp jobs since graduation
Relationship History: Vague. One exception; co-habited; now history
Other Skills: Good talker; great smile; fantastic tits

Inside Hot House, we get shown to our table by this foxy waitress in regulation short black skirt and tight white top. It's a case of eyes-right when she's on my left and eyes-left when she's on my right. Girls, I swear to God, can *sense* you scoping another female. Sixth sense. ESP (Enemy Skirt Perception). So as the foxette sits us down and gives us the menus to check out, I consciously develop a blind spot for her. She doesn't exist. Only Amy. *Honey, I only have eyes for you . . .*

I bluff the wine menu, select a mid-price bottle and take the lead by ordering the cheapest main course on the menu, hoping she'll take the hint and not order lobster. We tuck in and we talk. I let her in on my life: surface stuff; rehearsed; my standard girl chat. What I paint. Where I hang out. I do the politician: let her talk and discover what she's into, then bounce it straight back at her. Subliminal message: I'm your man. Vote Jack Rossiter for a Better World.

'What about *you*, though?' she asks.

'What do you mean?'

'You. Y O U. What makes you tick? What do you want from life?'

'That's a big question,' I stall.

'So, give me a big answer.'

Of course, I do have an answer to that question. Everyone does. And the answer's always the same: love. There are things I want, things I don't tell anyone in case they don't happen. But they're One Day things. As in, one day I want to fall in love. One day I want to marry the woman I fall in love with. One day I want a family and a home. one day I want my kids to come charging into the bedroom at six on a Sunday morning and wake me up the same as I did with my parents. But One Day isn't now. For all I know, One Day might never happen.

'I don't know,' I reply lamely. 'Fun. I suppose that's the main thing.'

'Okay,' she says, 'so what was the last proper fun you had?'

'Easy,' I say, a smile settling on my face. 'I went to Hamleys to get a birthday present for my nephew.'

'You've got a nephew?'

'Yeah, my elder brother's. He's cool. My nephew, that is. My brother, Billy, well he's a bit . . . I don't know. Me and Kate don't really have much to do with him.'

'Why's that?'

'Well, he's nice and everything. In fact, fuck it, he's really nice. But he's a lot older. He's into different stuff to us. Late thirties. Married and settled down before he was my age. Met this girl and fell in love and that was that. Next thing, he's got kids and his life's over. Crazy.'

'You're not into the love and kids deal, then?'

'Not settling down. Not now. No way.'

'I see.' She stares at me for a moment, and I can't work out what she's thinking. Then her face relaxes and she asks, 'So what did you get him?'

'Who?'

'Your nephew?'

'Oh, John. I got him this radio-controlled car. One of those American drag racer things. Goes like shit off a shovel. Me and Matt thought we'd better give it a test run before I posted it off. You know, in case it was crap, or something.'

'Right,' she says, stifling a laugh, 'in case it was crap. Not because you wanted to have a go.'

'Of course not,' I say, totally failing to hide my grin. 'We're adults, for Christ's sake. I was just thinking of John. I mean, there's nothing worse than getting a crumby present, is there? We had to make sure it worked.' Now she's shaking her head. 'Anyway,' I continue, 'we got it out in the garden and worked out the controls and gave it a spin. And then we set up a couple of jumps for it. And—'

Her jaw drops. 'You set up jumps?'

'Yeah. Nothing too complicated, though. Just these planks from the shed. We propped them up with bricks. Just to check out the suspension.'

'Have you actually got round to posting it to John yet?' she interrupts.

'Er, no. It's probably a good idea if I clean the dirt off it first.' I take a swig of my wine. 'And fix the wheel. The front one.' I grimace. 'It got sort of wrecked on the last jump.'

'For someone who's not into kids, you make a pretty good one yourself.'

The hours slide by smoothly, and before I know it Hot House is empty apart from us. I call over a tired-looking waiter and ask him for the bill. I even manage to pay for it and turn down Amy's offer of going Dutch without visibly wincing.

Her flat's only about a mile away and so, partly because it's the kind of hot summer night specifically designed for walking beneath the stars, and partly because I've only got enough cash left on me to pay for a cab to the end of the street, I say I'll walk her home.

'That stuff you said last week about not having had sex for ages,' I say. 'Was that true?'

This could piss her off. Luckily, though, it doesn't.

'Yep. Almost six months, if you want to know the gory

truth. Something of a personal record. Why do you ask?'

'I'm just surprised, that's all.'

'How's that?'

'I don't know,' I begin. 'You're good-looking, you know . . . And you're fun. You just don't seem the type to end up going without – unless that's what you want . . .'

She laughs, says, 'I've been out with my fair share of losers, and now I'm holding out for someone I really fancy.'

'A case of where are all the good guys, you mean?'

'Exactly.'

We turn off the main road into a side street, walk fifty or so yards in silence and stop outside a Georgian terrace block.

'This yours?' I ask.

'Yeah. Home sweet home.'

And I say, 'So . . .'

And she says, 'So . . .'

Suddenly wanting to be the good guy she's been looking for, there are certain events which I hope might occur at this juncture. She might:

a) Ask me if I want to come in for a coffee
b) Put on some music and sit next to me on the sofa in her living room, sipping her coffee and waiting for me to make a move
c) Forget the coffee and jump me

What I'm not expecting, but what, to my horror, she does, is:

a) Thank me for a lovely evening and for walking her home
b) Briefly kiss me before disengaging and taking a step back
c) Tell me to call her next week

And then she turns her back on me and walks to the entrance of Kit-Off Manor, opens the door and goes inside and shuts it firmly behind her.

I stand.

I stare.

77

'Fuck.'

That one word, I manage, but apart from that I'm left speechless.

So much for the good guys getting all the luck.

Getting In

'You're kidding,' Matt says.

It's the following morning. A couple of minutes ago, Matt came through to the kitchen to find me slumped over the table, gazing at the steam rising from my tea through sleep-starved eyes. My mental health was low, visibly so. He asked me what was wrong. I gave him the lowdown on the previous night's disaster.

'Do I look like I'm kidding?' I snap back.

He sits down opposite me and runs his hand through his bed-battered hair.

'No, mate, you look like you're losing your touch.'

'Thanks.'

He shrugs. 'So . . . what next? You going to call her?'

'Now *you're* kidding.'

'Why? She sounds keen enough. Probably worth a second go – if you're up for it. Are you?'

'Well, of course I'm bloody up for it. I wouldn't have taken her out last night otherwise, would I? Being up for it isn't the point.'

'So what is?'

'The point is, going out on a date is fine. That, I can handle. What I can't handle is getting blown out by someone who then expects me to call them up and take them out again. I mean, Christ, where's that going? Same thing might happen next time. And the time after that. Next thing I know, I'm living Groundhog Day – without ever getting the girl.' I light a cigarette. 'The point is, Matt, that last night everything went perfectly and she still binned me on the doorstep. The point is that I'm fucking pissed off.'

'It's not like it was a total blow out. You got a snog.'

'You're not listening. I didn't take her to Hot House and

78

cough out Christ knows how much just for a snog. Snogging's what kids do. I'm a consenting adult, for Christ's sake. If all I'd wanted from the night was somewhere wet to put my tongue, I'd have bought a fucking ice cream.'

'Only trying to help.' His grin doesn't convince me of his sincerity on this point.

'Well, you're not.'

'Don't take it so bad. There's probably a perfectly good explanation for her acting like that.'

'Such as?'

'I don't know. Maybe she's a bit old-fashioned. Doesn't want to look easy.'

'She's not old-fashioned. That's the last thing she is.'

'Well, maybe she's on. Off games week.'

This conversation's doing my head in, so I change it. 'What about you? How was the party?'

'Good,' he says, taking my cigarette and having a drag. 'Linda was there. Asked after you.'

Linda's a bunny-boiler, a one-night dream who turned into a six-week nightmare. Phonecalls, letters, emails . . . the kind of case study Freud would have killed for.

'What did you tell her?'

'Same as we agreed I would, if I ever bumped into her: that you've turned God Squad. Don't go out. Gone celibate. The whole deal.'

'And she believed you?'

'You questioning my ability to feed a girl a line?'

'Wouldn't dream of it.'

'Good.'

I take my cigarette back.

'What about you? Any luck?'

He doesn't need to reply. I hear footsteps heading towards the kitchen, then the door swings open and a girl appears. She's nice, I have to admit. Even with the pillow creases fresh on her face. Even with Matt's dodgy old dressing gown – his only sentimental and unfashionable item of clothing – wrapped round her.

'Hello,' she says to me, her voice husky from too many cigarettes and drinks, 'I'm Sian.'

'All right,' I mumble.

'Okay if I fix myself a coffee?' she asks Matt, heading for the kettle.

'Go ahead,' Matt replies. 'Only you'd better make it quick. Me and Jack here have got to leave for Bristol in about half an hour.'

She looks confused. 'Oh?'

'My mother's sixtieth. Surprise party. I told you last night. Remember?'

She doesn't, but then again why should she? This must be about the tenth surprise sixtieth Matt's mother's had to my knowledge. No matter. She says she'll hurry. I hang around for a few minutes, listening to their small talk shrinking towards microscopic, then excuse myself, saying I'd better get my bag together for Bristol. Matt winks at me, grateful for my participation in the scam. I can't bring myself to signal him back. To tell the truth, I'm a little hacked off with him. Purely on a jealousy level. He's got a doe-eyed, shagged-out girl in the kitchen. Where's mine? That's what I want to know. *Hey, Amy!* I want to shout. *Where's mine?*

This frustration hangs out at the back of my mind throughout the next day. At first, I do a pretty good job of ignoring it. But it doesn't last. Saturday night, I head out drinking with Matt, Chloe and Co. When Chloe asks me how it went with Amy, I tell her it was OK. When she asks me for details, I cut the conversation cold. I get blitzed and get talking to some girl. Only I can't get into it and so I cab it home alone.

I am, of course, aware that this is a Sign. What happened with Amy has shaken my confidence. You do everything right and it works out wrong. So what does that mean? That Matt's right? That I've lost my touch? That my pulling days are drawing to a close? That Amy's getting to me?

I don't like the answers I come up with.

Sunday afternoon I go for lunch at Zack's with Matt and he tells me to forget it. Just put it down as a bad experience. Don't dwell. So I won't. McCullen to look forward to on Friday. Concentrate on that. Only I then get back to the house to find a message from her, saying that she won't be able to make Friday because she's going up to Glasgow to watch Jons playing in some crappy student rock festival.

Come Monday afternoon, I admit to myself that I *do* have a problem. And my problem has a name: Amy. I keep catching myself staring at the phone. The urge to call her is there, no point in kidding myself it's not. This doesn't make sense. I try to analyse what's going on in my head. The only relief I find is that the main emotion I'm feeling is anger. I'm angry with her for leading me on. And I'm angry with myself for failing to achieve closure. Bollocks, I'm just angry. It's obvious she fancies me, so what's her problem?

I'm not going to call her.

But, as it turns out, I don't have to.

Wednesday night and I'm sitting in the living room, listening to the radio and reading the paper, when the phone rings and the answerphone message kicks in: 'Hi, Matt and Jack aren't here right now. Please leave a message after the tone and we'll get back to you.'

And I listen to the beep and then I listen to the caller's voice.

'Hi, guys. Amy here. Hope you're both well. This is a message for Jack. Just ringing to say—'

And then I do the strangest thing. I pick up the phone and say, 'Hi, Amy. How's things?'

When I replace the receiver and check out the clock, the surprise I feel when I see that I've been talking to her for over an hour is only surpassed by the overwhelming sensation of shock at what I asked her and what she agreed to. Dinner. My place. Friday night. Like, *hell-o*? Who's going to cast her from his mind and get on with his life? Who's not going to arrange another date? Not ever?

OK, so I've fucked up.

I've fucked up and I'm smiling.

Work that one out.

I give Phil, a mate of mine who also happens to be a top chef, a call. He owes me a favour for fixing him up with a date with Chloe last year. I call it in. One three-course meal for two to be delivered here on Friday afternoon. Nothing too complicated. Something I can chuck in the fridge, then oven it when Amy arrives and make out what a great cook and all round nineties guy I am.

Sorted.

Nothing can go wrong.

I will get my woman.

I will make amends for my failure last week.

Friday evening comes and Amy arrives on time. I lay it on thick. She wants romance? That's what it's going to take? Fine. I'll be her Valentino. The table's already laid in the living room, the curtains drawn. Ella Fitzgerald's singing about hearts and hurts. Candlelight flickers across the walls. As I serve up the food (Phil's) and pour out the wine (Matt's), I'm almost convinced of the situation myself.

But not quite. Because Jack the Lad is back.

We wine.

We dine.

I feed her lines.

I know, deep down, she will be mine.

But my cynicism doesn't last. Maybe it's the booze. Maybe I'm just not as immune to the effects of candlelight and wine and a beautiful woman as I thought I was. Maybe it's because, halfway through the meal, she gets up and changes the CD. Only puts on Cat Stevens. Only puts on the one CD everyone I know hates and I adore. Or maybe it's just that I *like* her. Our conversation's indicative of this decline in my predatory standards. It doesn't stop. Not once. Topic runs into topic, an endless row of dominos. I've got to admit it: she's a find. I can't remember having talked this much for ages, not since I was a kid and my imagination ran wild. Not to Chloe. Not even to Matt.

'So why did you chuck her?' she asks, kicking her shoes off and sitting back on the sofa beside me.

She's just finished drawing me the heart-chart of her life,

telling me all about her shithead of an ex, and now it's my turn. I feel myself closing up. Talking about Zoe and why we broke up isn't something I'm good at. It's something I've avoided doing ever since it happened. It gives too much away, leaves me exposed.

'Just because,' I say

'You can't just chuck someone you've been seeing for two years *just because*.' She studies my face, shakes her head. 'Or maybe you can.'

I'm about to change the topic, but then our eyes meet. And, suddenly, I can see right through her and I know it's OK to let it all out. There's no wolf lurking there, waiting to eat me alive, no judgement waiting to be passed. I look down at the floor and I don't know whether it's the booze or me that's doing the talking. I don't even care.

'I loved her. Right up to when we broke up. That's the fucked-up thing. I still wanted to be with her, even when I was telling her that I was leaving. It doesn't make much sense, does it?'

'These things never do.'

'It's just that I knew she wasn't . . . all that stuff people say about there being someone out there who's made for you, someone who fits you perfectly. She didn't. She was wonderful and she was beautiful. But she wasn't the one. And I wasn't the one for her.' I light a cigarette, take a swig of my wine. 'Whatever. It wasn't meant to be. History.'

'And since then? You found her?'

'Who?'

'The woman who fits.'

'No,' I admit, 'I haven't even come close.'

'I guess we're both due some luck, then,' she finally says.

And the real me knows that this is my cue to lunge. The real me is holding up a flashing neon sign, which reads, ENTER JACK THE LAD. NOW! MAKE YOUR MOVE. This is where I should think that the only luck worth considering is mine, and the only consideration is that it's now officially In. So how come when I look at her and she smiles, all I manage to do is smile back?

Why am I afraid that if I pounce and she's not ready, then all this might come to an end, that all this talk will have been just that: talk? And how come I believe that what she's saying might be true?

Because Matt's right, that's how. Because I'm losing my touch.

She gets up from the sofa and walks to the window, draws back the curtain and stares up into the sky. I stay where I am, try to shake the alcohol from my mind.

'This is one of life's good nights,' she announces.

'Yeah,' I agree, 'the kind of night you don't want to end.' And this is better. This is more like the old me. Feeling back on track, I say, 'The last thing you want to do on a night like this is end up sleeping—'

Alone. I'm about to say, *alone*.

But, before I can, Amy turns and walks towards me, her face suddenly animated.

'Really?' she asks.

'Really,' I confirm.

'Well, there's a party. An old college mate. We could go there, if you like. What do you say? Are you up for it?'

And, yes, I *am* up for *it*, but, no, I'm not up for *that*.

But she doesn't even give me a chance to reply. Before I can stop her, she's reaching for the phone and calling a cab, replacing the receiver and returning to the window.

Inside the cab, she gives the driver the address of the party and we head on up the street. It's dark outside and the radio's playing some dance track, and I'm thinking, *Why didn't you make your move before the cab turned up?* Two seconds, that's all it would have taken.

Bugger.

For a moment, stoicism descends. Maybe this whole Amy deal is jinxed, just not meant to be. Maybe that's why I keep on blowing it. Way things stand right now, I can see how the evening's going to pan out. We'll get to this party and Amy will know a million and one people and I won't know squat. She'll go schmoozing and I'll go boozing and, chances are,

Nothing Will Happen. The Moment Will Have Passed. I stare out of the window at the street lamps flashing by and I can feel her leg against mine. And I'm thinking that the only way I can rectify the situation is to do now what I should have done then.

And so I do.

I kiss her.

As kisses go, it's a good one. Not the best. That honour goes to Mandy Macrone, the first girl I ever kissed. *That* was electric. Literally. We both had fixed braces and when they touched it was like sticking a fork into a plug socket. Still, this is a good kiss. This is a kiss I want to last.

Shame is, it doesn't look like Amy agrees.

But after I hear what she says next, I'm quick to forgive.

What she says is: 'Let's bin the party, go back to yours instead.'

And I want to scream. I want to jump up and down. I want to graffiti *YES!* on every building in the street. I want to thank my teachers and my parents and my friends and everyone who's ever been there for me. Losing my touch? Fuck you, Matt Davies. Watch this.

'Good plan,' I say. 'Let's do it.'

The only person not happy with this turn of events is the cab driver. I tell him he can have his money anyway, just turn round and take us back. And then he's happy, too. Jesus, the whole world's smiling. He drops us back outside Matt's and I pay him and we get out. We go inside and I shut the front door behind us.

And then the fun begins.

It starts against the wall, moves down the corridor and continues at the bottom of the stairs. Behind us is a trail of clothing: my jacket, Amy's coat. Not that I'm not looking behind me. Forget that. I'm looking straight ahead, concentrating on the matter in hand (the matter in both hands, at least).

My fingers are off on autopilot, performing an exploratory mission. First, they scout under her top and under her bra, across her breasts. They hang around her nipples for a while, as she pushes against me and unbuckles my belt. Then they

85

move down, gripping her buttocks and pulling her close. Then round, over her thighs, under her skirt, inside her knickers.

The preliminary findings thus far relayed to Ground Control include:

a) Expensive bra
b) Expansive tits
c) Stiff nipples
d) Firm buttocks
e) Tensed thighs

Weather conditions on the lower terrain are described as moist. The overall message: Planet Inhabitable – Capable of Sustaining Human Life. Ground Control is satisfied and gives the thumbs up for full colonisation to proceed forthwith.

Meanwhile, Amy's undone my zip. Her hand slides inside. As she takes a firm grip on what resides therein, I break the kiss for the first time since I closed the door. I pull her top over her head and let it fall on the stairs behind her. Her eyes are closed and, for a moment, I just watch her face and listen to the rush of her breath. Then I unfasten her bra and she threads her arms free, chucks it over the banister.

She opens her eyes, smiles and whispers, 'Hi.'

And I am.

As in sky.

Just looking at her.

She's beautiful and, I've got to admit, it looks like this is going to be well worth the wait. I run my hands down her sides, over her hips, and hook my fingers under her skirt, ride it up to her waist.

'Lie down,' I tell her.

And she does, legs and bum on the floor, back against the stairs. I kneel beside her and unfasten her suspenders, peel her knickers down and off. Sliding her legs apart, I reposition myself and lower my head, brush my lips up her inner thigh, do The Tease by bypassing the groove my tongue was designed to fit, settle for a moment on the soft skin of her stomach. I hear her gasp, close my eyes. And I'm glad it's her. I'm glad it's the scent of her skin I'm breathing in.

Then down.

Deep down.

Because down is where it's at.

4
amy

I am in what you might describe as a sticky situation.

This is absolutely not what I planned. Less than ten minutes ago, Jack kissed me in the back of the cab and I don't know *what* he put in that kiss, but I think he must have had some sort of narcotic on his tongue, because I seem to have taken leave of my senses.

One minute I felt like I was the leading lady having the snog scene in a pretty straightforward PG romance and the next I've landed the lead in *Amy Does Tricks*, the porn blockbuster.

Hello Amy?

Earth to Planet Floozy?

I'm lying on Jack's stairs having abandoned my bra over the banisters and my legs are over his shoulders and whilst it feels oh . . . OH . . . YES . . . YES . . . THERE . . . THERE . . . ohhhhh-hhhhhhhhhhhhhhhhhhhhhhh . . . yes . . . yes . . . great, I'm also in a MAJOR PANIC. It consists of:

My Mother's Voice: You're behaving like a common slut. What kind of a girl will he think you are?

My Vanity: He's going to see my cellulite and think I'm a lard monster.

My Lungs: I can't breathe in much longer and WHAT IF HE LOOKS UP NOW AND SEES THE TRUTH ABOUT MY STOMACH!

My Paranoia: What if Matt walks in through the front door? And worse, much much worse . . . What if I . . .

if I . . .

smell?

I mean I can't do, because I wallowed in the bath until I was squeaky clean, but that's a scary one.

And to top it all, I'm just embarrassed and feel stupid for feeling embarrassed. I mean when someone sticks their tongue in . . . there . . . mmmmmmmmmmmmmmmmmmmmmmm . . . and starts gently licking you . . . ohhhhhhhhhhhh . . . there . . . it's not exactly an everyday occurrence is it? It's not something you invite every Tom, Dick and Harry to do to you. It's kind of intimate. Personal. EXPOSING!

And if Jack Rossiter thinks I'm going to have an orgasm with all this going on inside my head, he's got another think coming.

But on the other hand, I don't want him to stop. It's been so long since this happened and a girl's got to get it when she can. And anyway, Jack is Heineken Man – reaching the parts that other men don't reach.

This makes me pleased. Pleased because he's trying to pleasure me. Pleased because he wants to, and pleased because H will approve. No, H will be over the moon.

'At last,' she'll say. 'At long bloody last.'

My sentiments entirely. So long Mr Detachable Shower Head, hello bloke who gives good head!

A rarity.

A treasure.

A fucking miracle!

Because all the blokes I've had so far have been crap in this department.

Take Andy. Mr Wham Bam, put the kettle on ma'am (and you can iron my shirt whilst you're at it). After three months, it took all my courage to broach the there-are-other-things-we-could-be-doing-in-bed chat. I mumbled, fumbled and when Andy looked at me with blank confusion and carried on reading the Sunday papers, I was mortified.

But then the next day, out of the blue, Andy whisked me off to the futon when I got back from work – and *went down*. I nearly died of shock. I couldn't believe my luck. I wriggled encouragingly, groaned, praised the Lord, and just when I'd decided that I could marry Andy after all, he stopped. Just stopped. After about a minute. 'There,' he said with a smug look. 'That's your welcome home present.'

But Jack is different. Jack's into this. He's making noises. Horny noises. And so am I, but this can't go on. The poor guy will get lockjaw soon and, anyway, I want to touch him. Badly.

I grab his head, which is blessed with the essential qualities of good hair. It smells nice, it's cut well and, best of all, it's permanent-looking. I run my fingers through it and can't help moaning softly. Jack takes the hint. He looks up at me and gives me a soggy grin.

'You're gorgeous,' he says, and my heart does a loop the loop.

And then he kisses me. (Phew. I don't smell after all!)

But it's not just a kiss.

It's *the* kiss.

And right at that point, because he does have a toptastically amazing body and because I'm melting into his eyes and because he's bothered to go down on me and because I fancy him more than Mel Gibson, Brad Pitt and that bloke off *Neighbours* all rolled into one, I make an executive decision to shag him to within an inch of his life.

So I do.

But I actually now think that Jack *is* dying! Either that or he's about to come, which is fair enough because it has been a bit of a marathon sesh.

'I'm coming,' he gasps, and I watch as his forehead crinkles and his mouth opens. And then he does something wonderful. He says my name. Right as he's climaxing.

Cool.

He's got my name right!

He collapses on top of me and I can feel his heart thudding. I gently stroke my fingers up his spine and look up at the ceiling.

I'll give him a definite seven out of ten. No, that's unfair. Eight. But still, room for improvement.

Sex for the first time is always a disappointment. I always

expected it to be like all the novels I read when I was a teenager – knee-trembling, tunnel-vision passion with earth-moving simultaneous orgasms that went on all night. So when Wayne Cartwright (I still can't believe I lost my virginity to someone called Wayne) hauled something out of his Wrangler drain-pipes that looked suspiciously like turkey giblets, I had quite a shock.

A day later when I was skulking about by the common room, hoping to catch a glimpse of Wayne, I overheard him and his mates discussing the definition of excellent sex. I stopped rigid below the open window, fascinated. However, when they all agreed that the only thing that mattered was coming at the same time, I was thrown into a state of worried confusion. The odds that Wayne-pokey-penis-Cartwright would *ever* bring me closer to a physical sensation other than mild disgust were firmly stacked against me, but damn it, I was blowed if I was going to be labelled frigid. Thus, overnight, I reinvented myself as Amy Crosbie: Queen of the Faked Orgasm. Meg Ryan? Pah! Not a patch on me.

But faking is a dangerous game. I found myself getting more OTT just to see whether anyone would catch me out. But, surprise, surprise, they never did. Bastards!

So twelve blokes down the line (God, Jack is my twelfth) and I've come to my senses. I just have to live with the fact that I'm not one of those girls who have unaided vaginal orgasms. So what? They're all lying anyway.

Jack is making soft purring sounds and I continue stroking his back. Ideally, what I'd like now is for him to nose his way back under the duvet and to finish off what he started, but I know that's wishful thinking because there are two golden rules of sex:

Rule One: Blokes never, ever do that
Rule Two: Always make sure that you come first

And if you don't achieve number two, you can't blame the bloke for number one. So Jack is off the hook, even though my

91

nether regions are screaming, 'Me me me me me me me!'

Jack rolls himself to one side and strokes my hair. As we grin at each other, I'm overcome with affection. So overcome that my brain disengages with my mouth.

'Jack, I really, really like you. You're the best,' I whisper.

As soon as it's popped out, I know that I've won the cheesy declaration award of the decade. Why I needed to open my big gob and say something, I don't know, but in terms of cheesiness it's up there – it's Stilton.

Jack looks slightly alarmed and gently withdraws his (ten out of ten) penis from me, holding the wilting condom in place. In a nanosecond, he peels it off, ties a knot in it and drops it on the floor. (He's obviously done this before.)

'I'm knackered,' he sighs, flopping down beside me and taking me in his arms. I snuggle up to him, pressing my ear into the ruffle of hair on his chest. I'm desperate to take back my cheesy comment, or to find out what he thinks, what he feels, what this all means, and suddenly I'm in a frenzy and all I want is answers, answers, answers.

I'm aware that I'm being ridiculous. I've just spent the best part of two hours exposing every part of my flesh to this man, and I've counted no fewer than nine sexual positions, which isn't bad for the first time. So I think it's safe to conclude from all this that he likes me. He must do.

But I know that I've been had. Had in every sense of the word. I've lost a trick in our game of sexual relations and I can't go back. I can't un-shag him which means that I need to renegotiate my position, which is why I'm desperate to hear it, desperate for Jack to declare that this isn't just a one-night stand and that he will be pleased to see me in the morning.

Speak to me, at least.

'Jack?' I whisper, stroking the soft skin on his stomach.

But Jack is blissfully unaware of my inner turmoil, because Jack is fast asleep.

He totally passes out, as if he hasn't slept for a week. There's no getting through to him, so I lie suffocating for most of the night wondering whether he knows that one day he'll almost certainly be reincarnated as a starfish.

It's now nine in the morning and it's another scorcher, judging from the shafts of light through the blind. I really want Jack to wake up. I want to see his eyes, to duvet lurk and have a sleepy morning shag. But instead I'm lying here listening to him snore and my bladder feels like a space hopper.

I ease his arm from across my neck and sneak out of bed, slipping into his shirt on my way to the door. I look back at him tenderly as he grunts and rolls over, his hair all ruffled with sleep.

I'm still smiling with my conquest and with the relief of an empty bladder when I come out of the bathroom and bump into Matt, tits to chest. Whoops! I can feel myself blushing to my toenails as I stand self-consciously in Jack's shirt. It's only just covering my bum.

Matt is amused and I feel every inch the brazen hussy that he thinks I am.

'Jack still asleep, is he?' he smiles.

I nod, avoiding eye contact. 'Out for the count.'

'Come and have a cuppa then.'

'No I can't, I . . .' I begin. Matt is staring down at me. Close up, he's taller than I remembered and he's looking extremely handsome in baggy shorts and a vest. He's got a hard fit body and a great tan from somewhere and, despite myself, despite the fact that I've just left Jack's bed, I feel a guilty thrill of anticipation. But hey, I'm only flesh and blood, after all.

'Come on. He won't wake up for ages yet,' whispers Matt conspiratorially and I smile at him. His blue eyes seem to dance over my face and I nod in collusion.

I pull down the shirt, clamp my knees together and shuffle after him up the corridor like a Japanese concubine, admiring the way he strides along with a casual lope. He's got very nice feet. Nicer than Jack's at least.

After the dinner last night, the kitchen looks like a bomb's hit it. Matt gingerly retrieves the kettle from the pile of plates on the counter.

'Sorry about the mess,' I mumble. 'We didn't have a chance to . . . um . . . tidy up.'

Matt laughs. 'Good night then, I take it?'

He pushes down the bar on the double doors and the kitchen is filled with warm light and birdsong. I feel like I'm in an advert.

'It was great,' I say, leaning against the door frame and watching him.

Hello? Why am I breathing in?

'Jack's a fantastic cook,' I say.

Matt fills up the kettle. 'Isn't he though? I'm always trying to get him to enter *Masterchef*.'

'He should.'

'I know. Too busy though. You know these artistic types.'

'It sounds pretty hectic, all those models to deal with.'

He flicks on the kettle. 'It's a tough one. It takes it out of him.'

'Have you seen any of his work? Is it good?'

He nods. 'Excellent. I haven't seen his latest piece though.'

'Oh, the one of this Sally girl?' Curiosity gets the better of me. 'What's she like?'

Matt looks bashful. 'Oh, you know, um, how can I describe her?'

How sweet of him to protect Jack. 'It's all right,' I laugh, 'you can be as rude as you like. Jack's told me she's a right old trollop.'

Matt rocks his head back and laughs and the sun catches his face. When he stops, he looks at me and I start to feel all flustered.

'What?' I ask.

'That shirt suits you.'

'It's Jack's,' I say, fiddling with the hem.

'Hmm. I like that one,' says Matt. 'Normal or Earl Grey?'

He's flirting with me. He's looking at my legs!

'Normal please. I'll do some washing up,' I offer, side shuffling like a deformed crab towards the sink. I'm very

94

aware that I don't have any knickers on and I'm pretty sure that Matt's aware of it too. I can't meet his eye.

He stretches across me to get tea bags from the cupboards by the sink and I notice that he smells nice, not in a poncy after-shave way, but in a soapy clean way. Nice. His arm is so near I can see the fair hairs on it. He's got a scar by his elbow and without thinking I touch it. His skin feels warm.

'How did you get that?' I ask.

'I did it.'

We both twirl around to see Jack in the doorway. 'I booted him out of a tree house, if you really want to know.'

By the look on Jack's face, he's wishing he'd booted a bit harder. I pull the shirt down over my thighs self-consciously.

Matt flicks a tea towel over his shoulder as if nothing is amiss, but I'm caught in a firing range of looks and Jack knows it. And Jack knows I know.

'Tea, mate?' asks Matt.

Jack grunts an affirmative. Uh oh. So much for being in an advert.

Matt winks at me and rolls his eyes and I feel totally trapped. I move towards Jack, but he raises his eyebrows at my scanty attire and looks out into the garden.

Matt dunks the tea bags.

'What did you say you were doing today?' I ask Matt, groping around for conversation and trying to suggest every-thing is normal, but my voice chokes with guilt.

Matt shrugs. 'I'll probably stick around here and catch a few rays in the garden and watch the footie on the portable. Are you going to watch the match, Jack?'

Jack shrugs, obviously put out. 'Don't know. I'll probably work today.'

'Whatever,' says Matt, beating a hasty retreat, whistling as he exits the kitchen. I'm left alone with in an atmosphere so loud it's hurting my eardrums.

How do I reach Jack in the kingdom of the black cloud? Oh why oh why did I get out of bed? Why didn't I stay and wake up with him? He's looking at me like I'm a stranger, but I can't say I blame him. If I found him in my kitchen stroking H's elbow the morning after our first shag, I'd throw a wobbler. I think about saying something flippant about Matt, or explaining that I had no choice in coming to the kitchen, but even as I rehearse my speech in my head, I know anything I say will make me sound guilty, as if there's something going on.

'Sugar?' I ask feebly.

'No thanks,' he says, sitting down at the table.

I take his tea over. He's looking broody. I wish I could rewind and start all over again. This is a disaster.

'Do you have lots of work to do?' I ask.

'Yes.'

'Oh.' I stare at the floor.

Jack sips his tea. 'What are you up to?'

There's no invitation in his voice. I shrug. What can I say? If he chucks me out now, I'm going to spend the day wearing black and weeping loudly. I don't think he wants to hear this though.

'Not much, I guess.'

I sneak a look at Jack. Can't he see that I want to fling myself across the great divide between us and cling on to him for dear life, that I'm seriously thinking about a career change to a limpet? I can't cope if I've blown it.

There's a fraught pause before Jack speaks next. 'It's gorgeous out there.' He nods through the doors.

No, no, no. Don't give me polite weather conversation, *please*. I can't stand it. I swallow hard and follow his gaze. 'I hate being in London on days like this, the only place to be is on the beach,' I mumble, sipping my tea.

I look up at Jack now. I've got nothing to lose. I've got to ask and try, try not to make it sound like I'm begging.

'There's no chance that you fancy going to Brighton for the day is there? I mean, we could get the train and be there in a couple of hours.'

Thus spake desperate woman.

Jack narrows his eyes and looks at me. He looks non-plussed, but then shrugs and says, 'Why not?'

At first I'm not sure I've heard him right. I ogle at him with my mouth open until it sinks in.

'Cool!' I gush, like I've had an electric shock. I'm so grateful, I want to kiss his feet. How could I ever have thought that Matt's were nicer?

As we go back to my flat to pick up a dress (suspenders and heels not being suitable beachwear) I keep looking at Jack, checking that he's real. That he's here.

But he is here. In my kitchen. I've got a second chance! I feel that this at least justifies a headline or two in the national tabloids. WORLD EXCLUSIVE: ELEVENTH HOUR RESCUE FOR GIRL ON SHELF.

I leave him trying to extricate the ice tray from the polar ice-cap of W12 and waltz into my bedroom where I kiss my teddy.

'Ted, I've got a man doing man things in my kitchen!' I whisper. Ted looks back at me with his usual glazed expression. 'Well don't just sit there, what am I going to wear?'

I rip off my clothes and rummage round in the cupboard for my blue sundress, but when I put it on, I notice a red wine stain on the left tit. Typical. I revert to frayed shorts and a sun-top. Too casual? Too *Charlie's Angels*? Ted, help me out here!

Jack's travelling light. He's only taking what he's standing up in. How do blokes do that? How do they feel secure without a comprehensive set of grooming equipment and a cheque-book with them at all times? I don't understand. Before I know it, I've accumulated a pile of stuff on my bed that would do me for a three-week holiday, and that's only the essentials: hairbrush, make-up, bikini (dare I?), sunglasses, beach towel, jeans (just in case it gets cold), cardy and spare knickers (I am my mother's daughter), deodorant, baseball cap – they keep on coming.

I rummage round in my top drawer, aware that I'm humming 'We're all going on a summer holiday' like I'm Cliff Richard and knowing that I'd better get a move on because otherwise I'll move on to a rendition of 'The hills are alive with the sound of music' and that would be too embarrassing. I flip the lid off my perfume and engulf myself in a generous cloud, even giving my pubes a squirt for good measure.

I'm just about to ram the drawer shut when I spy the condoms. I grip the bumper box tightly, making a wish on them. Please, please, please make Jack want to shag me again . . . Hang on, these are extra long ones! Shit!

I know Jack is well endowed, but not abnormally so, not in a way that would justify super schlong johnnies. I fly to my chest of junk in the corner and locate a big paper bag full of supersonic extra extra safe ones in various flavours courtesy of the tight-lipped woman at the family planning clinic. They're probably all way out of date by now, but I've no time to check.

'What are you doing in there?' calls Jack from the kitchen.

'Two ticks,' I chirp, dropping to my knees and trying to find a bag under the bed. The only one I can find is gigantic, but it'll have to do. I pile in my stuff and empty the boxes of condoms into it as well (might as well be spoilt for choice). I breeze into the kitchen.

'What have you got in there?' asks Jack, handing me a glass of iced Ribena. 'A bucket and spade?'

'Of course!' I smile and down my drink. 'Come on, let's go.'

Despite the fact that I feel like I'm on speed, Jack's still being a bit distant and we stand awkwardly in the ticket queue at Victoria. There's four inches of uncrossable air space between our hands and I measure it with my eyes, wishing I had the courage to reach across it. But I don't. I'm too aware that the intimacy we shared last night can't be recreated in a public space, not with the tannoy going off all the time.

So Jack's being cool. That's OK, I can do cool too.

I think.

Except that he looks so bloody attractive in his T-shirt that I wonder how long I can keep it up without bursting. However, I've made a pact with myself. NO MORE CHEESY COMMENTS and NO BEGGING.

When we get to the ticket window, I grope around in my tardis bag for my purse, but Jack won't hear of me paying and casually throws down his Visa card. I sigh inwardly, listening to the whirring of his brownie points racking up in my brain.

At the kiosk we buy supplies: a bottle of water, chewing gum and fags. I stand behind Jack watching in awe. He's so assertive!

'What time's the train?' he asks.

A simple enough question, but I'm being such a teenager that I go all of a dither. I squint up at the departures board, but it's a blur. Is this because I need glasses or because Jack is standing so close and I can't concentrate on anything other than repressing my desire to grab him?

We have to sprint to make the train. He pulls me up through the door just in time and for a second I'm in his arms. I put my hand on his chest and he doesn't let me go when our eyes meet. I'm swallowed in his eyes and the train jolts forward and my stomach lurches all at the same time. I think Jack feels something too because he blushes and sort of laughs.

He breaks away and I follow him into the carriage, holding my breath. It's fairly empty and there's a whole set of seats free by the window.

'Here,' says Jack, reaching for my bag to put it into the overhead rack.

It's one of those moments where life goes into slow motion. I watch, horrified, as he swings it upwards by one strap which tips the balance and all of my belongings cascade to the floor between us. Everything. Including all the condoms.

There's silence as we both look down at them.

'Well, um, Amy,' he says, stroking his cheek. 'We're only going for the day. Isn't this a bit . . . enthusiastic?'

I feel sick. I drop to the floor and scrabble around to pick everything up. Even my split ends have gone pink.

'I didn't buy all these. I, I got them from the family planning . . .' I start, but I know that I'm making things ten times worse.

'That's very . . . forward thinking of you.'

Bollocks. What he means is it's very *forward* of me. Forward as in jumping the gun like a brazen, psycho woman forward. Roughly, I shove the condoms back in my bag. I feel like such an idiot, I want to do a runner down the corridor and hurl myself out of the train. I'm painfully aware that anything I say will just incriminate me more.

Jack just snorts with laughter and collapses on to the seat. I crouch down and bury my face in my hands. I can't look at him, but he starts to laugh so much that eventually I look through my fingers.

'You've gone *so* red!'

'Oh God. What must you think?' I moan.

He pulls me up on to his lap and cuddles me. 'I think I can't wait to make a start on them,' he whispers, and then he puts a cool hand on my burning cheek and kisses me with such intensity that I forget that I'm probably squashing him and spiral into weightless joy.

By the time we reach Brighton it seems incredible that there was ever any frostiness between us. We've been chatting like we're old mates, telling each other about past holidays and family stuff and it feels normal. Like we're friends. We're still babbling on to each other as we walk through the town to the beach. The sun is glinting on the water and there's people stripping off everywhere and you can smell the summer in the air, along with the wafts of waffle and candy floss from the stalls on the pier.

There's something about the heat that's so infectious, that in no time at all, I've regressed to childhood and I really do start wishing I'd brought a bucket and spade. All I want to do is muck about and Jack is obviously up for it. I grab his hand and drag him towards the pier and it feels like I'm five and he's my partner in crime and we're off to the swings.

We lark about on the pier and stuff our faces with ice lollies and laugh at each other behind the cardboard cutouts, and it may not be cool, and we may not be mentioning last night, but it doesn't matter. It's just great to be out of London, away from everyone else, and I start to feel so relaxed that I forget about being cool, or trying to impress him. It's enough that we're together.

By the time we hit the arcade, Jack's in his element and I laugh at him being such a big kid. It's amazing how much you can find out about a person when they hit a simulated racing game. It sort of distills someone's personality and I find out that Jack is:

a) competitive
b) a very bad loser

I vow never to play Monopoly with him.

'I'm going to whip your arse, girl,' says Nigel Mansell Rossiter, dropping his coin in the slot.

'Oh really? Is that a fact?' I adjust my seat. 'We'll see about that, shall we?'

And we're off, careering round the Monaco circuit, and I glance over at Jack being buffeted by the hydraulics and biting his lip with concentration and I resist the urge to melt into a pile of goo, because I want to beat him. And by sheer fluke, I do. Three times.

Thank you God, I owe you one.

Jack can't deal with it. He's seriously put out when I refuse another game and won't let him win.

'It's all about knowing when to stop. About quitting when you're ahead,' I tease, flouncing back into the sunshine. Jack's practically scraping the floor with one foot. I half expect him to yell, 'But you're only a girl!' but in some perverse way, I know he's impressed. I look over my shoulder at him and grin smugly. 'Don't sulk, Jack.'

That's it. He chases me and I run, squealing up the walkway, dodging round the kids and the grannies and I'm into the fair and running to the end of the pier and he catches me, trapping me against the balustrade. He sort of growls, but there's a big grin on his face and all of a sudden we're snogging like fourteen-year-olds, all clashing teeth and lashing orange-lolly-flavoured tongues. When a kid goes past us and shouts 'Urghhh' with his mates, we both giggle and Jack pulls away. There's a tent in his shorts and we laugh.

He leans on the railing and looks down at the water lapping round the pier. I turn the other way and rest back on my elbows. The rattle of the roller coaster car drifts towards us on the warm breeze, followed by delighted screaming as it plummets down the track.

'You're beautiful, you're amazing,' says Jack suddenly, 'you've got the most wonderful smile.'

I close one eye against the glint of the sun and look down at him. It's the first time he's paid me a sober compliment and I'm dumbfounded. He looks bashful and covers up the moment.

'It'd be nice to dive in,' he says, nodding to the water, but I can't say anything because a truck load of endorphins is jack-knifing across my nerve endings.

He takes my hand, but I've got sweaty palms and I try to wriggle out of his grip. Jack notices, but he just grips my hand tighter and kisses my knuckles.

'Come on, let's go to the beach,' he winks.

I think being a grown-up is just about the hardest thing you can do. It's much worse than exams or anything like that, and what's worse, no one ever prepares you for it. No one tells you that one day, sometime in your twenties, everyone will expect you to be different. A grown-up. An adult with responsibilities like bills and mortgages and decisions to make with no fuss. And there's only one thing worse than being a grown-up and that's being a single grown-up.

I know I shouldn't admit this. I know I should be just fine. I read enough sanctimonious women's magazines to realise that by being a woman in the nineties, I should be, by definition, completely relaxed with my own company and totally independent; self-sufficient in every area of my life, including things like DIY; successful in my career and financially sorted; able to withstand all forms of criticism; happy at all times because I'm nurturing my spiritual growth.

But it's all just crap. Most of the time I don't achieve even

one of these five. Because for the last six months I've sometimes felt like the fat kid who no one wants on their team. Or
if I have been invited on to the team, with most of the blokes
I've met recently, I've wanted to run as far as possible in the
opposite direction. It shouldn't matter, but it does. It really
does. Because from the age of about two, everyone knows it's
rubbish playing by yourself. It doesn't work. It's boring.

But when you're a kid you can always run inside and your
mum will give you a hug and a biscuit and it's all OK. And
then suddenly, you're a grown-up and there's nowhere to run
and you have to be stoic about it and go around like it doesn't
matter. And then you start to feel guilty for wanting someone
you like to play with. And you start to want it more and more.
And the more you want it, the more impossible it seems. You
wander round Sainsbury's with a basket, looking in awe at the
people with trolleys. The people with teams that you're not in
and you think, *Why me? What's wrong with me?*

So occasionally you have a melt down and people like H say
things like, 'Don't worry, it'll happen when you're not looking.' Whoever said that first deserves to be put up against the
wall and shot, because you do look. You look everywhere. You
don't see for looking.

And then out of the blue, it happens. Just like that. You find
togetherness. Like now, with Jack walking beside me falling in
with my stride, with his arm around my shoulder. It seems like
the most natural thing in the world. But how did it happen?
It's fantastic, but it's so unfair too. All these months of angst
and, look, it's easy. Easy peasy. But if it came this quickly, this
feeling of being in a team, surely it can disappear just as
quickly.

All of a sudden I want to freeze time. Freeze this moment,
because I want everyone to see this. I want everyone to know
that I'm much better being part of an 'us' than just plain old
me. I want to jump up and down and shout, 'Look everyone,
I'm in a couple! I can do it too.'

Jack stops by a surf shop. 'Come on, let's go jet skiing,' he
says, grabbing my hand.

I don't have time to argue before I'm dragged into the shop. As I watch him, I laugh to myself. Laugh at the fact that he has no idea what's in my head and wouldn't even come close to understanding. Because he's a bloke and he simply doesn't have these kind of thoughts. And he's right not to. I'm so jealous of how his life is so uncomplicated. How marvellous it must be to have all that brain space to concentrate on the here and now. I'd get so much done if I didn't spend so much time having existential angst. I'd have time to be impulsive like Jack is being now and my life would be fun all the time.

I remember how it felt when someone taught me how to tie my laces properly for the first time. It was such a revelation. All of a sudden, it made perfect sense. There was no need to trip over any more. Watching Jack in the shop, I feel like that again, as if he's shown me a way to be happy, and I feel like knocking my head and saying, 'Durrr. Of course, it's so obvious!'

The girl in the shop warns me that my excuse for a bikini is too flimsy and it'll be whipped off in a second. Instead she gives me a sticky rubber wet suit which doesn't exactly flatter my child-bearing hips. Jack, of course, looks like James Bond on a mission and I feel a surge of jealousy when the woman behind the counter eyes him up and down.

Oi you, hands off!

In the water, Jack's a natural. When I see the glint in his eye, I can tell he's seeking revenge for my triumph in the car and burns through the water, slashing it into big waves which make me wobble.

'Don't be scared, just let go,' he yells, and I pull on the throttle shooting off towards the horizon. It's so exhilarating that I screech as the water splashes up in my face. He catches up with me and shows me how to turn, and in no time I'm a *Baywatch* Babe. Tee hee.

I'm having such a laugh that the time goes in a flash. My throat is hoarse as I stagger up the beach and peel myself out of the wet suit.

Jack puts his arm around me as I emerge from the back of the shop. 'Fun?' he asks.

'Fantastic, but I'm starving now.' I pat my stomach, astonished that my body paranoia has vanished.

'Then I shall treat you,' he says grandly.

'Fish and chips?'

'You're so English,' he teases. 'No, I think we can do better than that.'

We stroll around the lanes and find a cheap and cheerful French restaurant with tables outside on the cobbles. Jack orders us a couple of beers.

'To us,' he toasts, and I clink his glass. The bubbles go up my nose.

I've spent so much time wondering what he thinks about last night, but now I've got the opportunity to ask him, I let the moment pass. I realise that I'm much more interested in finding out what he thinks about everything else.

'Do you like being an artist?' I ask when the starters arrive.

'I think so. It's the only thing I know how to do well. And anyway, it gets me out of having a nine to five job.'

'You're so lucky,' I sigh. 'I wish I had something I was really good at.'

'I can think of something,' he grins.

I blush. 'Apart from that.'

'You want success, you mean?'

'I guess so. Doesn't everyone?'

'What did you want to do when you were a kid?' he asks, breaking a bread roll and dipping it in his sauce.

'Something to do with clothes, I think. Men's clothes. I always preferred Ken to Barbie.'

'You just wanted to get his trousers off.'

I laugh. 'True. Although Ken doesn't have very exciting bits. No, I like men's clothes. The first time I saw you, I noticed your clothes.'

Jack looks up at me. 'Why don't you get into the fashion industry or something then?'

I look at the asparagus spear on my plate. 'I wanted to for ages, but I didn't get anywhere. It's far too competitive.'

'You'll never find out unless you try. There's loads of

talented people, but there's no reason why you shouldn't be one of them. If I thought about the competition, I'd have given up painting ages ago.'

'I suppose.'

'You've got nothing to lose. Anyway, you've got everything going for you.'

He looks at me and smiles. I feel so relieved and so happy that without even thinking about it, I trust him. Completely. I haven't talked about my career prospects to anyone apart from H and I feel like a big weight has lifted off me, just admitting my ambitions to him. I feel like I'm me again. Me with substance and a shape to my future. Maybe I will give it a go.

We stay and get pissed, watching people going by, and the afternoon dissolves into laughter. Later we stroll back down to the beach. It's emptier and we find a quiet spot. I'm pissed in a heady way and I feel that there's only me and Jack in the world. Jack skims pebbles across the waves towards the sinking sun and I watch as his body moves. I'm pathetically loved up.

He turns to face me.

'What shall we do now?' I ask.

'Do you want to go back?'

'No. Do you?'

He shakes his head.

We look at each other nervously and laugh. He taps his lips. 'I know somewhere we can stay. If you want to, that is.'

And I do want. I'm all of a want.

The man at the Casanova B&B treats Jack like an old friend. He throws him a key with a wink and a warning that breakfast is only served until 10.30 a.m. and leaves us to it.

Our room is very British Home Stores, with a floral quilt and a fluffy rug. But it's clean and there's an assortment of tiny packets of biscuits by the Teasmaid. I put my bag down on a chair by the TV and peek round the net curtain on to the small garden at the back.

It feels strange to be in this room with Jack. After the day we've had it seems illicit and grown up. We don't touch each other.

Jack goes into the bathroom and puts up the toilet seat. I can see his back as he takes a leak and, for some reason, I feel shocked. Now it's such a sure thing that we're going to sleep together, I feel nervous. Somehow it'll mean more than last night at Jack's house and I'm scared by how intimate this setting is. How *together* we are.

Jack flushes the loo and stands in the doorway. I notice he's put the seat down. Someone must have trained him well. I wonder who . . .

'I feel grubby,' he says.

I wrinkle my nose and ruffle my hair which has gone all curly with the salt water. 'So do I.'

'Shower?' he asks, and I nod.

He gets in first and I can see him adjusting the temperature through the glass doors as I undress. When he opens the door, I climb in.

I feel all geeky and awkward. It's very bright and, standing naked opposite Jack, I feel hopelessly exposed. It feels like the first time we've really seen each other. I suppose it is. I want to cross my arms over my stomach and curl up in a ball.

Jack looks at me. Really looks at me. All over, as if he's taking in every pore of my skin, and I know I'm blushing.

I try to grab him and kiss him, which would somehow be less intimate, but he pulls away and pushes me back. Without saying anything, staring right into my eyes, he takes a small tablet of soap and rubs it into a lather between his hands.

You wouldn't think that a pink plastic shower cubicle is particularly erotic, but right now it's up there in my list of all-time fantasy moments. Because Jack starts to wash me, turning me into a quivering mass of lather. As he strokes me, he pays such close attention to my body that it's almost as if he's drawing me. I can feel myself sliding against him, both of us enveloped in a cloud of steam. And I feel . . . WOMAN.

Wet woman.

Wicked woman.

I'm shaking all over before he crouches down and hooks one of my legs over his shoulder. He buries his head between my legs and I'm a goner. Everything is slipping, his hands over my body, my back down the wall, and my senses into the most awesome orgasm I've ever had.

Afterwards, it takes me ages to get my breath back and I kind of go all shaky. We still haven't spoken. I look at him through the steam.

It's my turn.

I sink down and he grips my hair as my tongue does all the talking.

'Amy?' he rasps after a while.

'Mmmmmmm?' I say. I can't say much else, I've got my mouth full. 'You're kneeling on the plug hole.'

We mop up the flood with most of the towels and lie on the bed to dry off naturally. Jack traces the tan line of my bikini top on my breast.

'You've caught the sun,' he says.

And I have. I feel warmed to the bones. We look into each other's eyes and I know then that we're going to make love. And the thing that really gets to me is that Jack reads my mind because he says, 'All night, all night and all tomorrow until you won't be able to walk.'

And he's as good as his word.

By the time we get back to Jack's on Sunday, I'm feeling knackered in only the way that too much sex, sun, sea and booze can make you feel.

'Happy?' he asks, as he unlocks the door. We've been playing around on the beach all day and the sun has made his freckles come out. He looks gorgeous. I reach out and stroke his cheek.

'Maybe,' I smile.

'Only maybe? What does a bloke have to do?' He pretends

108

to be outraged and picks me up, carrying me around the waist and walking with me to the kitchen. I'm giggling so much that I don't notice Chloe and Matt sitting on cushions on the living room floor.

'Well, well, look at this. It's love's young dream,' laughs Chloe.

Jack stops tickling me and springs away. I push my hair behind my ear, my laughter dying at the sight of Chloe. She's sprawled out as if she lives here with a bottle of beer in her hand. She looks sickeningly thin, her perfect legs careering out of her short sundress.

'Hi guys,' says Jack, brushing past me. He crouches down and kisses Chloe on the cheek.

'Help yourself,' says Matt, gesturing to some beers on the table. 'Where've you been?'

'Brighton,' I reply.

'Look at your nose!' Chloe wails at me. 'You poor thing.'

Jack laughs and hands me a beer. It's not funny. It's not my fault I look like Rudolf. I pull a face at him, but he seems distant and he doesn't defend me.

'So?' asks Chloe. 'Tell all?'

'We had a great time, jet skiing, the works,' says Jack, leaning back against the sofa and opening his beer.

'And you stayed over! Where's that shag haunt of yours, Jack?' teases Chloe. She clicks her fingers, looking at me. 'Don't tell me, don't tell me . . . the Casanova. That's it, isn't it? I hope you got a discount rate.'

'Shut up, Chloe,' he says, but he's laughing, revelling in being Jack the Casanova, and it all makes sense for a moment. I'm just another conquest to him. He's done all this before and I'm not the first. Who else has he moved the earth for in the pink plastic shower cubicle? The floor seems to sink from under my feet.

'Sit down, sit down,' says Matt, waving his bottle at the cushions, but I don't want to go anywhere near Chloe in case I accidentally stab her.

'Oh, Helen called me last night,' says Chloe, casually swigging her beer.

Warning siren. Why would H call Chloe?

'She was looking for you.'

'Shit.'

'Don't worry, I told her you were probably with lover-boy here.'

'Was she all right? What did she say?'

'Nothing much. Sounded a bit upset.'

'Can I use your phone?' I ask Jack.

'Sure, use the one in my room.'

I feel sick with worry as I leave them all laughing in the kitchen.

'H, it's me. Come on, come on, pick up,' I urge her answering machine.

There's a click. 'So you're back then,' she says curtly. She sounds really pissed off.

'I've been to Brighton.'

'Bully for you.'

This is horrible. She never takes this tone with me. I grip the phone. 'What's wrong?'

'I'm sure it's of no concern to you,' she spits, but her voice is shaking and she's making me feel frightened.

'Tell me,' I urge.

She lets out a suppressed sob. 'Leave me alone.'

The phone goes dead. I listen to the tone utterly gobsmacked. She's never put the phone down on me before, but then it's no surprise that she's pissed off. If I was her I'd hate me. We had plans for Saturday night which I blew out and I didn't call her all weekend and I'm guilty. Guilty of being a selfish cow, guilty of doing what I always promised I'd never do when it came to a bloke. And now she's having a crisis and I've deserted her in her hour of need. The thought of losing her fills my stomach with dread.

'Is everything okay?' asks Jack from the doorway. He walks across to me and puts a hand on my shoulder.

'Something's up, I've got to go and see her. You don't mind do you?'

'No, go ahead, it's no problem.'

I hate him for sounding so genuine. I wish he did mind, wish that he cared that our blissful weekend has fizzled out, but one look at him and I know that he's not going to. He's with his gang now and I don't count.

We have a public goodbye in front of Matt and Chloe, during which Jack treats me like he's seeing off his maiden aunt. I scan his face, but the Jack I've spent the weekend with has retreated into his fortress. The more I look at him, the more defensive he gets and he barely kisses me.

'See you then,' he says.

See me when? Tomorrow? In a week? In a month? In a year? *Ever Again*?

'I had a good time,' he concedes, but it sounds way too past tense to me.

'I hope Helen is okay,' says Chloe, joining Jack by the front door. Her voice is full of sympathy, but I'm not buying it for a second, especially when she wraps her arms around Jack's waist and gives him a hug. Anyone else would see it as a friendly gesture, but when she removes her hand from Jack's chest, I can almost see the brand she's left there: 'Private Property. Keep out'. I stumble backwards on to the street and before I'm out of sight, she's laughing and moving back inside the house with him. I look at the closed front door in disbelief.

My heart is thumping as I peg it over to H's on the tube and I'm nervous as I follow her into her darkened lounge. If there were smoking Olympics, H would have won gold, silver and bronze medals all by herself. She's surrounded by the debris of misery and she's listening to Leonard Cohen. It's a very bad sign.

At first she tries to keep up her pretence of being angry, but she can't and crumples back into the H-shaped dent in the bean bag. As I suspected, it's Gav.

'I've really fucked up,' she sobs.

'Shhh,' I soothe, kneeling down beside her. 'No you haven't.'

When I get her to calm down, she tearfully explains the latest trauma.

'We were lying in bed and I asked him if he wanted to get married. It was just a hypothetical question, I wasn't proposing or anything, but he went all strange. He said that he'd never get married unless he was going to have kids. So I said, well when *do* you want to have kids, and he said not for ages, maybe another ten years, there were things he wanted to do with his life.'

It sounds fair enough to me; a typical Gav reaction.

'But then it all got out of hand. I said that ten years sounded like a long time and where did that leave us, but he got the hump and said that he thought I was pressuring him and why couldn't we just have fun, but I said, what's the point?' She takes a deep, shuddery breath and her chin trembles. 'And what *is* the point? What's the point in being involved, of loving someone if all the time you know that they're going to piss off with someone else and not want babies until your ovaries have shrivelled into dried peas?'

I laugh and dry her tears with the last piece of loo roll. 'You can't predict the future, babe. You can't know for sure what either of you are going to be doing.'

'I know that now with Gav,' she chokes. 'It's going nowhere.'

'That's not true. It was going fine until you had this silly argument. You've got everything going for you both and you have a great time together. Why can't you just let it be?'

'You don't understand. Don't give me all that living for the moment crap, I'm not a fucking Zen Buddhist and neither are you,' she snaps.

She's not going to listen to reason. She's being stubborn, her true Capricorn colours showing through. The only way forward is to chivvy her out of it. Thank God I've got a Ph.D. in H Management Technique. I sigh and stand up.

'Okay, okay,' I surrender. 'Be a stubborn miserable old bag then. Don't get involved with anyone, just in case they don't turn out to be Mr Right. I know, I know, I know, I've got it!

What you could do is print up a questionnaire and get every bloke you fancy to fill it in giving his personal guarantee that he'll put his life on hold whilst you make your mind up what you want, because that'll *really* work.'

There's a smile playing on H's lips despite herself.

'Or perhaps you could just shackle Gav down. Chain him to the kitchen table and whip him until he proposes to you. Is that what you want? Are you absolutely positive that he's the one for you, for ever and ever until the end of time?'

'No,' she admits.

'Well then.'

'But I do love him and I do want it to work out.'

'And when did he say that he didn't want that too? H, you're being ridiculous.'

'It's too late now. He's gone.'

'Yes, back to his house probably.' I roll my eyes at her. 'He hasn't dropped off the end of the world. You'll probably be laughing about this tomorrow.'

She cheers up and we have a big hug.

'The worst thing was not being able to get hold of you,' she says. 'I was really worried.'

'I know, I know, I got carried away, I'm sorry.'

She asks me all about the weekend in Brighton and I tell her.

'So what's wrong? Why the glum face?'

'I don't know. I had a great time, but now I feel all jangled by Chloe. She was such a bitch.'

'Maybe she's right to warn you.'

I'm immediately suspicious. 'Why? What did she say?'

H sighs and pulls an it's-too-bad kind of face. 'Nothing much. I don't want you getting hurt, that's all. Chloe knows Jack pretty well. She says that he's a real womaniser and the whole prospect of a relationship would make him run a mile.'

'So what are you saying? You're believing Chloe now are you?'

'No,' corrects H. 'All I'm saying is that you shouldn't get your hopes up.'

'So that's it then is it? It's not going to work. Well I'm glad everyone has decided for me and saved me the trouble.'

H tuts and forces me to sit down. 'Who knows. Only *you* know what feels right. You'll just have to see how it goes.'

And she's right of course, but I hate it when she gives me back my own advice. It's so hard to take.

Back at my flat, I lie on my stomach on the sofa and stare at the carpet. My head is truly in a mess. Before my date with Jack on Friday, I was so sussed. I thought I had my strategy all worked out. I was going to be cool and take things slowly and I definitely wasn't going to sleep with him. OK, so I'll admit it, I bought new underwear – even suspenders (fucking uncomfortable) – and splashed out on new make-up, perfume and a dress on the never never, but I still had no intention of blowing it. I just wanted him to want me to the point where it lasted, to the point where he realised that I was someone he could have a relationship with.

And now I've ruined it. All before it's started.

But then I remember Brighton and the memories seem so fresh that they sting my eyelids. Was it only this morning that I was curled up so tightly with him? How could it not mean anything to him? How can he dismiss it so quickly? How can he treat me like a quick shag he was throwing out after that?

I run a bath, but it's no comfort. I'm cold and sunburnt and deserted and even when I wrap myself in clean towels, the feeling of desolation doesn't go away. There's no point in staring at the phone, I know he's not going to ring. Why should he? He's got Chloe to amuse him.

I douse myself in moisturiser, but despite the fact that I'm so tired, sleep is elusive. I fold my arms over the edge of the duvet and stare at the ceiling and the weekend is running through my head like a set of photographs. In every one I'm over exposed.

So much for my great expectations. I've had it all and lost it all in a day. In years to come, when I'm sitting in my flat like Miss Haversham, covered in cobwebs, people will say, 'Ah yes, poor thing, she was happy that one June day, but that was her lot.'

And even though Jack hasn't died, he might as well be on the moon. I'm torturing myself with what he's saying right now:

'Amy, she's a good lay. We had a laugh, but there's plenty more where that came from. Onwards and upwards.'

'Why should I see her again? My friends are more important and I want to be young, free and single. What's the point of being tied down?'

This is intolerable. I can't stay in bed with his voice in the room and I drag my bones into the kitchen to make a hot chocolate. I sniff the milk. It'll do. It's only when I close the fridge that I notice that my kids' magnetic letters have been moved. And there it is, in pink, green and orange:

I push my face against the white door and smile, because the message can only be from Jack. Whilst I'm standing here, waiting for the milk to boil, I don't feel quite so bad.

5
Jack

New Dawn

My morning begins with a riddle:

Question: What smells like cheese, tastes like cheese, but isn't
cheese?
Answer: Matt's foot.

Now, Matt's a nice guy. Correction: Matt's the *best* guy.
We've been through a lot together: from childhood piano
lessons in Bristol with the untamed, child-hating shrew, Miss
Hopkins, to puberty and our first purchase of dirty magazines
and cheap cider, to our current preoccupation with mas-
querading as mature, responsible members of society in
London. And I can say without doubt that there aren't many
sacrifices I wouldn't be happy to make in his interest. If I only
had one cigarette left in my pack and we were miles from any
shop, I'd share it with him. If he fell overboard in a storm, I'd
dive in after him. If he needed a kidney, I'd give him one of
mine. And, if pressed, I *would* give him my last Rolo. But even
the very best of friendships only goes so far. And waking up to
find the sweaty big toe of his left foot wedged firmly against
my teeth is, quite frankly, *too* far.

I remove the offending stump of flesh from my mouth and
wipe my lips on my arm. Or, rather, on my sleeve. Because I'm
still dressed. I'm still wearing the clothes I crashed out in last
night at around 3 a.m. when I drifted off to sleep to the sound
of Supertramp's 'Breakfast in America' (an irony not lost on

my sleep-deprived brain, either then or now). I attempt to sit up and immediately capsize, lie back on my side and wait for the swell that's seized control of Matt's house to subside. After a few seconds, it does, and I get to my feet, make a lunge for the sofa and successfully clamber aboard and arrange myself into a sitting position. It's only then that I risk assessing the situation.

One word comes to me: Apocalypse. The Four Riders are all present and correct on the field of Armageddon that was once Matt's living room: Matt, Chloe, Jack Daniels and Jim Beam. The first two are lying beneath me, side by side at the foot of the sofa, spooning like lovers. The others are empty shells of their former selves. Jim's glass neck is broken from where Chloe knocked him off the table round 2 a.m., spilling his guts all over the rug in the process. Jack is empty, quite literally having had his spirit sucked dry, pointing at where I was sitting while we played Truth or Dare. Looking at this scene of decadence, depravity and almost total futility, I reach the conclusion that my life sucks.

Something, I decide, has to change.

I run a quick self-diagnosis:

Taste: Stale alcohol, cigarettes and barbecue beef-flavoured Pringles
Touch: Unstable/clammy
Sight: Blurred
Hearing: Matt's snoring; my heartbeat
Smell: Matt's feet

And my worst fears are confirmed. My life; shit. Shit; my life. Right now, it's pretty hard to spot the difference. I drink too much. I smoke too much. I don't do enough work. This has been my life for the past six months. This is the way I've chosen to live. And this is no longer what I want.

I hear a cow fart and then realise that it is, in fact, Matt. His expression contorts into a pained wince as his eyelids prise themselves apart. It's impossible to tell whether this is an upper-body reaction to his butt's bovine behaviour, or a simple deduction, based on the weak light filtering through the curtains, that, yes, it is Monday morning, and no, he's not in a fit state to go to work. He groans, checks his watch and mumbles something incoherent. Then, with his eyes sealed tight once more, he gently shakes Chloe awake.

Matt: 'Ugudehgedub.'

Chloe: 'Uhg. Wotzatsiksmell?'

Matt: 'Eyedoanowotyertawkingabowt.'

Chloe: 'Uhg. Uhg-uhg-uhg. Eyedoanoweareyeam.'

Matt: 'Weergunnabelait. Werk. Weergunnabelaitfuhwerk.'

Chloe: 'Fukwerk. Eyemgunnadeye. Meyehedsgunnapop.'

Matt: 'Lisnclowee. Ugudehgedubnow. Okay? Ugunnagedub?'

Chloe: 'Okay. Aislegedub. Tenmorminitsandailgedub.'

Matt: 'Okay. Tenmorminits. Budthenweergunnagoatoowerk. Okay?'

Chloe: 'Okay.'

Luckily, my cultural and linguistic skills include the capacity to speak fluent Hangover. As a result, I'm able to translate their intellectual exchange of views and conclude that they've made the decision to stay put for the time being. This is good. Because my hangover is moving into overdrive. I need a bath. I need a long, hot soak.

Five minutes after lowering my aching body into the bath, I'm still suffering a living death. Coupled to my hangover is a profound sense of depression and self-loathing. Forget Frankenstein's monster. Nosferatu, eat your heart out. I'm the genuine article. I'm the accursed creature destined to walk the earth in agony till the end of time. Dante's Inferno had nothing on this.

Physical proof of my ungodly condition lies in the facts that:

a) The percussionist of the London Philharmonic Orchestra is performing an amphetamine-fuelled solo inside the concert hall of my skull

b) My stomach is twisting and growling like I've swallowed

a rabid terrier

c) The bath's water level is visibly rising as a tide of sweat seeps from my brow

In a desperate bid for redemption, I therefore turn to religion. I become a pilgrim and the bath becomes my Lourdes. I chant Praise Be to God for the Gift of Hot Water. I hallelujah over the Cleansing Spirit of Soap and the Bounty of Bubblebath. And verily do I bless this bath and all who slump in her.

But it's no good. In this, my hour of need, the God I haven't believed in since I was twelve years old has obviously decided to return the compliment. I'm left with no option other than to accept the grim truth that my body is not a temple, but a pig sty. And a rather shabby pig sty, at that. But then I remember Amy's advice from the other day about the Banana Recovery Plan and, with this in mind, I temporarily abandon the bath, drip across the bathroom floor and grab a couple of Nurofen from the shelf. I down them with a handful of water from the tap and return to my watery cocoon.

Lying here, waiting for the chemical cure to run its course, I grab my mask and snorkel from behind the taps and put them on. A change of environment could well be the key to my recovery. Some people use meditation as a means of sorting their heads out. Others, drugs. For me, though, it's the mask, snorkel and lying face down in the bath every time. So be gone, dry land, and all your earthly cares. Bring forth Atlantis.

I submerge myself fully beneath the water and play the old game, the game I've played since I was a kid. With my eyes closed, I visualise a seascape through which I'm drifting. Brightly coloured coral reefs below, warm currents all around. I imagine myself having the ability to breathe under water. Fronds of seaweed stroke my skin, fish flash past. And above me, above the waves, I picture a perfect, clear blue sky.

But there are times when escapism just doesn't work. And this is one of them. The imaginary scene dissolves and all I'm left with is murky bathwater and Mr Matey foam above my head. It's a concentration thing, I suppose. And I'm distracted.

As in *totally*. It's the old problem. The BIG problem. Life. And where it's going. And how come it hasn't got there yet. I'm twenty-seven years old and what have I achieved? Answer: nothing. Being aware that this paranoia I'm suffering from is largely a result of my hangover doesn't make it any less real. I'm wasting my life, and I know it.

Something *definitely* has to change.

At the end of last year, I made a decision. I would quit my job and become an artist. I would leap from the stern of the good ship Comfort, forsaking the security of its complimentary salary, pension scheme and low-pressure, nine-to-five regime. Man Over Board, I would take my chances with the sharks and strike out for the mythical Isle of Fulfilment. And so, on 1 December 1997, I reared up from my work station in the art department of ProPixel Ltd, Wembley. On my Mac screen was a half-completed packet design for Chick-O-Lix™ ('The tasty chicken bits kids love to dip and lick.'), which, as a parting gesture of solidarity towards feathered fowl the world over, I erased from existence. My resignation letter, typed on Matt's PC at home that night, stated that my reason for leaving was 'to get a life'.

I gave myself a year to achieve this goal. Sink or swim. And if it was sink, then so be it. I had enough experience and contacts to walk back into another crap job with another crap firm. And that would be fine. Because at least I'd have tried. At least I wouldn't have settled for mediocrity. And, even feeling the way I do right now – with half my allotted year of freedom gone and still no sight of land – it's not a choice I regret. What is getting me down, though, is quite how much of this year I've wasted. If ambition is critical to success, then mine, I fear, is critically ill. And that's what's nerving me out. Solution: I must get down to work. Today. Today will be the day I get on with getting a life. A new painting. On cue, an idea racks up in my mind. I feel a rush and tell myself that this could be the start of something great.

I smile. One good thought. One good thought is all it takes to drive the paranoia away. Just like Peter Pan, one good thought and I can fly. And it's not like I only have one good thought, either. I have two. I have getting stuck into my work. And I have Amy. I run the Brighton episode through my mind, pausing on the good bits: mucking about on the pier, the French restaurant, the hotel shower . . . all that cool stuff. Amy is nice. Amy is clean. Amy is all the things that I, right now, am not. Amy is definitely someone I should hang out with more. As a friend. As a friend I also happen to sleep with.

Girlfriend.

The concept leaps out at me like a jack-in-the-box (or a you-in-the-box, as Chloe says). Same as last night when we were playing Truth or Dare. I remember the instant Chloe spun the Jack Daniels bottle and it pointed directly at me. Matt had been caught telling numerous whoppers, and had paid Dare penalties of swallowing three spoonfuls of olive oil, as well as removing all of his clothes. He was sitting by the sofa with his genitals discreetly tucked between his legs, looking like a woman. Chloe, a more accomplished fibber, had merely had to surrender her jeans. And I, priding myself on having very few secrets kept from these my closest mates, had yet to suffer a single Dare. Until the bottle pointed at me, that is. Until Chloe started enquiring about Amy.

'Would I be correct,' she asked, a mischievous grin spreading across her face, 'in describing Amy as your girlfriend?'

'No.'

'Liar,' she reacted, looking to Matt for confirmation.

'Liar,' he concurred.

Chloe held out her hand. 'Shorts. Now. Hand them over.'

'No bloody way. I'm telling the truth. We've only just met. We're mates, okay? Nothing more. And certainly not *that*. Not the G-word, for Christ's sake.'

Chloe tut-tutted, glanced at Matt again. 'Me thinks he doth protest too much.'

'Agreed,' Matt said. 'Shall I prosecute?'

Chloe sat back, waved him on. 'Go ahead, my learned friend. After all, you are the lawyer.'

Matt made to stand, then, remembering his naked state,

settled back down and placed his hands over his pubic triangle. 'I put it to you, Mr Rossiter,' he began, 'that you have spent a whole weekend in the company of one Amy Crosbie. I further put it to you, that that weekend was not spent indulging in any of the usual behavioural codes of single people, such as going, if I may use the vernacular–' his voice quivered with distaste '–out on the pull and clubbin' and largin' it up with the express intention of getting laid by a total stranger. Why no, sir,' he moved swiftly on. 'Quite the reverse, I think. Did you, or did you not, for example, invite this Amy Crosbie to this very house for–' he made a melodramatic show of clearing his throat '–dinner?'

'I did.'

Matt frowned heavily. ''Tis as I feared, ladies and gentlemen of the court. And did you then not compound this error by taking the same dinner guest to a house of dubious repute in Brighton by the name of the Casanova?'

'Yeah,' I admit, 'but so what? You both know that isn't the first time I've taken a girl there. It doesn't mean a thing. Doesn't make her my girlfriend, does it?'

'In that case,' Matt pounced, 'could you kindly explain to the court how it was that when we encountered you earlier today, walking into this very room, you were chuckling and giggling and carrying the aforementioned Amy Crosbie wrapped around your waist?'

'It was just a bit of fun.'

Matt stifled a snigger, then collected himself, lowered his voice. 'Oh, no. It was far more than that. Was it not the action of a man with feelings – nay, emotions – for the woman he was holding on to oh so tight?'

'No.'

'You're crap,' Chloe interrupted, laughing at me. 'You're into her. You're serious about her. Why can't you just admit it?'

I avoided their eyes. 'Because it's not true.'

'So,' Matt continued, 'even in the light of the evidence presented before this court, you're still not going to hand over your shorts?'

'No.'

'Contempt of court, then,' Chloe said. 'Game over.'

'Who gives a toss?' I muttered. 'It's a crap game, anyway.'

Girlfriend.

The word's still there, in spite of my protestations to the contrary last night. It's weird, but at the time I meant what I said about Amy just being a mate and all that. Only I don't now. And, more bizarre still, I feel guilty about describing her that way to Matt and Chloe. I feel like I've betrayed her in some way – which, I suppose, I have. I was drunk, but that's hardly an excuse, is it? I knew then, like I know now, that it *was* a good weekend. Bullshit; it was a *great* weekend. So how come I said all that stuff about her? And how come I switched off once we got back from Brighton and did the nonchalant act? What's the score on that? Maybe it was her leaving, shooting off to see her mate, and me being back with Matt and Chloe. The Triumvirate. Same as it ever was, getting drunk and talking shit, not needing anyone else.

Girlfriend.

It's not going away. Because I know I'm going to see Amy again. Because it's something that I want. Soon.

The thought occurs to me that maybe I should have handed my shorts over to Chloe after all.

I breathe in, but nothing comes. Panicked, I spin round on to my back and burst to the surface. Chloe's sitting on the edge of the bath, laughing, holding her guilty hand up.

'Find any mermaids, sailor?' she asks

Matt, wrapped in a towel, stumbles into the bathroom and looks at me with suspicion. 'Why do you *do* that?' he asks me, scrunching his face up in distaste.

I remove the snorkel from my mouth. 'Do what?'

'That getting up thing. That peeling yourself off the floor downstairs and achieving a state of wakefulness. Why do you do that when you don't even have to go to work?'

'Because, my brother,' I say, removing my Amphibian Man gear, becoming a mild-mannered twentysomething once more, 'I do have to work.' I pull the plug on my imaginary ocean, stand up and step out of the bath, brush past Chloe with her averted eyes and grab a towel. 'And that's exactly what I'm going to do right now.'

Park Life

Thursday morning arrives with a surprise: a dream of Amy. We're sitting on a tropical beach and the sun's melting across the sea, pulling a starry sky down behind it like a blind. It's warm, but still I pull her close.

'This is good,' she whispers, her head resting on my shoulder, her hair tickling the side of my face. 'I could stay here for ever.'

'Yeah, this is—'

But before I can say anything else – and there *are* things I want to tell her – there's this high-pitched whining noise. I look behind me, but all I can see is the line of palm trees further up the beach. Then the whining's shifting into rabid barking. I turn to Amy and, as I do, she looks up. At first, I'm too shocked to form a reaction to what I see: a wolf's head sprouting out of Amy's neck, saliva dripping from its fangs. I'm paralysed by the sight and the noise coming from her mouth, now pitching into a howl. But then I'm moving, throwing her back, turning, running across the sand, screaming out for help, desperate to escape.

I wake with sweat running from my brow on to the pillow I'm clinging to. Even here, though, with my eyes wide open, back in my bedroom, the howling keeps coming. Then my heart slows as I realise what it is: Fat Dog, my alarm clock. I reach out and grab it from the bedside table and hurl the furry fiend across the room. There's a yelp of pain as it hits the wall and drops to the floor, then silence.

Fat Dog was a present from my gadget-freak of a brother last Christmas. When it goes off, it starts with a quiet panting noise, then rises in volume into a growl, through to a whine and a frenzied bark, before peaking in an ear-splitting howl. The card that accompanied it read: 'A new girlfriend for you'. Ho, ho, ho. Big Bro' Billy. Always the wise guy. Still, as Billy presents go, it's not a bad one. Certainly better than the previous year's offering of an electric sock warmer, anyway.

As for the dream intrusion thing, it's not the first time Fat Dog has put in an appearance. This is a relief, because it would be pretty easy to get all Freudian about it otherwise. It would be tempting, for example, to interpret my dream as follows:

a) The tranquil beach location represents my basic need for security and emotional exchange; Amy's transmogrification into a wolf, at the very moment I'm about to express an emotion, represents my fear of surrendering my independence; ergo, I'm emotionally immature and scared shitless of even entertaining the thought of committing myself to a relationship

b) Amy's a bit of a dog herself and I don't really fancy her

The direct correlation between the rigidity of my penis and time spent thinking about sex with Amy over the last few days of not seeing her throws the second of these interpretations out of the window. Which leaves me with option (a). But I can't be dealing with that. I'm not emotionally immature. I've got as many emotions as the next guy. It's just that I'm choosy about what I do with them, that's all. And I'm not afraid, either. What have I got to be afraid of? I've been calling the shots so far, not Amy, right? I mean, it was *she* who called me Tuesday afternoon. OK, so it was me who didn't want the call to end, and kept whipping off new topics to chat about. But that's pretty normal; I'm just a sociable guy. I'm in this as deep as I want to be, no more. I can pull out anytime I want. It's no big deal. Surrendering my independence? Crap. I'm as independent as the day I met her.

So much for Freud.

I reach for the phone. 'Hi, Amy,' I say. 'It's Jack. How about lunch?'

There's a long, soft – and, yes, it must be said, very sexy – moan from her end of the phone. 'Jack?'

'Yeah, you know, the guy you spent most of the weekend with.'

That moan again, then, 'What time is it?'

'Round eight-thirty.'

She clears her throat. 'So . . . so, how are you?'

I hear Matt coming out of the bathroom. 'Oh, you know, pretty good. How come you're not up?'

'Not working today. Top Temps let me down.' She sounds depressed.

I say, 'Sorry,' then, 'Shit, I've ruined your lie-in, haven't I?'

'No, no – well, yes.' She laughs. 'But it's okay. It's good to hear from you.' There's a silence and I listen to the sound of her moving in her bed. I get a visual of her lying there, hair messed across the pillow, eyes all scrunched up. I wish I was there. 'Lunch,' she says. 'Yes, that would be great. Where?'

I look out of the window. 'Well, Amy, it looks like it's going to be another sun-sunshiny day. So how about Hyde Park? Sort out a picnic. Get ourselves a tan.'

'Sounds fab. What time? And where? Hyde Park's a big place.'

'One-ish. You can pick me up from work.' As soon as I've said it, I realise I've cocked up.

Right on cue, she sounds confused. 'What, your house, you mean?'

'Er, no,' I improvise. 'It's a gallery in Mayfair. A mate's gallery. He's away, and I told him I'd look after it for him. Just as a favour, yeah?'

'Oh, okay. Give me the address.'

We talk for a few more minutes and then I put the phone down, stretch and get up. I'm fizzing. Wide awake and clear of mind. It's down to what's happened since Monday, to how storming everything's gone. On Monday, I started working in the studio at eleven and, apart from lunch and a quick coffee with Matt when he got back from work, I stayed there till gone ten. No TV. No lazing in the garden. Nothing but work.

I got going on this idea that had hit me in the bath while I was still nursing my hangover: a boys' toys thing. I rummaged

126

through Matt's *GQ* collection and cut out all these photos of fashion accessories and pinned them into an arrangement on a board. Then I borrowed Matt's car and got a canvas from ArtStart over in Chelsea. Three foot by eight. Had to put the roof down on the Spitfire to get it back. I spent the rest of the day on preliminary drawings, groundwork for copying the cutouts on to the canvas. And then I got stuck in. And it was a buzz, like I knew that what I was doing was actually going somewhere for a change. Same went for Tuesday and Wednesday nights, once I got back from working at Paulie's. No ducking down the pub. Even blew Gete and Paddy out for a West End crawl. Just work. Just what I should have been doing these last six months.

'What are you looking so pleased with yourself for?' Matt asks when I walk into the kitchen.

'Just life, Matt. Just life.' I grab a bowl and sit down opposite him at the table, pour out some muesli and drown it in milk.

'Yeah? You got something good planned for today?'

'Not really. Just down the gallery. Same as usual.'

'Uh-huh. Oh, yeah,' he adds, 'there's a message on the answerphone for you.'

I look down at my food, disinterested. 'Who?'

'S&M.'

I can feel him watching me. 'What does she want?'

'Well, not your body, if past form's anything to go on.'

Despite myself, I smile. 'Oh, hearty-ha-ha.'

'No, she was asking if it's still on for her coming round tomorrow. The modelling bit, you know.'

'Oh.'

He waits for me to say more, but I don't. 'So, you still reckon you're in with a chance, then?' he asks.

'We'll just have to wait and see, won't we?'

He raises his eyebrows, nonplussed. 'Yeah, right.'

'What's that meant to mean?'

'Take a guess. Three letters. Starts with an A, ends with a Y.'

Amy. I look back at my bowl. 'What's she got to do with it?'

'You tell me.'

'Nothing. How's that?'

'So you're not going to see her again?'

'I didn't say that.'

'So you *are* going to see her again,' he states.

I rest my spoon on my bowl, finish my mouthful. When I look at him, I can't tell whether he's joking or being serious. 'I didn't say that either.'

'What are you saying, then?'

'I dunno. I haven't made my mind up.'

'So you're not meeting her for lunch today, then?' He laughs when he sees my expression switch to surprise. 'Sorry, mate, but I couldn't help overhearing you talking . . .'

This pisses me off. 'Eavesdropping, you mean.'

But Matt's not reacting. He just keeps on smiling at me. 'Got to hand it to you, though . . .'

'What?'

'Picnic in the park. Very romantic.' He pronounces the word 'picnic' like it's some sort of contagious disease.

'A picnic,' I point out, 'is a form of lunch. A park is a place where people eat picnics. There's not necessarily anything romantic about it at all.'

He shrugs nonchalantly. 'Your call. Whatever you say.' He finishes his coffee. 'Personally, though, I'd call it a romantic date. Personally, I'd take it as yet more evidence that Amy is developing into something more than a "mate". Personally, I'd advise you that, if this is indeed the case, you should be extremely careful about your behaviour towards S&M.'

'Meaning?'

Matt stands up and puts on his jacket. 'That it might be decision time,' he says, heading for the door.

I cycle over to Paulie's Gallery and get there early. It takes me a couple of minutes to get in. Someone unsuccessfully tried to break in on Tuesday night and made a complete mess of the door in the process. So now there's a new door and new locks and, more importantly, Paulie owes me the money I forked out to pay for them. I haven't heard from him for a week, not since he jetted off for a climbing holiday in Nepal. Money owed aside, though, I'm not complaining. Paulie, truth be told, is a bit of a prick. Mid-forties, ex-City, multi-millionaire with an arrogant streak the size of the Panama Canal and a personality the size of a rat shit. When he interviewed me for the position, it became apparent that he didn't give a toss about art, and the only reason he owned a gallery at all was because it gave him something to talk about at dinner parties. Still, as Chris, who I used to work with at ProPixel, counselled me at the time: 'It's a job. It pays. Just do it.'

I tell myself that Chris's advice is no less relevant now than it was then. So what if this job is terminally boring? It's a means to an end. It pays the rent. I can cope. So I do. I go inside, I make myself a coffee, I station myself at the table by the door, and I smile at people who look in through the window, and generally concentrate on looking professional and approachable.

This lasts all of five minutes. Then I'm pacing round the kitchen at the back of the gallery, radio on, having a cigarette, dwelling on the conversation I had with Matt this morning. He does, of course, have a point about McCullen. Or, rather, he has a point about McCullen and Amy. Because it's the same point. And it's razor-sharp, too. It's fidelity.

For the two years I was going out with Zoe, fidelity wasn't an issue; I was faithful to her and, as far as I know, she was faithful to me in return. My thinking on the matter was very clear-cut:

a) The difference between sex with someone you're going out with and someone you're not is its emotional content
b) If you experience emotional sex with someone, then you care about them
c) If you care about someone, why would you want to deceive them?
d) If you're at ease deceiving the person you're going out with, then you no longer care about them
e) If you no longer care about them, then you shouldn't be going out with them

f) If the person you're going out with is unfaithful to you, then they're not worth caring about in the first place

This isn't to say I disapprove of infidelity across the board; I don't. And it's not to say I haven't been involved with other people's infidelities; I have. Between Zoe and now, I've slept with one married woman and two with long-term boyfriends. But in each of these cases, it wasn't me who made the decision to be unfaithful, it was them. The way I see it, the betrayal stops at their front doors, not mine. Single people are predatory by definition. Once I broke it off with Zoe, I became a free agent. I owed sexual loyalty to no one. Just because I wouldn't be unfaithful myself if I was in a relationship didn't mean I shouldn't be extremely grateful if other people chose to do just that with me.

But I'm fully aware that my single status is in jeopardy right now. I *do* have emotions for Amy. I'm not saying they're big emotions. It's not like I'm some love-crazed troubadour who's going to impale himself on his sword or anything. But, still, seeing her in a few hours is a good thought. And everything has to start somewhere. And if this is where Amy and I start, then continuing to hunt McCullen will probably be where it stops. So decision. Just what Matt was banging on about this morning. The question I have to address is this: Do I want to make a go of things with Amy? Because if I do, then for however long it lasts, I *will* be faithful to her. Which means no more hunting McCullen. Which means no more hunting at all.

And *that's* a very big decision indeed.

Amy arrives at Paulie's at four minutes past one. I know this because I've been monitoring the clock on the table for the past nine minutes, ever since I struck up this arty pose in preparation for her arrival: feet up, an illustrated copy of the history of Dadaism studiously rested on my lap. She raps her knuckles against the window pane and I look up casually, then smile, stand up. She's wearing mules and this brightly patterned, knee-length dress, and her hair's tied up. My mate Andy's dress rule applies one hundred per cent: 'You know a woman's well-dressed when all you can do is picture her naked.' I walk to the door and open it for her. For a second, we just stand here, all nervous smiles, and then I lean forward and our lips meet.

When she pulls back, I stroke my finger down her nose. 'The sunburn's gone, then . . .'

She blushes, screws up her face. 'Five jars of Nivea later.' She looks past me into the gallery, grins up at me. 'So what's it like doing an honest day's work for a change?'

At this point, the Clean Conscience Brigade marches to the front of my mind, all starched white uniforms and mops and buckets of warm soapy water. *Look at the state of this place*, they mutter in disgust. *Isn't it about time we cleared up some of this bullshit?* And they *do* have a case: I *would* feel a lot better about myself if I just fronted up to Amy and told her the truth about working here for real three days a week.

But just as I'm about to speak, to blurt it all out and tell her that it was just a chat-up line and that I feel I can tell her the truth now, because I know she'll be cool with it, I chicken out. What if she's not cool with it? What if she thinks, *He's lied to me once, he'll do it again*? Then it'll be over. It'll be over before it's even begun. Besides, it's not like I'm going to be doing this job for ever. It's just a stop-gap. And the people who know the truth, Matt and Chloe, are old hands at backing up my lines. Amy need never know.

'Put it this way,' I say, opting for ignoring her question, rather than lying outright, 'the sooner we're out of here and in the park, the better.'

I flip the sign on the door round to closed, lock up, and we set off towards Hyde Park. We chat about the weekend and what we've been up to since. Then we pop into a deli and grab a couple of sandwiches and some soft drinks. As we're walking from the deli to the park our hands brush, and the next thing I know her fingers are knitted between mine. I can't help flinching. Spooked is not the word. Stupid, I know, because our hands have been on far more intimate parts of our bodies before. But that's been behind closed doors, or drunk, or out of London. Not here in the sunshine on my home turf. It's the significance of the action, I suppose, that's freaking me out. It's the whole, hey-world-this-is-me-and-this-is-her-and-we're-together deal.

'What?' she asks, laughing at me, stopping and staring down at our joined hands.

I bite the inside of my cheek, then say, 'Nothing. It just feels weird, that's all.'

'We don't have to, if you don't want to. In fact,' she adds mischievously, slipping her hand from mine, 'it's probably best if we don't.'

I stand here confused, suddenly feeling off-balance, with the shopping bag in my left hand and nothing in my right. 'How's that?' I finally ask.

She narrows her eyes, challenges, 'What? Do you think I'm stupid? I know how these things work.'

I'm still clueless. I can't even tell if she's being serious any more. 'What things?'

'Things like holding hands. My mother warned me all about men like you. First it's holding hands, then it's a peck on the cheek. Next thing I know, you'll be trying to have sex with me and I'll be pregnant and you'll be shacked up with some other floozy.' She pouts at me. 'Well, let me tell you, Jack Rossiter, I'm not that kind of girl.'

A snort of laughter escapes from my mouth. 'Okay,' I apologise, 'point taken.' I hold out my hand, but all she does is raise her eyebrows in an invitation for me to say more. 'Please,' I say, 'I'd like to.'

'Certain?'

'Certain.'

And, as she puts her hand in mine and we walk on, I have to admit it feels pretty good.

The bits of the park near the main roads are packed by the time we get there. All the office workers are out on their lunch hours, getting their daily allowances of unfiltered oxygen and sunlight. It's all hitched-up skirts, rolled-up sleeves and loosened ties. Empty bottles of Evian and Prêt A Manger wrappers litter the grass, and Amy and I navigate our way through these obstacles until the people thin out and we find a quiet place near the centre of the park. We settle in the half-shade of a tree and eat and drink and talk.

To begin with, the whole scene seems pretty unreal to me. I find myself play-acting, laughing at Amy's jokes, firing off question after question, getting under her skin and letting her know it's a good place to be. Doing, in other words, all the stuff girls like – or all the stuff I've learnt to make girls like me, anyway. But after a while, the act slips. It's no longer me playing Jack the Lad, or Jack the Listener, or any of the other personas I've developed since I split up with Zoe. I end up just being Jack the Me. And it's a relief. I find myself relaxing. We're lying here side by side, staring up through the pattern of leaves at the sky, and suddenly, there's a conversation I want to have with her, a conversation I haven't had with anyone since I first met Zoe.

'That thing with the hands,' I begin.

She touches her fingertips against mine. 'This thing?'

'Yeah,' I say, folding her hand inside mine, 'that's the one.'

'What about it?'

'I don't know. It's just, well, you know . . . it means something. It's a link. I mean, when you look at two people holding hands, you make assumptions about them, don't you?'

'That they're together . . .'

'But it's more than that, too. You assume that they're happy with the situation, that they're comfortable with it.'

Still holding my hand, she props herself up on her elbow and stares down at me. 'And are you? Is that how you feel when you're with me?'

'I think so.'

Her brow wrinkles slightly. 'Only think?'

I try to explain. 'Well, you can't know, can you? Not yet.' I falter. 'I can't, anyway.'

She looks disappointed, but when she speaks, her voice is

133

stoical. 'You feel what you feel, Jack. It's as simple as that. It's not something you plan. It's just something you do.' The way she says it makes her sound like she's been here a hundred times before.

'I'm being crap, aren't I?' I conclude.

'What do you expect? You're a bloke. It's part of your job description.'

'It just feels fucking weird opening up to you like this.' I grimace. 'Or not opening up to you, which is probably more accurate.'

'You don't have to tell me anything you don't want to,' she points out.

'I know. But that's the deal, Amy: I *do* want to tell you stuff.'

'What stuff?'

'That I had a fantastic weekend and I'm having a fantastic day and . . . and I want there to be more. I want to do this again.' She doesn't say anything, because she knows I haven't finished. And she's right. But still, I'm apprehensive. This might not be what she wants. She's keen, sure, but how keen? Maybe for her this is just a fling-thing. Maybe me telling her I want it to be more, that I'm finally *ready* for something more than a serial shag, will scare her off. And then there's me. I'm scared of me, too. Maybe I've just caught a dose of summer madness and two weeks down the line I'll find myself trapped in a relationship I no longer want.

Her grip on my hand strengthens. 'Do you know what I feel?'

'No, tell me.'

'I feel comfortable with this.' She shakes her head, smiles. 'Fuck comfortable. I feel great.' She holds my hand up before my face. '*This* feels great. *This* feels right. *This* is what I want.'

'And if it doesn't go anywhere?'

'Then it doesn't go anywhere.'

And there it is. A tidal wave of relief washes over me. There's no pressure. We see how things go. We do what millions of people do every day: we throw the dice and wait to see how they land.

'Okay,' I say, 'so when people look at us holding hands and assume that we're together, they'll be right, then.'

'Yes.'

When we kiss, it feels different to the times we've kissed before. As our lips touch, it's like putting a physical seal on the verbal pact we've just made. It's scary and amazing at the same time. *This is it*, I'm thinking. *This is the end of one part of your life and the beginning of the next.* Just as our tongues are entwined, I realise that so are our lives. But when this kiss breaks, we won't. That'll only happen if one of us decides it. That will only happen if we stop believing in the words we've just spoken to one another. And who knows? Maybe that's on the cards. But that's the kick, I suppose. But then there's the possibility that this is for real. And it's a possibility that leaves me smiling as we settle back on the grass and I wrap my arms around her and drift into sleep.

I get back to the gallery round four, still drowsy from the sun, still woozy with what's gone down. There's an envelope wedged in the letterbox and I open it and read the letter inside. It states: *Call me on my mobile now. Paulie.* Shit. Shit, shit, shit. I can't believe my luck. The one day I do a bunk, he has to turn up. I go inside, brace myself and dial his number. He's not in a good mood. Wrong, he's homicidal. He explains, through a staggering variety of expletives, that he's been made to look a fool in front of his new girlfriend by not being able to get into his own gallery because the locks have been changed. But this, I discover, is merely the build-up to the seriously bad news.

Me: 'Listen, Paulie. I messed up, okay? And I'm sorry. And it won't happen again.'

Paulie: 'You're damn right it won't, and d'you want to know why?'

Me: 'Why?'

Paulie: 'Because you're fucking well fired, that's why. I want you to shut the gallery now and take the keys round to Tim Lee in the pottery next door and then I never want to see or hear from you again. That simple enough for you?'

Me: 'And that's it?'

Paulie: 'That's it.'

Me: 'Well, actually, there *is* one thing I don't understand.'

Paulie: 'What?'

Me: 'Just how come the reception on your mobile's so bad?'

Paulie: 'Because I'm in a helicopter. Though what the fuck's that got to do with—'

Me: 'So where exactly are you?'

Paulie: 'Halfway to Paris.'

Me: 'Oh.'

Paulie: 'What d'you mean, Oh?'

Me: 'I mean, Oh, well you'd better turn round, because I'm leaving your stupid keys in your stupid door, and I'm leaving your stupid door wide open.'

I don't, of course, carry through my threat. Partly on the grounds that Paulie can afford a better lawyer than me, and partly because I'm feeling more down-and-out than up-and-at-'em. Instead, I dutifully lock up the gallery for the last time and drop the keys off with Tim.

As disasters go, this makes the Hundred Years War look like a harmless squabble. The effect it's going to have on my life is barely quantifiable. No income = No way of sustaining my current lifestyle = No option other than to take a one-way ticket back to Crapjobsville = The end of ambition and the beginning of a life of meaningless drudgery.

Whatever control I had over my life has just vanished and, as I get on my bike and set off for the home I can no longer afford to live in, I'm overwhelmed with a feeling of impotence. I've never felt this way before. Well, almost never.

* * *

Confessions: No.4 Impotence

Place: my room, student digs, Edinburgh.

Time: 11.30 p.m. 2 October 1991.

Ella Trent was a babe. Understatement. Ella Trent was the *best* babe. The legs of Julia Roberts's body double in *Pretty Woman*. The face of Uma Thurman when she's dancing with

John Travolta in *Pulp Fiction*. Jamie Lee Curtis's tits in *Trading Places*. And the cool charisma of Lauren Bacall. If there was a school whose entrance policy was based on beauty rather than IQ, then Ella Trent would be the girl they'd put on the cover of the prospectus. This woman didn't just turn guys' heads when she entered a room, she broke their necks.

And I'd just pulled her.

It should never have happened, of course. There was her, and there was me. North & South. Sweet & Sour. Beauty & Beast. Never should the twain have met. Ella Trent wasn't destined for the likes of me. A film or rock star? Yes. A date in some exclusive Hollywood bistro? Yes, again. But Jack Rossiter outside The Last Drop in the pouring rain? No. No to the power of infinity.

Not that I was complaining at this unlikely twist of fate. I was nineteen years old, in the second year of my Art degree at Edinburgh. The sole reason I'd passed my first year had been down to the fact that Ella Trent worked on the same floor in the library as me. In between staring at my books, I'd stared at her. I'd stared and I'd planned and I'd plotted. And, finally, I'd plucked up the courage to speak to her. After much subtle work (biro borrowing and the likes), I'd successfully engineered a nodding-of-heads-in-mutual-recognition relationship.

But it wasn't the contents of her pencil case I was interested in. My top five sexual fantasies at the time – always run in reverse order, for titillation purposes – were:

5. Three-in-a-bed sex romp with Hayley and Becky, twins on my course
4. Being held captive by a tribe of beautiful Amazons for breeding purposes
3. A spanking with a wet halibut, administered by Mademoiselle Chaptal, my school French teacher
2. Being the only male survivor of a plane crash on an uninhabited tropical island, where the female survivors happened to be the contestants for Miss World

1. Achieving a simultaneous orgasm with Ella Trent after a lengthy bout of stroke-inducing sex

Excepting the fish fetish thing at number three (attributable, I now suspect, to cod and chips being the staple of my student diet), I think it was a fairly standard list for a young man. But the order says it all. Ella Trent above an unlimited supply of Amazons? I mean, really. But there she was: numero uno. There was nothing I could do about it.

And there I was, back in my bedroom, after snogging her outside The Last Drop and all the way back in the cab. I stared at her as we undressed, savouring every moment. For me, this was the opportunity to fulfil the fantasy of a lifetime. And if, for her, it was the result of being stoned, having lost her glasses, and having mistaken me for Brad, an Australian exchange student who she fancied, so what? At that moment, as far as I was concerned, her presence in my bedroom was the direct result of a splendidly fought campaign. I'd done my ground-work in the library. I'd spotted her in The Last Drop. I'd accidentally bumped into her at the bar. And I'd chatted and charmed and schmoozed her as if my life had depended on it.

And my plan had worked.

Here she was in my bedroom, and soon there she lay, naked on my bed. I had conquered. I had seen. And soon I would come. Or, rather, just as my fantasy dictated, we would come together. The shag was in the bag and nothing was going to go wrong. And not just any shag, either. The Shag of the Century. It was going to be sexellent, screwpendous and screwperb, all rolled into one. I would be her Clint Eastwood, her Sean Connery and her Richard Gere. She'd remember me. My ego demanded it.

And, to begin with, that's exactly how it was. We groped and rolled and grunted our way across the sheets. We stroked, we poked and we pried. Forget foreplay. This was fiveplay. Sixplay. This was the most horny I'd ever felt in my life.

'Now,' she said. 'Now. Get a condom. Do it now. Please, do it now.'

But if my plan to live out my number one fantasy was working, something else, I became excruciatingly aware as I pulled the condom on, wasn't. It could have been the eight pints of lager it had taken me to pluck up the nerve to make a move on Ella that was responsible. Or it could have been insecurity, just looking down at her incredible body and knowing that I could never live up to its standards and expectations. Or it could have been plain shock, achieving something I hadn't ever really thought possible.

But whatever the cause, the results were the same: a sinking sensation in my gut, accompanied by a shrinking sensation in my groin. I watched my condom-covered cock shrivel like a burst balloon. No. This can't be. No way. Not now. Not her. I won't allow it. I began to panic, desperately running through fantasies two to five. But my dick had other ideas. For the first time since birth, it didn't have a life of its own. Instead, it had a death. And a rapid one at that. Ella and I watched as it stooped and drooped, wilted and died.

'I don't believe it,' I said.

'Don't tell me,' she replied, getting up and snatching her knickers from the floor, 'it's never happened before.'

I covered my face with my hands, mumbling, 'I blame it on my mother.'

'What?'

My Australian accent was thicker this time. 'For calling me Brad. I've never felt comfortable with the name.'

* * *

Talking Pictures

Most times, I reckon, change is a slow process. It's so slow you don't even register it happening. Like puberty. One minute, you're eleven years old without a single pube to your name, and then it's ten years later, and not only have you got enough hair down there to stuff a cushion, but it's sprouting out of your knuckles and nostrils as well. And you ask yourself, *How did I get like this? Just when, precisely, did I change from soft-*

skinned boy into hairy-bellied man? And you've got no reply to these questions, because it didn't happen overnight, it happened over years.

Sometimes, though, it's different. Sometimes change is an express train, picking you up at one stop and dropping you off further down the line only seconds later. And it leaves you staggered. It leaves you staggered and stunned, because you can see the distance you've travelled and you know you can never go back.

Take now. Take being here in my bedroom at 8 a.m. Take lying here with my arm around this beautiful girl, with her sleeping head rested on my chest and the sound of her breathing synchronising with mine. A couple of weeks back, my reaction to this would have probably been:

a) There's a *girl* asleep in my bed; excellent, I've pulled
b) There's a girl asleep in *my* bed; shit, that means I can't do a runner
c) There's a girl *asleep* in my bed; better wake her up – but what the hell's her name?

But I *do* know this girl's name. This girl's name is Amy. Today is Sunday. It's a week and a half since I got fired from Paulie's Gallery. It's a week and a half since I had that conversation with Amy in Hyde Park and we moved from a Me and a Her to an Us. And my reaction now to her being here is:

a) *Amy's* asleep in my bed; excellent, I've pulled
b) Amy's asleep in my bed; good, I don't want her to be in anyone else's
c) Amy's *asleep* in my bed; great, because waking up without her on the nights we spend apart sucks

In spite of my initial resistance, I've come to the conclusion that change isn't necessarily a bad thing. This is just as well, really, because the change doesn't stop with my attitude to waking up with Amy beside me. Change, as the hippies

140

sensibly pointed out, is all around. All around my bedroom, at least. The old faithfuls – my favourite *FHM* pin-ups, my *Die Fly, Die!* collection of squished insects on the window pane, and my rogue socks and boxer shorts – have been respectively torn down, wiped off and vanquished to the washing machine. And if change is not a bad thing, then it's *definitely* a bed thing. My sheets and duvet and pillow cases are freshly laundered. My bedside ashtray contains four, rather than forty, cigarette butts. And my March '71 edition of *Playboy*, a twenty-fifth birthday present from Matt, has been removed from beneath the mattress and stashed in a box on top of the wardrobe.

But change *can* suck. And when that change is do to with my job, it *does*.

My first thought after getting back to Matt's house after being fired was to construct an effigy of Paulie out of jackal dung, mark out a chalk pentagram on the paving stones in the back garden, and stab knitting needles through his vital organs whilst chanting the Lord's Prayer backwards. Dismissing this on the grounds of impracticality (jackal dung is a total nightmare to come by at this time of year), I then got practical. I boosted my ego, telling myself that I was good at the job I used to do and shouldn't find it a problem sorting out some freelance work. There are times, though, when the world takes it upon itself to prove its superiority by crushing your ego like an ant. Ten phone calls to old contacts and ten noes later, I concluded that this was, indeed, one of those times. So I bit the bullet. There was only one honourable course of action left to me: begging.

I drew up a list of potential benefactors:

a) My father. Dad said goodbye to me, Kate, Billy and Mum about a week after my eighth birthday. Two kids and a wife he no longer loved, coupled with the pressures of commuting from Bristol to London, left him susceptible to the dubious charms of Michelle Dove, his then secretary. Despite my mother's predictions to the contrary, Dad and

Michelle are still happily married. They live in a mansion house in Holland Park and divide their time between spending the ludicrous amounts of cash Dad's property development company made in the eighties boom, and raising their two children, Davie (14) and Martha (13). Dad and I meet twice a year (birthday and Christmas). Probability of him giving me cash: zero. Probability of him lending me cash: slim. Probability of him repeating his offer of getting me a start in the City: high.

b) My brother. Billy Boy, in keeping with his fascination with all things technological, does marketing for a software development firm in the Docklands. Billy has a mortgage and a family. He does OK and he's happy. But he's got a future. He's got his kids to think of. I shouldn't be pressuring him back into the role of Acting Dad he pulled off so well when me and Kate were kids.

c) My mother. Asking Mum for money would put me in the same league as Nero on the decency front. She works as a typist in a bank in Bristol and, after the mortgage payments and bills, there's not much left. Sure, she'd find the money, same as she did when I was a student, but I'd end up feeling shit about it.

d) My sister. Student. Like asking a corpse for health tips. Forget about it.

e) Matt. Tricky one this. Because Matt's stacked cash-wise. And he's my best mate. And I'd do the same for him, but he's so generous anyway, I'd feel pretty shoddy about borrowing cold currency off him. It comes down to self-respect, I suppose.

Not exactly what you'd call a dream selection. But desperate times call for desperate deeds. Working on the theory that a slim chance was better than no chance at all, it was Dad who got the call. His receptionist was hostile, but Dad, bizarrely enough, was receptive to my suggestion of a meet. We duly arranged to hook up for lunch on Tuesday afternoon.

It went well. Relatively well. It went well for a meeting with the one relative of mine who can't help sighing at the very sight of me. We talked the talk for a while, caught up on each other's lives. Then I cut to the chase and asked him if he could lend me some money and he told me I should be standing on my own two feet. Then I told him about losing my job and he told me he could get me an introduction to a perfectly good stockbroking firm. Then I told him that I wanted to make a go of the art and he sighed and returned his attention to his lobster salad. And then he did something I didn't remember him ever doing before: he came up with a solution that wouldn't involve compromise by either of us. He told me he'd commission me to do a piece for the reception of their new Knightsbridge office. And I did something I'd never done in return: I thanked him and told him I wouldn't let him down.

Friday morning, and Willy Ferguson, Dad's marketing director, rocked – or, rather, rolled – up at Matt's house. I'd cancelled Sally's modelling session for the second week running, telling her I had to go to Bristol for a funeral. Last week, wallowing in a post-firing depression, I hadn't been able to face seeing her at all. And, of course, there was what had happened with Amy: our pact. I needed time to straighten this out in my head before I saw Sally and risked going on to autopilot and forgetting I was no longer available. She was OK about it and this was a relief, because despite my decision not to go for closure with her any more, I did want to finish her portrait.

Willy was mid-fifties, balding, and had a gut that only a lifetime of serious lunching could have produced. What looked suspiciously like a baked bean lay embedded in his thick moustache, just above the corner of his mouth. I showed him through to the studio, where I'd hung eight pieces of my work up for his critical assessment. He glanced over the paintings like he was reading a McDonald's menu.

'Three thousand pounds,' he finally said. 'One thousand up front and the rest on receipt of the goods. Make it big, because we're a big company. Big is what we're about. Same sort of size as that one,' he continued, waving at my boys' toys piece. 'But not so weird.'

'Have you got any ideas about what sort of thing you're looking for?' I asked helpfully.

'Something bright. Something to cheer people up.'

'Something bright . . .'

'Yellow.'

'Yellow?'

'Or orange. Orange will probably do just as well.'

'How about lime?' I asked, barely able to believe my luck at being privy to this, the inaugural exposition of the Citrus Theory of Art by Professor Willy Ferguson.

He considered this for a moment, before deciding, 'No, lime's no good. Looks like mildew. Don't want clients coming in and thinking our walls are riddled with damp. Stick to yellow or orange. Can't go far wrong with that.'

I made a mental note to call ArtStart as soon as he'd left and order a pot of their brightest yellow paint.

'Who's the bird?' Willy asked, clocking Sally's portrait and leaning forward to get a better look.

'Just a model.'

He tilted his head to one side and stood in wrapped contemplation for a moment. 'Amazing,' he finally concluded.

I felt myself swell with pride. 'You like it?'

'Bloody right. I haven't seen a pert pair of tits and a nice tight arse like that for years.'

So there it is. With the good (Amy), comes the bad (having to go to Dad for help), comes the ugly (whatever yellow monstrosity I whip up to adorn the reception of Dad's firm). But I mustn't complain. There's money in the bank. I can afford to live again. I wanted a change, and that's exactly what I've got.

So deal with it.

I look down at Amy. She's still asleep. It would be good to join her, but too much thinking's gone down in my head for me to slip back into a dream state. It's tempting, of course, to slide beneath the covers and wake her up with an early morning present, but last night was a late one, so I'll let her be. Instead, I slip out of bed and dress, go to the deli down the street. Back in the kitchen and I'm slicing up the smoked salmon and layering it on the bagels. OK, so it's extravagant. Just like insisting on paying for that dress Amy tried on yesterday. But gestures like that are what make life sweet. What better use for money is there?

The bed's Amy-less when I get there, so I put the tray down on the messed-up sheets and go and check out the bathroom. This, too, is an Amy-free zone. I stand in the corridor and call out her name, but there's no reply, so I go downstairs.

I finally find her in the studio. The French windows are closed and it's oppressively humid, like a jungle. She's sitting cross-legged on the floor, dressed in white knickers and my black Hendrix T-shirt. Very Yin-Yang. But it's not what she's wearing that grabs my attention. It's what she's staring at. The half-completed painting of Sally McCullen. The half-completed painting of the quite apparently beautiful Sally McCullen. The half-completed painting of the quite apparently beautiful Sally McCullen, with a pair of tits and an arse the likes of which Willy Ferguson hasn't seen for years.

'I can explain,' I say.

Amy doesn't look round. 'This is Sally, then. This is Sally, your model.'

'Really,' I try again, 'It's not—'

Amy holds up her hand. 'Maybe I'm wrong,' she says, still staring at McCullen, 'but didn't you tell me that she was – and I quote – "A total moose. Wouldn't touch her with a shitty stick. But that's the point with nudes, isn't it? They're meant to be *interesting*, not attractive. Otherwise it's just pornography. It's just some sad pervert getting his rocks off by looking at some naked girl."' She finally turns round to face me. Her expression would cause an SAS squad to perform a tactical trouser-soiling manoeuvre. 'That *is* what you said, isn't it?'

'Well, yes, but—'

'But what, Jack? That you lied to me? That she *isn't* stunning? That you *aren't* some sad pervert? Well? Which is it? Come on, I'd like to know. What's the matter, Jack – cat got your tongue?'

I stare at my feet. The cat doesn't just have my tongue. The cat has chewed my tongue up, digested it, and shat it out into the kitty-litter. I mean, what *can* I say? Yes, I *have* lied to her. Yes, Sally McCullen *is* stunning. And, yes, I probably am a bit of a pervert.

Eventually, I say the only thing I can say in the circumstances. I say, 'I'm sorry.' And I look down at her and hope she'll forgive me for being such a prick.

6
amy

I have never been more humiliated.

Ever.

I am the secret love child of Attila the Hun and Darth Vader; I'm *that* cross.

I look behind me at the door through which I've been ejected and fire a volley of two-fingered vitriol with both hands. It's all I can do to stop myself kicking the door.

I stomp up the road under bruise-coloured clouds, muttering under my breath. By the time I reach the station, the heavens have opened and I'm soaked.

Amy Crosbie: all washed up.

I didn't think it was possible to get fired from a temp job. I thought, as a light drifter through the ranks of the employed, I was untouchable. But evidently I was wrong.

Being in the wrong seems to be a new skill of mine.

I don't like it.

OK, so I shouldn't have blagged to Elaine that I knew every switchboard under the sun. I should've told the truth, but you never get anywhere unless you lie about your skills. That's the first rule of temping: tick every 'yes' box on the introduction form. When Elaine called me and told me there was a highly paid two-week job in the headquarters of a big law firm, I told her immediately that I'd do it. She looked me up on the filing system.

'That's good. You've worked an Elonexic 950 XPCZ 150 digital pci system 2 before,' she said brightly. 'You'll be fine.'

'Yes, yes,' I said, not listening to a word as I mentally totted up my wages and thought about the funky shoes I'd seen in Red or Dead last week. After all, how difficult could it really be? Reception work? I can do it standing on my head.

So it didn't cross my mind that I might not be qualified for the job, even when I was schlapping across London to the City, or when I was striding across the acres of plush atrium to my new desk. Or even when I wriggled my bum back into the space-age chair and introduced myself to Angela from Personnel.

But I did think about it when I was left alone with something that looked like an air traffic control system. Then it dawned on me that this time, I'd blagged once too often. Red, orange and yellow lights flashed angrily, the vast silence of the reception area interrupted with the insistent buzzing of jammed lines.

'Right,' I muttered, looking at it and rubbing my hands together, but I could already feel an earthquake under the foundations of my temping confidence. After twenty minutes, I'd failed to answer any calls and I was starting to get panicky. After an hour, Angela must have sussed. She was back down from one of the many floors above me, strutting out of the lift in her sharp pinstripe suit.

'Having problems?' she asked.

'No, no,' I smiled, realising that my headset was on back to front. 'Everything's fine.'

She nodded, evidently not satisfied. I watched her go. I was determined not to give up. I had a physics O-level. This should be easy.

It wasn't.

Soon, there was a barrage of frustrated callers on my hands and I was having an extension line crisis. By eleven o'clock the switchboard looked as if it was about to explode. I started jabbing buttons indiscriminately.

'Shit, bollocks!' I panicked. 'Go away, you idiots. Stop calling! Call somewhere else. Fuck *off*!'

Two minutes later the lift pinged open and a balding man in an immaculate suit was running towards me. At first I assumed that there was a fire, since he was flapping his arms so wildly, but it soon became apparent that the only hazard in the building was me.

'What on earth do you think you're doing?' he shouted, skidding to a halt in front of me. 'How dare you swear into the telecom system! Do you realise that we've got some very important clients in the boardroom? Your foul language has been heard on every floor! *Every floor!*' His bushy eyebrows quivered with indignation and his goggly eyes seemed to be in danger of popping out of their sockets.

I stood up abruptly, my headset trapping me to the system and yanking me down again.

'Where are you from?' he barked, as I fumbled to unplug myself.

'Shepherd's Bush,' I squeaked, noticing the intercom button for the first time. I punched it and it went out, as did the green light on the microphone directly above my big mouth.

Angela burst through the doors by the stairs. She rested her hand on her heaving chest as she gasped for breath.

'Which agency is she from?' demanded the man, pointing at me as Angela rushed to his side.

'Top Temps,' she gulped. 'They'll be hearing about this.'

I wasn't even given a chance to talk my way out of the scrape before the man had me by the arm and was frogmarching me to the door.

'Ow!' I yelped.

'Get out!' he said, looking at me as if I'd just urinated on the carpet. 'I never want to see you again. Do you realise . . .' He couldn't finish his sentence, and for a moment I thought he was going to boot me up the backside as he shoved me through the door.

I throw myself into the underground, taking solace from being subterranean. It seems to be the best place for me. I change lines at random, letting the jumble of faces and posters soothe me whilst I think about all the things I should have said. In the end, I have five expertly honed retorts that would have left Angela and her henchman stunned with the deadly accuracy of my tongue.

It's pointless, though. I'm never going to have a chance to explain myself. I have to accept it: I ain't the winner here.

I decide that what I need is a change of scenery, and get out at Green Park. I dawdle up the gravel paths, feeling the weight of the world on my shoulders. It's still cloudy, but at least it's not raining. I pull my damp jacket around me and slump into one of the empty deckchairs.

I close my eyes and watch the dots on the inside of my eyelids float about. I know I'm going to have to confess to Elaine. I draw my knees up and hug them. Why hasn't someone invented teleportation yet? This is one of those occasions I'd like to be beamed up. A remote island off South America would do.

H is away filming somewhere and I don't want to phone Jack. After finding the picture of Sally, I'm feeling slightly detached from him. Even though he spent at least an hour explaining it all and apologising, I'm still annoyed that he didn't tell me the truth before. He must have thought I was too flimsy to cope with the fact that he was painting someone he obviously finds attractive. What did he think? That I'd crumple into a heap of jealousy? I might have done, but that's not the point. So now I'm trying to be cool. But I'm not feeling cool at the moment. I'm feeling like a lump of jelly.

I can't turn to anyone else for sympathy either. I've well and truly burnt my bridges there. For the past week, I've spent all my free time calling everyone I know to extol Jack's virtues and rave about how wonderful my life is. Now that I'm officially a girlfriend, I've been spreading the word of love and exuding positive vibes around all the people who are lucky enough to be in my Filofax. That's what I told myself anyway. But who do I think I am?

Let's face it. There's nothing sharing, caring or honourable about my intentions. I just want to make everyone else green with envy.

I positively gloated to Susie, my best mate from college, which was pretty insensitive, given the fact that she's in a floundering relationship with a married man. After my monologue about having found meaning in the world, Susie sighed miserably down the phone.

'You're so lucky.'

'You could be too.' I paused for effect. She knew what was coming. We'd had this conversation hundreds of times before. 'He's never going to leave her. You know that, don't you?'

'I know, but I love him.' She said this in a pathetic cockney accent, like some weathered soap star and, as usual, we ended up laughing.

'I'm really pleased that everything is going so well for you,' she admitted at the end of our call. 'Despite the fact that I'm choking with jealousy. I'd be over the moon if a bloke was that romantic. Keep hold of him, Amy, whatever you do.'

Whilst I felt smug, I also felt guilty having peppered my description of the relationship between me and Jack with some Oscar-winning movie moments. At the same time, I generously embellished his character with more wholesome qualities than he's ever likely to possess. For starters, I told Susie that when Jack turned up to my flat, he was bearing a colossal bunch of pink roses and that we had caviar and champagne on our picnic.

The picnic was great as it was. And anyway, caviar makes me puke.

But I know why I'm doing it. I've been so keen for Jack to be IT that I've invented and exaggerated things about him to convince my friends, and therefore in the process me, that he is.

I look up at the trees and listen to the distant jingle of an ice-cream van. I take a deep breath.

The truth is that my life isn't wonderful and Jack isn't perfect.

I think about it for a moment and then, just to complete my self-destruction, I substitute a because: my life isn't wonderful because Jack isn't perfect.

Maybe I'm thinking this because I don't know if I'm going

to spend the rest of my life with him. That's normal, I guess, for a relationship that's as new as this, but I'm in a panic about it, nevertheless. I've been waiting for the right bloke to come along for so long that I've lost sight of reality. I thought that when my love interest eventually deigned to show up in my life everything would be clear. Love. Marriage. Babies. No mucking about.

But the bloke I've been waiting for isn't Jack. The bloke I've been waiting for is perfect. He's IT.

He's also a figment of my imagination.

So I've got Jack instead. And whilst Jack is real, he certainly isn't perfect. There are things about him that really annoy me. Enough things for there to be a list.

- He's vain. I mentally cross this one out. It's not really fair. I'm only thinking that because he's got this habit of holding his chin and looking at both sides of his face as if he's in a shaving advert. Ridiculous, but hardly vain.
- He's ridiculous.
- He's childish. He farts and thinks it's funny, he swings his balls from side to side when he comes out of the shower and he sulks when he doesn't get his own way. But then, I'm not such a model specimen of adulthood.
- The foot thing. Every time I'm trying to get to sleep, he twitches his foot in bed. It's a nervous energy overspill, but it makes me think I'm sleeping with Alan Shearer. When he does it against my leg, it annoys me even more because of his bad foot maintenance. Why is toenail filing only restricted to girls?
- He seems to be more committed to his friends than he is to me.
- He paints beautiful nude girls for a living.

Grrrr.

So Jack isn't perfect. I'll have to live with it. I can't blame him for my misery. The fact that my life is rubbish is my fault. And it's mine to sort out, before I freeze to death.

I slope up to Oxford Street for the inevitable showdown with Elaine. She's not a happy camper. She sits sternly behind the desk in the 'private' office we've come into for our 'chat'. She tells me that I've let her down, that she's extremely disappointed in me and enquires how it's possible to be so careless etc., etc. I stand with my hands crossed humbly in front of me, nodding and shaking my head in time to her comments until it's going in a circle, apologising profusely and generally looking as meek as I can. Eventually, Elaine's bollocking comes to an end. She stubs her cigarette out in the gravel around the plastic rubber plant. There's about ten in there already. Maybe she's having a bad temp day.

'This is very serious, Amy,' she says, sucking in her pockmarked cheeks as if she's about to decide my punishment. The thick foundation stops in a tan line under her chin. 'In the circumstances, I don't feel comfortable placing you anywhere else.'

There's been a funeral bell tolling in my head, but now as I look up and our eyes meet, there's an almighty clang, as if Big Ben has just fallen down its tower.

Elaine doesn't know it, but with her last sentence she's cleared away the fog in my life. She's jabbering on, but I don't hear her.

It all becomes incredibly clear.

One word.

That's all it takes.

Placing. Elaine doesn't feel comfortable *placing* me.

I don't need *Elaine* to place *me*!

I'm astonished that it's taken this to make me realise what my life's become. When I first met Elaine, I sucked up to her, but for all my smiles and diligence, I knew I was going to use her. Temping was going to be a stop-gap for a couple of weeks until I sorted out my life and then I'd never have to see her again. But over the weeks, then the months and now years, Elaine has become a permanent fixture in my life. I've placed all my faith in her to find me work, because I've become too complacent to think for myself. When did it happen? At what point did I hand over my power and start to rely on her so totally?

All this time, I've been pretending that I'm detached from it all, that I'm above being a temp and I'm in control. I've been contemptuous of all the jobs I've had and people I've met and mostly of Elaine herself, but it was all just a smokescreen. The contempt has been for myself.

So it's got to stop. Standing here like a naughty schoolgirl, I face up to the fact that H has been right all along. I'm coasting along in my life and I'm using Jack to provide me with feelings of connection. What kind of attitude is that?

A weak one.

And I'm not prepared to be weak any longer. Not me. I may not be able to work a switchboard, but there's loads more I can do. And from now on, I'm going to stand on my own two feet.

Amy Crosbie, this is your life.

Once I've placated Elaine, I leave the building, buy a Kit Kat and a magazine and take the number 94 home. On the way, I do the 'How Well Do You Know Your Boyfriend?' survey and find myself guessing most of the answers. When I tot up my score, I fall into the 'Mostly Cs' category.

You don't trust him yet. You need to spend more time getting to know your man and find out what really makes him tick. Your relationship will blossom if you base it on honesty and truth.

I know these surveys are ludicrously general, but my good mood is temporarily jangled. When I get home, I strip off, have a shower and then call Jack.

'You're home early,' he says through a yawn. 'Hang on a minute.' He puts his hand over the receiver and I hear some rustling about. In a second he's back on the line. 'So why aren't you at work?'

'The job didn't work out. But the good news is, I'm never going back. What are you up to?' I ask.

You call him at home at an unexpected time of day. He doesn't sound thrilled to hear from you. Do you:

> *A. accept that he's doing something else and is naturally distracted?*

'Just a bit of work. I might come over in a bit,' he says. 'If you're in.'

I didn't mean to think C. I was A all along. Honest.

Being a girlfriend is much more stressful than I remember. It takes up so much time. I now live in a permanent state of Just In Case. Just in case I see Jack, I now find myself shaving my armpits and legs nearly every day, which is leading to a stubble management crisis; trimming my pubic hair over the loo, which is a nightmare because pubes take ages to flush away; tidying up my bedroom and putting my clothes in the wardrobe instead of leaving them on the floor; re-washing my one nice duvet cover, rather than putting on the embarrassing floral spare; shopping in a supermarket so that I have edible supplies in, rather than existing on Pot Noodles and toast, and wearing exposable underwear.

This last one causes me by far the most angst. During LBJ (Life Before Jack) I thought nothing of flinging on my grey, holey mummy pants and an equally tatty bra. I've also got a truly disgusting selection of manky G-strings that provide a service of genital flossing rather than anything remotely comforting.

I once read an article on single girls who wore sexy underwear just for themselves. Bullshit! In my opinion, they're either desperate for a shag or too rich for their own good. Anyway, I've never met one. I don't know one girl who'd give their gusset-stained underwear collection to Oxfam, even if there was an international knickers crisis.

I don't know why I'm making such an effort in the underwear department. After all, I spied Jack's washing hanging on the line in his garden the other day. And there it was, a pair of threadbare Father Christmas boxers. He's no angel, either.

However, I'm determined not to be caught out and hence

me and my handy Visa went underwear shopping last week. Two-thirds of the way through the trip, I was collared by a moustached woman in M&S who tutted loudly.

'What bra size are you, love?' she demanded.

'34B,' I replied, clamping two hands to my chest as if I'd been caught in a Carry On film.

'Never! You're more of a 32D, if ever I saw one.'

'32D!' I exclaimed, as she pushed into the cubicle and started threading her tape measure around my back. She tugged at the tight loop around my boobs.

'Just as I thought,' she nodded.

32D! But I've always been a 34B, ever since I grew tits. When did I transform into a Page 3 girl?

I pull on my new over-the-shoulder-boulder-holder and adjust myself in it. I feel very trussed up. I look in the mirror and feel perplexed.

What else shall I wear?

Dressing to go out is no problem, but how do I dress for being at home? I usually slob about in leggings and a grotty T-shirt, but Jack's coming round. How shall I present myself *au naturel*? Do I:

A. Dress for sex
B. Dress in my usual slobby clothes
C. Dress for going out?

I remember my A resolutions and opt for a pair of Calvin Klein knickers and a white vest top. I ditch the bra.

I spend ages applying my make-up so that it doesn't look as if I've got any on, tidy up and pace about the kitchen. I think about cooking something, but decide against it. It's bound to go wrong and I'm determined that nothing else is going to go wrong today. I'm new. I'm independent. And Jack's going to know about it.

I paint my toenails, watch the TV and wait for him to arrive. I've dozed off by the time the door buzzer goes. I shed the blobs of cotton wool from in between my toes as I hurry to press the button. I feel a swell of excitement as I hear him coming up the stairs.

'Hi,' I say, wrapping myself round the door as he bounces into view.

He kisses me and smiles. 'Aren't you going to put any clothes on?' he asks, glancing at my knickers.

'Of course,' I stutter. 'I was just, um . . .' I point to my bedroom.

'Don't let me stop you then,' he smiles. He raises his eyebrows at me and I have the feeling I've been rumbled. I slink away to hide my pink cheeks.

'I thought we could go out,' he says, walking into the sitting room. He picks up the TV zapper and flicks through a few channels.

'Okay,' I reply, from my bedroom.

As I yank open my wardrobe and root about for my jeans, I can hear the channels. Jack scans through a games show, the news and stops on the football. For a moment, I think he's going to stay watching it, but he drags himself away and comes in and sits on my bed.

'Why don't you put on that dress you were wearing the other day?' he asks. 'You look great in that.'

'Sure,' I say, pulling it from the hanger. I turn my back on him and take off my top. Suddenly, I feel him behind me. He's obviously crouching down, because I feel his lips at the base of my spine. He kisses all the way up, until his breath is on the back of my neck. Then he reaches round and cups my new novelty 32Ds.

'On second thoughts . . .' he whispers.

It's dark by the time we finish having sex. I go and get a bottle of wine from the fridge and the matches. I stumble about, trying to light some candles.

'Why don't you turn the light on?' asks Jack, watching me as he opens the wine.

'Because I hate this room. It needs decorating, but I haven't got round to it.'

'What are you going to do to it?'

'I don't know. Something different. Now I've got some time on my hands, I'll have a think.'

I lie back down with him and we sprawl on the duvet, our naked limbs entwining in the shadows.

'How come you've got so much time all of a sudden?' he asks.

I tell Jack about my day and he laughs so much that he spills wine all over my stomach. He leans down and licks it off, before resting his chin in my belly button. He looks up at me.

'I was fired once,' he says, 'if it makes you feel any better.'

I can't imagine Jack being sacked. He's far too cool. When I press him for details, he tells me that he worked at a gallery a couple of years ago and had to change the locks after a break-in. Apparently, his boss came back and went ballistic because he couldn't get in.

'What did you do?'

'Left him to it. It was the best thing that ever happened, really,' he says, leaning up and tracing a circle on my stomach. 'It made me realise a few things. That I wanted to be an artist and that's what I should throw my energy into.'

I take a sip of wine. ' You know it's such a turn on.'

'What is?' he asks.

'You being a success as an artist. It's one of the things I like most about you.'

Jack sort of growls and buries his head in my neck. I love it when he's bashful and I hug him.

'The question is, what am I going to do?' I ask.

'Something will come up,' he says. 'I know it will. And if it doesn't, then you'll have to pack your bags, because I'll take you sailing round the world.'

'Maybe I won't type up my CV after all then,' I laugh.

*

But despite the temptation of Jack's fantasies, I do. I spend the next week finding out names and addresses of companies and fine-tuning my plan of action. To my surprise, Jack turns out to be incredibly supportive and helps me design my CV on his state-of-the-art PC that he's lent to Matt. At first I feel embarrassed sharing all my details with him, but he's so fired up with enthusiasm on my behalf that I don't have a moment to feel insecure.

'You should run seminars on Positive Mental Attitude,' I tease, when he calls for the third time on the one evening we've agreed to spend apart. 'Or at the very least, found your own religion. You're very believable.'

'You won't be taking the piss when you're earning a fortune.'

'Jackism,' I mused. 'Hmm. Suits you.'

'Okay, smart-arse. What's the first rule of Jackism?'

'Enlighten me, great Guru.'

'All my disciples have to have sex with me.'

'I might have known,' I laughed.

'Ah, but you're my only disciple, so far. So I'll expect you here in half an hour.'

'You'll be lucky. I don't do religion.'

'Oh, go on. You know you want to.'

And I do want to, because the truth of it is, I love spending every night with Jack. If I ever had him down as being commitment shy, I'm proved wrong time and time again. After a week, he's become so integrated into my life that I can't remember what I ever did before him. I'm also not sure how I ever had time to work.

I'm so happy with my new life that it comes as quite a shock when Elaine calls at nine o'clock the following Tuesday. She already seems like a blast from the past.

'I'm giving you a second chance,' she announces. 'Only because I'm desperate.'

I'm thrown into confusion. In the last week, I've mentally moved on from temping. I can't bear the thought of being sucked into the vortex again. Jack rolls over and puts the pillow over his head.

'I'm not really available at the moment, Elaine,' I say. 'Sorry.'

'Hear me out,' she says. I can hear her scrabbling around as she inhales on her cigarette. I stroke Jack's arm which is lying across my stomach and roll my eyes at the ceiling. My life has been so much more tranquil without Elaine and her stress in it. All I want to do is curl up with Jack and go back to sleep.

'Right, got it,' she says. 'It's with Friers. They're some kind of fashion house. I need you to get there as soon as possible. The girl I asked to do it hasn't turned up—'

'You're kidding! *The* Friers?' I interrupt, sitting bolt upright. The pillow stirs and Jack lifts his head.

'What's going on?' he moans, his face crumpled with sleep.

I put my fingers to my lips and jump out of bed to find a pen. I scribble the details on the back of an envelope.

'Elaine, you're an angel,' I say, as I end the call.

Jack sits up in bed and stretches. 'What are you looking so pleased about?'

'Friers.' I wave the envelope at him.

'Who?'

'I applied to them about three years ago and never heard anything back. I've got a job. Thank you Elaine.' I kiss the envelope.

'I thought you weren't temping any more.'

'Yes, well I wasn't, but this could be my big chance. I've got to be there in an hour.'

I rush about getting ready and make Jack a cup of tea, but he doesn't seem to be too enthusiastic about moving. I turf my spare keys out from the depths of the fruit bowl in the kitchen.

'You can let yourself out,' I say, kissing the part of his head that's visible from under the duvet and jangling the keys by his ears.

He leans up on one elbow and takes them. 'Are you sure?'

I laugh at him. 'Yes. I'm not asking you to move in, if that's what you're worried about. It's practical reasons only, but you might as well keep hold of them. I'm always locking myself out.'

'Great,' he smiles. 'I can have a good snoop around. Where are your diaries?'

'You're not going to find anything,' I say, looking at him in the mirror whilst I put my lipstick on. 'So don't go looking for things you can't handle.'

'Would I?' He pretends to look outraged.

'Yes. But I trust you. So don't blow it,' I warn.

He grabs me and kisses my lipstick off. 'Jack!'

He smears it round his lips. 'I don't know why you bother. Your lipstick looks far better on me.'

'You big girl,' I laugh, hugging him goodbye.

'Have a good day at the office, darling,' he says, rolling back under the duvet. 'Don't worry about the kids, I'll pick them up from school and do the shopping.'

I put my hands on my hips and smile at him from the door. 'That's it, is it? All this help getting me a job is just so that you can be a house husband?'

He picks up my teddy bear. 'Damn,' he says to Ted. 'She's sussed.'

The Friers offices are above a café on Charlotte Street. I'm quite nervous by the time I get there. It's an unusual feeling and I take a deep breath to calm down before I ring the buzzer. I've no idea what to expect, but if there's the faintest whiff of a permanent job, I'm going for it. This is my second chance and I'm not going to blow it.

The office is cluttered with desks, laden hanging rails, half-clad dummies. A radio blares in the background above the ringing phones.

'Bloody hell!' A tall man, wearing a pink checked waistcoat and ridiculous black glasses with yellow tinted visors puts up his hands in frustration and marches through the office. 'Where's the temp?'

'I'm here,' I say.

He struts towards me. 'At last! I do hope you're reliable, darling,' he says, looking me up and down.

'I'll do my best,' I say.

'Jenny, Jenny!' he calls. 'Salvation here at long last! Make the most of it.'

He flounces through to a small office and slams the door.

'Take no notice,' says the woman walking towards me. 'That's Fabian. He likes to throw his weight around, but don't be intimidated. I'm Jenny.' She smiles at me and I immediately like her. 'Welcome to the mad house.'

She shows me round and introduces me to everyone. There are about ten of us sharing the office and they all seem friendly and fairly laid back. Jenny is about thirty-five and has, from what I can gather, spent most of those years dedicated to the kind of hardcore partying that would have left me in a coma by now. She's from Lancashire and has a top accent which, of course, I find myself mimicking when I talk to her. She doesn't seem to mind.

She makes me tea in the kitchen before showing me to my desk. She instructs me to answer the phones and gives me some letters to type.

'It's pretty boring secretarial work, I'm afraid,' she says. 'But we'll find you something else to do later on. We're a bit snowed under.'

'No problem,' I say. 'Pile it on.'

Jenny works with Sam in the cutting room next door. As H would say, they're PLUs (People Like Us) and it's quite a relief. At about eleven o'clock Sam bursts through the swing doors with a big grin on her face. She's wearing a leather mini-skirt and an oversized jumper which makes her tits seem enormous. After the 32D scandal, I seem to be obsessed by other people's busts.

'How are you getting on?' she asks.

'Fine. Is there anything else I can do?' I volunteer. 'I've finished the letters. Here.' I hand them to her.

She looks through them approvingly. 'Excellent. Someone with a bit of nous at last.'

Nous Schmous. She doesn't realise it yet, but I am SUPERTEMP.

Sam's carrying a big pile of magazines in one arm. 'I brought these out for you,' she says. She fishes out a typed list from the pages of the first magazine. 'Can you go through and check out all the photographs by these guys?'

'Sure.'

'Boring, I know, but it'd really help.'

'No problem.'

'You'd better come for a fag break first.'

I follow her on to the cast-iron fire escape at the back of the cutting room. Jenny is already there. By joining them, I know I've been recruited into their gang. Cool.

I've been sitting on the fence for so long in every job I've got splinters in my arse, but this job could be different. I want to get to know these people. I've only been here a few hours, but I already know that this could be my kind of place. We chat for a while. They've both got it in for Fabian.

Sam untangles her sunglasses from the knot of curls on her head with difficulty. Jenny watches her before helping.

'I don't know what's going on, but I doubt if he's going to mince around here much longer,' Jenny says.

'Why?' I ask.

Jenny taps the side of her nose and we huddle together as she shares her secret. I love being included like this. 'There'll be a takeover. You mark my words. I reckon we're about to be bought out and if we are, Fabian will be out on his ear.'

Sam makes suitably shocked noises. I'm just about to ask more when the phone rings.

'I'll go,' I say, stubbing my cigarette through the grille.

I spend the rest of the day sorting out a courier crisis, helping Andy when his computer crashes, picking up some samples from Berwick Street and generally being as helpful as I can. I must have turned over a new leaf, because I don't call anyone all day. I'm astonished when I realise that it's six-thirty.

'Promise that you'll come back tomorrow,' says Jenny.

'I'll be here,' I say.

'We couldn't have got through today without you.'

I'm still smiling to myself as I walk down the road. I'm knackered, but I don't feel like going home yet. I've been trying to find out about Friers all day. I've got a patchy idea of the type of clothes they're producing for this season. They mainly do casual wear for men's chains, but they've got their own line in a boutique in Covent Garden.

I decide to have a look and walk through Soho and up St Martin's Lane. I look in the window of every clothes shop and make mental notes of the displays, getting a general picture of what's in fashion at the moment.

I have a good nosey round the Friers boutique. I like the clothes, but only the most outrageous cuts are in the window. I'm surprised by how classic most of the range is when I get inside. I eavesdrop on the shoppers and sales assistants, before I realise that they're waiting to close up and I have to leave.

It's late by the time I get home and my head is brimming with ideas. Jack has made the bed and done the washing up. There's no note or message on the machine from him, but I like the feeling that he's been in my flat without me. I take the big pile of men's magazines I've bought to bed and study all the fashion pages. For the first time in ages, I feel genuinely purposeful. When I turn off the light and put my head down, my pillow smells of Jack and I fall asleep with a smile on my face.

The next couple of days pass by in a blur and I enjoy myself. I feel like I fit in at Friers.

'It's a shame Karen is back next week,' says Sam when we pop to the pub on Thursday lunchtime. 'It'd be great if you could stay on.'

'I don't want to leave,' I say, honestly. 'There's no permanent jobs going are there?'

'Believe me, if there were you'd be the first to know. Have you got a CV we can keep?'

'Sure. I've just done one. I'll leave it with you this afternoon.'

'I'll see what I can do,' she says.

I hope she means it. I don't want to leave. I've been so busy helping out with the secretarial work, I haven't had a chance to show them how interested I am in the business.

On Friday morning, everyone gets called into a company meeting and I'm left alone in the office. I look around me, feeling nostalgic already. I'm really going to miss this place.

Elaine calls.

'They like you,' she says, as if it's the biggest surprise in the world.

'I like them too,' I admit. 'You haven't got any more jobs up your sleeve like this one, have you?'

'Nothing. It's all gone quiet.'

Back to square one then, I think, as the door buzzer goes.

'Everyone's in a meeting,' I say to the man when he comes up the stairs. 'Can I help at all?'

'I'm here to see Fabian,' he says, looking around the empty desks. 'Do you mind if I wait?'

'Not at all,' I smile, showing him to the sofa by the window.

He can wait any time he wants. He's extraordinarily good looking, with short blond hair, sexy stubble and a honey-coloured tan to match. He must be in his late thirties, judging from the laughter lines around his eyes. 'Can I get you a coffee?'

'Please,' he says, relaxing back, as I make for the kitchen.

A model. Definitely a model. Can't be anything else. I can see why Fabian wants to see him, he's perfect for Jenny's new collection.

There seems to be no point pretending to work with everyone in the meeting, so when I return with his coffee, I sit on the edge of the desk and smile.

'So, what's Friers like?' he asks.

'It's a brilliant fashion house. The clothes are fab – the classic stuff anyway – and the people are great. I've only been here a few days,' I add, 'but I wish I wasn't leaving.'

'Leaving?'

I shrug. 'I'm just the temp.'

He raises his eyebrows at me. I know I shouldn't talk to him, since he's a complete stranger, but I'm feeling so depressed after my conversation with Elaine that my frustrations are out before I know it. I tell him all about sending in my CV three years ago and how I'd hoped that temping here now might lead to something permanent.

'So why here and not some other house?' he asks, after a while.

'Potential. There's so much I'd love to do here.'

'Like what?'

I tell him about my ideas and my shopping expedition. When he keeps asking questions, I launch into my theories on window dressing and how Friers should go upmarket. I tell him about the conversations I overheard in the boutique and my magazine research. I even tell him about the clothes that Jack wears.

He nods as I burble on and I feel overwhelmingly flattered that someone is listening to me at last. Shame he's just a model.

'Just a few ideas,' I say when my monologue has ended.

'Have you told Fabian what you think?' he asks.

'Fabian! God no! He hasn't said two words to me. I'm just the temp,' I remind him.

'You're wasted,' he says honestly.

I nod, my attention distracted by the people filing back into the office. I jump off the desk.

'Sorry to go on to you,' I say, smoothing down my skirt.

'The pleasure's all mine,' he says, inclining his head. I like his American accent. 'What's your name?'

'Oh, um, Amy,' I say. 'I'll tell Fabian you're here.'

I turn to go, and then stop abruptly. I turn round slowly and screw up my face.

'Your name would help.'

He stands up. 'Jules. Jules Geller.'

Once everyone is back at their desks, it's obvious that the atmosphere has changed. When I get a moment, I go through to the cutting room. Jenny, Sam, Andy and Louise are out on the fire escape.

'What's going on?' I ask, standing by the door.

'Just as we thought,' says Jenny. 'Friers have been bought by A&M.'

'Who are A&M?'

'They're another fashion house. They're mostly based in America, but their collections have been selling well over here,' explains Sam. 'They're bringing over a new boss.'

'I can't believe we're going to get *him*,' says Jenny excitedly. 'He's fantastic!'

'I'm sure he'll get rid of Fabian, if he's going to head up the whole thing from London,' adds Andy.

'Did you see the collection he did in Paris?' asks Louise.

'I know. He's really good. God, I hope he keeps us all on.'

'Who?' I ask, as they all continue their conversation.

'Jules Geller,' says Jenny, finally taking some notice of me. 'Jules Geller is our new boss. Isn't that great!'

I stumble back to my desk. Jules Geller is the new boss.

The same Jules Geller I have just spilled my guts out to.

Well done Amy. No, well done. You've really made a good impression there. Upstart temp, pitching your ideas to a man who from the look on Jenny's face practically owns the whole bloody industry.

Shit.

I keep a low profile for the rest of the afternoon. Fabian's meeting seems to go on for ages and Jenny and Sam are called into his office. I avoid eye contact with everyone, trying to ignore the tension in the office. When I come back from the post office, I'm not sure whether Jules has left or not, but I've decided that, come what may, I'm going to hide under the desk rather than let him see me.

At five-thirty, Jenny comes in and I give her the latest batch of work I've done along with my timesheet.

'This is the last time I'll be doing this,' she says with a sigh.

'To be honest, it's just as well I'm going,' I say, before explaining what I've done. She shakes her head at me and laughs.

'Nothing is ever as bad as you think.'

'No, it's worse,' I say, tucking my timesheet in my bag.

'You'd better say goodbye to Fabian before you leave.'

She hugs me goodbye and there are thanks all round. Everyone seems to be looking at me strangely. Either I've got a stamp stuck to my chin, or I'm being paranoid. I check my chin.

Paranoia it is.

'We'll keep in touch,' promises Sam, crossing her fingers at me. They stand by the door, smiling at me as I knock on Fabian's door.

'Is he in there?' I ask, turning round to them. They look as if they're about to crack up laughing.

'Go on,' urges Jenny.

I push open the door.

'Ah, just the person I wanted.' Jules is standing behind Fabian's desk. 'Come in,' he says.

'I came to see Fabian,' I stutter.

'Fabian, I'm afraid, has gone. You'll have to talk to me, instead.'

I ease myself down into the chair. I know I'm blushing and he smiles at me with genuine amusement.

'I shouldn't have said anything earlier. I didn't know you were the new boss, or anything. I never usually—'

Jules puts his hand out to stop me. 'It's okay, Amy. You don't have to apologise.'

'But—'

'No buts. I happen to think your ideas are great. I also happen to know you're just what I'm looking for. I need a personal assistant to help me set things up here and I think you'd be perfect. How's your typing?'

I'm about to go into autoblag, but stop myself. I close my mouth abruptly. This is real, I'm not going to bullshit this time. 'Not great,' I reply, 'but I'm sure I could brush up.'

'I've had a word with Jenny and Sam and they both seem to think you're the best organiser there's ever been around here. I've also been having a look at your CV.' He holds it up. 'I'm impressed.'

Thank you, Sam.

'So how about it? Are you going to save me the hassle of

interviewing some terminally dull secretaries, or will you give me a go?'

Will *I* give him a *go*?

After celebrating in the pub with Jenny and Sam, I rock up to Jack's with a bottle of champagne.

'You'll never guess what,' I announce, when he opens the door.

'What?'

I pull out the champagne from behind my back. 'You can be a house husband, after all!'

Jack and Matt are delighted with my news. We sit in the kitchen drinking whilst I gush on about Friers.

'When do you start?' asks Matt.

'That's the best bit. Not for a couple of weeks. Which means we can go on holiday.'

'Holiday?' asks Jack.

'Of course. Why not? Once I start the job, there'll be no time. I thought about it on the way over. Let's go somewhere hot for a week.'

'Isn't that a bit sudden?'

'Well you've got a week to think about it,' I say. 'Come on, Jack. You can afford it, we'll have such a laugh.'

Jack doesn't seem convinced.

'You can't go next week,' says Matt. 'It's Alex's stag do.'

'I know,' says Jack.

I've been on such a high, emotional and alcoholic, that it takes me a moment to notice the eye contact between them. I have a feeling I'm missing something.

'I'll work something out,' says Jack to no one in particular. He gets up and goes to the fridge.

'I'm off out,' says Matt, suddenly.

'Don't go,' I say.

'Sorry. Have to. Enjoy yourselves,' he says before leaving. He shuts the door behind him.

'Did I say something wrong?' I ask.

169

'No, don't worry.'

'You don't have to come on holiday if you don't want to.'

'Of course I want to. Alex is more a friend of Matt's than of mine. I'll sort things out with him.'

'Excellent.' I slip off the stool and give Jack a big hug. 'I'm so excited.'

'Me too,' says Jack, but he doesn't sound as convinced as I want him to.

Why is it that my social life only happens on about seven of the 365 days in the year, and on each of those seven, forty billion things compete for my time? This Saturday is a prime example.

I'm stressed even before I wake up. Having a hangover doesn't help.

It's Aunty Vi's fiftieth birthday party in Hemel Hempstead. An event I have been invited to with Jack (Mother's scheming influence, I suspect), but I'd rather die than introduce him to my cousins. I don't want him to draw premature conclusions about my dodgy gene pool. Aunty Vi is quite a laugh though, and normally I'd be looking forward to seeing her. She's having a bouncy castle in the back garden.

I've told mum that I'll go, but as I go back to my flat on Saturday morning, I know I'm going to have to ring her and duck out. She's not going to be happy.

Aunty Vi's clashes with H's dinner party which she's having tonight for Gav's birthday. H has been banging on about menus and guest lists for ages and she'll flip if I don't go. I've also promised that I'll help her cook.

However, the real problem is that Chloe is having a barbecue and Jack got really grumpy this morning when I told him I was going to H's.

'But everyone will be there,' he said. 'You've got to come. Matt and I are cooking.'

'But I promised H.'

'It's not her birthday. It's only dinner. She won't mind if

170

there's one less mouth to feed.'

'She will.'

'Go then,' Jack sulked. 'I think you're being a bit selfish though. I'm giving up a stag weekend to come on holiday with you, the least you could do is come to this with me. I want to show you off.'

There are three messages on the machine from H when I get through the front door. I know that I'm going to go to Chloe's, but there's no way I can tell her the truth. I feel shit about it, but I'm going to have to lie.

When she calls again, I put on my most miserable voice.

'Where've you been?' she asks. 'I've been trying to get hold of you all morning. We're going shopping, remember?'

'I don't feel well,' I answer.

'Is Jack there?' she asks, sceptically.

'No. I've been throwing up.'

'Hangover?'

I'm dying to tell her about my new job, but I've already started on my lie. 'I don't think I'm up to coming shopping.'

'But you promised.'

'I know, but I feel awful. Honestly.'

She sighs. I can tell she's pissed off. 'Okay, but get better for tonight. Jack's coming, isn't he?'

'He can't. His aunt's birthday, or something.'

'But I've planned it all! You could have said.'

'Sorry. I've got to go, I'm going to throw up again.'

I go into the bathroom and stick my tongue out at myself. I've made myself feel ill. I know I've created a mess and have a nasty suspicion it'll get worse. I never lie to H. And anyway, I've bought Gav a birthday present. I'll have to 'get better' for tonight. Jack will have to lump it.

I mooch around all day, feeling disgruntled. Jack calls at six o'clock. He's on Matt's mobile.

'Where are you?' he asks.

'I'm just getting ready . . .'

'Be here soon. The food's looking great. I've told Chloe you're coming.'

'Jack . . .' But he's already rung off.

For a while I think about going to H's and then leaving to go to Chloe's, but the more I think about it, the more I know it'll just make things worse.

I'll have to blow H out. I can't let Jack down. Not after everything he's done for me recently. I rehearse my lines before I pick up the phone.

'How are you feeling?' she asks.

'Worse.'

'Have you eaten anything?'

'No. I can't keep anything down. I think it must be a stomach bug. There's been one going round at work.'

'Do you want me to come and get you? You can stay here if you want. It doesn't matter if you don't eat anything.'

'I can't H.'

'But it's Gav's birthday.'

'I know, but I feel dreadful. I'd be no fun. You're better off without me.'

'You're not coming then?'

'I think it's better if I just go to bed.'

'I'll call you later then to check you're okay.'

'Don't worry. I'll probably be asleep. You have fun. Give my love to Gav.'

That's it. I'm going to hell.

It takes me ages to get to Chloe's and I'm not in the mood for a party. Her flat is on the ground floor of a large Victorian house. When she greets me at the door and shows me through to the garden, I look through to the living room. It's all stripped floorboards and tasteful art. Even the garden is perfect.

Jack and Matt are doing their chef thing by the barbecue and there are about forty people milling about the garden. The stereo is blaring Aretha Franklin and everyone seems to be pissed.

'Glad you made it,' says Jack, kissing me.

'Good,' I reply, looking around the garden and seeing H's

brother, Martin. He's talking to a group of people and when he sees me, he waves his glass. I wave back, feeling sick. I've really done it this time. He's bound to tell H I was here.

I turn back to Jack.

'Want some food?' he asks, his mouth full of the hot sausage he's just bitten into.

'No thanks, I'm fine.'

Jack puts his arm around me. 'Cheer up. It's a party.'

Cheer up? With my social life now up in flames?

I smile weakly at him. 'Who is everyone?' I ask, forcing myself to make an effort.

He points out people around the garden.

'That's Stringer, he works in the gym. Damien, old mate from school,' he starts, reeling off a list of names I'm never going to remember.

'Oh, and that's Jons,' he says eventually, having done a tour of the garden. He points to a bloke in leather trousers. He's very good looking, but obviously knows it by the way he's standing. 'Watch out for him. He's coked off his tree. Oh God, they're coming over.'

The girl walking towards us with Jons looks vaguely familiar, but I can't place her. Maybe she's a model or something because she's very thin with long blonde hair and the kind of good looks that make you want to give up and have a sex change.

'Jack, you're doing a great job,' she smiles, flashing him a bright smile.

I bet she's never had lipstick on those teeth before.

'Aren't you going to introduce us?' she asks, looking at me curiously.

Jack looks shifty. He turns over a steak on the barbecue.

'Course. Amy, this is Jons.' He waves a fish slice between us.

'Hi,' I say, looking at Jons. Jack's right. Just from looking at him you can tell he's taken far too much coke.

'And Sally,' mumbles Jack.

It takes a moment for it to sink in and then a horrible feeling lurches in the pit of my stomach. Jack has painted *her*? With no clothes on?

173

'Oh!' I gush. 'You're *the* Sally, the one in the painting. I thought I recognised you.'

I'm surprised I don't slap my thigh to accompany the false trill of laughter that issues forth from my mouth. Sally is looking at her feet, but damn her if she thinks *I'm* going to be embarrassed.

'What painting is this?' asks Jons.

'Oh you know!' I say, smiling as if my face is going to crack. 'The nude Jack's doing. It's really very good—'

'Woah!' Jons interrupts, holding up his hand. He's wearing a particularly nasty silver skull ring on his index finger. 'Woah!' he says again, shaking back his hair.

'Oh God!' I say, clasping my hands to my face. 'Was it meant to be a surprise? You were going to give it to him?' I grimace at Sally. 'Of course you were, it is kind of . . . well . . . intimate.'

It's come out wrong.

Very wrong.

Very, very wrong.

Sally is staring at Jack, her face like thunder. There is a split second of silence and then Jons loses it. He looks as if his head is going to explode. He grabs Jack by the neck of his T-shirt.

'YOU FUCKING PIECE OF SHIT,' he yells as he takes a swipe at Jack.

I can hear the gasps around me as he misses and crashes on to the barbecue. He flails out one hand, and pulls over the table, sending burgers flying and coating himself in barbecue sauce. There is an almighty crash as the barbecue collapses under his weight, followed by the loud hiss of his leather trousers sizzling on the grill. He yelps.

'You've really done it now!' screams Sally at me, pushing me so violently that I fall back, impaling myself on a rose bush. She rushes over to Jons who is staggering out of the mess on the patio.

'Calm down,' shouts Jack.

Jons shoves Sally away. 'You fucking whore!' he yells as he staggers upright. Then he grabs the barbecue fork and rushes towards Jack. The people behind scramble to safety. Jack picks up the plastic garden chair and they joust for a moment until Jack bats the fork out of Jons's hand. Jack crouches and puts his hands out defensively as if he's about to do a kung fu move.

'Just calm down,' he shouts again. For a moment Jons turns away. His hands fall to his sides and Jack stands up straight. 'Let's just talk about this,' Jack says, advancing towards Jons.

But he can't see Jons's face. I know instinctively what's going to happen and try to run forward, but my dress is caught.

'Watch out!' I scream, which distracts Jack for a second. This, of course, is the second that Jons throws his punch. I watch as it lands slap bang on Jack's cheekbone. I can hear myself screaming as Jack's skin splits open under the skull ring before he staggers backwards on to the trestle table, knocking it over, sending bottles and plates into the air.

Matt and Damien and Stringer rush in and grab Jons by the shoulders.

I rip myself away from the thorns and scramble to Jack.

Jons is still shouting obscenities as Damien and Stringer frog-march him to the gate. Sally runs after them and then the noise fades away.

I crouch down beside Jack who is now sitting upright. 'Are you all right?'

He's far from all right. He holds his face and waggles his jaw. I put my hand out to touch him, but he shoves me away.

'Leave me alone!' he hisses, with such viciousness that my breath leaves my body as I topple back on the grass. I watch him stagger up and walk inside the house.

'Jack!' He ignores me.

I cover my face with my hands. Matt crouches down beside me.

'Don't worry,' he says. 'Give him a few minutes to calm down. He's just been hit. He didn't mean to do that.'

Everyone is looking on stunned. Matt helps me to my feet and puts his arm around me as Chloe stomps over. She's furious. Everything is wrecked. The garden looks as if a hurricane has passed through it.

'Where's Jack?' she snaps.

I nod dumbly towards the house.

'Jesus!' She rolls her eyes at me, before marching up the garden and into the house after Jack.

Minutes later, I stumble into the bathroom and close the door behind me, reeling from the scene in the garden. I don't know how long I sit on the toilet seat, but suddenly I can hear a soft knocking on the door.

'Amy?' It's Matt's voice. There's another knock. 'Amy, let me in.'

'It's open,' I croak.

He comes in and the look on his face makes me start to cry.

'Don't,' he says, sitting on the edge of the bath beside me. 'Come on, it'll be all right.'

He puts his arm around me and hands me some loo roll. I blow my nose.

'I'm sorry,' I sniff.

'Don't be. It's okay. Things like that scare the hell out of me too.'

The door bursts open.

'Oh, so you're here,' says Chloe, pursing her lips at me. 'Just as well. You're not exactly flavour of the month.'

Matt and I stand up.

'How is he?' I ask.

'Don't worry. *I'm* looking after him.'

Jack appears in the doorway, his hand over his face. I can see his eye is already swelling. Chloe barges past Matt and opens the cabinet on the wall.

'I've got some witch hazel in here,' she says, before fishing out the bottle and pulling off a big wodge of cotton wool. 'Come here, Jack,' she commands.

'I can manage,' he says. He doesn't look at me. 'Will you leave us alone for a minute?' He looks at Matt who nods and then at Chloe, who looks as if she's about to stamp her foot. She stares at him, as he takes the bottle and cotton wool from her. 'It's a bit crowded in here, that's all,' he adds.

Chloe glances at me as if I'm a bug she wants to squash

176

before following Matt through the door and slamming it behind her. Jack walks to the door and turns the lock. He leans back against it and closes his eyes for a moment. Then he looks at me.

'I'm sorry,' he says. 'I didn't mean to push you like that.'

'You don't have to be sorry. It's all my fault. Oh God, Jack, I'm so sorry.'

'Come here,' he says, and in one second I'm in his arms.

'He's such a wanker!' he says.

I look up at him. His eye makes me wince. I lead him to the bath and sit him on the edge. I take the witch hazel and cotton wool and kneel in front of him.

'Does it hurt a lot?'

Jack doesn't answer. He leans forward and puts his arms on my shoulders and his forehead touches mine.

'What a mess!' he sighs.

'It's over now.'

'I didn't mean to—'

'Shh.' I put my finger to his lips. He looks at me and I look straight into his eyes. And all at once it makes sense. Nothing else matters, not Sally, not Chloe, not Jons. Nothing except Jack.

'I love you,' I whisper.

7
Jack

She Loves Me, I Love Her Not?

Not, *I like you*. Not, *I fancy you*. Not even, *You're my friend*.

None of the above.

Just, *I love you*.

As sentences go, it's a biggie. It's up there with *Before we go any further, I think you should know that I haven't always been a woman* . . . (Michaela/Mike to Matt, 1995); *When I told you I wasn't married, I wasn't exactly telling the truth* . . . (Graham King to Chloe, 1997); and *I think it's time we started thinking seriously about getting married* . . . (Zoe to me, 1995).

Not, in other words, something to be taken lightly.

Various traditional evasion tactics are, of course, at my disposal at this critical juncture:

a) The contemplative 'Mmmmm' (best accompanied by a slow nodding of the head and a constipated expression)
b) The incoherent 'I urgh you, too' (the drunker, the better)
c) The panicked 'Oh Christ, I think I'm gonna puke' (ditto).
d) The therapeutic 'Thank you for sharing that with me' (follow-up hand-squeezing essential)
e) The arrogant 'I know' (full eye contact, smug smile/sneer optional)

But I'm not feeling tactical right now. I'm far too confused for that. I'm looking at Amy and I'm thinking that, yeah, maybe these *are* words I want to hear from her. I'm feeling flattered and I'm guessing that her telling me this translates into her having made some monumental female decision that I'm the right man for her. There's a part of me that wants to stand up and be counted, take her hand and look her in the eyes and say, 'Yes, I *am* your man. Yes, I *do* love you. Yes, I'm happy because you love me, too.' I mean, that's what everyone wants when it comes to the crunch: to love and to be loved. Just having one side of the equation doesn't seem right.

Right?

But I'm thinking other stuff as well. Insecure stuff. Stuff I don't like admitting, even to myself. Like, how well do I really know her? Enough to take her declaration of love at face value? Do I *really* trust her enough for that? And what happens if I do and I'm wrong? What happens if I let go now and take this mess of emotions I'm feeling for her and christen them Love?

My past record on such matters, as with most matters, doesn't exactly inspire me with confidence. For a start, I've only ever (relatives and pets excluded) said 'I love you' to one person. That was Zoe. It was at Heathrow Airport. We'd been stuck there waiting for our flight to Ibiza for six hours. Fatigue had set in three hours before. Terminal boredom. I was sitting on this plastic bucket seat, gazing at the information board, waiting for the letters to flick over to read, NOW BOARDING. Zoe was asleep, her head resting on my lap. I remember looking down at her, with her hair falling across my thighs and her eyes pinched up, and this huge surge of protection washing over me. She was beautiful, peaceful. I'd never experienced a comfort zone like it before. I leant down and kissed her forehead and the three magic words just came out in a whisper. I'd been seeing her for six months and I thought I meant every one of them.

But today, here in Chloe's bathroom, with witch hazel burning my cheek and my eye swelling into a dead ringer for the winner of a poached egg lookalike competition, I feel differently. I'm not a kid any more. Love isn't a protective urge. Love isn't comfort and complacency. Love's a decision. It's reaching the conclusion that this is it and there isn't anything else. I'm not one of those guys who says it because it's easier than not saying it. And I'm not one of those guys who'll use it like some security code to gain access to a girl's knickers. (I'll say anything, but not *that*.) But, at the same time, I'm not afraid of it. I'll say it when I'm sure. And looking at Amy now, I'm not sure.

Bottom line: our future's still an *if* and not a *when*.

So, instead of taking her words and issuing her with the expected receipt of 'I love you, too' I walk the track beaten by indecisive men's feet for generations: I wimp out.

'Your dress is torn,' I tell her, breaking eye contact, peering at the material.

There's a few seconds' silence and I hear my heart beat and wonder if she can hear it, too.

Finally, she asks, 'How are you feeling?'

'Fucked off,' I tell her.

Thankfully, she realises I'm talking about what went down in the garden, rather than what she's just said. 'It was stupid of me,' she says.

I squeeze my arm tighter around her, pulling her into me, and kiss the side of her face. 'No, it was stupid of me. Stupid of me to lie to you about what Sally looked like. Stupid of her not to tell Jons. And it was stupid of that crazy, coked-up fucker to lose it and try and knock my head off.'

Amy's head dips. 'Yes, but you can understand why . . .'

'Bullshit, you can. No one's got the right to behave like that. Too much of this,' I say, making a snorting sound and pointing at my nose, 'and not enough of this,' I add, tapping the side of my head. I hear my breathing coming heavy, Jons's face suddenly in my mind.

'What if you were in his situation? What if you found out someone was painting me in the nude? Wouldn't you freak?'

This is, of course, a reasonable question, but it's not one I want to get into now. I shake my head adamantly. 'No. I wouldn't freak, because I'm not a prick. And . . . and because I trust you.'

'Did you know she hadn't told him? Before tonight, I mean.'

I consider lying, telling her that I'd assumed that Jons was cool with the situation. But what would be the point? You only have to see Jons from a distance to know that he wouldn't be cool with another guy sitting next to Sally on a bus, let alone anything more intimate. So I tell her the truth: 'Yeah. She said he'd freak if he found out.'

'Same as I did when I saw the painting.'

'Yeah,' I sigh, 'same as that.'

'It comes down to honesty, I suppose,' she considers. 'I was suspicious and assumed the worst.'

I shift round on the edge of the bath to face her. Her eyes are puffed-up from when she was crying. I feel like it's all my fault. And why not? It is.

'Is that what you thought when you found the painting?'

'What, that you were sleeping with her?'

'Yeah.'

'Well, I'd be lying if I said it didn't cross my mind.' I feel her running her hand through my hair. 'It did. A lot.' She cocks her head and looks at me. 'Does it piss you off that I thought that?'

'No.' I've hesitated too long before I've said this.

'Not even a little?' she probes.

'Okay,' I admit, 'a little.'

'I'm sorry. It's a jealousy thing. I do trust you, Jack. Completely. You know that, don't you?'

I'm feeling shit about this. And not just standard shit either. Something way lower than that. Something that you might find caked on a cow's tail, or in a bluebottle's underpants. Same as I have done since we patched things up in the studio after she found the painting. Now would be the right time to come clean and tell Amy that she was right to suspect that my motives for painting Sally were more to do with me being a tart than being into art. Just get it out in the open and move on.

But what's the point? Why should I be accountable to Amy for what I was thinking pre-her? Why cause more grief? It's not relevant now. It's Amy I'm into, *not* Sally. There's no need for her ever to know that things were ever any different.

'I don't know,' I tell her, sticking to the broader issue. 'I mean, what makes your thinking that any different to what Jons thought just now? You reacted the same as him.'

'I didn't hit you,' she says. 'That's got to count for something.'

Despite myself, I smile. 'I suppose so. And I didn't fry your leather trousers. That's got to count for something, too.'

She grimaces. 'It sounded painful.'

'Awesome,' I say, unable to prevent myself from grinning. 'Like bacon in a pan.'

Her voice goes all serious again. 'This is something we've got to sort out, Jack.'

'What, the trust thing?'

'Yes. But not just that. The whole past. So there aren't any secrets or lies. So we don't go getting in a mess like this again.'

And she's right: we do have to deal with this. But not here. Not now. Not with our emotions running so high.

There's a knock at the door and I let Matt in. 'You feeling better now, Elephant Man?' he asks, wincing at the sight of my face.

'Yeah,' I say, turning round and smiling at Amy. 'Let's get this party back on the road.'

Baggage

Tuesday evening and Amy's already sitting at a table on the pavement outside Zack's by the time I get there. We're stopping here for a drink before moving on to some mate of hers' party. Still a few yards away from her, before she's spotted me, I stop and look at her. It's a game I used to play with Zoe when I was going out with her. It's called, *Would I still fancy her if she wasn't my girlfriend?* I stand here and try to imagine that she's a total stranger, and that I'm just some guy out for a stroll. Now that I've laid eyes on her for the first time, the pertinent question is, *Would I like to lay her, too?*

The physical information's processed first: hair, build, clothes. All are compatible with my type. She doesn't have a wet perm, a shaved head, or a beard. There are no obvious signs of either a wasting disorder, lard addiction or anabolic steroid abuse. Clothes-wise, she's not wearing fluorescent lycra leggings, stilettos or a Michael Bolton Fan Club T-shirt. She also falls within the correct age range: no more than five years younger than me (thus enabling cool nostalgia trips centring around cult TV programmes of the seventies and eighties – *The Dukes of Hazzard*, *The Rockford Files*, *C.H.I.P.S.*, etc.), and no more than ten years older than me (thereby reducing the possibility of serious baggage – failed marriage, children, Pink Floyd/David Soul vinyls, etc.). So far, so funky. Next comes the peripheral visual information. She's reading a glossy magazine (literate – good), wearing designer shades on the top of her head (expensive tastes – bad), and has two glasses and an iced bottle of wine in front of her (meeting someone, possibly a boyfriend – very bad). Overall analysis: real potential; shame about the boyfriend.

And if this *was* the first time I'd seen Amy, then I'd have to reluctantly walk away. But it isn't the first time. And the fact that she's got a boyfriend doesn't bother me either. Because I *am* that boyfriend and that second wineglass has got my name written all over it. I walk towards her with a smile on my face, because the answer to my original question is a resounding *Yes*.

The first thing I realise after I've kissed her and sat down and poured myself a drink is that the glossy magazine she's reading is, in fact, a travel brochure. The second thing I realise, as she's asking me how my day's been, is that the travel brochure is for holidays in Hawaii. The third thing I realise, as Amy remarks on the fact that she hasn't been abroad for two years, is that she's labouring under the illusion that I'm filthy rich and probably hang out in places like Hawaii all the time. But the main thing I realise, as she points out that I've got yellow paint in my hair, is that I'm well and truly fucked.

'So what do you think?' she asks, turning the brochure round and showing me a picture of a particularly exclusive resort.

What do I think? As in the truth? I think that after I've paid off my overdraft and my rent and my living expenses with the money from doing *Study in Fucking Yellow* for Dad's company, there won't be enough left for a bus ticket to Clacton-on-Sea, let alone anywhere more exotic. I think that it's gorgeous and hot over here, so why bother going abroad at all? I think that, in an ideal world, Amy would have a mortal fear of flying and we'd just have to spend the summer chilling out in the UK. But Amy doesn't want to hear the truth. Or, at least, *I* don't want her to hear it. As I open my mouth to speak, it occurs to me, not for the first time in my life, that lying is rather like masturbating: once you've started, it's pretty hard to stop. In spite of these thoughts, though, I amazingly manage to keep the look of abject horror from my face, and instead adopt a blasé, worldly tone, and say, 'I don't know. The trouble with Hawaii is that when you've gone there once, you've kind of done it.'

'Oh.' There's no attempt on her behalf to hide her disappointment. 'I didn't know you'd already been.'

'Oh, yeah,' I say.

And this *is* true: I *have* been there before. Just because I was six months old at the time and spent the whole time in a pram when Dad got a business freebie doesn't make it any less relevant. When it comes to Hawaii, I can claim to have *Book 'em, Danno*'d with the best of them. To back this up, I make vague paddling actions and start humming the tune to *Hawaii Five-O*, hoping that my performance will distract Amy from her mission.

It doesn't. I'm hardly into my first *ba-ba-ba-ba-baaa-baaa*, when she cuts me short, asking, 'And you don't want to go back?'

My arms fall limply to my sides. 'Well,' I continue to bluff, 'it's all sun, sand and surf and not much else, really.'

'Sounds terrible.' She slaps another brochure down on top of the first. I look at the cover: Rainforest Tours. 'How about this, then? Done one rainforest, done them all?'

A quick glance at the extensive library of brochures sticking out of her bag tells me that even Alan Whicker would have a tough job claiming he'd visited all these places. Time for some quick thinking, then, because there's no way I'm getting out of this. I've already told her I'll go on holiday with her and any retraction now will almost certainly be viewed as a signal that all is not well chez Rossiter and Crosbie. And I don't want a relationship crisis discussion. Because there is no crisis. Apart from me lying to her about how much money I make from my painting. Apart from me continuing to lie to her about this when I've sworn to her that I'll never lie to her again. Crisis? Ha! What crisis? These are details, mere smudges on life's great plan – nothing to get freaked out about at all.

I gently nudge the brochure to one side and say, 'I was thinking of somewhere a bit closer.'

'Why?'

'We-ell . . .' And then it hits me: 'Because by the time we book it, we'll only have a week before you start your new job.'

But she's not being fobbed off so easily. 'That's okay,' she says, opening a Bahamas brochure. She runs her finger down a list of prices that look like national economy outputs, and points at the departure and arrival dates. 'See – they do loads of one-week deals.'

Deals. Ha! Try telling my bank manager that.

'I know,' I counter, 'but think how long the flights are. Jet lag, and all that kind of stuff. By the time we get there and sort ourselves out, it'll be time to come back again.' I see her mouth open, preparing to contradict me, so I plough on. 'Europe. What's wrong with Europe? Europe is good at this time of year. Europe is – I don't know – Europe is *fun*.'

Her eyes narrow as she repeats the word. 'Fun?'

'Yeah,' I enthuse. 'Loads to do. Places to see . . .' I nod my head in agreement with myself. 'Fun.'

She sits back in her chair. Her body is communicating with me. It's saying, quite clearly, *Europe is* not *fun. Europe is not fun, because I've been to Europe loads of times and I want to go to Hawaii.* 'Okay,' she says aloud, 'so which part of Theme Park Europe do you want to have *fun* in?'

I think cheap flights, cheap accommodation, cheap food and cheap booze, and the word 'Greece' just slips out.

'Greece?' Her lips are so tightly pursed as she utters the

word it's a wonder it gets out at all.

'Yeah, Greece. As in the birthplace of Western culture. As in the Parthenon and Homer and that groovy Greek stuff.'

She considers this for a moment, looking from me to the brochures in her bag. I get the distinct feeling that if it came down to a them or me situation I'd come out a poor second. 'Okay,' she finally says. 'Greece it is. Do you want to book it, or shall I?'

'Leave it to me,' I say, a heavenly vision of bargain bucket travel agents filling my mind.

Thankfully, the conversation moves on. Thankful, though, isn't a very appropriate word to describe my feelings towards what comes next. Anxious, yes. Paranoid, yes. But thankful, no. The words 'frying pan' and 'fire' spring to mind. Because what Amy starts talking about is what I narrowly avoided discussing with her in Chloe's bathroom at the weekend: the past.

Now, I've got a funny attitude towards the past. On the one hand, I'm easy with it. I'm where I am/who I am because of what's happened to me – a sum of my experiences and all that. Like the first night I met Amy. We talked about the past then and that was just dandy. But it was the clean past, the censored past, the kind of past you could show to a kid without worrying about giving them nightmares. On the other hand, though, there's some stuff I've done that's probably best left where it is. Like sex. Like the other people I've had sex with over the past few years. Sex is a dangerous issue. When you tell someone about your sex life, they draw conclusions.

Take Christine. Christine is a girl I had the major hots for at the beginning of last year. She was a mate, a real mate, in that we told each other everything, swapped love life stories like football cards. And this was great. This was open and this was honest. Problem was, when I finally got round to propositioning her, she wasn't having any of it. Why? Not because she didn't fancy me – she admitted that she did – but because she didn't fancy becoming another sad statistic in the Jack Rossiter Hall of One-Night Stands.

And this is my worry with Amy. Will she judge me? If I

admit that I've spent the last God-knows-how-long perpetrating sexual hit and runs, will she take a leaf from my book and run a mile herself? It's a risk, but it's a risk I'm going to have to take. Because there are no more lies, right? If Amy's going to accept me, then she's got to accept me for what I am. It's a love-me-or-leave-me kind of a thing.

I just hope it's the former.

So, after a bit of humming and hahing, we sit here and get down to discussing our past relationships. Only I'm aware that we're not really discussing our past relationships at all; we're using them as models, as testing grounds for whether we're compatible. In everything we ask one another there's a pretended meaning and a *real meaning*. Amy, for example, asks me:

Have you ever been unfaithful to someone while you've been in a long-term relationship? (*Are you likely to be unfaithful to me?*)

When you've broken off relationships, have you just come out and told the other person it's over, or have you engineered intolerable situations, so it's looked like both parties have been to blame? (*Are you a man or a mouse?*)

With any of these girls did you ever consider marriage, even as just a remote possibility? (*Does the thought of commitment terrify you?*)

And I, in turn, ask Amy:

If any of these guys had asked you to marry them, would you have accepted? (*Would you marry me because you like the idea of marriage and it's the right time in your life, rather than because you're head over heels in love with me?*)

Have you ever committed an act of revenge on a former lover? (*If things don't work out between us and I dump you, are you likely to go all* Fatal Attraction *on me?*)

Have you ever had a lesbian experience? (*Any chance of a threesome?*)

187

And, bit by bit, we sound each other out, both of us no doubt considering whether we like what we hear.

Then things get more specific. It starts with the usual question: How many people have you slept with? I can't vouch for Amy's response to my answer (twenty-five-ish). But, as I watch her close her eyes and count her conquests off on her fingers, and announce, 'Twelve,' mine is definitely one of surprise. I immediately insert this information into the Promiscuity Equation that Matt and I invented in one of our more bored moments. It takes into account all the relevant factors necessary to calculate an accurate Promiscuity Rating (♥) which is the average number of people you've slept with per year while single: Number of People Slept With (W); Current Age (X); Age at which Virginity was Lost (Y); and Number of Years Spent in Long-Term Relationships (Z). The equation reads:

$$\frac{W}{X - (Y + Z)} = ♥$$

I apply this to Amy:

$$\frac{12}{25 - (17 + 4)} = 3♥$$

And to myself:

$$\frac{25}{27 - (17 + 2)} = 3.125♥$$

And there it is: even though she's slept with fewer people than me, our ratings aren't actually that different. In her single, sexually active years, she's got laid, on average, three times a year, compared to my 3.125.

I'm not quite sure how to react to this. There is, of course, relief that we're similarly experienced and that I'm no more of a tart than her and vice versa. I'm also, however, shocked. I regard myself as a bit of a loose guy, so does this make Amy a bit of a loose woman? And is this something I should worry about? I don't trust myself too much when it comes to women, so should I trust her when it comes to men? Or am I just having a male ego crisis, stressing over the fact that she's more than capable of having fun without me?

Whatever, at the very least, I'm intrigued. I want to know more. And so I ask. And I get. Name by name. Lay by lay. From her first (Wayne Cartwright, behind the bike sheds, Elmesmere High), to her last (Martin Robbins, six months before she met me, at a wedding in Wales). From her youngest (again Wayne Cartwright, aged 17), to her oldest (Simon Chadwick, a forty-year-old musician). I hear about her worst (Alan Wood, a thirtysomething suit in the middle of a marriage break-up), and her best (Tommy Johnson, a West End set designer). She tells me more about her longest mistake (Andy, the City trader who she moved in with), and less about her shortest ('Jimmy or Jonny Something. I was pissed and stoned. I don't really remember much about him.').

And somewhere in the middle of all this, even though I'm matching her confession for confession, an unusual feeling grips me. It comes from nowhere, but once it's here, it just won't go away. As she continues to describe and I continue to listen, I start to feel nauseous. It's the visualisation thing that's getting to me. I can't help picturing her with these other men, doing the stuff we do together, the stuff that makes her mine and me hers. It's crazy, I understand, but it's still painful. I haven't had to deal with this kind of thing for a long time. I haven't had to deal with it, because I haven't given a shit. Most of the girls I've slept with have been one-night stands. I've known next to nothing about them. And those histories I have known about haven't bothered me. Why should they have? It wasn't like I was going to be hanging around and having to cope with them. We had no future together, so why waste time worrying about the past?

But this is different. As in radically. I've been thinking about what Amy said to me in Chloe's bathroom a lot these past few days. Those three little words. And I've been thinking that maybe I should've answered differently. Because I *do* care for her. A lot. And I think I *am* falling in love with her. And that's why hearing this stuff hurts so much. I want her. I want all of her. And I know that means hearing the truth about her as well, because I'd rather know it than have it kept from me. But still, I don't want to hear about her being unfaithful to other people. I don't want to hear about her getting drunk and ending up in bed with someone, just because she's too wasted to get in a cab and go home. I don't want to hear about any of this stuff that I would have been more than happy to take advantage of when I'd been out on the prowl. And the reason I don't want to hear about any of these things is because I don't want them to happen to me.

I bite it back down and tell myself to stop being such an arsehole. She must be feeling this, too, over the encounters I've told her. So don't be pathetic. Don't be insecure and don't be jealous. Don't be all the things you despise. Fight this bad feeling. Be glad you've had this conversation. It's been unadulterated and it's been honest and, above all, it's been normal. Accept the fact that, short of marrying a virgin, this is something everyone the world over has to come to terms with at some point in their life.

'But they're all out of the way now?' I ask, once I've dealt with number twenty-five and she's done number twelve.

She looks me dead-set in the eyes and says, 'Yes.'

'No hangers on? No unfinished business? No unclaimed baggage waiting to be picked up?'

'No.'

'Good,' I say, trying to conceal the relief from my voice. 'I'm glad.'

'And you?' she asks tentatively. 'Anyone you haven't told me about?'

'There's no one,' I assure her. 'Just you.'

'No Zoe? No residual feelings there?'

'No.'

'No Sally?'

'No.'

She stares at the table. 'Has she called you?'

'No, I don't think I'll be hearing from her again. Kate says she's up in Glasgow with Jons, trying to patch things up.'

She nods her head, seemingly satisfied, then looks up and asks, 'What about Chloe?'

I doubt I'd look more shocked if she asked me to drop my trousers and piss in the middle of the street. I attempt to say 'What?', but what actually comes out is, 'Wuh?'

'She fancies you.'

'Crap, she does. She's one of my best friends.'

'So? Friends have been known to sleep together, you know.'

'Yeah,' I say, coming on all defensive, no doubt sounding guilty as sin, 'well we haven't, all right?'

'And you don't want to? That's the main thing. Not whether you have, but whether you will.'

'I haven't and I won't.'

She leans forward and kisses me. 'Good,' she says with a smile. 'I'm sorry, but I had to ask.'

'Why?'

'Why? Because if you did feel anything for her, then I could never be friends with her. I wouldn't want her within spitting distance of you. You do understand, don't you?'

'Yeah. But it doesn't matter now, does it?'

'No.' She lifts the bottle out of the ice bucket. It's empty. Then she looks at her watch. 'Come on,' she says. 'Max's party. We don't want to be late.'

Party On

Max's party is a relief. A total laxative. A Maxative, no less. Max's party should be bodily advertised on prime time TV as a miracle cure for anal guys like myself who are paranoid about meeting their girlfriend's friends *en masse*.

The moment Max opens the door to his flat, the knot of worries inside my stomach dissolves. He's all smiles and, 'Wow, so this is your new man,' and he doesn't give me the once over I was expecting, but just jams a chilled can of beer into my hand, hugs Amy, shakes my hand and waves us through.

There are probably around sixty people already here. Ages vary: twenties and thirties. I check out the people in the room and feel pretty comfortable. Outwardly, there's nothing to fear: no gathering of Satanists sacrificing goats in the corner; no writhing mass of rubber-clad bodies on the floor. Nothing, in other words, to make me suspect that Amy's anyone other than the person she's been with me.

We stand just inside the door for a few minutes and Amy gives me a quick briefing on the assembled cronies. Then we get stuck in. It's like the Amy & Jack World Tour, with stopovers at all the groups and cliques assembled, and I'm smiling and joking and racking up the names, and Amy's whispering in my ear between groups, filling me in on the gossip. And it's exhausting, I've got to admit. I find myself fighting this urge to grab her and get the hell out. Just for five minutes. Because I am on show here. She's known some of these people since she was a kid. To them, I'm probably just another boyfriend, not a permanent fixture in Amy's life, not like them.

'So what do you think of them?' she asks me, cornering me an hour or so later.

'Most of them are great,' I tell her, looking over her head at the surrounding people, thinking of a few notable exceptions, but generally meaning it.

'Honestly?'

I smile. 'I wouldn't say it otherwise.' Obviously, this is a lie. If I thought they were the biggest group of weirdos outside of the Cuckoo's Nest, I'd still tell her I liked them. Because she's the important one here, not them. And it's important to *her* that I like them.

'Thank God for that.'

'Don't sound so relieved.'

'I am, though.' She frowns. 'Shame H isn't here. I can't believe you still haven't met each other.'

She gazes across the room and I catch her in profile for a

192

moment. The same thought crosses my mind as when I spotted her about half an hour back when I was chatting to her college mate, Sue. Amy was laughing as she talked to some guy by the French windows, and I thought to myself: *You're a lucky man.* Standing here now, it's all I want to tell her. That she's great. That I'm proud of her. That she's made my life a place I really want to be, the kind of place I can envisage building a home in and sitting on the porch and watching the sun go down. I lean across and whisper, 'Kiss me,' in her ear.

'Oh, my God!' she squeals, pulling away from me and pushing me aside.

My first reaction, as I turn and watch her weave through the crowd, is that there's been some sort of malfunction in whatever connects my mind to my mouth and that instead of whispering, 'Kiss me,' I've actually bellowed, 'Fire! Everybody get the fuck out!' This concern, however, lasts just about as long as it takes me to suss that it isn't the doorway that Amy's making a beeline for, but the figure that's just come through it.

As I move a few paces closer to get a clearer view, I realise that 'figure' is a grossly inadequate word to describe what's just appeared. This is no stick-drawing. More like Adonis. He's about six foot three, athletic and tanned, with the sort of thick dark hair and flashbulb smile that belong bang centre in a Chippendales line-up. I glance around the room, but no, it's not there. No flashing neon sign. Nothing at all, in fact, to warn the assembled guys that a Great White Shark has just entered the room and they should grab their womenfolk from the shallows and run for the hills. But maybe they don't need to. Maybe he's already spotted his victim.

Or maybe she's spotted him.

When he catches sight of Amy's rampaging approach, he drops his backpack on the floor and holds out his arms to welcome her. Keep cool. They're probably just old friends, right? There's no reason why you shouldn't be *totally at ease* with the situation. He's got a backpack and a tan, so he's probably just been off travelling and they're pleased to see each other. This is logical. This is OK. This is nothing I should worry about.

And neither should I worry about Amy literally launching herself at him now. Or him catching her smoothly like an old dance partner – just so. These, too, are things I should continue to be *totally at ease* with. Same as her wrapping her legs round his *slim* waist – just there – and her arms round his *broad* shoulders. Same as him spinning her round – like that – supporting her weight by gripping her – right there – with his hands. And the same as him lowering her now and keeping his arms on her as they chat, holding her tight. I should remain *totally at ease*, because I'm secure and confident and happy in my relationship.

It takes me just under three seconds to cross the room and loudly clear my throat in Amy's ear.

When she lets go of him, her eyes are shining, her cheeks flushed. It's the kind of look you sometimes see in movies, the kind that tells you in no uncertain terms that *this* girl likes *this* guy. His arm stays rested territorially across her shoulders as she says, 'Jack, this is Nathan, a really good friend. He's been trekking in Asia for the last six months.' She turns to Nathan. 'And this is Jack.'

'Her boyfriend,' I add, since it's obviously temporarily slipped her mind.

Whatever, this new piece of information has the desired effect on Nathan. He removes his arm from Amy. I assume he's done this because he's about to shake hands with me. Consequently, I hold up my own in readiness. Nathan's hand, however, has more important business to attend to, namely slowly pushing his glistening locks back from his face. With his eyesight cleared, he looks me briefly up and down, before grunting, 'Uh,' and turning his attention back to Amy and checking, 'Jake, right?'

'Jack,' she repeats.

'Uh-huh.' Nathan glances at me, as if to ensure this information checks out, then looks back at Amy once more. 'Boyfriend?'

'Right.'

Time to take control of the situation. Standing here like a

lemon is starting to make me feel sour. I make out that my still-ignored hand was going somewhere by grabbing a bottle of beer from the table next to me. I twist the top and shove it towards Nathan. 'Beer, mate?' I ask, all fresh and friendly, slipping my hand into Amy's and pulling her arm behind my back.

Nathan observes this public show of affection and then looks down his perfectly straight nose at me, again mumbling to no one in particular as he accepts the beer, 'Uh-huh.'

Uh-huh? Who does this guy think he is, fucking Elvis? Not wanting to cramp his style, should the urge to start gyrating his hips whilst whistling Dixie overcome him, I move back a step. Naturally fearing for her safety, too, I take Amy with me. It's only then that *Nelvis* deigns to address me directly.

'So what do you do?' he asks, disinterested. His accent, now he's made the decision to speak in sentences longer than two syllables, is Home Counties via Eton. It's pure money.

'I'm an artist.'

His eyes spark with interest. 'Oh, really?' He glances at Amy knowingly. 'Successful?'

'Yeah,' I say, then, suddenly feeling cautious, I add, 'reasonably so.'

'What's your surname?' he asks. 'Only my father's a collector and he might have some of your work. He encourages a lot of up-and-coming people.'

I tell him, even though I know it won't mean a thing to him – unless, that is, his father's called Willy Ferguson and happens to specialise in commissioning studies in yellow.

He snorts dismissively and announces, 'Never heard of you.'

And that's exactly what I want to say to him. Or, more specifically, to Amy. Just who is this guy? Just how come, if he's such a great mate, you've never mentioned him before?

Amy, as if reading my mind, squeezes my hand and intervenes. 'Nathan and I were at college together.'

What? I feel like asking. *And that makes it OK, him treating me like a piece of shit he's just picked off his shoe, does it?* But I don't say anything, because giving guys like Nathan a reaction is giving them exactly what they want. It's all to do with territory. He fancies Amy. I'm with Amy. He wants me out of the way. So long as I sit tight, there's nothing he can do.

His upper lip curls into what can only be described as a charming sneer. The charm bit's intended for Amy, the sneer's all mine. 'We've known each other for years,' he tells me, pulling rank. 'How about you? How long ago did you meet Amy?'

Correction: Max's party is no longer a relief. It's turned to grief. If this guy's trying to wind me up, then somebody should award him a scholarship. At some Poison Ivy League university. I stare at him with such concentrated hatred that I half-expect lasers to blast from my eyes and frazzle him from existence. Nathan, I decide, isn't just a name. Nathan's far more than that. Nathan's a verb, as in, *I'm terribly sorry, but I appear to have* Nathaned *all over your toilet seat.* And Nathan's a noun, as in, *I knew I shouldn't have had that extra chilli sauce last night, my* Nathan's *on fire.*

I'm not going to say this to his face, though. *I* have manners. *I* don't need to put other people down in order to feel secure within myself. *I'm* also significantly shorter than him. In reply to his question about when Amy and I first hooked up, I therefore mention a rough date and Amy corrects me and starts to tell him the Story of Us. Nathan listens for a while, but it doesn't appear to be a subject he has much interest in. Then this thirtysomething, ponytailed media-type comes over and tells Nathan there's some coke going down in the conservatory.

'I'll catch you later, Amy,' Nathan says with a wink, excusing himself and pushing past me.

Nelvis is leaving the building. Consider me officially all shook up.

'What an arsehole,' I mutter to Amy.

But she's not listening. She's just watching him go.

Round 2 a.m., the party's winding down, and I say goodnight to the people I'm talking to in the living room and go looking for Amy. I come across Nathan in the study at the back of the flat. The smell of dope hangs heavy in the room. A couple of girls are crashed out on the floor, unconscious. Nathan hands a spliff to some guy with dreadlocks, whispers something, and tilts his head towards me. 'Hi . . .' he mumbles, his forehead crinkling into an exaggerated frown. 'I'm sorry. I've forgotten your name.'

'Jack,' I say.

'Oh, yeah – the artist guy.' He blinks heavily, nods to himself. 'Amy's boyfriend.'

'You seen her?' I ask.

He mutters something that sounds like, 'Sure I have. Every last bit of her,' and the guy he's sharing the spliff with rolls on to his side and cracks up laughing.

I take a step closer to Nathan 'What did you say?'

He literally wipes the smile from his face with the back of his hand. 'Nothing, man, nothing.'

I stare at him for a couple of seconds, then turn to go.

'Hey,' he calls out as I reach the door.

I don't turn round. 'What?'

'When you find her, remind her I'm taking her out for dinner Friday night.'

This I ignore. This I ignore and don't ask him to repeat. This I ignore and don't ask him to repeat, because if I don't and he does and he is saying what I think he's saying, I'll be duty-bound to break his fucking nose. He shouts something else after me, but I'm not listening. I just want out.

Now.

I find Amy in the garden and she's pretty wasted and ready to go, so I call us a cab and we sit on the doorstep in silence, waiting for it to rock up. On the way home, she sobers up and asks me if anything's wrong and I tell her no. Then she asks me why I'm being so quiet and I tell her I'm tired. It's not till we're back at hers, with the lights out and the curtains drawn, lying on opposite sides of the bed, that I spit out what's bugging me.

'Were you going to mention it?'

'Mention what?' she asks drowsily.

'That you're going out for dinner with Nathan on Friday.'

'Oh, that . . . yes, of course I was.'

'So how come you haven't?'

'What?'

'How come,' I say *very* slowly and *very* deliberately, just in case part of what I'm saying isn't crystal clear, 'you haven't?'

'I was going to tell you tomorrow. It's no big deal.'

'It is a big deal,' I correct.

'What is?' She sounds confused. I have to admit, I'm genuinely impressed with this show of innocence.

'That some guy walks into the party tonight and you run squealing across the room into his arms like you're Fred and fucking Ginger.'

'I already told you – he's an old friend. What's your—'

'Such an old friend that you forgot to mention him,' I interrupt. 'Fine, so you're best mates with Johnny Depp's *better-looking* brother and you kind of forgot to mention that, too. Despite the fact that only this evening we sat down and went through the process – the very painful process – of telling each other all about our pasts. That's cool, Amy. That's just great. Were I on butt-clenching, groin-grinding greeting terms with the likes of Cameron Diaz and Kylie Minogue, and it slipped my mind, I'm sure you'd be just delirious about it.'

I hear her struggling into a sitting position. She half sighs, half growls. 'I didn't tell you about him because he was out of the country. The first I knew about him being back was when I saw him tonight. I didn't think he was coming back till Christmas.'

'Oh, right,' I say, suddenly enlightened, 'so honesty's now a time issue. You'll tell me things when you deem the time's right. Is that it?'

'You're being ridiculous, Jack. I haven't thought about him for ages. *That's* why I didn't tell you about him.'

'So let me remind myself: you're just good friends with him?'

'Yes,' she snaps, exasperated. 'How many times do I have to say it? He's a *good, close* friend.'

'So you've never slept with him, or anything like that?'

She sighs as if this is the stupidest question in the world, and tries to curl up to me, saying, 'No.'

Great, so now she's not just hiding things from me, she's lying to my face. I push her away.

'How come, then,' I say, 'when I was looking for you at the end of the party, and I asked him if he'd seen you, he cracked some shit joke about having seen *all* of you before? Was he being *ironic* perhaps? Was it some sort of an *in-joke* that I've totally misread? Maybe you guys used to go skinny-dipping as kids and it's all innocent and cool.'

This time, there is a pause.

A long one.

'Okay,' she finally admits, 'I've slept with him.'

'How many times?'

'What does it matter? It was ages ago.' Her voice is becoming shaky.

'Believe me,' I tell her, ' it matters.'

'I don't know, half a dozen times. All right? I went to bed with him half a dozen times when we were students. Happy now? Do you want the details as well? Do you want the dates? Is that what you want?'

'No,' I say quietly. I feel no triumph over having made her admit the truth. I just feel crushed over her lying to me. I just feel sick. 'I want to know why you didn't tell me about him,' I manage to say.

'I told you: because I haven't been thinking about him. Why would I?'

'So why are you going out for dinner with him?'

'I don't still fancy him, if that's what you think,' she asserts. 'I haven't for years. Not since I left college.' I feel her hand touching my arm. I don't respond and her voice becomes more urgent. 'I'm going out for dinner with him because he's a friend and I like him. There's nothing more to it than that.'

I jerk my arm away. 'Yeah? And why precisely not? Because he's, like, really ugly? Because he's, like, not seriously rich and the son of one of the wealthiest men in the country. Shit, yeah, I can understand you not fancying him. I can completely relate to that. Jesus, what have I been worrying about? Of course you don't want to sleep with him. Only a moron would want to sleep with a guy like that.'

'Why are you being like this?'

'Because you've lied to me.'

'I'm sorry, okay? I'm sorry.' Her hand's back on my arm. It's shaking this time and I can't bring myself to push it away.

'Why did you do it? And don't tell me you forgot, or you didn't think it was relevant, or any other crap.' My voice is cold, because my whole body feels cold, because I know that this is how it starts, how every break-up I've ever been in starts: with the death of trust and communication. And I don't want this. I can feel the tears rising in my own eyes. I don't want to lose Amy. Not to Nathan. Not to anyone. I don't want this to happen. At the same time, though, I'm not going to kid myself. I'm not going to settle for a lie. I want it all, or I don't want it at all. 'Just tell me the truth.'

I hear her breathing coming heavy, mixed with the sticky sound of sobs. 'I didn't tell you, because what I'm saying is the truth. There's nothing going on between us.'

'So why was he winding me up? Why would he do that if he wasn't jealous?'

'You saw him. He was coked out of his face. He probably didn't know what he was saying. He's not normally like that.'

We drop into silence for a few seconds, then I say, 'I don't want you to see him. I don't want you to see him on Friday.' She doesn't reply, and so I go on. I ultimatum her. 'If you see him on Friday,' I tell her, 'then I don't know if I want to see you any more.'

There, I think. Run with *that*. But her reaction isn't what I'm expecting. It isn't what I want. There's no, *OK, Jack. You're right. I'm wrong. I won't see Nathan on Friday. I won't see Nathan ever again.* Instead, she just ultimatums me right on back: 'And – and if you want to stop me seeing my friends, then I don't know whether I want this either.'

'Are you telling me you're prepared to break up over me telling you not to see him?' I blurt out, astounded.

'No, but are you telling me you're prepared to break up over me telling you I am going to see him?'

Touché.

We lie in silence, Amy waiting for a response to her question and me trying to arrive at one. It's no easy task. The options are twofold. I can say yes, and break up with her. Or I can say no, and stay with her. And it's a case of Mind vs. Heart. My mind's telling me, *Chuck her. Bin her and get up and get out. She's putting Nathan above you. She's already made her choice, so don't hang around and make an arse of yourself.* But my heart's got another argument. It reads: *Trust her. That's all you've got to do. If you don't trust her, then what you've got means nothing.*

So there it is: trust or bust.

The choice is mine.

I choose the former; I say, 'No.'

'Well . . .' she says.

'Well, it looks like you're going for dinner with Nathan, then.'

'It does, doesn't it? And you're happy with that?'

Happy isn't quite the word I'd choose, but still I say, 'Yes.'

'Good.'

She spoons up against me and, despite my reservations, I suddenly feel warm and secure. As I listen to her breathing arranging itself into a sleep pattern, I consider that this is the first time since I was with Zoe that I've had to trust anyone else. And I realise that while this means surrendering my emotional independence, it also means that I'm no longer alone.

Playing Away

Wednesday's spent hunting round various dodgy travel agents for bargain package holidays in Greece. I eventually discover a deal being offered by a company called FunSun in a one-room office near Paddington. It's a week on the Greek island of Kos, flight leaving from Gatwick this Saturday. OK, so it's not the mainland. The tourist attractions are more likely to be cheesy discotheques than Hellenic architectural triumphs. But what the hell? It's still abroad, isn't it? It'll do.

Mandy, the FunSun sales rep, is somewhat reticent about a few of the finer details of the holiday. Like accommodation, for example, which we'll be told about when we get there. And transport to and from the airport, which we'll find out about on arrival. And proximity to the beach, which, according to Mandy, can't be that far on such a small island, can it? But no matter. Any misgivings I have are soon knocked off by the glossy photos in the brochure that Mandy waves enticingly in front of my face, but won't let me take home. Plus it's cheap. As in chips. Which is the main thing. So I go for it. I sign the disclaimer, prohibiting me from suing FunSun should my holiday turn out to be anything other than funny and sunny. Mandy then gives me the tickets and shows me to the door, locking it behind me and switching the sign round to CLOSED.

Sorted.

Early Friday evening and I'm lying on my bed, watching smoke curl up from my cigarette to the ceiling. I'm feeling a darker shade of blue. My room looks like the aftermath of a plane crash: the contents of my wardrobe and chest of drawers are littered across the floor and bed. In my role as Back of the Wardrobe Investigator, I've uncovered some particularly nasty fashion crimes from the last ten years of my holidaying life: ankle-length surf shorts, gonad-hugging briefs, palm-tree-patterned flip-flops and a baseball cap adorned with the legend I WENT POTTY IN LANZAROTE. But it's not this sight that's getting me down. It's more what I can't see. Amy. And where she is. And what she's doing.

I issued myself with a mental order last night. It was about five in the morning. I was lying next to Amy, round at hers. We'd had a great evening together, starting with some am-dram play one of her mates was in, followed by dinner with the cast, and topped off with a sextathlon back at her flat. She was sound asleep, but I hadn't slept a wink since we'd crashed. Nathan was on my mind. Or rather, Amy and Nathan. The thought of them together. It wouldn't go away, no matter how many times I told myself that I had nothing to worry about. Outside, it was getting light. Blackbirds were making blackbirdy noises and the first commuters were driving past. And here I was, sleepless and stressed. I was desperate. So I issued the order: I commanded myself *not* to think about Nathan. I told myself that whenever he popped into my mind, I was to think of something more pleasant. *Anything*. And it worked: I slept.

And it's working now.

In the last half hour, thoughts of Nathan have soiled my state of well-being on no fewer than eight occasions. In response, I've thought about eight things more pleasant than Nathan. These have included:

a) Bat droppings
b) Lice
c) Dog slobber
d) Haemorrhoids
e) Death

Which, while not exactly making me feel good either, have succeeded in preserving me from a general collapse into mind-melting paranoia. I check my watch. It's seven on the dot. Amy should be meeting up with Nathan right about now. Bastard. I quickly add varicose veins to the More Pleasant Than Nathan list.

'All right,' Matt says, appearing in the doorway. He's dressed in his oldest shirt and jeans: combat clothes for Alex's stag night. 'How's the packing going?'

I flick my empty Gladstone bag with my foot. 'Shit. How about you?'

He pats the toothbrush sticking out of his shirt pocket. 'Travelling light,' he says with a grin, coming over and sitting down next to me on the bed. He lights a cigarette. 'What time are you off?'

'Tomorrow morning. Quarter past nine flight.'

'Yeah? Amy crashing here tonight, then?'

'No, she's out with a friend.'

'What,' Matt laughs, 'and she expects you to make it to the

airport on time on your own? She must be mad.'

'I'll be there.'

My tone of voice causes him to look at me strangely. 'Everything all right, mate?'

'Sure,' I tell him. 'Why shouldn't it be?'

'No reason.' He looks at me sceptically. 'Only you don't exactly sound too thrilled about things. I mean, here you are, blowing out the opportunity of a top stag weekend in Edinburgh, because you're going away instead with the woman of your dreams, and yet you're looking about as happy as a pig in a slaughterhouse.'

'I'm fine,' I tell him. But I'm not. And he's right: I'm not making much sense right now. I want to tell him what's bugging me. I want to tell him all about Nathan, and all about Amy lying to me about him. I want to tell him that I feel insecure, that my ego's at rock bottom and burrowing deeper by the second. But I can't. Because he's my mate. Because I know how gross insecurity looks to other people. Because I don't want his pity. Same as I don't want Amy's. Same as I don't want anybody's. So I do the only thing I can do: I change the subject. 'Look, Matt,' I say, 'I'm sorry.'

'About what?'

'Alex's stag party. About not coming.'

'Forget it.'

'You're not pissed off at me?'

He glares at me. 'Of course I'm pissed off. You've chosen your woman over your mates. You should be shot.' He relents, rests his hand on my shoulder. 'But I'll give you a reprieve – so long as she's worth it, okay?'

'She is.'

'Good. That's all I wanted to hear.' He gets up and walks to the door, then hesitates in the doorway and looks back. 'Oh, yeah,' he says, 'help yourself to some clothes from my room. Dress in any of that shit and she'll drop you out of sheer embarrassment.' He salutes me goodbye, saying, 'Have a good night.'

But I don't. I have a shite night. I manage to kill an hour or

204

so choosing clothes from the Matt Davies Summer Collection and stuffing them into my bag, along with the plane tickets and my passport. After this excitement, though, it's all downhill. It's just me and a bottle of vodka and a jug of freshly squeezed lime juice and the kitchen table. And it's a steep ride down.

As the minutes flick by, and Churchill eyeballs me from the table top, the More Pleasant Than Nathan list grows. By eight-thirty, when Amy and Nathan are probably arriving at whatever overpriced, dick-swinging restaurant he's booked, it's approaching the fifty mark and it's getting kind of obscure. Tooth plaque, for example, has made the list. As have dirty socks and bad breath. By eleven, when they should have finished their post-dinner coffees, I've hit a hundred, and it's becoming plain ridiculous. Tailenders include fish scales, nuclear power stations and mud. And in between all this list making and booze swigging, I'm calling Amy's flat. Repeatedly. But she's not there. She's still with *him*. Midnight comes and goes and I give up on the list altogether, and start repeatedly throwing darts at an imaginary picture of Nathan on the dartboard. I blow out the lime juice, too, plugging direct into the vodka – or what's left of it, anyway.

But then it happens. Just before one. The doorbell goes. And I laugh. I laugh out loud, and if there's a tinge of hysteria to my laughter, then so be it. I'm not proud, just relieved. Right now, all that matters is that Amy's come round to see me, and all this worrying's been nothing but a waste of time.

Having consumed enough premium strength vodka to qualify as a Russian denizen, rather than rushing into the arms of my loved one, I settle for lurching down the hallway to open the front door.

* * *

Confessions: No.5. Infidelity
Place: Matt's house, London.
Time: Now.

I open the front door.

'Hello, Jack.'

'Sally?' I ask. I have to ask, because whoever this willowy female slumped against the doorway is, isn't immediately clear. There's too much blonde hair hanging over her face, too much madly patterned dress covering her body. And this, combined with my alcohol-induced Blur-O-Vision, makes identification almost impossible.

'Hello, gorgeous,' she says, pushing her hair back, revealing that it is indeed Sally McCullen.

I put my hand on her shoulder to steady her. Since I'm far from steady myself, this has the unintended effect of leaving each of us gripping on to the other for support. 'What are you doing here?' I manage to ask.

'What do you think?' She lurches forward and attempts to kiss me.

'You should go home,' I tell her, gently pushing her back.

She stares at me, confused. 'Why?'

This is a good question, and one which my addled brain isn't well poised to deal with right now. She is, after all, cute. And I am, after all, pissed off at Amy. So why, indeed, shouldn't she stay? But the answers to these questions aren't long in coming. Because it would be wrong. Because it's Amy I wanted to be at the door, not Sally.

'It's late,' I mumble, starting to close the door on her. 'I've got to get up early tomorrow. I'm going to bed.'

But she just grins and brushes past me into the hall. I turn and watch her disappearing, shaking my head, confused. Why me? Why now? And, more to the point, why not a couple of months back when I was in a position to oblige her? I close the door, accepting the fact that there's no justice in this world, and follow her through to the kitchen. By the time I get there, she's standing by the cooker, looking round the room. I watch her eyes settle on the vodka bottle.

'You not going to offer a girl a drink?' she asks, her eyebrows raised expectantly. 'You always used to offer me a drink,' she adds slyly, walking over to the table and taking a long swig from the bottle. She looks at me sideways. 'So what's changed? Don't you want me any more?' She takes another swig and pouts at me, leaning back against the table. 'Is that it?'

I remember her lying there in the studio. I remember the curves of her body, the shades of her skin. I close my eyes for a second and will the vision away. Time's moved on. I'm different. Sally's right. I don't want her any more. Just Amy. I just want Amy back safe and sound.

'You're drunk,' I slur. 'I'll call you a cab.'

As I head past her towards the phone, she grabs me, pulling me into her. 'I don't want a cab,' she tells me. 'I want you.'

'I've got a girlfriend, Sally,' I say, suddenly feeling incredibly tired. Too drunk. I want her out of here. I want to go to sleep.

But she hasn't finished. 'So what? When I had a boyfriend, it didn't stop you trying to get me into bed, did it?'

'No,' I admit, 'but you didn't sleep with me then, and I'm not going to sleep with you now.'

She lets go of me and wanders to the sink, fills a glass with water and drains it. 'He's dumped me, you know,' she says, sitting back down and turning to face me. 'Because of what that girl you were with at Chloe's party said. He says I'm a slag, doesn't want anything to do with me.'

'I'm sorry,' I say.

But I'm not. I know she's better off without him. Now, though, might not be the best time to point this out. She may disagree. Or, worse, she may think I'm hitting on her, assume that by my telling her she's too good for him, I'm actually implying she'd be better off with me.

'Was that her – that girl – is she your girlfriend?'

'Yeah. Amy. Her name's Amy.'

'Didn't look your type.'

'How's that?' I ask, glancing at the phone, waiting for an opportune moment to suggest calling a cab again.

'Physically.' She puts her legs up on the table. Her dress slips down over her perfectly toned calves and thighs.

'Well she is,' I tell Sally, starting to get pissed off with her. 'She's great. She's exactly my type.'

'Yeah? So where is she?'

'What?'

'Where is she?' She makes a show of looking round the room before getting up. 'Where is this great woman?' She opens the fridge and wags her finger at it. 'Not in here,' she says, taking out a can of beer, opening it and drinking. She puts the can down. 'What about in here?' she mutters, opening a cupboard and peering inside. She swings round drunkenly to face me, chiming, 'I don't think so . . .'

'She's out.' No sooner have I said this than incontinent old men the world over are celebrating their inclusion on the More Pleasant Than Nathan list.

Sally raises her eyebrows. 'When the cat's away . . .'

I don't even bother asking Sally if she wants to go this time. I've heard enough. I walk to the phone and pick up the receiver, read the cab number off the board. But – maybe because I've done it so many times already this evening that it's the only telecommunications function my fingers are capable of initiating, or maybe it's because I've just noticed from the clock on the wall that it's now gone one – I don't ring the cab company. I ring Amy. I ring Amy and yet again there's no reply. There's no reply because she's still out.

Still out with *him*.

'Before you order me a cab,' I hear Sally saying behind me, 'why don't you turn round and see what you'll be missing. Not,' she continues, as I look over my shoulder, 'that you haven't seen it all before . . .'

She's stepping out of her knickers, the rest of her clothes already discarded.

'I'm going upstairs,' she says, turning her back on me. 'See you in a minute.'

But she doesn't. Not in a minute. And not in an hour. Because I don't move from the kitchen. It's like I'm paralysed. I just sit here, wondering what the hell I'm going to do. I'd be lying if I said I didn't want to. I mean, look at her. Sex personified. And gagging for it. The perfect pull. A once-in-a-lifetime opportunity. But there's Amy. And I meant what I said to Sally: Amy *is*

208

exactly my type. Everything about her. It's 2 a.m. on the dot and I give Amy one last call: again, nothing. OK, so she's still not home, which means she's still out with Nathan. But so what? I don't *know* that anything bad's going on. Anyway, even if she *is* screwing around on me, it doesn't give me the right to screw around on her. This isn't some tit-for-tat kids' game we're playing. The decision to be faithful to her has to be made by *me*.

And I've just made it: I will be.

Sally's lying on her back on the bed when I walk into my room. I set Fat Dog to go off at six, giving me plenty of time to get to Gatwick to meet Amy, then slip into bed next to Sally. She's asleep. Euphemism. She's passed out. For the count. And this is a relief. There's not going to be a scene with her attempting to get it on, while I'm attempting to get her out. All there's going to be is sleep. I'm knackered. I'm drunk. Loneliness washes over me. The need for comfort's almost overwhelming and, even though I know it's stupid and is exactly the kind of action that can be horribly misinterpreted, I snuggle up next to Sally and, careful not to wake her up, fold my arms around her.

I'm woken by a groan.

My own.

I don't move for a minute, just lie here savouring the sensation spreading from my groin across my body. My lips move, forming the word *Amy*. I reach down with both hands and run my hands through her hair. The noise of her movements fill my ears. I shift my hips up towards her, groan again. I feel her tongue flicker and feel myself twitch involuntarily against her. I want her. I want to be inside her. Now. I hook my hands beneath her arms and pull her up my body. Her lips press against mine and I open my eyes and look deep into hers. Then suddenly, just for an instant, I don't know whether I'm coming or going.

But then I do.

And I freak.

Because it's Sally, not Amy, and I realise I've just made the biggest mistake of my life.

* * *

209

8

amy

Jack is two hours late. That's 120 minutes . . . 7,200 seconds.

I know.

I've counted.

Sonia, the FunSun rep, has ticked off everyone else on her clipboard and has tottered off to passport control. I'm left alone by the check-in desk (about to close), desperately searching faces in the other queues around me. Even though my new sandals are busy chewing up my feet, I can't stop myself pacing.

Emotionally, I've covered every angle:

7.15 a.m.: No show = mild amusement (predictable bloke shabbiness)

7.30 a.m.: No show = irritation (duty free shopping time jeopardised)

7.45 a.m.: No show = anger (start of holiday ruined)

8.15 a.m.: No show = worry (danger of missing flight increasing by the second)

8.45 a.m.: Still no show = panic (the plane leaves in under half an hour)

Now I'm just plain frightened.

Jack's dead. There's no other explanation for it. He's been brutally murdered on the Gatwick Express and is lying, unrecognisable, in a pool of blood. The tannoy interrupts my morbid train of thought.

This is the last call for Flight CB003 to Kos. Would all remaining passengers go to gate D46 for boarding.

'Okay God. Listen up,' I mutter aloud before starting again, attempting to be more reverential. 'Dear God. Now I know I haven't been a model specimen of purity and compassion so far, but I'm willing to change. I promise you *right now* that I'll go to church every Sunday if you will please, please, make Jack turn up. Just this one favour. Please.' I look around me desperately. 'And I'll give all my money to Christian Aid.' I grimace at the woman behind the check-in desk. She shrugs at me, looks at her watch and shakes her head. 'I'll become a nun. Will that do?'

'Amy!' I hear Jack's shout before I see him sprinting towards me, tickets flapping in his hand.

Damn! I shouldn't have said the nun bit.

'Sorry, sorry,' he gasps, sweeping past me without so much as a kiss.

'What happened? Where've you been?' I shout, torn between the urge to smother him with relief and the equally strong urge to rugby tackle him.

The woman at the desk looks sceptically at Jack as he rummages frantically through his bag before producing his passport. He takes a moment to catch his breath. The woman checks Jack's passport photo and looks back up at him. I can understand her difficulty equating the well-groomed (and, yes, I must admit, cute) snapshot to the bedraggled, wet-haired mess before her. But then Jack remembers his first-class honours degree from the University of Charm and flashes one of his supersonic knee-trembler grins at the woman.

'Too late to check in your bags, you'll have to take them with you,' she says, reluctantly, but I can tell she's won over. 'You'll have to hurry.'

'Thanks,' smiles Jack. 'Come on,' he orders, hoisting the strap of his bag on to his shoulder. I can barely lift mine. Despite H's advice, it contains practically every item of clothing I possess in it, along with half of Boots. Jack doesn't notice. He's already halfway across the hall, barging through the holidaymakers.

'Jack! Wait!' I yell, but he doesn't.

As life is operating by the principles of Sod's Law this morning, the boarding gate is the furthest one from the baggage check. I spend several minutes trying to flag down one of the buggies that are ferrying around fat blokes with golf bags. Surely my need is greater? They all look like they could do with some exercise.

But it's no use. It's official: the age of chivalry is dead. I start my waddling run after Jack, who is clearly in earnest training for the London Marathon. Approximately five miles later and still only a third of the way to the gate, I collapse on the moving walkway. My heart is pounding in my throat.

'Come on! Get up,' yells Jack. He has the audacity to sound cross. 'We'll miss the flight.'

'I can't, I . . .' I'm gasping for breath. 'My bag, it's . . .'

I slide towards Jack and he yanks it from me. 'Amy! What've you got in here?'

'Bricks,' I yelp, as I'm deposited on to the carpet.

'Bricks?' he asks, as he heaves up my bag on to his other shoulder.

'To build the fucking hotel!' I sneer, wanting to kill him. I pull off my sandals and stand up. I've got a stitch the size of the Bayeux Tapestry.

Sonia tuts loudly as we lunge through the concertina walkway on to the airplane. Her deep orange tan has a green tinge in the light. 'You won't be able to sit together,' she announces, before snapping on her smile. 'Enjoy your FunSun holiday.'

Momentarily I can see what she'd look like with her front teeth kicked in.

Jack and I are sitting opposite each other across an aisle. I struggle into THE MOST economic of economy class seats in aviation history and wedge my bag into the footwell.

My heels are shredded, my shoulders aching and I'm panting like a thirsty bloodhound, so it takes me a moment to realise that the seat next to me is occupied by the Toddler From Hell. A gene pool sampler from Satan himself. He grins at me demoniacally, before opening his mouth and emitting a scream so loud that for a moment I think that even the wings of the plane might curl themselves up over the top in protection.

'Oi! Shut up!' yells the bottle blonde in the window seat, as I recoil with horror. She rummages around in the pink sports bag at her feet and produces a dummy. She wipes it up and down on her stone-washed denim mini skirt before cramming it into the kid's mouth. 'Any more nonsense, Darren, and you're out of the window,' she snarls, looking like she means every word. 'Do you understand?'

Darren promptly flobs the dummy into my lap and pukes up lumpy orange juice over my arm. Remind me to have my fallopian tubes tied in a childproof knot.

Usually I love flights. I love the rubbish food and all the parcels and packages they give you with it. I love the naff, duty free teddies and the pointless articles in the airline magazines. I love the air-conditioning nozzles and the headset channels. I love the bottles of pongy perfume in the loos and the pedal taps. I love the double whammy excitement of take-off and landing. I even love the occasional bit of fairground turbulence to spice things up a bit.

But today I hate it. I hate everything about this stinking, lousy airplane. Flight AMY1 to Fantasy Island has crashed and burned.

There are no survivors.

It's a bit of a bummer, because I've been planning our trip there for days. I had it all worked out: the romantic early morning meeting at Gatwick like illicit lovers, the lingering smooch around duty free, the giggling and cuddling as Jack spends a fortune on my favourite perfume. I'd seen us strolling hand in hand on to the plane and snuggling up together by some private window seat. I'd even gone as far as assuming that we'd have sex in the toilets and join the Mile High Club.

And that was just for starters.

However, the slushy seventies soundtrack accompanying my fantasy trip now stops with a terrible scratch.

'So? Why were you so late?' I ask Jack icily, once I've mopped up.

He adjusts his bag by his feet. 'Hangover.'

!

'I see.' I clear my throat. 'What were you doing last night?'

'I could ask the same of you,' he retorts, as one of the air hostesses shimmies between to perform the safety routine. I crane forward to look around the striped skirt stretching over her buttocks. Jack ignores me, taking his seatbelt and following the air hostess mechanically, as he clasps it together and tightens it.

I lean back, ducking out of the way as she motions to the emergency exits. 'What's that supposed to mean?' I hiss.

Jack gets out his Walkman from his bag and stuffs the foam ends into his ears. 'I called you last night, through until two this morning. Nice dinner was it?'

'I was at H's,' I protest, far too loudly, frantically trying to get Jack's attention.

The air hostess is in mid-mime. She's doing the whistle on the life jacket bit. When I raise my voice, she accidentally blows and the shock of the shrill blast sets Darren off. He's obviously not going to be outdone on his personal quest to conquer the sound barrier.

Jack raises his eyebrows at me, then presses play, deliberately cutting off my chance to explain. I watch him smirk at the air hostess and he closes his eyes. He's asleep before we've even taken off.

'How could you?' I scream in silence. 'Just because you couldn't get hold of me on the phone, you assume I was with Nathan. What did you think, Jack, that I was shagging him all night? Is that it? You're so insecure and jealous that you can't trust me for five God-damned minutes?'

I suck in my cheeks, fold my arms and scowl at my fold-down table. I'm aware that my indignant outburst would make a good audition piece for the diva in a daytime soap, but I'm not put off. I let rip with my argument, my foot tapping ominously.

214

'Go ahead then, you moody, irritating, vindictive, insecure git. Ruin my holiday. Turn up late, just to punish me. See if I care. You can play your small-minded, pathetic games all you like. Nathan means nothing to me . . .'

I'm halfway through my vitriol when it occurs to me that Jack hasn't mentioned Nathan. He suspects, that's all. And I'm acting every inch of the guilty party he thinks I am.

I give up and slump into misery.

When the breakfast arrives, I refuse it. Instead, I watch Demon Darren flick scrambled egg at his mother. I check the back of his head to see whether he's got 666 tattooed behind his ear.

The truth is that it was Nathan, not me, who did the dirty last night. I'd been looking forward to seeing him. I was determined that Jack's ridiculous paranoia was not going to become the marker for my social life. After all, my social life has been around a lot longer than Jack.

I'd waited almost an hour before Nathan showed up at the bar in Soho. I don't know why I bothered to be on time, or why I felt so nervous sitting there. One of Nathan's trademarks is his unfailing ability to be late.

'I've got a date with this amazing girl,' he smouldered, as finally I felt his hand on my shoulder and his lips on my cheek. A flattered flush ran through me. After all, I had spent an hour getting ready. 'She's exquisite,' he continued, as he straddled the stool next to me at the bar.

Despite myself, I could feel myself patting my hair. 'Oh Nath,' I tutted, smiling as I reached out and pushed his knee. I'd forgotten how piercing his green eyes could be.

'Marguerite,' he whispered dreamily. 'She's Spanish, and so . . .' He paused for effect. 'I'm telling you. This could be the one.' At this point, he ordered two glasses of champagne, whilst I hastily brushed down my ego from its slip on the banana skin of my vanity.

'Great, Nathan! That's great!' I trilled, smiling tightly and remembering in a rush of *déjà vu* all the reasons that I'd never got it together with him in the first place.

'I'm taking her clubbing. So I won't be able to do dinner. You don't mind, do you?' he asked, not waiting for an answer. 'Look at you, anyway. All in love with what's-his-face. It's so sweet.'

I let him talk on, oohing and aahing at the anecdotes of his latest trip round the Himalayas. I hardly said anything, but as I went round to H's after he left me at the bar an hour later, I wished I had.

I wished I'd had the guts to stick up for my relationship with Jack instead of letting Nathan patronise it. I wished I'd told him that the way he chases beautiful women and falls in and out of love every two seconds isn't impressive. I wished I'd told him that he's not roguish and irresistibly charming, as I thought he once was, but immature and patently scared of commitment. I wished I'd told him to treat people with more respect and to stop being such a selfish brat. I wished I'd told him that standing me up was rude and insensitive. But most of all I wished I hadn't gone to meet him in the first place.

However, the necessary humility required to tell Jack how stupid I feel as a result can't be achieved on a plane full of FunSun holiday makers. It'll have to wait until we get to the hotel.

I glance over at my dishevelled and incommunicative travelling companion. He's snoring quietly and, for a moment, I feel tremendously relieved. The thought of another show-down makes me feel like hurling myself at the pilot and begging him to do a U-ey, so that I can run away to join a nunnery after all.

All I want is for things to be simple.

My life was so easy when I was in the Gobi desert of single-ness. There were no rows, no tantrums or misunderstandings. So, I might have been bored occasionally, but at least I knew where I stood. There was me, and there was me: we under-stood each other perfectly. Now I spend all my time in a com-plex tangle of emotions, constantly trying to justify myself.

Take H, for example. She wouldn't speak to me after she'd found out that I'd been to Chloe's barbecue. I spent all of last week leaving messages for her and worrying. I even wrote a postcard to her, but she still refused to communicate. In the end, I knew I had to see her. I'm too superstitious to leave the country knowing there was bad feeling between us. So last night, having left Nathan, I sloped round to her flat.

She wasn't having it when I stood on the doorstep saying 'Sorry' thirty times without drawing breath.

'Don't you think you owe me some honesty?' she asked, grabbing the bottle of wine I was holding out as an olive branch. I stopped mid-sorry. She's *really* scary when she's angry.

'How do you think I feel?' she continued, as I followed her sheepishly into the flat.

'Like you want to tear out my throat and garrotte my boyfriend?' I ventured.

H wasn't in the mood for humour. 'Something along those lines,' she said. She picked up the zapper and paused the *Friends* video. I knew then that she was serious. 'Does the word "respect" mean anything to you?' she asked, not offering me a seat.

Of course it does. H's respect means everything to me. I couldn't have a stand-up row with her, so I crumpled on to the bean bag and fessed up. I told her about how lying to her about being ill made me feel ill, about how I felt torn between her and Jack, about how I messed things up at the barbecue and how I'd been feeling dreadful ever since.

She listened until I'd eaten so much humble pie I wanted to throw up.

Eventually, she folded her arms and shook her head at me. 'When I said respect, I meant self-respect, you idiot,' she said, flooring me with her sympathetic tone. 'I don't care what you do, as long as you do what *you* want. You don't have to please me, or anyone else for that matter. Your sense of yourself is one of your best qualities, Amy. Don't lose it now, just because you've fallen in love.'

'How do you know I've fallen in love?' I asked, flabbergasted. She's never even met Jack.

'The truth's the truth. Sometimes it's very obvious,' she replied.

She had to forgive me then, because I started weeping. Weeping seems to be one of my new special skills. It's not one I knew I had before and it occurs to me that maybe I should use it to better effect. Maybe I should audition for one of those Hollywood romantic comedies where the only acting ability the heroine requires is to blub in every scene. I could make a fortune!

I don't know why I started to cry. It was just such a relief that H understood how I felt: that I am a Woman In Love and therefore, to some extent, my behaviour is understandable.

'Stop it,' tutted H, as she poured me a large glass of wine.

'I'm sorry,' I sniffed.

'And stop apologising. It's all right.' She kissed me on the cheek and thrust the glass of wine into my hand.

I knew then that everything was back to normal, especially when she sat down and said, 'You *stupid* cow.'

'God, I've missed you,' I laughed, crawling on to the sofa to curl up next to her.

She clinked glasses with me. 'Come on then, blockhead, spill the beans. I want to know everything.'

So, over the next few glasses of wine, I told her everything. I told her about my job, about Jack, about Nathan and the party and eventually about the holiday. We had so much to talk about that it was two a.m. before we stopped.

'It's late, you'd better call lover boy,' yawned H. 'Tell him you're staying the night.'

'I can't stay. I've still got things to pack!'

She waggled her finger at me and licked the red wine crust on her lips. 'You always take far too much. All you need is two pairs of knickers – wear a pair, wash a pair – a bikini and a couple of dresses. You'll be laughing.'

I leant down, picked up the phone, feeling guilty as I punched in Jack's number. I should've called him earlier.

H stretched like a cat. 'You can get a cab in the morning. Not there?'

'Engaged.' I replaced the receiver.

'Don't worry about it. You've got a whole week of him,' she said.

Whoopee do.

There's a spontaneous round of applause from my fellow passengers as the plane finally lands in Greece after an hour's delay. I don't join in. I'm not in a jubilant mood. My feet are swollen, my eyes are puffy and I've dehydrated into a prune.

Jack, on the other hand, looks refreshed as he steps into the blanket of heat at the top of the steps. I break out into a full-scale, all-over body sweat as he sniffs the air approvingly.

'Weather's okay,' he says – as if the meteorological conditions are somehow a personal victory.

Sonia ushers us into the terminal. I'm not fooled by Jack's remarks about the weather. When Hamlet said that there was something rotten in the state of Denmark, he should have tried Kos.

By the time we've got through customs, waited for everyone else to collect their luggage and taken our seats on a coach that would be refused entry into even the dodgiest scrapyard, we've lapsed into silence. In terms of sulking, we've reached a stalemate. When you've got intimate knowledge of the smell of someone's genitals, pretending to be strangers doesn't work. It's like sitting an exam when you haven't revised.

I take in the sights of Kos through the splintered, filthy glass and chew my cuticles. I'm in a sort of holiday hell trance.

Fantasy Island, this most definitely ain't.

By the time the coach finally shudders to a halt in the main resort, my eyes have glazed over. It's only lunchtime, but there are plenty of people milling about. Judging from the high incidence of raw sunburn, they're mostly British. They must be. Why else would they be oblivious to the thumping music coming out of the Bulldog pub on the corner?

The feedback from the coach microphone is deafening as Sonia grabs her clipboard.

This is her moment.

'One two. One two,' she announces in a sing-song voice, as if she's compèring the Royal Variety Performance. 'All right everybod-ee! This is Villa Stephan-o. Welcome to your FunSun holi-day.'

Sure enough, sprouting above the pub and the shops, there's a building that could just about pass as a hotel, even though the grey concrete balconies look as if they have been squashed on to it as an afterthought. Rusting steel rods poke out of the top, waiting for the next floor to be built. The two workmen on the roof, leaning against the broken Villa Stephano sign, are smoking cigarettes. They eye us tourists suspiciously.

This *must* be a drop-off point. Jack *can't* have booked *us* into this dive.

Can he?

Sonia is still busy roll-calling names. The Russell family next to us, all in matching red soccer strips, bustle down the gangway towards her, arguing about the fluorescent plastic sombrero that the youngest is wearing. It's far too big and he can't see. He crashes into all the seats, spilling his can of Coke, as he's shouted forward by his irate father. Following closely behind is Demon Darren. He's carried sideways under his mother's arm like a rugby ball, squirming and dribbling green goo.

I realise that Russell comes after Rossiter in the alphabet and that Sonia hasn't mentioned us.

Phew, we're off to the posh resort.

But then, my worse than worst fears are realised. Trust Sonia not to know her alphabet.

'Come on, this is us,' says Jack.

I yo-yo my head between the view of Alcatraz and the view of Jack's navel as he reaches up to grab our bags.

No.

It can't be.

We're in Greece. This is my holiday. And if this is my holiday, there are simple bare necessities, such as:

- Remote, detached, balconied apartment

220

- Large double room with en suite bathroom
- 360-degree view of the sea
- No other tourists in a five-mile radius
- Easy access to romantic, reasonably priced, family-run tavernas
- At least one deserted beach to claim for duration of one's stay

I've seen the TV holiday programmes. *I know my basic consumer rights*.

What's going on?

Leaving Jack to organise things, that's what's going on. Jack, who couldn't organise a shag in a brothel.

The football kids are already running riot in the reception area of Villa Stephano by the time we've booked in and have been handed our FunSun holiday schedules. KARAOKE EVERY NITE – LIVE reads a big sign above me.

Live?

I'll be dead by the end of this.

There's no light in the corridor on the fourth floor. I stand in the dark by an abandoned bag of cement whilst Jack fumbles with the lock to our room. There's an overpowering smell of mould. After two minutes of fiddling, Jack growls in frustration and flings his weight against the door. It swings open and he stands aside to let me pass. As I do, a cockroach scuttles in the opposite direction.

Great. Even the cockroaches can't wait to get out!

'It's not that bad,' says Jack defensively, as if reading my thoughts.

Well no. The slums of Calcutta are bad.

I place my bag on the floor and slowly look around. The two single beds are separated by a stand with a broken lamp on it. Crammed against the wall is an oversized table. It has a cracked vase on it and I put my hand out to finger the dusty plastic flowers.

'Thoughtful touch,' I manage, wanting to hurl them across the room.

Jack opens the window on to the balcony and looks out at the stunning view of the building next door.

Perfect.

And so close.

In a second, the room is filled with the heady aroma of frying food and rancid drains.

I glare at Jack before retreating to the bathroom to calm down. I sit on the toilet seat and count to twenty. Breathe. Come on. Deep breaths. You can handle this.

Jack's unpacking his bag when I come out.

'All right?' he asks.

No. I'm not *all right*. You've brought me to the worst holiday destination in the known universe and I'm truly gob-smacked at what a cheapskate you are, I feel like saying. However, I don't because I'm a mature adult. Instead, I sulk. But next to Jack, I'm clearly an amateur.

'Jack?' I ask eventually.

'Yep?'

'Are you going to talk to me?'

'I am, aren't I?'

I'm determined not to give up. 'Come on. It's ridiculous having this atmosphere between us.'

'What atmosphere? I'm not the one creating an atmosphere.'

I put both hands to my head and push my hair back. 'Will you sit down for a moment?'

Jack chucks his T-shirt on the bed and sits in the chair. He folds his arms and pouts. He looks like a dodgy criminal being questioned in a police station.

'I was really worried when you didn't turn up this morning,' I start.

'I told you. I had a hangover,' he interrupts. 'I was up drinking with Matt.'

'I thought Matt was at a stag do.'

'He went at about eight.'

'So what did you do?' I know I'm sounding like the Spanish

Inquisition, but I can't help it. What he's said doesn't add up.

'I stayed up drinking alone.' Jack looks up at me, his eyes narrowed scornfully.

'You got drunk because you couldn't get hold of me?'

'I got drunk, Amy, because I wanted to.'

The bitterness of his tone startles me. 'Oh Jack, you're thinking the wrong thing,' I say. 'I mean, what I think you're thinking isn't actually what—'

'Just spit it out. Whatever you want to say, just say it.'

'There isn't anything to say. You *know* I saw Nathan last night.' Jack looks away and sucks in his cheeks. 'But only for a few drinks,' I continue. 'Not even dinner. I left him at half past nine because he had a date with another girl at a nightclub. So I went to H's.'

'How gutting for you.'

'Jack, *please*. I'm telling you the truth. I wanted to see Nathan to catch up. Nothing happened between us. I told you. He's a friend. Like Chloe is your friend.'

'I've never shagged Chloe,' he reminds me.

We stare at each other for a moment and I know I've lost. I have no choice but to dismount from my moral high horse. I let my hands fall to my sides. 'Jack, I'm sorry. I shouldn't have gone. I realised that when I saw him.'

'Very platonic and innocent, was it?' His voice is dripping with scorn.

'Yes it was.'

'You could have called me.'

'I know. I meant to, but I lost track of the time. Then I did call you from H's. It was two o'clock. Your phone was engaged.'

Jack rubs his eyebrow with the heel of his hand. 'Well, that all sounds very plausible to me.'

'It's true!' I protest. 'Ring H, if you don't believe me.'

'There's no need. I'm sure she'll back you up.'

I grab his arm. 'Jack.' I force him to look at me, but he turns his head away and I drop my hand away from his arm. I can feel the tears swelling in my chest.

'This isn't fair. I'm not putting up with you punishing me

223

when I've done nothing wrong.' I look up at the ceiling and laugh bitterly. 'You know the ironic thing? *I* trust me. When I saw Nathan, the only thing I could think of was you and how much I'm committed to you. I shouldn't have gone because I knew you didn't feel okay about it. I was being stubborn, Jack. I admit it and I'm sorry. But I've done nothing wrong. I wouldn't do anything to hurt you. I thought you knew that.'

I have to get out of here before I suffocate. I pick up my bag.

'Amy, wait.' Jack stands up and leans against the door to bar my exit. 'I'm sorry. Okay? I don't want you to go.'

I try to stop my chin trembling as he gives me his explanation, but it won't. It's just as I suspected: Jack overslept. I spent two hours this morning squeezing myself through an emotional mangle and all the time he was asleep!

Sometimes, I really hate men.

'Do you want to go?' he asks.

I shake my head and let my bag drop to the floor. 'No! All I want is for today to start all over again,' I blurt.

'I'm sorry, I'm sorry,' whispers Jack, enfolding me in his arms. He plants kisses in my hair as he rocks me. After a while, he pulls me down on to the bed, yanking the blanket over the top of us.

'Close your eyes,' he murmurs in a hypnotist's voice. 'In a moment the alarm will go off. When it does, you will wake up and remember nothing about the last few hours. You will experience a feeling of lightness, of calm and tranquillity. Your boyfriend will have ceased being a wanker, your holiday will begin with joy and laughter, your sense of humour restored. Brrrrrrrrrrrrrrrrrrrrrrrrrrring!'

'Okay, okay!' I laugh, pulling the blanket away, gasping for oxygen. I kneel up and straddle him.

'I'm sorry,' he says again. He looks back to normal. He looks like my Jack.

'Me too.'

'Friends?'

'Friends,' I nod, before lifting up his T-shirt. I shuffle backwards and lean down to kiss his stomach. I can feel his muscles tense as I turn my face and rest my cheek on his skin. I breathe in his smell, relief overwhelming me.

'What's that?' I ask, noticing a red mark near his belt. I put my finger on it.

'What?' asks Jack, sitting up abruptly. He looks horrified as he pulls the skin of his stomach taut and looks at the mark.

'Don't worry,' I say, laughing at his vanity. 'It won't spoil your tan. It's probably just a mark from carrying the bags.'

I push him back down on the bed and kiss the red blotch, before repositioning my head. Jack feels tense and I can tell he's staring at the ceiling.

'Are you thinking what I'm thinking?' I ask.

'I dunno. What are you thinking?'

'That this is the worst hotel room I've ever been in.'

'No, I wasn't thinking that.'

'What then?'

Jack sits up and swings his feet off the bed. 'Food. I'm starving.'

Jack's hypnotist's skills work. After a massive breakfast, our good humour is restored fully. He announces a holiday policy of maximum fun, minimum time in the hotel room. At first, I'm reluctant and beg him to change hotels. In *Fantasy Island*, we would've spent every afternoon in bed, lazing around in air-conditioned bliss, before drinking Martinis on our private beach at dusk. But Jack's not familiar with *Fantasy Island*. He won't hear of moving. Actually, I don't know what's got into him, but he won't hear of anything. Jack is . . . Motor Mouth.

'Sod the hotel. I know it's basic, but that's the point, we'll use it as a base. Let's explore. It'll be fun,' he gushes.

'But—'

'Oh no. *Please* don't tell me you're one of those girls who wants to spend every day on the beach reading soppy novels? Please, please, please. Tell me you're cooler than that.'

'I—'

'It's settled then. We'll hire a moped and we'll go and see

225

what there is to see. I mean, there must be places to see. This is Greece. Birthplace of art. This is myths and temples and stuff.' He waves his arms around and grins at me maniacally.

'But Jack—'

'And you mustn't worry about me driving. It's fine. Because I know sometimes safety is an issue, but I'm very safe. I promise you.'

'I wasn't—'

'Excellent. Let's go,' he says, standing up and holding out his hand.

I look at him quizzically. 'Are you okay?'

'Totally. Never finer. Raring to go.' He grabs my hand and my fingers automatically fold through his. He closes his eyes for a second as he kisses my knuckles. 'You'll see. This'll be the best holiday, I promise.'

After a while, Motor Mouth calms down, but I'm still conscious that something is different about him. It's not that he's odd towards me – he couldn't be more flattering or tactile – but for three whole days we don't have sex. He treats me as if I'm his playmate, not his lover. It could be to do with the fact that we arrive home each night exhausted. Single beds and sunburn don't help either. But still there's a nagging doubt that he doesn't believe me about Nathan.

I decide to go along with it and not to push the issue. He's a bloke. And if I know Jack, it's only a matter of time before his hormones get the better of whatever's bugging him. Besides, there are fringe benefits to this period of abstinence. Because Jack and I talk. Really talk. And we have fun. The space that we would otherwise have filled having sex is filled with exploration. Not just of the island, with all its fragrant olive groves and dusty tracks, but of each other. Jack may not give me his body, but he gives me something far more valuable in those first few days. He gives me information. Over the jugs of sangria in the small tavernas we find, he tells me about his ideas for his pictures and how he hates having to do commercial commissions to keep himself financially afloat. By the time we drive back to the hotel each night, I've fallen for him a little bit more.

But on the fourth day, everything changes. Because on the fourth day, our quest for the perfect beach is over. We both spot the small cove at the same time from the coastal road and for ages we can't work out how to get there. Eventually, we abandon the moped and climb down through the rocks, until we find some rough steps cut into the cliff.

When we get to the bottom, it takes my breath away.

Fantasy Island, eat your heart out. This is paradise.

Within seconds we've stripped off and we're racing each other into the sea. The water is turquoise blue and so clear I can see my toenails. Jack dives under the surf and comes up from beneath me, grabbing me as he surfaces. It's the first time our bodies have been in such intimate contact for days. I hook my legs around his waist. His eyelashes are clumped together and his eyes sparkle in the reflection of the water. I smile at him.

'This is gorgeous,' I sigh, looking back towards the shore. There's not a soul in sight.

'*You're* gorgeous,' he replies.

I push my hand back through his hair and kiss him gently. I can't stand it any more. This abstinence thing is killing me. Anyway, it might be dangerous. Perhaps you can damage yourself permanently if you go around feeling this horny.

'Come with me,' I whisper, pulling him back through the water.

'Where are we going?' asks Jack.

I've seen *10*. I've seen *Against All Odds*. I'm determined to have sex in the shallows. Even if it means rape.

But it's not rape. It's as far from it as you can get. When we start kissing, the waves lapping at our legs, I can feel something change in Jack. It's as if all the passion he's been holding back for the last few days is released. I don't know how many times we've had sex since we've been together, but they all pale into insignificance compared to this.

Jack makes love to me. As if he's all my idols rolled into one. And it might be sandy and it might be too hot, but when we come together, it's catapulted up there into the number one slot.

This is my best shag. EVER.

'Wow!' gasps Jack, when our senses finally come back to earth. He kisses my eyelids, my nose and my cheeks, as if I'm the most precious thing in the world to him. I touch his face and he opens his eyes. That's when I feel it rush through me like adrenalin.

Jack's eyebrows knit together. He looks as if he's about to cry as he pushes a sandy rat's tail of hair out of my face. 'Amy, I . . .' he starts.

'Shhh.' I smile, putting my fingers to his lips. Because for once, there's no need for him to say it. Because I know.

The next couple of days are spent in beach bliss. Late one after-noon when we get back to the room Jack massages moisturiser all over me. I feel so relaxed that before I know it I've fallen asleep, naked on the bed.

I wake to a soft scratching noise.

'Don't move,' says Jack.

My whole body tenses. 'Please tell me it's not a spider!'

Jack laughs. 'No. Just stay still, I'm nearly finished.'

'Finished what?'

'Wait and see.'

The scratching noise continues for a while and then I hear Jack coming to the bed and sitting down next to me.

'Is it all right if I move now?'

'Yeah,' he says, and I roll over to face him. 'Here you go.' He hands me a piece of paper.

I stare down at the pencil drawing he's done of me. It's won-derful.

'Do you like it?' he asks.

I reach over and kiss him. 'I love it. How long did it take?'

'I don't know. You've been asleep for about half an hour. '

I look back down at the sketch. Do I really look this happy when I'm asleep?

Jack is watching my face. 'I haven't done you justice. You looked so beautiful.' He reaches out and strokes my cheek.

The thought of him painting Sally flashes through my head, and I can't help wondering if he was this intimate with her.

'I bet you say that to all the girls,' I tease, but fail to conceal the edge to my voice.

'There aren't any other girls. Not any more. Just you.'

I put the drawing down on the table and pull him towards me and we lie together on the bed. I believe him. Fully. I believe he's mine and, as I breathe him in, I've never felt so content.

We kiss and I fondle his hair. 'Thank you,' I whisper. 'Come on, I'm going to treat you to dinner.'

Jack smiles at me and sits on the edge of the bed. I watch him as he pulls on his shirt. I pick up the drawing again. I can't decide whether to kiss it, or kiss him, they both mean so much.

A week is never enough for a holiday. Everyone knows that. But I only remember when Friday comes around in about five minutes. I'm just relaxing, I've just got a good tan, and we've got to go home. It's not fair.

On our last night, we dress up and have dinner at our favourite taverna.

'Stop sulking,' teases Jack, as he pours me some retsina.

'I don't want to go back, ' I moan. We're sitting on the terrace above the bay. The only light comes from the candle on the checked tablecloth and the full moon hanging like a lantern above us.

'Yes you do,' he laughs. 'You've got the new job to look forward to and a top tan to show off. You'll love it, once you're back.'

The waiter comes and we chat for a while. He asks us about our holiday and we tell him it's been amazing. He gives us a big show of disappointment when we tell him we're going home tomorrow.

When he's gone, we both lean on the wooden balustrade and look out at the canopy of stars.

'You're right,' sighs Jack, eventually. 'Let's just pack everything in and stay here permanently.'

'You're on,' I say, sitting up and turning round to face him.

'We'll find a villa up in the mountains. You can spend all your time dedicated to growing warts and a moustache,' he jokes, 'and I can make sculptures out of goat dung.'

'What if we get bored of each other?'

'Well if we do, there's always the goats for me. And I'm sure there'll be lots of young fishermen happy to attend to your needs.'

'Excellent. Let's stay.' I lean over and kiss him.

'It wouldn't work. I'd have to keep you locked up, just for me,' he whispers.

I hold his hand against my cheek. 'Thank you for keeping your promise.'

'Which promise was that?'

'To give me the best holiday.' I kiss his palm. 'It has been.'

Jack puts his finger on my nose and smiles. 'Hey you. Don't get soppy on me, we've got a feast to eat yet.'

We drink two carafes of wine before we notice that it's gone midnight. I'm as stuffed as the stuffed vine leaves I've consumed.

'We should go back,' says Jack eventually, when the waiter hands us our bill. As usual, we're the last to leave.

'I don't want to.'

'What are you talking about? We can't miss the FunSun disco. Anyway, I want to try my hand at the karaoke.'

'You don't,' I laugh.

'Didn't you know? You're looking at the Karaoke King.'

'What would you sing?' I ask.

'"Summer Nights" – *obviously*.'

On the way back to town, I hum it as I rest my cheek against Jack's back. I'm so happy, feeling the warm breeze through my hair, that it takes me a while to notice that we're on the wrong road.

'Where are we going?' I ask, sitting up, as Jack turns off down a track.

'You'll see,' he says, stopping the bike and pushing down the stand.

He leads me through some rocks, until we come out on to the cliff top. 'I had to have one last look,' he says. Below us, framed between two olive trees, is our beach. I've never seen it from this angle before. I stand, mesmerised by the moon and the silver shimmer of the water. Jack stands behind me and puts his arms around my waist. I breathe in, the air thick with scent and the sound of cicadas.

This is perfect.

At last. I've found the 'it' I've been looking for.

'Jack?' I whisper.

'Hmm,' he says. I can feel him bury his nose in my hair.

'Do you feel it too?' I ask.

'What?'

I can feel my heart thumping. 'That this is right. That we should be together. That this is serious?' I can't believe I've said something so important, but I mean it. More than anything I've ever said.

Jack squeezes me tighter and his head drops to my neck. I reach up and fondle his hair, but he takes my wrist to stop me. I turn around to look at him, taking in the features of his face and the way the moonlight falls across his cheekbone. I know that he's about to say it. This is better than any of the movie moments I've had in mind. My knees are trembling as I hold my breath. 'I think we should go,' he says, not looking at me.

'What?'

He lets go of my wrist. He still doesn't look at me. 'It's late. We'd better get going.'

I sit behind Jack on the bike, barely daring to hold on.

I just don't get it.

Why? That's what I want to know.

What's so wrong with me?

I thought everything was great. We get on brilliantly, we

make each other laugh, we have great sex, but still it's not enough for him to be able to tell me that he cares.

Perhaps I pushed him too far. Perhaps the thought of us being together frightens him. Perhaps he's not ready. Or perhaps he doesn't think I'm the one for him. Perhaps I've got it all wrong. Perhaps he wants more. But how can I be more? I've given him as much of me as I can. There isn't any more to give.

So what do I do? Dump him? Shrug it off and carry on our relationship on a non-serious basis? Try to change?

I can't work out how we've reached this crisis point. How can everything be perfect one minute, and ruined the next? I don't understand. What have I done?

There's such a barrage of questions in my head that I don't notice that Jack has been steadily speeding up.

'Slow down!' I yell, gripping him tightly as he takes the last corner before the descent to the town. We swerve out into the road, but the angle of the curve is too tight. I can feel Jack tense as he squeezes the brakes.

'Watch out!' I gasp, but it's too late.

The next thing I know, I'm lying on the ground, my arms stretched out in front of me. It feels sandy. My elbows hurt. Everything is very quiet and dark.

'Amy?' I can hear Jack's choked scream, but I feel very disorientated. 'Amy? Are you all right?'

I can't speak. Jack is crouching down next to me. He looks terrified. 'Put your arms around my neck,' he whispers, lifting my arms and putting them around him. He lifts me until I'm standing. It's then that I notice that he's crying, and that I'm supporting him.

'Jack?' I croak. 'Are you okay?'

'I thought I'd killed you,' he sobs. 'I thought I'd killed you.'

'Shh,' I say, holding his shoulders, so that he can see me. 'See, I'm fine.' He's shaking his head madly and it starts to frighten me. 'Jack, calm down. Everything is all right. We've fallen off, but it's okay. I'm fine.'

232

Jack's gasping for breath. He puts his hands up to his head and grabs clumps of his hair. 'You don't understand. There's something I've got to tell you. It's been eating me up. Ever since you asked me what I felt . . . Whether it was right . . . And I wanted to tell you . . . I wanted to tell you . . . but I couldn't . . .'

I reach out to him, as relief floods through me. It's going to be fine after all. He does love me. I knew it. It might have taken a bike crash to knock some sense into him, but he's realised after all.

He breaks away from me, shaking his head.

'Tell me,' I urge.

He's racked with sobs and I can feel myself welling up in sympathy. I've never seen anyone this upset.

'I've fucked up. I've fucked everything up.'

'No you haven't,' I soothe. 'It's all right. You mustn't be afraid of saying it.' Jack's breathless like a child. 'Calm down,' I urge.

He shakes his head. 'McCullen. Sally McCullen,' he chokes. 'The girl in the painting . . . the girl from Chloe's party . . .'

He pauses, gasping for breath. He looks at me, tears coursing down his face. He looks as if he's cracking up, but it's amazing how instinct can kick in. I back away from him.

'What about her?' I ask. He hasn't said it, but already I know it all.

Jack sniffs loudly. 'Something happened. Last Friday. I thought you were with Nathan and I called and called you. But you weren't there. I was drunk.' He gulps heavily. 'And she came over. I'm sorry . . . I'm so fucking sorry.'

I don't hear any more. Everything slots into place: him turning up late at the airport; his odd behaviour when we arrived; his not making love; the mark on his stomach . . .

The *love bite* on his stomach.

I feel Jack lurching towards me. 'It wasn't my fault. I was going to tell you.'

I now understand the expression 'to see red'. I can't hear what Jack says next because my knuckles are firmly embedded in his face.

233

He yelps with pain and staggers backwards, but I'm running. Running as fast as I can. I find the bike on its side further down the road. The engine is still turning over. It takes all my strength to pull it upright. I sit on it, just as Jack reaches me.

'Amy!' he implores, reaching out to grab me.

'Fuck off!' I yell, kicking my foot into his groin, as hard as I can, before driving away.

Self-preservation is an amazing thing. Despite the fact that I feel as if my whole world has been blitzed, I still make it back to Villa Stephano in one piece. I calmly park the bike outside. Vasos, the bar owner, is compèring the karaoke and everyone looks in a jolly mood. Darren's mother is giving an abysmal rendition of 'Karma Chameleon' whilst performing a pissed can-can with one of her mates. No one notices me as I walk through the bar to the stairs. Why should they? I'm showing no outward signs of my very dodgy mental health.

Once I get to the room, however, I lose it. At first I just cry, but then I really go for it. I hurl Jack's clothes out of the window, shouting obscenities, until I've exhausted myself.

It was obvious something wasn't right when we met at the airport. I should have known.

But how could he?

How could he do this to me?

I slump on to the bed and put my hands on my chest. It feels painful. Perhaps my heart is literally breaking.

After a while, my sobs subside to a whimper and I can hear the karaoke downstairs. But all I can think about is:

How?

What?

Where?

Why?

When?

I don't know how long I sit in the dark, staring at the wall, as I invent answers to each of these questions, but eventually I'm conscious of a knocking sound.

'Amy?' It's Jack at the door. 'Let me in.'

I squeeze my eyes closed.

'I'm not going away. You'll have to let me in,' he says, knocking harder.

I cover my ears.

'Come on.' Louder this time. 'We've got to talk. I know you're in there.'

'Go away,' I sob. I want to die. I curl up in a ball on the bed. I don't want him to see me.

'Amy. Please,' begs Jack. He's banging harder now.

I ignore it, wishing I was home. Wishing I was in my bed. Wishing I was safe. Wishing I'd never been stupid enough to get involved with Jack in the first place. Wishing that I'd had the sense not to trust him. Wishing that I hadn't made myself vulnerable. Wishing that I was someone else, somewhere else, in another place, in another time.

Later – I don't know how long – I realise that the banging has stopped.

I know Jack hasn't gone away. I know he's there, as if I can see him. And that's the problem. I can see him.

I can see him in my head.

I can see him kissing me on our beach. I can see him looking at me in the moonlight. I can see him laughing with the wind in his hair.

I can see all these things.

But I still can't see him with Sally.

I yank open the door. Jack is slumped on the stairs, his head is in his hands. When he looks up at me, his face is badly bruised, his eyes bloodshot.

'What do you mean *something* happened?'

He looks at me blankly.

'Tell me now. What happened?'

Jack doesn't move. 'I didn't fuck her,' he whispers.

I'm shaking. 'So what did you do?'

'I didn't do anything. It was her. It was all her.'

'TELL ME!'

Jack buries his head in his hands again. 'I was asleep. I woke

235

up and she was giving me a blow job. I swear, that's all that happened.'

'Oh! She only gave you a blow job!' I shout. 'Poor you.'

Jack stands up. 'It wasn't like that.'

'So tell me? What was it like? *Just how precisely did she land up with her mouth wrapped around your dick?*'

He can't say anything. I look at him with the kind of disgust I'd reserve for an overflowing sewer.

Because now I can see it. I can see his face contorted with pleasure. From someone else.

'I never want to see you again,' I gasp.

I slam the door and throw myself on to the bed. I cover my head with the pillow as Jack pounds on the door. He's shouting my name so loudly that he must have interrupted the FunSun disco. I can hear a row outside as he's told to shut up.

Then everything goes quiet. I don't know if Jack has been taken away, or whether he's still outside. I don't care.

I take the Walkman off the table and put the headphones in my ears. I press play, cranking up the volume to drown out the sound of my own tears. It's the Beatles song, 'Come Together'.

Fucking typical.

9
Jack

Chucked

'She did what?' Matt asks incredulously, staring at my bruised face.

'Chucked me,' I repeat, and then, just in case this expression isn't one with which he's familiar, I add, 'binned me; trashed me; dropped me; dumped me.' At this point, it occurs to me that each and every one of these terms could equally be applied to rubbish. This is no coincidence. For rubbish is what I am. Rubbish is how I feel. Were a cockroach to walk into Matt's living room right now, I have little doubt that it would make a beeline for yours truly, and upon arrival, declare itself at home.

Matt, however, is having a hard time taking this information in. He slumps down on the sofa next to me. 'But that's impossible.'

His statement, combined with his look of consternation, momentarily reminds me of Spock being confronted with some scientific aberration aboard the Starship *Enterprise*. And I can understand this reaction. What's happened is indeed illogical and contrary to life as I know it.

Of course, I'd like to go with Matt on this one. Really, I would. I'd love to sit here and assure him that, under the known laws of the universe, it *is* impossible that a nice girl like Amy could have chosen to trash a nice guy like me. I'd like to tell him that since this is so blatantly impossible, I must be undergoing a delusional episode from which I will soon awake and discover that everything is well in my world. But I've never been big on denial, so instead I tell him, 'Shit happens.'

Because it does.

I know.

It's just happened to me.

'But it was all going so well,' Matt complains. 'You two were really into each other.'

'It was and we were.'

He stares at me for a few seconds, before asking, 'Well?'

'Well, what?'

'Well, who did the dirty on who?'

'What—'

'One of you must have,' he points out. 'That's why people break up. Most times, anyway.'

'That's not true,' I protest. 'People break up for millions of different reasons.' He waits for me to elucidate, so I do. 'One of them might snore and the other one can't stand it. They might support different football teams. I don't know . . . anything. They might just run out of things to say.'

'So it was you, then,' he concludes

There's no point in shitting him on this point; he knows me too well. Besides, I need a sounding board. I need someone to tell me that I don't have to nail the lid down on my life just yet. 'Yeah.'

He nods. 'Thought so. You want to tell me about it?'

And I do. I take him through it step by step. I start with Amy and me swapping our baggage outside Zack's and how good it felt not to be carrying that stuff around any more. I take him through Max's party and my fit of jealousy, and my ultimatum and Amy's stand. I describe Black Friday and Amy's date and my continuing paranoia. I detail McCullen's arrival later that night, along with my rude awakening the following morning. I tell him about showing McCullen the door and telling her I never wanted to see her again. And, finally, I tell him about the holiday, about the bike crash, and about what I told Amy and what she told me.

After I conclude my tale of woe, the first thing Matt says is, 'That Nathan guy sounds like a real prick.'

I appreciate that Matt's trying to cheer me up, but it's not working. Still, more out of habit than any continuing sense of loathing, I nod my head and remind myself to add people who eat their bogeys to the More Pleasant Than Nathan list.

The second thing Matt says, in view of my lack of response to the first, is, 'Why the hell did you tell Amy about S&M?'

This question comes as no surprise. It's the same question that first occurred to me after the bike crash, in the brief yet startlingly unpleasant interlude between Amy punching me in the face and kicking me in the nuts. And it's the same question I've been asking myself ever since.

After all, there was no *need* to tell her. Sure, there'd always have been the worry of her finding out through some other means. Maybe I'd talk in my sleep. Maybe McCullen would start mouthing off. Or maybe I'd join some extreme religious cult where I'd have to confess to everybody I'd ever lied to in my entire life. But, quite frankly, each of these scenarios, then, as now, seemed pretty unlikely. The plain fact of the matter remains that, if I'd just kept my big mouth shut, I would have got away with it.

Same as I've been doing all my life.

The consequences of this would have been obvious and uniformly beneficial. There'd have been no bike crash, for example. Neither, of course, would there have been any miserable journey home on the plane with her refusing to speak to me. Instead, there would have been the two of us standing there on that cliff top, arm in arm, gazing down at the moonlit beach. And not just any beach, either. *Our* beach – as in the place where we made love. As in her, me and the sea. As in poetry, for Christ's sake.

But – oh, no – not Jack Rossiter. Jack Rossiter had other plans. Like ignoring her on the cliff top when she asked him if he felt it, too. Even though he did. For the first time in years. Even though, for the first time in years, he found himself in a situation with someone that felt like a wish come true. The problem was, it *felt* too good to be true. And that's because it *was* too good to be true.

'Honesty,' I suggest to Matt. 'I wanted to be honest with her.'

'Honesty?' Matt queries. He looks at me like I've just farted.

'Yeah, honesty. As in telling the truth.'

'I know what the word means, Jack.'

'So, what's your problem?'

'My problem is, I fail to see what it has to do with relationships.'

'It's got *everything* to do with relationships,' I say, exasperated.

He stares at me blankly. 'Not with mine, it doesn't. And not with most people's.' His look turns to one of suspicion. 'You haven't been reading my copy of *Ten Steps to Lasting Love*, have you?'

'Your what?'

Matt gets up and walks to the window. 'Nothing.'

'I didn't want to bullshit her,' I continue. 'It didn't feel right. She trusted me and I lied to her and the longer I left off telling her the truth, the worse it was making me feel.'

Matt turns round and faces me with narrowed eyes. 'What, like a conscience thing?' he queries. 'Like, whenever you laid eyes upon her, you felt an unrelenting sense of betrayal coursing like poison through your veins? And each time you kissed her or made love to her, you felt like you were betraying her afresh? Almost as if each new intimacy you shared no longer meant anything, because it rested upon foundations of deceit?'

'Yeah,' I say, realising that Matt's put his finger on it, 'that's *exactly* how it was.' A wave of relief washes over me. *Someone*, it seems, understands.

But that someone, it turns out, isn't Matt. 'In other words, you did it to make yourself feel better. Wouldn't it have made more sense to cope with your guilt on your own and learn your lesson never to do it again?' he asks, returning to the sofa and sitting back down.

It takes me a few seconds to recover from my disappointment that Matt and I are not about to undergo a seminal male bonding moment. But I cope with it OK. To begin with, tree-hugging's never really been my idea of fun – too much mildew and squirrel shit, for a start. And as for hunter-gathering – well, I got kicked out of the cub scouts for smoking when I was nine and never looked back, so I'd better steer clear of that, too. Mainly, though, I cope with it, because I'm not pissed off with Matt. More me.

I mean, it's not like his reaction to my behaviour is abnormal. Quite the reverse. Were I, for example, to carry out a quick vox pop in the street outside Matt's house and ask the following questions of members of the public in steady relationships

a) If you got drunk and got laid by a stranger who you'd never see again, would you tell your partner?
b) If you started an affair with someone, only to realise that you were actually in love with your present partner, would you tell them about the affair?
c) If you could shag someone and get away with it (and yeah, yeah, Hollywood stars *are* included), would you turn them down?

I have little doubt that the answers would be a uniform 'no'. I mean, infidelities aren't something people own up to these days, are they? Sure, you tell your friends, but not your lover. What would be the point? There isn't one. Not unless you wanted to break up.

Or, at least, that's how I used to think. Even with Zoe. Even though I never was unfaithful to her, I reckon that if I had been, I would have kept schtum about it. Too much grief, otherwise. When I tried it on with Amy, though, it just didn't work. Hence my starring role in the classic of Greek cinematography, *Confessions of a Moped Driver*. Honesty, it seems, got the better of me. Like Matt, however, I'm not buying into the honesty angle on its own. It's too simple. Too easy. Sure, honesty's important, but it's only important in that it's a symptom of something else. Honesty's just the fall guy. He must have been working for someone else. And not just anybody, I now realise, but Mr Big himself. And when it comes to emotions, there's only one Mr Big. It just amazes me it's taken me this long to recognise him.

I look Matt straight in the eyes. 'I love her,' I tell him. 'I told her about McCullen because I love her.'

Matt raises his hand. 'Hold it right there, my brother.'

'What?'

'You know exactly what. The L word. You just said it.' He wags his finger at me. 'You did. You did. You know you did. Don't even attempt to make out that you didn't.'

'I'm not.'

Matt cocks his head to one side. 'You're not?'

'No, I'm not. I said it and I meant it. I love her.' I listen to the sound the words make as they leave my mouth. It's a good sound. It's the kind of sound I could do with hearing again. 'I, Jack Rossiter,' I tell Matt, 'being of sound mind –'

'A matter of opinion,' Matt mutters.

'– love her, Amy Crosbie.'

Matt looks hard at me for a very long time. 'That would explain it, then,' he concludes.

'Explain what?'

'Why you've been acting like a complete dick.' We stare at each other in silence for a few minutes. 'I suppose we'd better work out a way of getting you out of this mess,' he finally says.

Being a lawyer, Matt approaches the problem like a lawyer: he starts with the facts. After checking one or two of them with me, he falls silent and I watch his expression set in a mask of concentration. I imagine his ruthlessly logical brain at work, tweaking, tugging, toying with the problem. Confidence flows through me. If anyone can find a path out of this hideous Minotaur's lair, it's Matt.

'Accidental fellatio,' he eventually considers aloud. 'That's a tough one.' He scratches his chin and frowns. 'A total bummer, in fact.'

This is not the solution I've been craving. 'No, Matt,' I correct him. 'It's not a *bummer*. Losing my wallet would be a *bummer*. Getting a parking ticket would be a *bummer*. *This* is an unmitigated fucking disaster.'

242

Matt waits patiently for my outburst to subside. 'The crux of the matter,' he ponders, 'is whether you have or have not been unfaithful. Technically, I suppose the answer must be yes. You were indeed blown. The tip of her tongue did indeed touch the tip of your tool. That brings us to intent. Though, in the eyes of the law, ignorance is no excuse, it can be argued that, in your semi-conscious state, you were completely unaware that the tongue in question belonged to any other than your beloved Amy. Hence, your gaining pleasure from the motions of this tongue would not constitute emotional infidelity.'

'Great, mate,' I interrupt out of sheer frustration, 'try telling that to Amy. Just a case of mistaken identity, darling. Happens all the time. Nothing to get worked up about. Yeah, Matt, she's just going to love that.'

Matt looks at me sidelong. 'You really must learn to channel this aggression, you know. It's not good for you.'

'What?'

'Take a deep breath,' Matt says.

'What?'

'Relax. Calm down. Float downstream a while.'

I'm not in the mood for any hippy shit right now – especially from a City lawyer who wouldn't know a lentil from a loofah 'Relax?' I snap. 'How the fuck am I meant to relax? I've just been chucked, for Christ's sake.'

He gives me a few seconds to calm down, before saying, 'Listen, mate, nothing's ever as bad as it seems.'

'Mind telling me how exactly?'

He purses his lips in consideration, then suggests, 'Objectivity. You've got to be objective about this.'

'Objectivity?' I splutter.

'Yeah,' he explains, 'you know, like when you go and stand on a hill and look down on a town and it appears completely different, because you've put some distance between you and it.'

'Matt,' I say, 'I sincerely doubt that standing on a fucking hill is going to be of much help.'

He rolls his eyes. 'Just hear me out, okay?'

'I'm listening.'

Matt lights a cigarette and takes a couple of drags. 'The objective view,' he begins, 'is this. The love of your life no longer wants you. She's discovered that you've been slipping your dick into another woman's mouth behind her back. As a result of this, and the fact you didn't tell her about it straight away, she now thinks you're a low-down, no-good piece of shit who deserves to burn in hellfire for eternity. Suffice to say, she never wants to see you again.'

'Thanks, Matt,' I tell him, beginning to have serious concerns about his counselling skills. 'Why not just hand me a razor blade and go run the bath for me?'

'Okay,' Matt says, 'forget objectivity. You're right; objectively, you're fucked. Still,' he says, after a pause, 'things could be a lot worse.'

For the first time, he's said something that makes sense. 'Yeah,' I agree, 'I could be in the middle of the Sahara without a drop of water. I could be being eaten alive by maggots. I could even be being forced to watch every episode of *Dynasty* ever made. Aside from these, though, I really think there's very little *worse* that could happen to me.'

Matt studiously ignores this volley of sarcasm. 'Seriously, mate, it could. You're still alive. So's she. Shit happens. It happens to us all from time to time, doesn't it?'

'No, Matt,' I interrupt, 'I don't believe it does. I don't believe, for example, that it happens to *you*. Does it happen to you, Matt? Well? Does it? I mean, do feel free to correct me if I'm wrong, but answer me this: have *you* ever been dumped by someone you're in love with?'

'No.'

'Right, so it doesn't happen to us all. It happens to some people. And that I acknowledge. That I don't have a problem with.'

'So what *is* your problem?'

'My problem it that it shouldn't have happened to *me*,' I snap.

'Why not?'

I hold my head in my hands. 'Because I *trusted* her, Matt. *That's* what's really killing me. I've spent my whole life lying to women, keeping stuff back. But not her. I trusted her and I told her the truth. I told her the truth because I love her. And what did it get me? It got me dumped. She didn't even give me a chance to explain.'

'Do you really think it would make a difference,' Matt asks, 'if she could hear your side of what happened?'

'Yeah,' I mumble, 'I do. I really do. But what's the fucking point? I've been calling her all day and she won't even pick up the phone.'

Matt puts his hand on my shoulder. 'Maybe she just needs some time to calm down,' he suggests. 'Give her some space. Believe me,' he assures me, 'she can't go on hating you for ever.' He stares into the middle distance. 'Like they say,' he adds, 'if you love something, set it free. If it returns, it's yours for ever. If it doesn't, it never was.'

For Matt, this is pretty profound. I can only conclude that it's going to take a stroke of genius to get me out of this one.

The Waiting Game

'I know you can hear me,' I say. 'Yes, you, Amy Crosbie, I'm talking to you.'

I wait a few seconds for a reply, but none comes. I'm not backing down, though. I'm here on a mission. I'm a Guerrilla of the Heart. And Guerrillas of the Heart don't go chickening out at the first sign of resistance. We're committed, fearless. We relish the challenge, knowing that victory, when it comes, will be twice as sweet.

'Fine,' I call out loudly. 'You can skulk all you like. I'm not going away. Do you hear that, Amy? I'm not budging. Not one inch. I'm staying right here until you come down and give me a chance to explain.'

Still nothing.

Suddenly, my resolve takes a dramatic turn for the worse. I press my lips up close to the intercom and whisper, 'Please,

Amy. I love you. I love you and this is killing me.' I wait again, but all that answers me is silence.

An old guy on the bench across the street rolls his eyes at me and takes a swig from his bottle of Thunderbird. He looks like he's seen it all before. But I don't care. I mean what I say: I *do* love her. And I couldn't give a damn who knows it. She's the girl. The Uberbabe. She's the one I've been looking for all this time.

Ever since I told Matt last night that I was in love with her, she's all I've thought about – almost like saying it out loud to him made it real to me. No, I don't give a damn who knows. I want everyone to know, but most of all Amy.

And that's why I'm here.

It's just gone ten-thirty on Sunday morning and I'm standing on the steps of her building. I've been here since nine. Apart from the old guy, the street's deserted. With the pavements on either side coned off for roadworks, there aren't even any cars. Above me, in keeping with my mood, and for the first time in weeks, the sky is grey. I take a couple of steps back and crane my neck and look up the building to the top floor where Amy's flat is.

There are no signs of outward aggression. No boiling oil pouring down the battlements. No archers at the ready. But no signs of imminent reunion, either. No white handkerchief fluttering in the breeze. No waving hand, beckoning me up, nor Rapunzel hair tumbling down. Not even so much as an open window. But that's OK. I'm certain she's in there. I'm prepared to wait. If she wants me to lay siege to her, then that's precisely what I'm going to do. If she wants proof that I love her, then here it is. And if she doesn't – well, tough, I'm going to give it to her anyway.

I return to the door and press my finger down on the intercom. It makes a noise like an angry wasp. I hold it there and picture Amy inside, listening to it. It must be driving her mad. I hope it is, anyway. Sounds harsh, I know, but I don't care. The only thing I care about now is getting a chance to give her my side of the story. This is a democracy, after all. People don't go getting convicted without a trial. Justice decrees that she has to listen to me. I screwed things up. I know it. But everyone makes mistakes, don't they? And I've learnt from mine. I won't ever allow a situation like the one with McCullen to occur again. I won't ever lie to Amy again, or deceive her the way I did. All I need is a chance – just one – to let her know that I love her and that I'm hers, and that I don't want to be with anyone else. As in ever.

Still no response.

Take heart. I'm better equipped to deal with this state of affairs than she is. For a start, there's food. What's she going to eat? I know Amy. Stocked cupboards aren't her strong point. Those two cartons of Long Life milk and the past-the-sell-by-date tub of hummus in the fridge aren't going to keep her going for long. And then there's the new job. She's not going to blow that out just to avoid a confrontation with me. It means too much to her. No, she can't hide for ever. She's got to get tired soon, let me in, or at the very least come down and listen to what I've got to say. Logic dictates that the odds on this one are definitely stacked in my favour. Especially with the preparation I've put in. As temporary MD of Sieges Я Us, I've brought along the ultimate Relationship Survival Kit:

a) Twelve pink roses (granted, they're wilting, but rich with romantic potential nonetheless)

b) Food: one family-sized packet of Chick-O-Lix TM (the only item left in the twenty-four-hour garage's fridge); Kendal Mint Cake (standard army issue); and two bags of dry roast peanuts (protein rich)

c) Beverages: two cans of Toxoshock (isotonic energy-boosting drink, containing caffeine, taurine and guarana); plus one carton of Nutroshake (strawberry-flavoured)

d) Vestments: jeans and FCUK T-shirt (both Matt's); desert boots (ideal for rough terrains)

e) Other: two packs of Marlboro (Lights); one windproof lighter (petrol)

Apart from my choice of clothing – I glance up at the sky; it's darkening down – I reckon I have the capacity to last out here for hours, if not days. Amy, in other words, short of constructing a hang-glider out of her bed sheets and miscellaneous household items and launching herself from the roof, has little chance of escape. Like it or not, I *will* have my say.

With a valedictory, 'I'm still here,' I let go of the buzzer and slump back down on the steps. I feel something on my face and, looking up, notice that it's started to rain. Shuffling back against the door, I take the box of Chick-O-Lix from my rucksack and nibble at one unenthusiastically, before discarding it and lighting a cigarette in its place. Down the road, the church bells start ringing out, calling people in for morning service.

Say a little prayer for me.

I didn't sleep last night. Not a wink. I just lay there, staring at Fat Dog, watching the minutes flick by. Needless to say, it was Amy who was keeping me up. Or, rather, the lack of her. Because, obviously, she wasn't there. She wasn't there because she hated me. She thought I was scum. And why not? In her position, I would have thought exactly the same. Reverse psychology. How would I feel if *she* told me some guy had gone down on *her*? Angry? Jealous? Disgusted? Yes, all of these. But most of all, betrayed. Only I didn't betray Amy. I didn't set out to hurt her. I just fucked up. Acknowledged: bad. Not that this made me feel any better. It didn't. As I lay there, not even able to hold on to my pillow for comfort – because it still stank of McCullen – I just felt gutted. Devastated. I felt like someone had torn my heart in two.

Even my dick agreed. And this was not a dick-like thing to do. Normally (the Ella Trent incident excepted), come fair weather or foul, my dick's constitution is unassailable. I didn't think it was capable of letting me down in this way. Yet there it was, slumped between my legs like a hibernating creature. If it could have talked, I suspect that our conversation would have gone something like this:

Jack: 'What's up with you, then?'

Dick: 'Nothing's *up*. That's the point.'

Jack: 'What point?'

Dick: 'Exactly.'

Jack: 'Do you feel like talking about it?'

Dick: 'I don't *feel* like anything. Apart from numb, that is.'

Jack: 'I take it you're talking about Amy?'

Dick: 'Well, I'm hardly talking about McCullen, am I? Not after that pathetic excuse for a blow job.'

Jack: 'I can't even remember it. Was it really that bad?'

Dick: 'Put it this way, Jack: as blow jobs go, it sucked – and I don't mean that kindly. There I was, psyching myself up for a cracking wet dream. It had all the makings of a classic. You and me sitting in this sauna, steam all around, and in walks Amy in her school uniform . . .'

Jack: 'Her school uniform? I don't even know what her school uniform looks like.'

Dick: 'Dramatic licence, Jack. Give me a break.'

Jack: 'I see. What happened next?'

Dick: 'Bloody McCullen turns up. In she marches and, without so much as a by-your-leave, pushes Amy aside and takes over the whole shooting match.'

Jack: 'It doesn't sound *that* bad. For a fantasy, I mean.'

Dick: 'Yes, well that shows all you know. Take the word of a pro, Jack, it's not much fun driving a Mini when you're used to a Rolls-Royce. But even then, I coped. *All right*, I said to myself, *let's make the most of a bad job*. But – oh, no – you weren't having that, either. You weren't prepared to stop at duping me with the wrong girl. You had to go one better. Just when things were starting to look up again, you pulled out. Pulled out, Jack! That's just sick. That's just so . . . amateur.'

Jack: 'I'm sorry, Dick. I won't let it happen again. Can't we just be friends, like we were in the good old days?'

Dick: 'The good old days. Ah, yes, I remember them. Just you, me, the bottle of baby oil and a copy of *Hustler*. Not forgetting, of course, the occasional one-night stand to which I was treated. A quick plunge into 3D paradise, only for it to be snatched away once more the following morning. Great days, indeed. All the same, do forgive me if I don't start jumping up and down at the prospect.'

Jack: 'I said I was sorry.'

Dick: 'I know, I know. It's just that I miss her, Jack. She fitted, you know? She felt right.'

For once in my life, I had to admit it, my dick definitely had the upper hand.

I started thinking about Matt's advice – all that crap about giving Amy space. Space might well be the final frontier, but as far as I was concerned, it was for wimps. I didn't want to *give* her space; I wanted to *share* her space. And as for all that, if-you-love-something-set-it-free nonsense, well Matt could stick that, as well. Why would I want to do that? OK, so setting her free was a right-on enough concept, and, yes, one with which I could deal with on a purely theoretical level. Or even practically – were I talking about mynah birds, or pet tigers. But I wasn't. I was talking about Amy. I was talking about the woman I now realised I loved. And the way I saw it, if I *did* go setting her free, then the least I could do was let her know the facts. The decision she'd made had been a unilateral one. What I had to do was restore the democracy. There'd be no point in her flying off on her freedom thing if she didn't know I wanted her back. I mean, she might have just kept on flying and where would that have left us? Her homeless, and me home alone. Blues times two. I didn't want to set her free. I wanted to win her back. And if that meant I had to fight for her, then I would. All ten rounds. Muhammad Ali. Like a butterfly. Like a bee.

Or, alternatively, by just sitting outside her door.

In the rain.

Sleep-starved and cold.

I curl up closer to the stone and close my eyes.

It's a quarter past three when I wake up. My mouth feels like it's lined with wallpaper paste. Having seen the ingredients when I worked at ProPixel, I can only assume that this is a side-effect of the Chick-O-Lix TM I consumed earlier.

I struggle to my feet and flex my legs for a few seconds, forcing the cramp from them. I look up: the sky's now clear. The black clouds, it seems, have taken refuge inside my head.

I turn and give the buzzer another go. Yet again, Amy ignores it. I glance across the road. Nothing's changed. The old guy's still there, as are the road cones and the road workers' tools. A nostalgic smile spreads across my face as I remember the summer holiday I spent with a road gang when I was a student. We were laying cable for TV, same as has been going on here, digging up the road, sealing the cables in, then painting the lines back on the tarmac once it had set. My smile spreads wider as an idea lands slap bang in the middle of my mind.

'Okay, Amy,' I shout into the buzzer, 'you want to play rough? Watch this.'

I march across the road. The old guy, noticing that a fellow slumberer has turned active, puts down his bottle and salutes me. I salute him back, because, yes, this is a male thing. This is something men the world over will be able to relate to. I am, indeed, about to make a grand statement. It'll be romantic. It'll be cool. It'll be the kind of gesture other men will wish they'd had the balls to make.

It doesn't take long to break the lock off the line-painting machine that's sitting at the side of the road. A couple of deftly aimed whacks with the crowbar I find in the workers' tent is enough. Then, freedom! The carriage is mine. I flip the handle down and walk it a couple of paces forward. Sure enough, it's loaded: a white line, two feet long, trails on the road surface in my wake. I flip the handle off and walk the roller to the middle of the street. Then I begin the real work: the writing of the message I want Amy to read next time she looks out of her window. Various options run through my mind:

a) Amy 4 Jack (too teen)
b) I love you (too obvious)
c) Take me back (too cheesy)

Instead, I settle for a classic – the kind of line that would leave even Cyrano de Bergerac lost for words. I run my roller along the street, spelling it out. It's tricky work, of course. This machine's designed for straight lines. I have to shuffle it round for each stroke of each new letter. But this is a labour of love. I know no fatigue. And, there, twenty minutes after I start, the message is complete. And just in time. The paint runs dry on the last stroke of the last letter. But, hey, so what? It's readable, at least. And who could ask for more?

I return the roller whence it came. Then I cross the road to Amy's side and take in the enormity of what I've done. It looks good. It looks great. Even if I say it myself, it looks like *art*. And I'm not the only one who's impressed. The old guy is, too. Out of the corner of my eye, I notice that he's deserting his bench for the first time today. He takes a couple of steps forward and slowly moves his head from left to right, checking out my handiwork. Then he's heading for me. Like a bee to a flower. He sees the beauty of what I've done. He wants to check it out. Not wanting to seem ostentatious, I stand still and allow an impassive look to settle on my face. My public awaits.

'All right, mate,' he says, reaching out his hand. 'The name's Clifford.'

'Hello, Clifford.' I take his hand and shake it. 'So what do you think?'

Clifford stares at the road for a moment, speechless. And I can sympathise; coming to terms with a gesture of this ambition will never be an easy thing. He opens his mouth to speak and I allow myself a moment of pride. Just how, exactly, will he phrase it? How will he manage to put into words the emotional upheaval he's undergone as a result of reading my few and simple words?

Like this: 'You working for the Electricity Board, then, son?'

I stare at him. Then I stare at the half-drunk bottle of Thunderbird in his hand. Then I stare at him again. Finally, I smile, making out that I share his sense of perspective on the world – which I genuinely doubt I do. 'Electricity Board?' I echo. 'No, Clifford, I don't.'

He looks me up and down, before making another guess: 'Gas, then?'

'What makes you say that?' I ask.

'What you've written there, son,' he goes on. 'Sounds like an advert, doesn't it?' He takes a swig from his bottle. 'Heat an' that. If it's not the electricity, then it's got to be the gas, hasn't it?'

'Really,' I say genially, because let's face it, at times like this, it's no real skin off your back just to humour someone.

'S'right, son. Quite catchy, really,' he reflects, before nodding his head at his bench. 'Fair's fair,' he adds. 'If I had electric central heating an' I read an advert like that, I'd switch to the gas, no problem.'

There comes a point, though. And the point is now. 'What the hell are you talking about?' I ask him.

He looks at me like I'm mad. 'Read it,' he says, pointing down at the street. 'Right there.'

I follow Clifford's hand and do as he suggests. 'Still not quite with you,' I conclude.

Clifford shakes his head. 'It's got to be an advert, hasn't it?' he says. 'Otherwise, it just don't make sense.'

Up until this moment, I've been labouring under the assumption that Clifford has a reading disability. But the more I look at the letters I've written on the road, the more I realise he doesn't. Quite the opposite. It's not Clifford who has a reading disability, it's me. Or, rather, a writing disability. Because when I look at what I've written, this is what I see:

MY HEAT BELONGS TO YOU

Not, *MY HEART BELONGS TO YOU.* Not the grand gesture I intended. Not anything that even makes sense. My first reaction is to laugh. No way. There's *no way* I could misspell a word like that, just go leaving a whole letter out. My second reaction, however, is to gag. Because Clifford's right – what I've written *does* look like an advert for a power company. I rush to the offending word and scuff my foot across it;

nothing. I try again; not so much as a blemish on its smooth, white perfection. I drop to my hands and feet and try rubbing with my hand; still no result. And the roller's out of paint. I can't even cross it out.

I stand stock still for a whole minute, trying to come to terms with the monumental cock-up I've just perpetrated. Then I turn to Clifford and ask, 'All right with you if I have a swig?' and, before he has a chance to reply, I grab the bottle of Thunderbird from his hand and drink it dry.

Sign Off

Monday goes by in a blur of mental and physical exhaustion brought on by the weekend's events. My time's spent mostly in bed, either asleep, or lying on my back and staring at the ceiling, listening to CDs. I don't shave. I don't wash. I don't change my clothes. I try not to think about anything. Instead, I quietly rot and, short of urinating in my pants, successfully leave all vestiges of civilisation behind. With Matt away on business, my contact with the outside world is zero. And I don't care. All I want is for the days to pass, to form a buffer between me and Amy, because that's the only way the pain I feel is going to get any easier to bear.

Tuesday afternoon and my stomach forces me to surface from this advanced state of nihilism. I reach for the phone and call up a pizza. As I chew my way through it, it occurs to me that perhaps I'm going about this all wrong. After all, moping isn't going to get me anywhere. And just because the road painting outside Amy's flat turned into a débâcle, it doesn't mean that any other plan I might come up with will come similarly unstuck. I was close, for God's sake. *Damned* close. Just one letter out. That's what I've got to remember. Not how much of a failure I am, but how near I was to success. All I need is another plan. A new angle. I collect a bottle of vodka and return to my room to give this further consideration.

Tuesday evening arrives and I'm still in my bedroom – or my creative hive, as it's now known. I've resolved on a plan. It's so simple that I can't believe I didn't hit on it sooner.

Especially with it staring me in the face all along.

My guitar.

There it was, up against my wardrobe, untouched since the five lessons I took last summer. A song. Of course. To serenade her with. What better way to make her sit up and see how much I care? And it's going well. Far better than I would have dared to imagine. The lyrics were slow in coming at first, but soon they took on a life of their own. And the tune's great, too – especially considering I only know three chords. Everything feels perfect. The joss sticks are burning. I've got Elvis crooning at me from the stereo for inspiration. And the finishing touch: a bandanna round my head *à la* Springsteen.

By eleven, I'm ready to give it its first outing. I put my half-finished vodka bottle out of harm's way on the floor, then sling the guitar round my neck and announce from the doorway, 'And now, coming at you live from the Hollywood Bowl, we're proud to present the one, the only, Jaaaaa-ckieee Rossiter.'

I stride across the room and take centre stage in the middle of the bed. 'This is a little number,' I say, giving it my best Southern drawl, 'I wrote about a little lady I know. A little lady called Amy. A little lady I love very much.' I wipe my hand across my brow. 'It's called, "Don't Reckon I Can Take It No More".'

I strum the first few chords, then let rip:

> Don't reckon I can take it no more.
> My life, girl, without you's a bore.
> I miss you so bad,
> And feel such a cad,
> My heart's just dropped straight thru' the floor.

Then on with the chorus, designed to be sung by a backing trio of hip-swinging cowgirls:

> Don't reckon he can take it no more,
> Girl, since you walked out his door.
> Please won't you come back

To your good man Jack?
Without you his life's just a chore.

And on to verse two. I'm really getting into this now.

Don't reckon I can take it no more.
I'm drifting without sight of shore.
Oh, please rescue me
From this dark, cruel sea.
This lost soul, you mustn't ignore.

But I don't get as far as the second chorus. Instead, I hear:

'Just what the *fuck* do you think you're doing?'

I look up and see Matt standing in the doorway, a look of utter astonishment on his face.

'Singing,' I reply. 'What does it look like?'

He considers this for a moment, then says, 'Like somebody in real danger of being institutionalised.'

'You're entitled to your opinion.'

He looks slowly round the room. 'I take it from this display that she hasn't taken you back.'

'Correct.'

'Then face facts, Jack: she isn't going to.' He shakes his head. 'It's over. Accept it.'

'Nothing's over.'

'It is tomorrow.'

'What?'

'Tomorrow,' he informs me. 'This shit stops tomorrow. No more crap dirges. No more self-hatred.' He glances down at the vodka bottle, before looking back at me with disdain. 'No more drinking yourself into a stupor. No more, do you under-stand?' I say nothing. 'You'd better believe me, my brother,' he warns, 'because that's the way it's going to be.'

And with that, he walks out and slams the door behind him. I stare at it for a few seconds, before strumming my guitar defiantly and picking up where I left off.

I don't know what time I crash, but I wake to a stinging

hangover and the sound of Matt's voice: 'Radiohead . . . Nick Cave and the Bad Seeds . . . Portishead . . . Bob Dylan . . . Nick Drake . . . Do I see the Smurfs? No, I don't. Do I see the St George Junior Church Choir Christmas Carol Compilation? No, I don't see that, either.' I briefly open one eye and see that the light's on. Matt's crouched down on the floor, examining the CDs I've been playing over the past few days. 'What we do have, however,' he concludes, 'are all the signs of a self-pity binge.' He claps his hands loudly. 'Well, this is where it ends. Now get up.'

Bright sunlight fills the room and I open my eyes to see Matt standing by the window. I lift my head from the mattress and look at Fat Dog. It's Wednesday morning, 8 a.m. I groan and bury my head beneath the duvet.

'I mean it,' Matt continues, grabbing the duvet and ripping it off me. 'It's like I told you last night: this shit stops here.'

It's only now that I react. I grab the retreating corner of the duvet and try heaving it back. But Matt wins hands down. 'Fuck off,' I tell him, pushing my face into the pillow.

'Charming.' There's silence for a moment, then Matt says, 'There are two ways we can do this: easy, or hard. You can either get up of your own accord, or I'm going to force you to get up.' He waits for a response, but I don't give him one. 'Fine,' he finally says, 'we'll do it the hard way.'

I listen to him walking out of the room and a vague sense of unease creeps up on me. I know what Matt's like when he's made his mind up to do something. He does it and he does it efficiently. But then I relax. Short of holding a gun to my head, there's bugger all he can do to make me move. And Matt wouldn't do that. He's a lawyer. He's got too much to lose. Forget about it. He's bluffing. Then I remember the scar on my eyebrow from when he shot me with the air pistol when we were kids. But it's not something I have much time to dwell on.

The water, when it lands, is not only freezing, but plentiful. I'd scream, if it wasn't for the fact that the shock of it hitting my body had already blasted the air from my lungs.

'You piece of shit,' I snarl, turning on him. 'I'm drenched.'

'A not altogether unexpected condition,' Matt observes, idly swinging the now empty plastic bucket in his hand.

I sit up, water trickling from my hair down my face. The T-shirt and jeans which I've failed to remove since Sunday are soaked through.

'I suppose you think that's funny?' I glare at him.

'Coffee,' he says, nodding at the bedside table.

Reluctantly, I reach out and take a swig. 'There,' I say. 'Happy now?'

'It's not my happiness that's the issue here,' he points out. He watches in silence as I finish the coffee. 'Now stand up,' he orders.

'What?'

He narrows his eyes. 'Just do it, Jack. I haven't got all day. I've got to be in the office in an hour.'

Resigned to the fact that he isn't going to stop until he gets what he wants, I get to my feet.

'Look at the state of you,' he says.

I catch my reflection in the mirror behind him. I have to admit, it's not a pretty sight. The neck of Matt's FCUK T-shirt is grey with grime. My fingernails are black, like I've been digging through earth with my bare hands. And what I can only assume is a piece of pepperoni is cemented to my forehead. But it's my eyes that really freak me out. They look like some kid's taken a red pen and scribbled all over their whites. Not that any kid with half a brain would dare come near me looking like this. They'd be calling the police, letting them know a crazed killer was at large.

'You're a disgrace,' Matt announces, continuing to look me up and down in disgust. 'An embarrassment.' He fixes me with a stare. 'I'm ashamed to be living under the same roof as you. What have you got to say for yourself?'

I look down at my feet and mumble, 'Okay,' I say, 'so I'm not looking my best at the moment.'

'Not looking your best? You're not even looking your worst. You're looking like something your worst would turn its nose up at.'

'Okay,' I snap. 'I'm a total bloody mess.'

'Good,' he says, sounding pleased. 'Recognising that you have a problem is the first step towards recovery. Now, repeat after me. My name is Jack Rossiter.'

'What are you—' I begin to say, but the warning look he shoots me brings the bucket of water splashing back into my mind. I remind myself that this man is an animal, capable of anything. 'My name is Jack Rossiter,' I repeat, as instructed, making sure to sound as bored as I possibly can.

This he ignores. 'I am a man,' he goes on.

I do the robot voice again. 'I am a man.'

'I'm a strong and independent man,' he says.

'I'm a strong and independent man.'

'I don't need a woman to define me.'

'I don't need a woman to define me.'

'I can be happy on my own.'

'I can be happy on my own.'

'Not only am I a man, but I'm also a very dirty man.'

I find myself smiling for the first time in days. 'Not only am I a man, but I'm also a very dirty man,' I manage to repeat.

'And I need a good wash.'

'And I need a good wash.'

'And a change of underwear.'

'And a change of underwear.'

'Because I smell.'

This last line I don't manage to complete, because I'm too busy laughing. He produces a bar of soap from his pocket and slaps it into my hand. Then he steers me to the door and points down the corridor towards the bathroom.

Later, as I'm drying myself off, he pokes his head round the bathroom door. 'I'll be back around six,' he informs me. 'And if I catch you pulling any of that Bastard-Child-of-Bon-Jovi shit like last night, I'll ram that guitar up your arse.'

'Don't worry,' I say. 'The ghost of Hendrix will walk no more.'

He nods. 'Oh, yeah. One other thing.'

'What?'

'Chloe rang last night. She's expecting you for dinner at eight.' He winks at me. 'Part of your rehabilitation programme, so don't be late.'

The rest of the morning's spent tidying up my room, the afternoon immersed in the task of completing *Study in Yellow*. So therapeutic was my session with Matt this morning that I successfully resist the urge to paint it black. But the therapy's not complete. Thoughts of McCullen keep flashing through my mind. It's probably just being here in the studio that does it. I keep catching her portrait staring at me from the corner of the room. Eventually, I decide enough's enough and I cross the room and pick it up. I open the French windows and walk into the garden.

Outside, by the bonfire, the burning canvas and paint combine to produce a satisfying smell. I feel no regret. It holds too many memories. And not just of what happened between McCullen and me on the night before the holiday, either. Too many memories of *me*. Of the person I *was*. All that chat. All that scheming and manipulation. It's worthless, and I know it's worthless now, because all that Don Juan bullshit put together hasn't helped me get the one thing I want: Amy's forgiveness, or, more specifically, Amy. She's made her decision, and if it's final, then that's just the way it is. I can't force her to think any differently. And I was stupid to think that I ever could. I watch the canvas curl in on itself and crumble into ash. Then I turn my back on it and head inside.

I get to Chloe's at eight on the dot.

'Matt wasn't kidding,' she says when she opens the door.

'About what?'

'About you, you poor baby. You look like shit.'

So much for my pre-dinner shower and shave. I smile weakly. 'Thanks,' I say, checking her out. 'You look great.' She does. Stunning, even, in a short black number. Not that it does much for me, the way I'm feeling right now.

'Come here,' she tells me, putting her arms round me and squeezing me tight. 'Let me give you a hug.' She keeps me close for a minute, then leads me by the hand through to the dining room. 'I hope you're hungry,' she says, pouring me a glass of wine. 'I've cooked enough for ten.'

Looking around the room while she's off in the kitchen, this doesn't seem entirely inappropriate. With the effort she's made, there might as well be a full-scale dinner party going on. The posh cutlery's out on show. Soft music's playing from the stereo and a candle burns low. I look down at my crumpled shirt and faded jeans and feel guilty as sin. Then I remind myself: it's only Chloe. She wouldn't give a toss if I was wearing a nun's wimple and a stetson. And I'm right to think this. She appears a few minutes later with the starters and a grin as wide as the Grand Canyon. And she starts talking and she doesn't stop. She manages to steer round the topic of Amy all the way through the meal. Even I manage to forget for a while. But then, when we're sitting on the sofa, sipping our coffees, the black dogs return once more and I fall into silence.

'So, tell me,' she says. 'What happened to Jack the Lad?'

'Gone. Departed.' I shrug. 'On a sabbatical, at the very least.'

'When's he due back?'

'I wish I knew.' I struggle for words. 'Everything's changed. None of my rules seems to apply any more.'

'What do you mean?'

'I don't know. Women. I thought I had them sussed. I thought I knew what made them tick.'

'And now you don't?'

'No. I haven't got a clue.' I tell her about Amy not returning my calls, about my going round there on Sunday, the works. I even tell her what Matt caught me doing last night.

'There'll be others,' she assures me. 'You're attractive. You *will* find someone else.'

I close my eyes for a second, but all I see is Amy at the side of that road, tears running down her face. 'I don't want anyone else.'

Chloe rolls her eyes and digs me in the ribs. 'Now you're being melodramatic. This is reality. We take a knock and we pick ourselves up and we start again. That's how it works.' She rests her hand on mine. 'You're going to have to get a grip on this, Jack,' she sighs. 'It's not going to be easy, but it's something you're going to have to do sooner or later.'

'It's hard, Chloe. It's really fucking hard.'

She runs her hand through my hair. 'I know, baby,' she says. 'I know it is. But you'll get over it.'

'Yeah, well I can't see how.'

We fall silent for a minute or so, then she says, 'I can help you, if you want.'

I turn my head towards her. Her face is only inches away from mine. 'How?'

She moves in closer, whispering, 'Like this,' and I feel her lips pressing against mine.

'Don't,' I tell her, pushing her back. 'This isn't what I want.'

She must see from my face that I mean it. I watch her as she sits back, lights a cigarette and stares across the room. 'I'm sorry,' she says, turning back to me. Her face is flushed.

'We're friends, Chloe,' I tell her, as gently as I can. 'Good friends. But that's all.'

'I know. I'm being stupid. Too much to drink.' As if to prove this, she gets up and collects her wineglass, fills it to the brim. 'I'm sorry.'

'It's okay,' I tell her, meaning it. 'It never happened.'

'You really love her, don't you?' she asks, after she's finished her cigarette.

'Yeah, I really do.'

'Then write to her. Tell her how you feel. Maybe that'll work for you. It must be worth a go. After all, you've tried everything else.'

'I will.'

'Promise?'

'Promise. I'll do it tonight and drop it round to her tomorrow.'

Chloe comes over and leans down and kisses me on the cheek. Then she stands up and smiles, shaking her head at me. 'The Bastard Child of Bon Jovi, indeed. What *are* you like, Jack Rossiter?'

Matt's still up when I get back, sitting in the kitchen, reading a magazine.

'You're early,' he remarks. 'I thought you two would be chatting all night.'

I sit on the edge of the table. I'm not going to tell him about what went down with Chloe. It's a dead issue. There'd be no point. 'I'm exhausted.'

'All that rockin' and rollin' last night take it out of you, did it?'

I smile back at him. 'Sorry about that. And thanks for sorting my head out this morning. I needed a good kick up the arse.'

'The pleasure was all mine.' He checks my face. 'You're okay now, though?'

I nod my head. 'Yeah. Well, no, but that's how it goes. It'll just take time.'

'And meantime?'

'Meantime?'

'Meantime,' Matt informs me, 'we're going to have fun.'

'Fun?'

'Yes, fun. You remember that. Going out. Having a laugh. Getting laid.'

'To tell the truth, Matt, getting laid's the last thing on my mind.'

'I'm not talking about *you*. With a face like that, you've got about as much chance of pulling as the Hunchback of Notre Dame. I'm talking about *me*.'

I stand up, yawn. 'All the same, mate, I think I'll be giving it a miss for a while.'

'Fair enough,' he says. 'You've got till Saturday. Because then you're coming out. With me. You're coming out clubbing and I'm going to remind you what it's like to have a good time.'

Upstairs, I sit down at my desk and take out a sheet of paper and a pen. *Dear Amy*, I begin. And then I stare at the sheet. It seems so small compared with what I've got to say. But still, I try. I try and I fail. Because I don't know how I'm even going to begin to tell her how much I love her and how much I miss her, or set the record straight on what happened that night with McCullen. But also because I don't want this to end. And this *is* the end. Of that, I have no doubt. This is the place where I sign off. Whatever happens next is down to her, and her alone.

10
amy

'If you think I'm going out clubbing on Saturday night, you're very wrong,' I say for the last time.

H has her lips pursed around a beer bottle and she stares despairingly at me from the other side.

'I'd be no fun. I'm just not in the mood,' I continue, shovelling up the last dollop of korma on some nan bread and cramming it into my mouth.

We're sitting on my living room carpet, the remnants of our Indian take-away between us. H insisted on bringing it round earlier. She thinks all the trauma of the last week is going to make me too thin.

I wish.

H burps and undoes the top button of her jeans. 'What have we just spent the last hour discussing?' she asks, but she doesn't wait for an answer. 'You've got to move on. You can't put your life on hold.'

'I'm not,' I say, weariness spreading over me. I lean back against the sofa and look at the ceiling.

'You are. You've been working every hour that God sends—'

'But it's a new job,' I interrupt.

'Bullshit! You're avoiding thinking about Jack. You have to get over it. And the best way is to go out and have some fun. Look, the tickets are free. It's a new bar, and there'll be music and dancing. We've got to go, it'll be a really good laugh.'

I pull up my knees and wrap my arms around them, whilst H prattles on. I feel sick. It could be to do with the fact that I've just consumed enough food to feed the population of Milton Keynes, but it could also be the recurring feeling of nausea I experience every time Jack's name is mentioned.

I can't blame H for taking the practical route. I can't blame her for cajoling me into going out. For the last week, I've been festering like the kind of forgotten matter you find under a cooker. If it was H who was behaving as if the end of the world was nigh, I'd do the same as her. I'd suggest drowning my sorrows. But going to this new bar she's harping on about?

I'd rather eat my own head.

I know I'm being mean, but half the reason H is so enthusiastic about going out is that Gav's going away and she's determined that he's not going to have a better time than her. He announced unexpectedly that he was off for a week on some corporate hospitality jaunt with his company. It's to help all his team 'bond', according to H, who is very sceptical about the whole thing. She thinks that quad biking and golf competitions are for tossers.

I think she's jealous.

As a result, since I returned from HFH (Holiday From Hell), H has gone all Girl Power on me. And whilst I love her to death and value her support, I do wish she'd piss off and leave me alone. I don't want to be chivvied out of my bad mood. I want to die. And H just doesn't get it.

She hasn't got a clue.

For starters, how can she think I've been avoiding thinking about Jack? I've done nothing *but* think about Jack for a whole week. In fact, I'm so pissed off with him being in my head that I'm considering booking myself into a mental institution for some electric shock treatment.

He crowds into my every waking hour and blocks out all the sleeping ones. I've done everything to make him try and go away. I've thrown myself into my new job, like a matador into a bullring, but it's taken every ounce of my concentration to pick up even the smallest of instructions. Because if I stop concentrating for just one second, it hits me all over again.

Like now.

'Oh babe,' says H, letting out a hopeless sigh. She reaches forward and holds my hand. 'Stop it.'

'I'm sorry. I can't help it,' I gulp, trying to curb the onslaught of yet more tears. Where are they all coming from? That's what I want to know. Surely it isn't possible for one person to have this much spare water inside them.

'Listen. This is exactly why we've got to make plans. You can't sit around here all weekend, blubbing.'

'I can,' I sob, failing to keep control.

'But you've worn out "Winner Takes It All".'

I sniff loudly and wipe my nose. 'I like Abba.'

H screws up her face at me. 'You should get out more.'

'Shut up.'

She blows out a deep breath of concern. 'You know, I bet Jack isn't feeling this miserable.'

H has got her war face on again. She's taken Jack's behaviour as such a personal slight that I'm glad she's never met him. I think if she bumped into him in a public place, she might garrotte him. I can just see the article in the *Evening Standard*:

MAN ASSAULTED IN CHECKOUT QUEUE

Twenty-seven-year-old lothario, Jack Rossiter, was brutally beaten with a packet of frozen peas in Tesco earlier today. Unremorseful assailant Helen Marchmont of Brook Green denied temporary insanity. 'He deserved it,' she railed at shocked shoppers, before being escorted to Shepherd's Bush police station. Rossiter was later discharged from hospital following a two-hour operation to remove a frozen corn on the cob from his personage. Surgeons said that he would always walk with a limp. Yet following a statement by Ms Marchmont, angry crowds, brandishing a variety of root vegetables, gathered outside Rossiter's bachelor love den and riot police had to be brought in . . .

I nod and blow my nose to calm H down. The general smothering of my face with kitchen towel will also stop her from guessing what I'm thinking. Because I don't want to admit it. I don't want to tell her that I bet Jack *is* feeling as miserable as me. He might even be feeling ten times worse. And despite the fact that he's hurt me more than I could imagine, the thought of *him* hurting makes me feel even more miserable.

Liberated Nineties Woman? I think not.

'I don't want to talk about Jack,' I say. 'Let's just leave it.'

But H hasn't finished.

'It's not as if he's banging down your door begging for forgiveness,' she points out.

'No, but—'

'He's called you a couple of times, and then what? Nothing. He's given up trying. He's broken your heart and he doesn't give a shit. In my book, it's all about respect and that, quite frankly, isn't remotely respectful.'

I hang my head in silence. She's right. There's nothing I can say, but despite myself I still feel defensive.

H can tell. 'Hello? Calling Amy? He was unfaithful to you.'

'He didn't sleep with her.'

'Oh, so that's okay is it? You want him back?'

I rub my temples. How can I answer this question? Because my heart screams YES. Of course I want him back. I've been through every emotion this week from murderous anger, to indignation, to utter dejection, but the fact remains that I miss him. And I love him.

Correction.

Loved him.

Yet despite that, I do want him back. But I want the Jack back I made love to on the beach. I want the Jack back who holds me all night. I want the Jack back who makes me laugh and makes everything all right.

But no, I don't want the Jack back who could sleep with Sally McCullen and, what's more, lie to me about it for a whole week.

And this is where I'm stuck.

Because both Jacks are the same person.

H knits her brow. 'If he's done it once, he'll do it again,' she warns. 'Blokes like that always do.'

'I know.'

I can tell she's about to give me a dose of tough love. 'If you want a relationship where you don't trust him, then go ahead. But don't come crying to me when it all goes wrong.'

'I don't want that. You know that.'

'Trust is the most important thing,' H rails on. 'If you don't have that you've got diddly squat. And Jack has blown it, it's as simple as that. It's hard to take, I know, but it'll stop hurting in time.'

'Will it?'

'Of course it will.'

'Why do I feel so confused then?'

'Because you think you miss him. But you only miss what he represented – security and all that stuff.'

'Oh,' I mumble. I feel like she's just explained the answer to a mathematical puzzle and I still don't get it. She's so annoying when she's on a therapy roll and, by the looks of things, it's only just started.

H stands up. She reaches down for my hand and hauls me to my feet.

'What are you doing?' I protest.

She drags me into the bathroom and turns on the light. 'Now then,' she says, folding her arms. She nods to the cabinet mirror. 'What do you see?'

I can see both our reflections. I look puffy-eyed and generally as if I've been dragged through a hedge backwards. I've also got a spot the size of Manchester on my chin.

'H, this is stupid,' I moan.

'No it's not.'

I roll my eyes at her and look at her in the mirror. 'What do you want me to say?'

H ignores me. She eyeballs me back. 'Meet Amy Crosbie. The girl who loves to get shat upon from a great height, because she's too weak to be on her own. This is the girl who'll go out with a lying, cheating bastard, who won't tell her that he loves her, who'll take her on holiday and almost kill her before he clears his conscience—'

'Stop it!' I interrupt, my hackles rising. 'I dumped him, didn't I?'

H sucks in her cheeks. 'Exactly.'

We stare at each other for a long moment. I think back to the holiday, but Jack has robbed me of all the good memories, because what he did totally negates the best week of my life. And the worst part of it all? I didn't even suspect. I was such a doting fool that it didn't cross my mind he was carrying a bombshell that would blow us apart. Finally, I see H's point.

'You're right,' I say.

'He doesn't deserve you.'

I sigh and shake my head. 'No, he doesn't.'

H gives me a long hug, before she breaks away. I follow her back into the lounge and watch her whilst she clears up the take-away cartons and dumps them in a corner.

'Right. Well that's it. I'm having no more long faces from you madam,' she announces. She goes to the stereo and throws in a CD. 'This one's for you.' She cranks up the volume.

'Once I was afraid, I was petrified,' she sings, screwing up her face as if she's Tom Jones.

She knows her tough love has worked, but just to make sure, she's doing what she always does. She's making me laugh.

'I spent so many nights feeling sorry for myself,' I add, feeling a surge of affection for her. H jumps on to the sofa and drags me up after her. We shriek over Gloria Gaynor, doing a ridiculous formation dance in the cramped space.

'Now go! Walk out the door, don't turn around now, you're not welcome any more.' We waggle our fingers at each other. I'm feeling immensely cheered up.

'Weren't you the one who tried to hurt me with your lies?' I slap hands to my chest. 'Well did I crumble? Did I lay down and die?'

We're bellowing 'I will survive' so loudly that it takes me a while to hear the door buzzer. I jump off the sofa and turn down the stereo. I'm sweating.

'Did you hear the door?' I ask H, lunging for the intercom.

'Nope.'

I shout down the mouthpiece for a while, but there's no answer, so I jog down to the front door. I'm out of breath by the time I fling it open. I look out on to the street, but there's no one there. I close the door and as I press the timer light again, I spot the letter on the doormat.

My heart is thumping as I carry it back up to my flat.

'What is it?' asks H when I get back to the lounge. She looks worried and turns off the CD. The flat suddenly seems very quiet.

'It's a letter,' I reply. 'From Jack.'

I look between the letter and her.

My hands are shaking.

Trust him to butt in, just when I was feeling strong again.

'He gave it to you?' she asks.

'No. It was on the mat.'

H comes over to me and we stare at the envelope. On the front it says **A. CROSBIE, TOP FLAT** in Jack's handwriting. He's written it in green ballpoint pen.

A. Crosbie.

Not Amy Crosbie.

Or just Amy.

There's not even a drawn-on stamp.

A. Crosbie – it could be any Crosbie.

Even my bank manager manages to address me as A. L. Crosbie. Amy Lauren. (Dad had a bit of a Lauren Bacall fixation going on when I was born.)

I stare at the letter, trying to divine its contents. I turn it over. There's nothing on the back either. No S.W.A.L.K written across the gum line. Nothing. I sniff it. There's no tell-tale waft of aftershave either.

So much for my mail smelling of male.

'Are you going to read it?' asks H.

'I don't know.'

And I don't. I don't know what to do. I'm not sure if I can

271

bear hearing what Jack has to say. It might make me feel even worse. I don't think I can cope with him telling me that I've made the right decision. I don't want to read that he's going to carry on seeing Sally. I don't want to know the sordid, slurping details. I don't want to deal with anything that will make him seem real.

H touches my arm. 'Think carefully. Is there anything that he can say that'll make you feel better?'

There's only one thing that Jack could say to make me feel better and it's totally improbable: 'I was lying, Amy darling. Nothing happened with Sally . . . it was all a practical joke.'

But even if he was to take it all back, I've been through too much. I'd just think he was a stupid twat.

'No,' I answer, decisively. 'Anyway, if he has anything to say, he should say it to my face.' I choose to ignore the fact that I haven't given Jack a chance to see my face. But that's mere detail.

It's the principle that counts.

'Right then,' says H, rubbing her hands together. 'It's time to exorcise him, once and for all. Come on. Bring the beers. I'll need you to assist.' She snatches the letter out of my hand and marches into the kitchen. At the sink, she snaps on my Marigold gloves. 'Saucepan!' she barks, like a surgeon.

She puts out one of her hands and I pull a saucepan off the hook and give it to her. She doesn't look at me.

'Lighter fuel,' she continues. I start to giggle as she takes it out of the spice rack. She dumps Jack's letter in the saucepan. She sneaks a look at me and there's an evil glint in her eye.

I nod at her.

H flips open the lid of the fuel and squirts it all over the letter.

'Matches!'

I hand her the box of Cook's matches, feeling as if we're Thelma and Louise. H strikes a match and drops it into the saucepan with a dramatic flourish. Jack's letter bursts into flames. We both stagger backwards and grab hold of each other.

'I can't believe you just did that!' I gasp.

'He's out of your life for good,' says H, picking up her beer and clinking bottles with me. 'Onwards and upwards.'

'Onwards and upwards,' I agree, but I don't feel as happy as I'm making out, because despite our white witch gestures, my thoughts are still ping-ponging between the ball-breaking feminist Amy and the Merchant Ivory heroine Amy:

Ball-breaker: I am a liberated woman. I am free. I don't need Jack Rossiter. He's history.

Soppy heroine: He was here tonight. He was on my doorstep. *He was breathing the same air as me.*

Ball-breaker: I've been single before. I can do it again. I have standards and Jack Rossiter doesn't meet them.

Soppy heroine: I miss him. Does he miss me too? What did he say in his letter?

Ball-breaker: He let Bitch Features Sally McCullen give him a blow job. What more is there to say? He can't wriggle out of that one, even if he's turned into the Poet bloody Laureate.

'I'm glad,' I say.

Yet later, when H eventually goes and I'm cleaning my teeth, I don't feel so glad. I go into the kitchen and look at the saucepan. I wedge the foamy brush in the side of my cheek and pick up the charred letter. Black flakes float up and out of the window.

Why were we so reckless? I want to know what Jack wrote. I want to hear his explanation. I want his voice to be filling the silence of this flat, however hard it might be. There's a part of me that knows I'm being weak, because I'm feeling lonely, but my instinct overrides my common sense.

For the first time since I left Greece, I do what I vowed I wouldn't do. I pick up the phone and ring the operator. I find out that if you don't want someone to trace your call, you dial 141 before their number. I do it and dial Jack's. I don't know what I'm going to say. I don't know how I'll explain that I've burned his letter. I just want to hear his voice.

He answers after one ring and, as I suspected, my heart does a somersault at the sound of his voice.

'Hello?' he says. He sounds suspiciously normal He's not racked with sobs, he's not having a nervous breakdown. And he's not vetting his calls. Does that mean that he's expecting someone to call?

'Is that you?' he asks, softly, after a short pause.

You? Who the fuck's you?

I'm so shocked that it takes me a moment to realise that *you* might mean *me*. And if *you* is meant to mean *me*, how *dare* he sound so smug! What did he think? That he'd drop a letter through my door and everything would be back to normal? That I'd ring him up and forgive him, just like that? I remember that I have a mouthful of toothpaste foam and make a strangled gurgling sound before slamming down the phone. At least he won't know that it's me that's called.

Thank God for technology.

Make-up doesn't work!

It's a con!

It's Friday morning and I've put on so many stripes of concealer under my eyes and across my nose that I look like Adam Ant, but the bags under my eyes are still glaringly obvious. Why can't I sleep any more? It's not fair. I used to be the Martini girl of sleep: I could do it anytime, anyplace, anywhere. It's all bloody Jack's fault. If this unrelenting insomnia carries on, I'm going to have to start doing Valium.

I scowl at myself in the mirror. There's no point. I already look like the girl on the anti-drugs poster.

I pick up my keys and I'm about to leave for work when Mum calls.

'Darling, how *are* you?' she asks. I can tell that she's settled down, ready for her morning instalment of *Daughters In Distress*, the real-life soap from W12.

Despite her good intentions, this mental image does nothing but irritate me. I rub my forehead, thinking what a fool I've been. I knew this would happen. I shouldn't have gone running home straight from the airport last week like a jilted thirteen-year-old. At the time, it made me feel much better. After leaving Jack, it was the only place I wanted to be. There's no one in the world that can provide TLC like your mum.

And mine rose to the challenge in clucking splendour.

I let her make me hot chocolate and tuck me up in my old bed, soothing me to sleep with a well-worn monologue on the blight that is mankind. On Sunday, she woke me up late with breakfast in bed, did all my washing and spent the whole day bolstering me back up to the point where I was desperate to escape. By the time I made it home on Sunday night, I was ready to face the world again.

As much as I love her for doing this for me, I wish I hadn't let her in to my emotional crisis. I'm twenty-five. Old enough to work out my problems by myself.

'I'm fine,' I say. 'Honestly.'

'Are you sure? You can come home for the weekend if you want.'

'No, Mum, I've got things to do here.'

She's not listening. 'Why don't you jump on a train after work tonight and I'll cook us a nice dinner?' she suggests.

I can tell she's got it all planned out. I close my eyes, willing myself to be nice. I don't need to be swathed in the blanket of her concern. I can't think of anything more claustrophobic. Besides, I'm over my meltdown, *aren't I?*

However, I shouldn't be horrible to her. Things are good between us at the moment and since I've got my job, she's stopped giving me grief. I don't want to blow it now by regressing into petulance.

I'm stronger than that.

'I can't, I'm sorry. I've promised H I'll go out with her tomorrow night. I think it'll do me good to have some fun.'

I'm shocked that I've said this with such conviction. I thought I was going to duck out of H's plan, but in the light of Mum's offer, it suddenly makes perfect sense.

'If you're sure, darling?'

'Positive, but thanks anyway. You've been such a star,' I add.

'What are mums for?' she says, and I can tell she's made up and I'm off the hook.

Phew.

I'm just locking my flat when I bump into Peggy, my neighbour, on the landing. Peggy is at least a hundred and fifty and a compulsive curtain twitcher. She's turned Neighbourhood Watch into a professional occupation. I've got the feeling she's been hanging around waiting to collar me for days.

'Did you ever hear from that weirdo again, dear?' she asks.

'What weirdo?'

'That down-and-out who was round here last Sunday.'

'What down-and-out?' I ask, wondering what she's harping on about this time.

'Well! He looked dreadful!' she tuts, plumping up her blue rinse hairdo. 'Soaked through, he was. Yelling down your intercom. I told Alf. I said, "You want to get rid of him." Here all day. But did Alf move? Did he 'eck. Glued in front of the snooker, he was.'

So now I'm privy to Alf's TV viewing habits.

Fascinating.

'I haven't heard anything,' I say, trying to dodge past her.

But Peggy hasn't finished.

'Must've got the wrong house, then,' she witters on. 'And then there's all that graffiti. I've got a good mind to call the council. This area used to be so nice.'

I smile blandly at her. She must be talking about that nonsense some idiot painted on the road. 'Kids these day, eh, Peggy,' I comment, making my escape.

I ponder on this new information, all the way into work.

What if it was Jack yelling down the intercom? Despite all my resolve, I start to feel guilty. I think back to kicking him in the balls. I think back to his battered face on the airplane and how I refused to talk to him. I remember wiping his messages off the answering machine and – the ultimate revenge – ringing up British Telecom to remove his number from my Friends

& Family list. And then I think about the scene in my kitchen last night and how we burnt his letter.

But then I think about his voice on the phone and I remember what H said. I shouldn't feel guilty. Even if Jack had declared undying love in his letter, why should I believe him after what he's done?

It's too late.

Much too late.

I'm still feeling out of sorts by the time I walk up Charlotte Street to the office. Why does everything have to be so confusing? Why can't life be simple?

Because it is so easy in theory.

In theory, you can split life into three categories: career, love life and life in general (this includes home, mates, etc.). The big problem is that you only ever get a maximum of two out of the three working well at the same time. It's like juggling. Whilst I was with Jack, the love life and life in general stuff was tickety-boo; the career was shit. Now the career's great, life in general is fine, but my love life sucks.

It's rubbish!

When am I going to have it all?

I only start to feel better once I'm ensconced at my desk. I do love this job. Jules has been in and out all week, which has been a relief. He hasn't been looking over my shoulder and it's given me a chance to find my feet. I've got a catch-up session with him later this morning. He's asked me to compile a list of my ideas, and now, as I put the finishing touches to it, I feel chuffed. This is the first piece of work I've done as a bona fide employee and not as a temp.

At last.

I'm permanent.

And I'm here to stay.

(Fingers crossed Jules likes it too.)

I'm so engrossed that I don't notice that Jenny is standing by my desk. She's going to a fancy dress party this weekend and she's wearing the get-up that Sam has been making for her. She's got a ridiculous Cleopatra wig on and a sexy lace bodice.

'How do I look?' she asks, doing a twirl whilst I laugh.

'Amazing! You're bound to pull.' I spot my camera on the desk. 'Stay there.'

Jenny poses whilst I take pictures of her. After three snaps, the camera runs out of film. She pulls off her wig and ruffles her hair, as the film rewinds. She sits on the edge of my desk and leans forward conspiratorially. 'There's a cute twenty-three-year-old I've got my sights on,' she whispers. 'He's a dead ringer for Leonardo Di whatsit.' She folds her arms and sucks in her cheeks comically. 'I think I'll be having some of that, thank you very much.'

'You're terrible,' I laugh.

'Always was, always will be,' she grins. She looks at me for a moment. 'How are you feeling today? Any better?'

Jenny and Sam have been brilliant this week. It was probably very unprofessional to spill the beans about Jack on my first day, but they didn't seem to mind. Instead, they've rallied round, not letting me get too blue. Andy calls us the Witches' Coven and every time we come back from a fag break, he yells, 'Run for cover, lads! They'll chop off your balls!' We all cackle demoniacally at this, but it's all a good laugh, especially since Sam fancies him.

I take the film out of the camera and look up at Jenny. 'He delivered a letter last night.'

She grimaces. 'And?'

'I burnt it. I didn't even read it.'

'That's my girl,' she grins, putting out her hand to high five me. 'I knew you'd see sense. There's no point in breaking your heart at your age, when there's so much fun to be had.'

'Don't worry, I'm taking a leaf out of your book,' I say. 'I'm going out tomorrow night.'

'Best thing for you,' she nods. 'Just remember: death before compromise.'

And that's why I admire Jenny. Because she takes no shit. Because she does what she wants and sticks to her decisions. She may be in her thirties, but you don't hear her bleating about needing a man or getting panicky about her biological clock. And if she isn't desperate, why should I be?

I can be Jenny too.

In spades.

With knobs on.

There's a good Friday feeling in the office. I join in with all the banter and for the first time since I came back from Greece, I feel myself again.

At eleven-thirty, Jules calls me in for our meeting. We spend ages going over all the work I've done and he's pleased. He tells me his plans for Friers and I feel a surge of confidence, because some of my ideas match his.

Things are definitely looking up.

'Let's go and get something to eat,' he says, eventually. 'I'm starving.'

I'm just about to agree when Ann, Jules's wife, calls. I gather up my things from the table.

'I can't,' says Jules. 'I'm taking my new secretary out. Okay, I'll see you later. I love you.'

Why can't I find someone like him? Why can't I find someone who's not scared of their feelings, who's decent and honest? They must exist somewhere. Jules is living proof of that. So where are they?

Married. That's where.

I'm still brooding about this when we take our seats in a trendy Soho brasserie. The maître d' is tripping over himself to serve Jules.

'Ah, Mr Geller. May I get you something to drink?' he asks.

Jules smiles at me. 'I think we'll have a couple of glasses of champagne, Tom.'

'What are we celebrating?' I ask.

'Surviving our first week.'

When the champagne arrives, Jules settles back in his seat. 'So how's it been?' he asks.

'Great,' I say. 'I'm really enjoying it.'

Jules spreads his napkin over his lap. 'Cut the crap, Amy. I've been watching you all week.'

I open my mouth in astonishment.

'It's all right,' he continues, 'I'm not having a go. The work you've done is brilliant, I'm worried about you, that's all.'

I can't believe he's saying this. Whenever he's been around, I've made a super-human effort to be chirpy.

'I've been around the block enough times to spot a broken heart when I see one. Do you want to tell me about it?' he asks.

'Is it that obvious?'

''Fraid so. You never know, I might be able to help, being a fellow human being, an' all,' he says, exaggerating his American accent.

I shake my head. He's my boss, not my therapist. Anyway, he's a bloke. What does he know?

'You don't want to hear about it,' I tell him.

'Try me.'

He does deserve an explanation, I suppose, since he's obviously sussed. I take a deep breath and look at him, before I start telling him all about Jack, our holiday and how I've been feeling ever since. I try to make it sound like it's not a big deal, but when he starts asking questions, I find myself giving him all the gory details.

'What bugs you more? The fact that he did it, or the fact that he didn't tell you?' asks Jules.

'I'm not sure. All I know is that because he didn't tell me, it makes the whole holiday – our relationship – mean nothing.'

'But he did tell you eventually, and in my book that takes a lot of balls.'

I should have known. This is such a typical male response. I don't want to hear how ballsy Jack has been. He's not brave in *my* book.

Our starters arrive.

'I had an affair once,' Jules says, after a while.

I almost choke on my food. Not Jules? Not wholesome family man, Jules? Not Mr Declarations Of Love To His Wife In The Office (before lunch!), Jules? Not him as well?

'Ann knows about it.'

'You told her?' I ask incredulously.

'Sure I did.'

'How? I mean.' I stare at him and then check myself. 'You don't have to tell me.'

'My affair was a lot worse than Jack's,' Jules admits. 'I slept with another woman for six weeks, and then it took another six weeks before I had the guts to tell Ann about it.'

'Why didn't you keep it a secret?' I try not to sound as pursed-lipped as I'm feeling.

'Because she suspected. Because I realised that by censoring the truth, I was being totally disrespectful. She deserved the truth and it was hers to deal with. She trusted me, so I had to trust her back.'

'But wasn't she terribly upset?'

'Of course she was, but she also realised that I'd risked everything in telling her. She knew that I could lose her, the kids, our home, everything. And she also knew that that was the last thing that I wanted.'

'How did you feel?'

'Wretched. I couldn't believe I'd hurt her so badly, or that I'd been stupid enough to have an affair in the first place.'

'So what happened?'

'We worked it out. It took time, but our relationship is much stronger as a result. The thing about the truth is that you can't argue with it. And if you trust someone enough to tell them the truth about things like that, no matter how hard it is, it means that you love them.'

I want to ask him if he thinks that Jack told me about Sally because he loves me, but I stop myself. Jules doesn't know Jack. He'd just be guessing.

Just like me.

'It sounds to me like you've been pretty harsh on him,' Jules says, quietly.

I twist my lips and look at him.

'You should have at least read the letter and found out what he had to say. I doubt if he had much more of an excuse than the fact that he's male, but you could have heard his side.'

'But how can I trust him again?'

'Why wouldn't you? He's told you the worst.'

281

'But if he's so *male*, won't he do it again?'

Jules laughs at my jibe. 'He might want to, but the point about love is that it's much more than just sex. And next time he'd probably think a little harder.'

'What does that mean? Would you have an affair again?'

'No.' He pauses. 'I don't regret it, though. It made me clear about my feelings. It also made me realise that you can't be complacent in relationships. You have to work at them.'

I push my knife and fork together on my plate. I feel confused.

'It's simple. Do you love him?' asks Jules.

'But—'

'If you love him, then you have to accept that he's human. I'm sorry, Amy, but this ain't the movies.'

When I get home, I unpack my shopping from Sainsbury's and steel myself to open the holiday photos. Jenny had the film developed at lunchtime and the pack of pictures have been taunting me all afternoon. It takes me a glass of wine before I have the guts to look through them. I make a pact with myself: I'm not going to blub.

But as soon as I open them, I start to feel wobbly. I look through them with an other-worldly sensation. Somehow they don't seem real. There's Jack on the bike, looking tanned, me on the beach, fast asleep. I hold my breath, willing myself to carry on. But each photo stabs a little deeper.

I'm nearly through the whole pack and I'm about to congratulate myself, when I come to the ones of both of us. And that's when it hits me. Because in the photos we're together.

Really together.

Together as if it would last for ever.

We're standing near the taverna and Jack has one arm around me and is holding the camera up with the other. I had no idea that the shots would come out, but they have. And as I look through them, my heart starts to ache, because here is Jack looking into my eyes and I can see my feelings suspended in the space between our faces. He's grinning, his nose touching mine, and I can't look any more. Because I can feel his arm around me and smell his skin. And my pact is well and truly broken.

Niagara Falls has relocated to my face.

I must have bawled myself to sleep, because it's late by the time I hear the phone. In my blurry state, I immediately think it's Jack. But it's not. It's Nathan. He sounds stoned.

After talking me through the dumping of the Spanish girl for an Argentinian polo heiress and his current two-timing situation with a girl from Glasgow, he finally cottons on that I'm not saying anything. He obviously takes this as a sign that I'm pissed off and starts apologising profusely for failing to take me out to dinner.

'It's okay,' I say.

'Cool.' Nathan sounds relieved that he's off the hook so easily. I can hear him taking a drag on a cigarette. 'How was the holiday with lover boy?'

'We split up.'

There's a pause. 'Oh man! That's too bad.'

I don't say anything. This news is obviously just *breaking* his heart.

'Look on the bright side . . .'

'Which bright side is that?' I interrupt, curtly.

'He wasn't exactly your type.'

It occurs to me that Nathan wouldn't know my type if my type punched him in the gob. In fact, Nathan wouldn't have the first idea what I want any more. He wouldn't even think to ask. Because since he's been away, he's changed. No, he's always been the same, he's always been this arrogant. It's me who's changed. And even though I hate to admit it, I've changed because of Jack.

'How do you know? You didn't speak to him,' I snap.

'We didn't have anything to say to each other,' he says defensively.

'And whose choice was that?'

'Hey! Don't take it out on me. I'm sorry, all right?'

'Whatever.'

He sucks his teeth. 'It's not a good time. Look, I'll call you.'

There's a long pause before he hangs up. I'm glad he does it first; it saves me the effort.

'Tosser!' I yell, as I slam down the phone.

I'm furious.

How dare Nathan judge Jack? What does he know? It's all his bloody fault, anyway. If he hadn't been so rude, Jack wouldn't have been jealous. And if Jack hadn't been jealous, he wouldn't have been with Sally.

But that's no excuse, either.

Men!

Ugh!

They're such a bunch of neanderthals. They haven't evolved *at all*. All they think about are their dicks and their egos, not that there's any difference between the two.

I shake my head, astonished at how stupid I've been. Even though I can see Nathan from Jack's point of view, it doesn't absolve Jack for one second. They're all the bloody same. Nathan, Jack . . . even Jules couldn't keep his dick to himself.

What hope is there?

I pick up the bottle of wine and down a huge slug. I put my elbows on my knees and bury my head in my hands. On the carpet is the photo of Jack leaning against the bike.

I pick it up and stare at it.

No wonder he looks so bloody happy. That bitch Sally wasn't the only one with her mouth full; he was having his cake and eating it all the time.

'How long had you been planning it, Jack? Ever since you perved after her in the nude, pretending it was all in the name of art? It was probably in the back of your mind all the time, wasn't it?' I ask.

Still the same smile.

I slug back more wine.

'So what happened, then? Tell me, I'm intrigued. You invited her over, did you, because you knew I was out with Nathan? What did you do? Cook for her? Chat to her? Ply her with wine? Hold her hand across the table and gaze into her eyes? What did you say? No, no, don't tell me, I can guess.'

I slug more wine.

'"You're beautiful, you're amazing, you've got the most wonderful smile." Did you? Did you, Jack? Did you tell her the same things you told me, because you were horny. Was that it? You just wanted a fuck, because you're a man and you have to sow your seed? Is that it?'

Still the same smile.

'And what did she do? Accidentally trip over and land up with your dick in her mouth?'

The photo shakes in my hand. I stare very closely at Jack's lips.

'What was she like to kiss? Because I presume you kissed her, didn't you? And what did you do? Keep your hands tied behind your back, I suppose? You didn't by any chance go down on her, kiss the parts you've painted? No, you wouldn't do that, would you, Jack, because you've never bragged about how pleasing women is as important as pleasing yourself! And what did she taste like? What did her skin feel like against yours?'

My heart feels like it's in my throat and I'm gasping for breath. I stare at the picture, feeling sick.

'Did you compare us, Jack? Did you hold me a few hours later and think about her? Did you?'

My eyes are brimming with tears and I wipe them away angrily. I finish the wine in one gulp and stand up. I'm very unsteady on my feet.

'But I shouldn't worry my pretty little head about it, should I? Because it doesn't count as infidelity. You didn't sleep with her. Silly me for getting so worked up.'

Still the same smile.

'You BASTARD!' I rip up the photo and hurl it across the room. Then I screw up all the others and dump them in the bin, before kicking it.

This time I've had it. I don't care what Jules says. Jules and all his psychoanalytical clap trap about trust. I'll never trust anyone ever again. It's not worth it. From now on I'm with Jenny. I'm going to use men. I'm going to use and abuse them. I'm going to have my cake and eat it, too. And if anyone thinks they're getting close to me, ever again, they can FUCK OFF!

On Saturday morning, I have a whopping hangover, but a sense of calm has settled over me. In fact, I feel strangely isolated from all the pain I've been feeling. It hasn't gone, but it's not immediate any more. I think my outburst last night was a turning point.

Because today is a new start.

Today I'm back to being Amy Crosbie. No more blubbing, soppy heroine. No more ball-breaking feminist. No more mental tormentor.

Just me.

Calm.

Tranquil.

Sussed.

Today, I'm going to reclaim the space in my head that has, up until now, been filled with Jack. From now it's just going to be filled with thoughts of me.

ME.

ME.

ME.

I dig out the tape of whale noises that I bought in my brief 1990 New Age phase, and run myself a huge bath. I'm on a mission to sort out my head. I idly blow blobs of suds around, stick my big toe up the tap and let my thoughts wander. As soon as I alight on anything remotely to do with *him*, I sound the whoop-whoop siren and retrace my steps.

It's quite hard, at first. I spend ages pussy-footing around my head, careful not to open the doors to any out-of-bounds memory banks. But after a while, I discover there's loads of things to think about. Interesting things, like the plot of *EastEnders*, the Eurovision Song Contest, the decorative borders I might paint on my walls and, eventually, shopping.

Shopping is key.

After my bath, I spend several hours pampering myself in preparation for the almighty Visa bonanza I have in store for myself. I wax my legs, pluck my eyebrows, give myself a facial, file and paint my nails, spend an hour blow-drying my hair and by the time I've finished, I feel human again.

I *look* human again.

No, I look great.

I must do, because the workmen chipping the graffiti off the road wolf-whistle me when I set out for the shops. I don't care, though. They're men. They don't count.

'Piss off!' I shout.

I'm not the world's greatest shopper, I have to admit. I've always been a bit of an impulse buyer and have, hitherto, chosen to spend my Saturday afternoons in other ways. Down the pub, or flanging around with my ex-boyfriend, for example. But as of today, all that has changed. Today is for me. Today is for shopping. Today I'm on a mission.

Five shops later and I've spent more money on my Visa card than I'll ever be able to pay back, but I don't care. I'm on a roll.

Who needs men, when you've got armfuls of groovy carrier bags?

I'm in New Bond Street, fully engrossed in deliberation about a spectacularly expensive dress, when it all goes horribly wrong. I'm holding the dress up against me and looking in the mirror when I spot a familiar face browsing through the rail behind me.

I freeze.

It's Chloe.

There's no way I can move without her seeing me. I stare at her, not daring to blink.

But, as usual, her sixth sense is fully operating. She sees me straight away.

'Hi!' she gushes, coming towards me.

'Hello,' I manage, my back teeth glued together.

She admires the dress. 'Wow, that'll look amazing on you.'

I'm stuck. My muscles won't work. I'm holding the dress up against me like an idiot, wishing it would hide me, or make me vanish, but it doesn't.

'You must get it,' she adds.

This is obviously my cue to move. I drop the dress on the floor.

'Maybe, I um . . .' I bend down and pick it up. My hands have gone clammy.

'How have you been?' she asks, as I stand up, fumbling with the dress.

It's a loaded question. She knows about Jack. She knows and I know she knows and she knows that I know that she knows.

'Fine,' I say, stalling for time. 'I've got a new job.'

She nods slowly, scrutinising me. 'How's it going?'

'Great. Just, well, it's amazing.' I trail off. 'How are you?'

'Fine.'

There's a long pause as I meet her eye.

'I heard,' she says, softly. 'I'm sorry.'

I nod, not able to speak. She's not sorry. She's not sorry at all. I squeeze my lips together and carefully fold the dress over my arm.

She knows how he is. She has all the answers to all the questions I've just spent a fortune to stop myself thinking about. And as much as I want to shake it out of her, pay her, if necessary, to tell me every detail, my pride takes over.

There's something about her phoney look of concern that makes me go cold. I'm damned if she's going to see that I'm upset, or that Jack has affected me in any way. And when she reports back, as I'm sure she will, she won't be able to tell him anything other than that I looked fine. That I am fine. That I've survived. That I've risen above it all.

Because I have.

'You know, I think I'll buy it,' I say, gesturing to the dress.

Chloe looks startled. I've scuppered her. Shut her out and she knows it.

'What's the occasion?' she asks, watching me as I gather up my bags.

'I'm going out tonight,' I say.

Stick that, Jack. I have a life. I'm out on the town.

'Anywhere good?' I can't read her expression.

'I've got tickets for the opening of a new bar in town.' I am super cool Amy.

The one you lost, sucker.

'Where exactly?'

What does she mean, 'Where exactly?' It's none of her business.

'Zanzibar,' I mumble.

'Zanzibar in Beak Street?' she asks.

'Mmm,' I nod.

'If it's any good, I'd love to hear about it.'

'Sure.'

'We must get together some time for a drink,' she says. She gives me a questioning smile.

'Okay,' I manage.

She leans forward and kisses me on the cheek. 'I'll be in touch,' she says, before walking away.

This whole encounter confuses the hell out of me. I pay for the dress in a daze and hail a cab.

I feel utterly depressed by the time I get home. My new purchases are of no comfort; I wish I'd never bought them. I drop my bags in the hall, kick off my shoes and collapse on my bed. Thanks to Chloe, I now have a whole new set of questions:

Will she tell Jack she saw me?

What will she say?

What if she doesn't tell him?

What if he never gets to hear how super cool I'm being?

What if that's it?

What if I never see Jack *ever* again?

What if I've burned my bridges with Chloe?

What if I've cut off the last link?

It's all too much. My karma is blown. I'm destined for a life of confusion and unanswered questions.

It's not fair.

When H comes round, I'm catatonic in front of *Blind Date*.

'Looking good, feeling funky,' she chirps, waggling a bottle of vodka at me and conga-ing into the flat. 'Looking good, feeling . . . what's up with you?' she asks.

I slump down on to a chair. 'I saw Chloe.'

H curls up her lip and grunts. 'What did she say?'

'Nothing.'

'Nothing?'

'I didn't let her.'

H pouts and puts her hands on her hips. I can tell she's making a decision about whether to pursue this line of conversation. I don't care. I ignore her.

'Show me what you've bought,' she says, abruptly.

'What?'

'Show me what you've bought. I want to see.'

I nod to the bags. 'It's all rubbish. I spent a fortune.'

H runs her tongue around her teeth and picks up the bags. She empties them on to the carpet and whistles. I still ignore her. She looks at all the clothes and picks out the dress and throws it over her shoulder. Then she stomps into the kitchen.

She comes back with two large vodkas and pushes one towards me. 'Drink.'

I blow out my cheeks.

'Drink!' she warns.

I take a sip.

'*All* of it.'

She watches me until I've finished it. I can feel the vodka warming my throat.

'Now listen, you. It's Saturday night and I'm not having any of your nonsense. Have you got that? *None* of it.' She thrusts the dress towards me. 'You've got fifteen minutes.'

Zanzibar is packed by the time we get there. I almost turn and run at the sight of the crowd, but H grabs my arm and pulls me inside.

We have a few drinks and dance for a while, but I can't really get into it. My heart's not in it, and I feel like I've got two left feet.

About an hour later, when I come back from the loo, I stand by a pillar looking around for H. The dance floor is crowded and I start to panic that I've lost her. I feel horribly exposed. I can't talk to anyone, I've got nothing to say.

'Amy! Over here!' I spot H waving at me, and I wave back, relief flooding over me.

'I've found some blokes for us,' she says, her eyes glittering with excitement.

'H!' I protest.

'Come on,' she says. 'I was talking to this bloke at the bar. He's really nice. And *he's* got a miserable mate with him, too!'

'Thanks a bundle!'

'They're upstairs. They're buying us drinks,' she says, grabbing hold of me, but I shake out of her grip.

'If you're trying to match-make me with some miserable git, I'll kill you.'

'Would I? I haven't even met the miserable one yet. It's the one at the bar I want you to meet. He's lush.'

'No!'

'Just come and say hello. For me. Go on, what harm can it do? If we don't like them, we can leave.'

I bite my lip as she drags me across the dance floor to the stairs. When we get to the top, my heel catches on the step. I turn round to unfasten it. H is waving.

'They're over here,' she says. I straighten up and follow her in the direction of the booth at the back.

'Here!' she says, satisfied, when I catch up with her. 'This is Matt.' She's looking at him. 'This is Amy.'

? ! ?

I can't breathe.

I can't breathe, because this isn't any old Matt, this is Jack's Matt.

But even weirder than him being here in the first place is that there's no look of surprise on his face.

Chloe.

It's got to be Chloe. She's the only reason that he could be here.

What's she trying to do? Embarrass me? Get me back for today?

How could she?

H is completely unaware of what's going on. She shuffles into the seat opposite Matt and pats the cushion next to her. She gives my arm a shake and frowns at me, before pulling me down. I land with a thud.

Everything has stopped.

Time has stopped.

Because where there's a Matt, there's usually a Jack.

And then I see him.

He's walking over from the bar, carrying four pints of beer. He's looking at them, concentrating hard.

'Here's our Rossy Boy,' says Matt, rubbing his hands together.

Everything is screaming 'Run!', but I can't move.

It's too late.

Jack reaches the table and puts the pints down. It's only then that he looks up and sees me. He turns quickly and glares at Matt. 'What's going on?' he demands.

I can tell from the way the colour drains from his face that if there is some sort of a conspiracy going on between Chloe and Matt, then H isn't the only one who's no part of it.

Matt is a picture of innocence. 'Nothing, mate. These are the girls I was telling you about.'

'Hi, Rossy Boy,' chirps H, cheekily, 'I'm Helen.'

Jack stares at her outstretched hand, before eventually taking it. 'Good to meet you,' he mumbles.

'And this is Amy,' Matt chimes. He waits for Jack to speak, but Jack says nothing. 'Aren't you going to shake hands, mate?' Matt prompts. 'Where are your manners?'

Jack sits down and for the first time he looks at me.

Right into me.

'Hello, Amy,' he says. His hand stays where it is.

H looks at Jack and raises her pint to him. 'Cheers. You must be the heartbroken one, then.' She nudges me in the ribs. 'Heartbreaker, more like.'

'No, you got it right the first time,' says Jack.

'Amy's an expert in heartbreak, aren't you, love?' H blunders on, failing to notice Jack's stony expression. 'You two should have a lot in common.'

Matt splutters on his pint, slams his glass down on the table and then launches into a coughing fit. Jack whacks him on the back, so hard that I think his teeth are going to fall out.

Fine. So Matt wants to play games? Let's do it.

'What's your sob story, then?' I ask, my eyes boring into Jack's.

'I got dumped,' he replies.

'It's a real shame. She was a stunner, wasn't she?' Matt says.

'She was amazing. I'll never meet anyone like her again.'

H tuts. 'Blimey, you're as bad as Amy. You can't let it get you down, you know. There are always plenty more fish in the sea.'

'Not like her, there aren't,' says Jack.

I look away from his intense gaze. 'Why did she dump you?' I ask.

'I love this track. Shall we go and dance?' interrupts Matt, looking at H.

H shakes her head. 'We can't leave now, we're just getting to the juicy bit.'

'Bollocks to it,' says Matt. 'Knowing this one, he'll be talking all night. Come on, let's leave them to it.'

H stands up to follow Matt. She leans down to whisper in my ear. 'You'll be all right, won't you? Come and grab me if he turns out to be a psycho.'

And then we're alone.

'So?' he asks.

'I think you owe me an answer.'

'What? About why she dumped me?'

'That'll do for starters.'

Jack takes a deep breath. 'Because I did something stupid. I made a mistake.'

'Just a mistake?'

'No, it was worse than that. I let her down. And I started to tell her what happened, but she wouldn't listen.'

'Do you blame her?'

'Of course I don't. It would have been a miracle if she'd hung around after what I told her.'

'So what did you do?'

'I rang and rang. Then I went to her house and waited for her, but she wouldn't answer the door. So I wrote her a letter to tell her exactly what happened, but she didn't reply.'

I can feel tears rising. 'Maybe she didn't read it,' I whisper. 'Maybe she was so hurt and so angry that she let her best mate burn it in a saucepan.'

Jack looks horrified. He strokes his cheeks, very slowly. 'Then she wouldn't know how I felt and how it actually was.'

'So, how was it? Actually?'

Jack looks straight at me as he speaks. 'I fell asleep next to another girl. I shouldn't have done it, but I was drunk and I was angry. And when I woke up, this other girl was going down on me. And I freaked. I pushed her away. I threw her out of the house.'

'And you'd expect your girlfriend to believe that, would you?'

'Yeah. It's the truth.' He pauses then, and I realise that our eyes are locked together again. 'But the worst bit is that I lied to her about it. And it nearly killed me, because I'd realised something,' he continues.

'And what was that?'

Jack's fingers touch mine. 'That I was in love with her. That I still am. Completely. That I want to be with her, more than anything else. But I couldn't tell her any of this until I'd told her the truth, even if that meant losing her.'

I think back to everything I've thought over the past week. I think back to all the advice I've been given and how I still ended up feeling confused. And now, I realise, it was because

I wasn't listening to my heart. I tried to stop believing in Jack and it wasn't possible. It wasn't possible because I love him. And now that he's told me the truth, it all makes sense. My heart was right all along.

But before I can say any of this, Matt and H are back.

'Are you okay?' asks H.

'Better than okay,' I smile, slipping my hand into Jack's. 'I've just been asked to dance.'

ALSO AVAILABLE

☐	Reading Between the Lines	Linda Taylor	£5.99
☐	Sally	Freya North	£5.99
☐	Lucy Sullivan is Getting Married	Marian Keyes	£6.99
☐	Truth or Dare	Sara Sheridan	£5.99
☐	Animal Husbandry	Laura Zigman	£5.99
☐	The Godfather	Mario Puzo	£5.99
☐	Silence of the Lambs	Thomas Harris	£5.99
☐	LA Confidential	James Ellroy	£6.99
☐	Night Dogs	Kent Anderson	£6.99
☐	Scalpel	Paul Carson	£5.99

ALL ARROW BOOKS ARE AVAILABLE THROUGH MAIL ORDER OR FROM YOUR LOCAL BOOKSHOP AND NEWSAGENT.

PLEASE SEND CHEQUE/EUROCHEQUE/POSTAL ORDER (STERLING ONLY) ACCESS, VISA OR MASTERCARD, DINERS CARD, SWITCH OR AMEX.

EXPIRY DATE .... SIGNATURE ....

PLEASE ALLOW 75 PENCE PER BOOK FOR POST AND PACKING U.K.

OVERSEAS CUSTOMERS PLEASE ALLOW £1.00 PER COPY FOR POST AND PACKING.

ALL ORDERS TO:

ARROW BOOKS, BOOKS BY POST, TBS LIMITED, THE BOOK SERVICE, COLCHESTER ROAD, FRATING GREEN. COLCHESTER, ESSEX CO7 7DW.

NAME ....

ADDRESS...

....

Please allow 28 days for delivery. Please tick box if you do not wish to receive any additional information ☐

Prices and availability subject to change without notice.